The War and Alex Vere

The War and Alex Vere

Alan Kennedy

Lasserrade Press

Lasserrade Press

www.LasserradePress.com

ISBN 978-1-9996941-1-1

Cover illustration: "The Love Letter", Spencer, Stanley (1891-1959) Private Collection Luisa Ricciarini/© Estate of Stanley Spencer. All rights reserved 2022/Bridgeman Images.

First published in the United Kingdom by Lasserrade Press 2023.

For Elizabeth

Part 1: A Time to Tell Lies

"I have done that," says my memory.
"I could not have done that," says my pride.
Finally my memory yields.

Friedrich Nietzsche
Beyond Good and Evil

Prologue

Friday October 16 1942
Saint Aunix, Gers

There's nothing to do in the Café Flore. Just a place to sit until Joël in the bar across the square takes the shutters down and leans them against the door. You'd think he'd shift them, but he never does. After the shutters you wait till the covers come off the billiards table, then the whole crowd shoves off. It had been Wednesday, two days ago. The usual crowd. The English woman was there. Squeezing past, struggling against her knees, he felt his coat snagging. Then he saw. Not snagging - her hand, very small, milky white, holding his coat under the table. A single tug, nothing more.

She waited till they'd all gone, Thierry leading the way, letting the glass door smash closed, gawping back inside, grinning. You could tell what he was thinking. *Why him?* That's what they were all thinking. He'd asked himself the same.

"Don't bother about them. Look here."

A nice voice. Really proper French, like the School Mistress. A little book in her hands. A book of poems.

"I'm going to write something inside. You can say your girl gave it you. What's your name?"

"Rémy."

"What's your girl called?"

"How'd you know there is one? Fabienne, if you want to know."

"Nice name. I'll put *For Rémy from F* – you don't want anything sloppy. Now, you can do something for me," shaking her hair back, glancing to the door. They were already halfway across the square, Thierry bent over, cupping his hands round his crutch, pretending to gag.

"Number eight. There's a brass plaque on the door. Knock just the once – d'you understand? Like this. Just one tap. Somebody will answer. Give him the book."

"You can do that yourself – it's just over there."

That was when she'd smiled. Little wrinkles round dark blue eyes.

"No, I can't do that, Rémy. It has to be Friday. I won't be here. That's why I'm asking you. Nine o'clock, remember. That's not late. Wait for the church clock, that would be best. Just one knock. He'll hear."

"What about the curfew? The Germans. Curfew's half past eight, I'll get myself done for that."

"Nine o'clock's not late, not really. Tell them you're going home. But nobody's going to ask. Everybody knows you – they won't make a fuss. You're a good boy. And there's this."

A banknote folded in two, a picture on the front, a woman with a squint perched up like a statue. Hell, a thousand! He'd never seen a note that big.

"I don't want that much. It's too much."

"No, you take it. Buy yourself something nice. Or your girl. You take it. Just do this for me."

One

There were seven of them – five men, two women. A truck picked them up at Strathcarron in a blizzard, the stiff tarpaulin cover whipping open, feeble light inside cutting yellow across tumbling swirls of snow. At Achnasheen they stopped to take on the last of the women then, as the snowfall eased, turned West to Kinlochewe, creeping along a narrow glen, impossible ice walls rearing into a night sky. At the far end of the valley, huge frozen stars hung low over the brooding hump of Liathach, all the time Alex thinking how odd it seemed to find the blackout in Torridon. Alright, there was a war on, but who the hell would want to bomb this place? Even finding it would be a miracle.

The driver nearly missed his turn, jolting them against each other on the slatted wooden seats. The sound of the engine changed, echoing back from rows of little stone houses. Alex pushed the cover aside. They had passed through gates, grinding up a gravelled incline, engine screaming. A rectangle of light reached out across the snow: a man framed against lamplight at an open door, rhododendrons banked high on either side closing over him.

At the top, the truck drove straight into a kind of barn, wooden doors flung back. They stumbled out one by one into the smell of cattle. As Alex jumped down, stiff with cold, he collided with the woman who had got on at Achnasheen, grabbing her arm with a gloved hand to steady himself.

"Sorry. Where the hell are we? Do you have the faintest idea? Only don't say Scotland – I worked that bit out."

"That's the best I could do, I'm afraid. I'd say a good long way from anywhere else. Will that do?"

She had a nice voice: deep, just the faintest hint of something foreign. Nothing unusual there, the whole lot of them were a little odd in the language department, all walking with a slight limp you might say, accent-wise. The little imperfections that had got them here in the first place, had got them through the training. The knowledge they were that bit special keeping them sane, more or less. This was the third training camp, his last, but he'd not seen her before.

"Were you at Ringway? Funny, I didn't see you?"

She shook her head. "Parachutes? No, did that ages ago. I'm here for a course. The bloke who gives it wouldn't come South. Hell of a way."

She turned to look at the distant house set against the steep slope of the hill: high mullioned windows, stone balconies, pepperpot turrets decked out with aerials. "Although I must say it's a pretty place with the moon like this."

"Only the best for us. SOE, Stately 'Omes of England and all that. Except it's not - England, I mean." It was an old joke, she didn't smile back. "They do us proud, don't you think? Reminds you of nice young women in drawing rooms debating whether the milk goes in first or second."

She reached out, letting one hand rest on his arm. "And you would know what, exactly, about nice young women?"

So that was how it had begun, the two of them watching the rest of the group, a little knot of weary people crunching through packed snow, dragging kitbags. Nearing the top of the drive a sudden splash of light sparkled out from an open door across the ice, wavering candles on polished mahogany, the glint of silver.

The two left behind stood together in an empty shed puddled with cowpats, neither making the first move. That was how it had begun. It's a mistake to fall behind, you get that drummed into you – it's a golden rule, it really is. But not this once. Falling behind paired them for whatever time they had left.

Her name was Justine Perry. She had grinned telling him, saying he could call her Just for short if he really wanted because she always tried to be. She had lived in France most of her life, getting out after the fall of Poland. Came home, she said, to do her bit. Married, he thought. At least, she wore a ring because she had displayed it in that first session when they'd gone through the usual *personal effects* rigmarole. Pulling it off with a jerk, ostentatiously dropping it into the cardboard box, putting up with the Instructor's predictable coarse joke. They smiled on cue. Best to smile, because you could see at once this one was a vindictive bastard. So they all smiled, even Justine.

He found a place next to her that evening at the dining table. The house must have been grand in its heyday: an Edwardian folly thrown up at titanic expense by a Glasgow brewer in search of a peerage. Glass fronted cases lining the walls of a deserted gun room bore witness to long-forgotten shooting parties, even Royalty, so they said. Before the Great War had put shooting to other uses, leaving the brewer with both his sons dead at Ypres.

Faint patches on the figured wallpaper showed where pictures had once been: fake ancestors, somebody on a horse perhaps, more likely some animal about to die. They should have left that one up, Special Operations Executive having its own brand of humour.

They were sitting at a massive table, borrowed regimental silver winking in candlelight. High above, cherubs blew kisses to muscular painted nudes inside three enormous plaster cartouches. Beyond the point where dusters could reach, cobwebs waved in the rising heat. Huge mirrors in gilded ormolu frames set off each end of the room, the glass speckled with age.

Someone had screwed a wooden plaque into the polished mahogany of the figured double door, declaring *Mess Room*, the tiny act of vandalism reminding those few who might doubt it that war changes the rules. The place was already blue with cigarette smoke.

"Really married?"

At first he thought she was going to snub him. Cold blue eyes, rather large for her face, insolently fixing his. Then she smiled, glancing down at her hand, accepting a cigarette.

"Looks like it."

So he had had to settle for ambiguity even at the start. Still accept it three nights later, lying hard against her in a bed big enough for Victoria herself, army sheets smelling of carbolic soap. Even then she had not elaborated, beyond saying she was here for specialised training. She had done all that boy scout stuff long ago. She was trained – made her sound like a performing seal, didn't it? Although this particular seal had a few last tricks to learn. Otherwise she was going to keep out of the cold. She already had missions under her belt - a*ye, and still alive, the noo*, mimicking the Highland accent of the Instructor.

Perhaps it was the nonchalant cruelty of that wiry little chap that drew them together. A gymnasium had been improvised in a dusty ballroom, but he had declared it useless, fit only for faggots. What the hell was the army coming to if you trained *indoors*? He managed to make the word sound blasphemous.

Training was conducted in a pitiless landscape, snow banked so deep that walking was impossible, air so cold breathing was eked out to spare the pain. Their days were spent cracking ice to drag themselves through water tasting of blood. Fumbling the silencer onto the Standard Model B, fingers bloated by frost, then screwing it in again, this time blindfold. Then firing the damned thing.

You'll never win a goldfish that way Captain Vere, sir. It's not a rifle. Don't look. Dip. Up. Point. Squeeze. Go for the body, man, always the body. Two shots, sir. Rat Tat. Better sir, much better. Except he's shot you by now. You're dead and he's half way to Paris. Get a move on for Christ's sake.

Their days were so coloured with violence there was no time to remember he had once thought it might have been different, might have been about something else. Knife work in the second week confirmed otherwise. A stubby little thing, the standard issue knife, barely longer than your fist. Double edged, what's more, the better to work both ways.

You're slitting throats Captain Vere, not stabbing anybody. Stabbing's for girls, begging your pardons ladies. Stab him and he'll take too long to die. Take you with him more than likely. No. Like this. Over the top. Pull. Head back. Slit.

The snow was so severe one day they crowded into the Mess briefly to consider traitors, a blessed relief to be indoors.

Now the manual says you have a choice. You pay him off, you warn him off or you kill him. I beg to take issue with the manual on this. Kill him. Search him if there's time. But kill him first.

Then codes: a tweed back all they saw of a supercilious man scribbling on a blackboard. *The Playfair Code is for boy Scouts. Broken like this. Now watch carefully please* - scratch – *and this* – scratch. *You see?* Not that they did. *Poem codes. Double transposition. Chose your poem. No Captain Vere, I'm afraid* Rule Britannia *is taken. The code's as good as the poem, so write your own. If they break it – and they will – you might as well send* en clair. *We're working on one-time keys. Printed on silk. Alas, not ready yet. Questions?*

Spared this, Justine lay on her bed listening to the sporadic crackle of live fire across the hills, watching snow nestle quietly into the corners of windowpanes, thinking of *A Christmas Carol.* Perhaps remembering what Mr Dickens had in store for her, curled up on granny's sofa a lifetime ago, when Christmas seemed to mean something.

She would smile at Alex and his day in the field, him telling her he could barely remember Christmas and he wasn't going to start now, not when the whole caboodle was about to go up. Not when you need a bath, she'd say, and call him a maudlin bugger, letting him burrow into the heat of her, letting him find a way to forget they didn't have all that long.

Six weeks, the little man said, seeming proud of the number, of its precision, strutting about in the uniform of an army major. Not that he *was* a Major in anybody's army: that fooled nobody. It's what you learn first in this enterprise, people are never what they claim. Then you remember that applies to you as well. That's when you understand all you have is pantomime to hang on to.

That first evening, seated in lines on hard chairs, wondering who this man really was, a rickety blackboard out of place in a forlorn room someone once had called a library, leather spines untouched for fifty years releasing a foxy smell into the air, Alex had shivered. The little Major on his dais, catching the movement like a dog scenting prey, fixed him with soft eyes: a doctor bearing bad news.

"It's Captain Vere, isn't it? An average, of course. Unpleasant, but true. Operational lifetime, six weeks. But look, we're here to change all that."

A quiet laconic style that somehow managed to suck the truth out of his words. Best not to believe a word this chap says – he'd be better off selling cars.

"We're getting better though. Quite a lot, lately. Thanks to what you pick up here. What McIntyre's putting you through is going to be worth your life, believe me."

Getting into his stride, the room wondering how many times he had said all this before. How many dozens of previous faces, dead now, their six weeks being up? They said he'd been driven across from Inverness. In a huge staff car, its grey anonymity shouting Secret Intelligence Service. Flown up that morning. Surely not just for a pep talk? Ian somebody or other: Major Ian somebody, SIS. If he really was a Major.

"If you're going to survive – and it's our job to see you do – you must believe in the system. We designed it to save your life ..." The theatrical pause for effect spoiled rather by a Sergeant's choosing that particular moment to bustle in with the stack of little cardboard boxes. He had to relieve the guard at the gatehouse. Could they be handed out now, sir?

Two pills in each box: Benzedrine, wrapped in a paper spill printed *as required*. Use it right and you might keep awake for thirty hours. Or not ... it wasn't a guarantee. And the other? The 'L' tablet in its little rubber shell. Well, bite that and you were fifteen seconds from eternity. Expected, of course, but all the same leaving them peering into their tiny pillboxes, thinking complicated thoughts, the flying Major quite forgotten.

Alex would always remember Justine at that moment, catching his stricken face, winking, twirling the little tablet between her fingers like something she might pop into her mouth any minute, finally poking it into the pocket of her blouse. Keeping the sweetie for later, her expression said. He couldn't even look in his box, he'd get round to that eventually. That was the difference between the two of them.

The Major, having lost his audience, was busy switching to another page of his script. He seemed almost too young to be in long trousers, although when he got going you could see why they had given him this job, nodding to the Sergeant, stepping just the right inch back, suitably solemn, gracefully ceding the floor, *of course. Carry on Sergeant, carry on*, his voice adopting the slightly parsonical register reserved for these odd bits of awkwardness.

"Perhaps a good time to say when to … er … *bite* is not a solely personal decision." He let the pause stretch out an uncomfortable beat too long, "Please accept that if there is no choice, there is no choice. That's the logic of the enterprise we're all committed to. Obviously, if captured - whatever your rank - you will not be in uniform."

He let his glance flick over the heads of the women, coming to land on Justine, "Ladies too … although in your case the uniforms of the First Aid Nursing Yeomanry. We have to trust to the FANY to give you the necessary protection of a uniform ..."

He seemed not at all discomforted by the embarrassed silence that followed, until Justine burst out laughing, calling out, "That name! It's a joke. Anyway, we're hardly Yeomen, are we? Hasn't anybody noticed? So we're to go to war with *Fanny* tied round our necks. I ask you! Women of pleasure – *filles de joie* - that the idea?"

It was a long time before he replied, turning aside to stare at the bleak landscape outside, waiting for the laughter to subside, the scrape of chairs to fall silent. "You work without uniforms. Obviously. But that's not to deny your right to one – man or woman – and the enemy should respect that right. They probably will not. If you are taken, you will in all probability be considered a spy. You will be coerced – tortured - activities outlawed under the laws of war. And you will succumb. That's why taking your own life is not solely a personal decision. A whole circuit may stand at risk."

The last day was a Sunday. Albeit the Sabbath, it seemed appropriate to squeeze Assassination in before breakfast: *Written orders in all circumstances.* Someone had pinned up a Notice in the hall, *Morning Service 1100 hours, Torridon Kirk. All welcome.* Alex and Justine walked through the snow in blinding sunlight to the tiny church, to hear the Reverend McClure rail against the Pope. It was hard to say what they had expected: perhaps that God, having an interest in the ways of Special Operations, had, after due consideration, suspended a commandment or two. Perhaps that God, reflecting on the distinction between lawful killing and the other sort might appreciate how their cause sanctified their deeds. But on that Sunday, God had other things on his hands. He had the perfidious ways of Catholics to reckon with – apparently a consuming preoccupation. At which Justine kneeled on the dusty boards to pray, the papist gesture drawing loud tuts from the old ladies sitting behind.

"How did the old fool know I wasn't one?" Walking back, clutching his arm, already thinking of bed.

"You mean Catholic?" thinking of the little pill. "Are you?"

"Could be … he wasn't to know. He was taking a risk with the six weeks brigade: *You're trained to kill, lassie – Aye, remember that.* I could have strangled him. I'm inclined to go back right now and do it."

Back at the house they traded black jokes about the Pope. About the time they had left. About brief lives. Traded jokes all through that last afternoon, drinking gin in bed, curtains open to the darkening sky, the window glass figured over with crystalline ferns. White feathers she said: they looked like white feathers. And he flying into a sudden temper asking what the hell she meant by that, she saying nothing, nothing at all, they just made her think of home. And which home would that be? Shouting for the hundredth time, importunate, thinking of *personal effects*, thinking of the ring. She flaring back, it's none of your business, pestering him into one last hopeless coupling, screaming drunken improvisations on the letter L into his ears as her breath grew heavy.

And that was the end of Justine. He thought never to see her again.

Two

He had thought never to see her again. After all, six weeks doesn't give much time for casual encounters. Yet, incredibly, here she was, pressing against him, squeezing a greeting on his arm through the stiff flying suit, the two of them restlessly perched on a wooden bench in a draughty hanger at Tempsford, the place reeking of paint and aviation fuel. Dressed for the drop, a full moon staring down through the hanger doors, frost outside turning the asphalt silver.

Only an hour before, Alex had been sitting alone in the harsh light of a single light bulb in a shabby little room, staring at a blackboard not properly cleaned. What teacher did with the class before, you couldn't help asking, could you? Someone had written *Dame souris trotte* in rather an illiterate scrawl. Presumably a Playfair key, no accents, which was useful. Verlaine, a poem called *False Impression.* Who said SOE lacked a sense of humour?

It was the Major, nodding a brief acknowledgement. "Captain Vere, isn't it? I'm to brief you." He glanced at the board, frowning, "There'll be two of you jumping," fretfully checking his watch, "your courier's been held up. On the way, I gather. You take off in an hour. The Whitley's on the other runway. There's a decent moon but I'll get somebody to lead the way. Your wireless operator's flying on ahead. A woman: name Simone. This is her first mission, so go easy."

"It's my first as well."

"Sorry, I didn't know. Simone will be with the reception committee sorting out the drop markers for you. She's joining the local circuit. Called *Colombine* – God knows where they get these names."

"The poems of Verlaine, apparently."

"Right. The reception will allocate someone to look after you. The exact date we get you back depends on settling Simone in – she's to let you know. You'll probably be coming back through Northolt, not that it matters. Now … here's the money."

Two chunky parcels pulled from a drawer, green oilskin, bound with tape. "I can't say how important this delivery is. If we're to keep the French playing for us they need liquid funds. They're taking the risks, of course, but I wish it wasn't this way … a bit sordid, things coming down to cash."

Alex stared at a package plonked onto the table. "French Francs. More than you think - take good care of them. And see you get a receipt. God, makes me sound like a bank manager, doesn't it?" Glancing across to the door, suddenly shifty, "And this ..." A parcel, much the same, only this one bound with a white tape, printed *RM* for its whole length.

"Our Intelligence people sent this. Baker Street. Apparently it's German currency. Reichmarks. We make them. De La Rue, I think."

"You mean they're forged?"

"Let's say *printed*, shall we?"

He was busy stripping off the white tape, tossing it into a wastepaper basket. "Just see your courier delivers the goods. They're expected. We have to keep a regular service. No need to tell you it's important – this is one of those *or else* operations, I'm afraid. You hand these to your courier ... when she turns up, that is. Alright?"

Alex nodded, clutching his parcels, feeling foolish, feeling locked out of something, as if he'd missed some essential piece of information, wishing the man would finish a sentence for once in his life.

After the briefing he stood in the empty hangar smoking a last cigarette, watching a dull black Lysander burst into deafening life. The Torridon Major followed him through another door with a little mouse of a woman in tow, clutching a leather case to her breast.

Woollen mittens briefly shook his hand, a tiny face framed in curls: a schoolgirl out too late, a schoolgirl fallen in with the wrong set. So this was the WT Operator. God help them all – she should have been at home swotting for her exams, planning for Oxford tea parties and Rupert Brooke. This bewildered little mouse should have been at school, not messing about with wireless sets in the middle of the night. He wished her luck, fearful eyes, bright blue, catching his own and looking away. They seemed only a touch away from tears.

As he watched the Lysander disappear, a car bounced over the tarmac, skidding to a halt. A woman jumped out, fishing her kit off the back seat, slamming the door. Justine, striding towards him before he had time to be surprised, wrapping her arms round him, beaming.

"They said it was you. I couldn't believe my luck. Now say you're glad to see me. Like the proverbial bad penny, that's me. Briefing done? I got mine driving down. We're delivering loot, I gather. And I'm to carry it. Lucky me. Hand it over, I'll have to stow it. A bit of a miracle I made it, there's one of those random raids. South of London. The docks I think. Briefing alright otherwise?"

"I suppose so. I don't like that chap."

"Who? The gallant Major? He's alright – a bit stiff, but alright when you get to know him."

"That what you propose doing?"

"I may get around to it. What number is this for you? It's my fourth. This one's special, though - I'm going back home. I used to live not far from the drop zone."

"Four! God – how did you manage that? This is number one for me. My first drop. Rather explains the quivering frame, so don't laugh. But seriously, you've done all that?"

"I'm a bit of fraud, really. I've been across twice in one of those." She waved towards the faint rumble in the sky, "A Lysander. Remember that training session, how they said they can carry three? Well, all I can say is, not unless you're a dwarf. It's as cramped as hell with two – you end up really good friends after an hour. But two of my so-called missions amounted to exactly three minutes in a damp field, somewhere called Fauquembergues, not far from Paris. Both times the reception committee was no-show. You get used to that – unreliable buggers the French. These pilots don't hang around, either. I think they resent ferrying the likes of us when they could be giving it to Jerry. Mine didn't even taxi down the other end for a run at it – simply took off. Back home for supper. That was it."

"What was the other mission?"

But she didn't reply, turning to watch a faint finger of torchlight sparkling on the grass, bobbing towards them. Justine pulled at him as he started forward.

"No, let him find us. I'm not stumbling about in the dark just because our precious Major wants to keep his shoes dry - John Lobb shoes, by the way. The Major wears bespoke shoes, isn't that odd? London though, not Paris. I notice things like that. Still, it makes you wonder doesn't it?"

But it wasn't the Major. A voice, a little out of breath, came out of the dark, a bulky form looming up close, "I'll carry your pack, Miss, if you'll follow me. Keep close. You too, sir. It's not far."

Across the field the cough of an engine made the three of them veer towards lights high up in the cockpit of the Whitley. Figures standing, bending over something. Two engines now, rumbling over the frosty grass towards them, a man leaning out of the long frame of the fuselage, pushing a ladder down.

Problems started almost as soon as they had taken off. An earnest Flight Lieutenant came staggering back from the cockpit, to bawl into Alex's ear, "Weather closing in. Looks like we'll lose the moon." The noise made speech impossible. Alex pointed up to the jump lights showing red – it was a question.

"Can't say, old boy. We've a good way to go yet. Skip's going to soldier on. Says sit tight."

Justine leaned over, pulling Alex in, her lips touching his cheek, "Don't tell me. Another bloody no show."

They looked across to the tiny porthole of a window as the plane banked to starboard, a huge moon illuminating endless prairies of rumpled cloud, the sky beyond jet black, limitless. Justine cushioned her pack against the grey ribbed metalwork, smiling to herself. She seemed almost content.

He had been dreaming. Incredible to sleep in this hell, but terror had seduced him into a kind of desperate anaesthesia, nestling on Justine's breast. Standing at his bedroom window looking down. Stiff with terror. Bedtime. Behind him darkness thick and black. The street below bright as day. Always someone standing looking up. The doctor again come to call. No reason at all for terror. He was calling for Mother to come and see. She would be cross: he ought not to be out of bed, not without slippers, not in this wind, not with Justine jerking him awake into a solid mass of noise, Flight's face looming down, misted with sweat, fumbling for his strap.

They had opened the jump hole, the Whitley tipping nose-down, taking your stomach with it, Flight hooking Justine's strap, tugging it, shaking his head as she struggled up, pushing her back against the cabin wall, pointing at the jump light. Red, pulsing like a heart.

A seated upright posture, ladies - the standard joke - N° 1 Parachute Training School, Ringway, the Instructor a fearsome Mancunian, rearing up seven feet high. *Back straight like this* – giraffe neck, a comic line - *or your stupid head will hit the jump hole. No Captain Vere, I didn't design the damned thing. Just try to arrive with your head attached. Can you do that one and all?*

The jump light still red, the Whitley banking, engines resenting the turn, clips rattling, fumes turning your stomach. Flight glanced along the fuselage to the open door of the cockpit, pulling Justine's shoulder, her body juddering with the plane. The jump light still red. Banking harder now, Flight bracing himself against her, swaying at the rim of the jump hole.

"He's making a go-around. Can't see a bloody thing. Cloud."

The engine settled to a dull drumming beat, straight and level. Straight and level in the wrong direction. A pass right over the drop zone could easily put them half a mile adrift. With a go-around you could make that five. Or ten. They were coming round, hydraulics to the flaps stuttering, screaming. Where the hell were they? Tipping to port, cloud caught the edge of the drop hole, pouring ice cold fog into the cabin space. Coming round ... coming round, the final bank steeper, too steep, the floor bucking under their feet. Level now ... straight and level, Flight tugging clips on the rail, mouthing, "On my go." The jump light still red.

It was green, suddenly green. And Justine gone. Dropping into nothing: upright posture, back straight. His turn: the shoulder tap almost a shove, a shadow running huge and dark above him, air hard in his mouth, stinging like sleet, hurting his nose. One thought tumbling with him: the Whitley had been too fast, far too fast. Something like frozen steam was tearing his nose. Tumbling faster, a ferocious wind ripping at his legs. Too fast, too fast, too fast. Surely it was all wrong? Candles ... don't they call them candles, dropping like this?

Something monstrous punched between his shoulders, jerking his head back with the strength of it, sweet silk, vast as the sky, billowing out over him. A rush of new thoughts: how low? Justine? The dark of trees below ... there shouldn't be trees ... trees suddenly gone, jerked out of sight ... tipping back ... the swell of a hill canting across his view, grass between the trees, a rushing black advance of solid nothing. *Legs together ladies – you know it makes sense. Legs together.* Thump. Roll. Thump. Legs dragging through wet grass, bouncing your breath out, boots gouging clods of clay, a mountain of silk heaving above, dragging you in its wake over wet grass. Everywhere, the sweet smell of wet grass.

Justine was standing on the rise of the hill, already bracing against the wind, hauling in. Alex hit the box release, the webbing pulling past his shoulders. Justine was looking down at him, the rumble of the departing Whitley filling the distant valley.

They followed a path across the field and jumped a ditch. A road sign proclaimed *Aste-sur-Torre* in red and white. Beyond that, two lines of sleeping houses, shuttered and silent. Barely a village.

The moon had gone again. Alex unfolded the map, risking the torch, squinting close to the paper, Justine nudging him aside, running her finger along the black streak of a road.

"It's alright, I know Aste. I know where we are – I lived not far from here." She stabbed a finger on the map. "The drop zone's here. Your Simone woman will be waiting."

"God, it's a hike. Why the hell does nothing ever go right? Will she wait?"

"It's not just her – there's a reception committee. They'll wait. They have to: we've got their money. About five miles I reckon, but easy walking on the road. And we're not late, just a bit adrift."

Burying their flying gear they realised how inadequately dressed they were. Alex went to drape his coat over her shoulders, but she shook him away, "No time for that. I'll warm up walking. I've got all that cash weighing me down, remember? But first I'm going over there ... and don't ask why."

She vaulted the low wall, slithering down a steep bank into the dark bulk of the wood. A dog started up, surprisingly close, setting off a chorus of answering howls. There must be a house somewhere in the trees. A single yellow square of light appeared suspended in the dark, sending him scuttling for the ditch.

But the other light was already on him. He had not seen the car running silently down between the houses, twin headlights sweeping shadows of massive platanes across the road. Alex stood helpless and blinded in light as bright as day.

The car came to rest alongside, a huge engine panting fumes into the night air. A face in the rear seat peered out: a mouse of a face set under girlish yellow curls, fearful bright eyes catching his own, twitching away. A single gloved hand pressed against the glass, little woollen mittens, sky blue, the kind a child would wear sent into the snow to play. No recognition – her anonymous expression filled with the resignation of defeat.

A door on the other side opened then slammed shut, slow footsteps clicking on the metalled road into the headlights, a figure blotting out the light.

"Your colleague? You were three. The other woman? Where is she?" He was no more than a black silhouette against the headlamps, tall, angular, no hat, light catching the frayed ends of a woollen jumper unravelling at the neck, the kind of thing farm workers wore. But you'd take your oath this chap knew nothing of farms. The voice settled it:

English with just enough of a controlled German accent. A cultivated voice, expensively acquired on English playing fields, mildly put out by the frailty of the forces assembled against it, a slightly peevish tone, as if somehow it had deserved better.

"She is with you? Please. It would spare us all a cold night."

They must have been waiting for the Lysander to land, dressed for the part, waiting for Simone. Without that go-around he would have dropped into the same trap, Justine as well. Thinking of her watching, Alex tried desperately not to glance into the woods, peering blindly forward. Best not speak at all. Once you start to speak it's hard to stop.

You must hold out for forty-eight hours, the Highland accent gentle for once, singling Alex out. *Captain Vere, sir – you understand me?* Alex nodding like a keen schoolboy, Justine was not even looking up, fiddling with her cardboard box, rattling the tablets inside.

Forty-eight hours to hold out, to give the circuit a chance to repair, time for those who could to escape. Forty-eight hours for Justine to slip the net. This man would not be scouring woods tonight.

Standing alongside the car Alex felt something in his stomach move and clenched against the worst. They always said your bowels would give you away. But then, they said a lot of things. *Forty-eight hours*. They started now, those forty-eight. He never imagined his first mission this way. Stillborn. At least he could give Justine something.

Three

A flag was all that marked it as the Gendarmerie. Grander than its neighbours only by virtue of a flight of stone steps and a double door. The hall inside reeked of sweat and Gitanes, cheap disinfectant not quite masking some other smell, vaguely disquieting, like children's vomit. They kept Alex in the car while Simone was bundled inside, the driver returning to haul her WT set off the back seat. By the time it was his turn to be prodded up the steps she had gone. He was steered into a room off the hall and allowed to sink down on a wooden bench. An old man in Municipal Police uniform glanced up then went on typing.

Alex saw his German for the first time. Surely not more than twenty-five, pale oval face, fair hair, thin lips. *People with thin lips are cruel* – didn't Mother always say that? Although this one didn't look cruel. Tired perhaps, pulling a grubby pullover over his head, wool muffling his voice, emerging to catch his breath, smiling.

"I suppose I speak to you in English?" There was a kind of weary superiority in the voice.

"You are English, aren't you? And now you are going to deny it. This …" holding out the papers Alex had helplessly handed over by the side of the car, "this says you are French. Born … let me see …

born in Toulouse. A pretty place, Toulouse. La Cité Rose, is it not?" He threw them back onto the desk.

"Have you ever been there? Do you really want to play this stupid game?" He was enjoying himself, sprawling into a chair, showing off in front of the old man who had stopped typing to watch.

"You know, most of you Britishers pretend to be Dutch. Did you know that? You pretend to be Dutch and we have to hurt you – just to discover you are not. Not Dutch. Or in your case, not French."

He waited, letting the silence spin out, the old man settling back in his chair to listen to the strange language. Faintly from down the corridor muffled voices reached them, perhaps a woman – too far to tell.

The German stood up.

"It's late. I have got better things to do than round up sheep. In the morning my superiors will need to know who you are, who sent you, why you are here, and where your missing colleague might be. You will have an uncomfortable night to think about it."

He came across to Alex, resting a hand on his shoulder, embarrassed. He seemed very young,

"Let me speak frankly. I am a soldier. You - you are a soldier? Pretend you can't understand, if you like, but I ask where is your uniform? Where is your identity token – your disk? You know perfectly well why I ask. Is this your idea of war? Giant Albion – isn't that what your poet called you? Parachuting women to do your fighting. Is that what the Giant has come to? Hoodlums and criminals firing pistols from ditches."

He perched himself on the edge of the desk, leaning forward, soft face excited. Unused to conquest, this one, having caught his fish, wondering what to do with it. Hard to believe he was long out of school.

"Listen. If you are helpful, it is possible you could become … how can I put this? Something other than a cheap bandit. A French criminal perhaps? It might be arranged. You have the night to think about it."

The squeal from down the corridor took Alex by surprise, a primal sound setting his heart racing. The old policeman stopped typing. For a moment it seemed that everything stopped. The second scream was louder, as if someone unused to screaming had decided to rehearse. The scream of someone who, in all her life, had never found reason to scream. A door somewhere crashed open, the sound billowing down the corridor, running feet halting, the scuffle oddly demeaning, someone intoning, *No, no, no*, over and over again, a tiny voice insane with fear.

The typewriter began again. Alex stared at the floor. *You're meant to hear this. You're meant to hear this.* Torridon said this would happen, said there were things you were meant to hear. They had even rehearsed it, roping Justine into the pretence, her screams that morning bringing complaints from the kitchens.

This is something you are meant to hear. Although no pretence could prepare you for a schoolgirl's screams. She didn't know how to scream, this little girl, not properly. The German was patting his pocket, looking for his cigarette case. He seemed embarrassed at these unpractised moans, sounds that tore your heart out.

Something heavy shuddered on the wooden floor, making the old policeman glance up, the silence broken by the scrape of a match. The policeman yanked sheets of paper out of the typewriter, watching the German light a cigarette. He shook one of his own from a crumpled blue packet.

The German was back in his chair, shuffling through papers, tossing them one by one onto the desk. He kept the passport till last.

"It is a remarkably bad forgery, you know. You English usually do better. Here, I will show you something. It will amuse you."

He drew a folder on the desk towards him, taking out a single sheet of paper, dangling it in front of Alex. "No? Very well, I will read it to you. ETA 0130 STOP HOME DELIVERY SIMONE STOP DROP GERALD AND MARIE STOP ETA 0210 WCP STOP ARCHER STOP END. You see it is in English. Well, a sort of English. Ah, perhaps you Dutchmen don't understand English. WCP, that would be Weather Conditions Permitting, would it not? And it appears they did permit because you are here. Frankly it was a surprise. We had been told of heavy cloud. Shall I call you Gerald? Tomorrow you will tell me who you really are and where we can find this woman Marie. I will discover her real name myself."

He turned away, the single word, 'Jorg!' barked at the top of his voice bringing the clump of hurried feet to the door, polished boots clicking a salute. A whispered exchange ended in a stream of muttered oaths, Alex risking a glance saw this shiny Untersturm*führer* was SS. Nobody said there were German troops here, just the Vichy police to deal with, London said. London was certain of it: somebody should have told the Germans.

His arms were being pulled hard behind his back, wrenching his shoulders.

"My regrets. The handcuffs remain. I am told the discomfort becomes less. It is too much trouble looking for wherever you have hidden your little tablet. We shall discover tomorrow. You English, always flirting with suicide. There was a boy at my school … no, I will tell you that story when we meet tomorrow. There will be time." He nodded to the soldier and turned away.

There was an odd faecal smell in the passageway. Through the open door Alex could see the chair Simone had been tied to. It had fallen with her. She lay splayed across a tangle of split wood, her blouse torn open, the pink brassiere, something a girl would wear, curiously innocent. Her head had lolled back at an impossible angle, the mouth crusted round with something white. This child had been sick before it died. Her eyes followed him as he stumbled past. They seemed fearful even in death.

The window in the room where they left him was barred but you would hardly call the place a cell. It must once have been someone's living room, scuffed linoleum worn through at a spot near the empty fireplace. An ancient horsehair mattress had been thrown on the floor. Apart from a bucket by the door there was nothing else. Alex crouched down and let himself fall awkwardly back onto his tethered arms.

Captives must fight the temptation to create a rescue myth. Odd he should think of that particular lecture now. They had dragooned a tame psychologist in to talk about fear, all of them faking attention, thinking how best to spin it out, anything for a few more hours out of the snow. The man spoke of myths of rescue, of their corroding effect, of the dangers of hope. Nonsense, of course. Alex had no thoughts of rescue. Hope had ended with that car sliding silently between the houses. Life had ended then. Your six weeks are up, Captain Vere. There was a peculiar kind of peace in that realisation.

Forty-eight hours to survive. He would focus on that. How many gone already? Four? Five? They had not taken his watch, but he had no way of looking at it. No way either of extracting the tiny lump from his coat lapel. Women sometimes put the L-pill in a broach – something to pin to your heart. High enough to get at, of course, if you were so minded. Poor Simone had been so minded.

There was a terrible racket in the night, shadows passing across the slit of light under the door, footsteps heavy on bare boards, the rattle of buckets. There were two of them, muttering to each other. Not police, though. They sounded aggrieved. Eventually, an outer door slammed and the place fell quiet. It must be six hours gone. But these were the easy hours. The German would come back, the one with thin lips.

Alex had been desperate for the bucket for ages, discomfort inexorably progressing to pain. Legs writhing in ludicrous efforts to stand, he somehow rolled off the lumpy mattress, inching himself upright against the wall, tottering across the room dragging urgently, hopelessly, at the back of his trousers. There was no point: a thick warm stream was already running down his legs into his shoes, piddling a thick black snake across the floor. A blissful, shameless, shameful relief.

Humiliation by the removal of clothing or denial of personal hygiene. Torridon had had words for this as well. Hardly a consolation, if you think about it, more a perverse validation of the process. Yes, they said, you will feel humiliated. And he did.

A church bell had started up, not telling the time, just clanging slowly a long way off. That bit of Verlaine about the mice came back to him, hadn't he composed that in prison? *Dormez, les bons prisonniers.* He thought he would never sleep on that stained mattress but sleep can be born of misery easily enough.

He awoke dreaming of Simone's terrified face, oddly indistinct with its halo of curly hair, the bang of a distant door jerking him back to terror.

Still early, a little winter sunlight red on the houses opposite, shutters propped open a crack for the air, the occupants surely still asleep. What did they make of all these stumbling people dragged up their neighbour's steps? What did these sturdy French burghers think of all those goings-on? Did they even wonder? Probably not. You got used to things in France now, even screams.

A cockerel behind the house started to crow, got into its stride, and couldn't stop.

Someone was making coffee, a wireless punching out snappy bits of morning news, louder as a door opened, feet thumping past his door, his heart thumping in step. *Get on with it. Get on with it.* Forty-eight hours was two days. Get through today and that would be one gone: he would be into the second. And what then? They were going to kill him, but you can still ask how. When you are this close to death, *how* is all that matters. What thin lips that German had – you notice things like that.

With thoughts of death off the leash Alex lingered over them, wondering why fear refused to come, why it had stayed so stubbornly aloof. What was the matter with him? All he felt was an odd numbness about the heart. Perhaps there is a point beyond which fear cannot grow? And Justine? She was free. Of the three of them, one caught, one dead, one still free. Would he betray her? Could they bring him to that?

He stood at the window, looking out across the vacant street, wet trousers draped cold against his legs. She was free. At least they had secured that much. And he was going to die. All he had left to discover was how.

He would be having his breakfast, that German with the thin lips. He had asked for a name. Surely any name would do? Why should the German care what Alex called himself? What would be lost in telling? Nothing at all. What was the point of torturing him for that? Perhaps he did not need a point. Perhaps torture would be satisfaction enough. If so, nothing in God's world could help him – nothing at all. *You will succumb.* Oh, there was truth in that. If only they would not hurt him, he would succumb alright. Hurt him how?

A million secret thoughts invaded him, fear as he'd never known it curling over him, doubling him up, pressing him crouched into the corner, fettered arms shaking, crying *No, no, no* into the pointless air, his little tablet wedged out of reach. Dear God, he would bite it now. Oblivion was more desirable than anything he had ever known: even than Justine.

Her name is Justine Perry. Her name is Justine Perry. She's a spy. We're both spies. Get on with it. Open the bloody door. Get it over. Only please God, don't hurt me too much. Please, not that.

The wireless clicked off. Real voices now, one lighter than the rest. That German with the oval face must be back. He seemed dreadfully young, this man with thin lips. Was he here already? New voices talking, the old policeman with his smoker's cough, clearing his lungs, somebody laughing as the door opened, feet thudding along the corridor, taking their time, a key in the lock.

He wouldn't get up. Crouching, knees pulled up, face buried in the stink of his trousers, they could leave him here, a little foetal lump, not worth the taking. The old policeman pulled at his collar, dragging him to the open door, casually prodding him to walk ahead, trousers flapping wet against his shins. At the door he leaned past Alex pushing it open, shoving him inside.

A tall man in the uniform of an officer of the Gendarmerie was standing by the door spitting out French words in barely supressed fury. Justine, a heavy purple overcoat incongruously draped over bare shoulders, stood listening with the air of someone patiently waiting for a storm to blow itself out. She had rested one hand on his sleeve in a curious proprietorial gesture, tugging it slightly as Alex came in.

The man prised her hand off, turning away, staring out of the window. They stood together, their backs to Alex, in urgent whispered conversation, voices barely audible. Finally, the man erupted with a snort of laughter and swung round to stare at Alex, the old policeman scuttling back against the door, standing erect.

For a split second Justine's glance flashed danger and Alex knew – although God knows how – she was begging him not to speak. On tiptoes, lips inches from the tall man's ear, she murmured something that drew another reluctant smile.

Alex could only guess who he was, this tall man with his crisp uniform, elegant fingers unconsciously paddling Justine's bare arm. Clearly somebody - undeclared authority reason enough for the old policeman to stand nervously eyeing his cigarette burning itself out.

There must have been an order given, no more than a nod, Alex wincing with relief as he saw the handcuffs for the first time, surprisingly small, tossed onto the desk. He watched as a bundle of papers was pressed into Justine's hands.

She was already tugging his arm, pushing him ahead through the door. In the corridor, the double entrance doors stood wide open, the street beyond bathed in cold sunlight. The same cockerel was crowing.

As they came out, two women on the pavement looked up then went on talking. Alex stopped, consumed with a sense of anti-climax, Justine murmuring, "For Christ's sake, what now?"

At the foot of the steps she suddenly pulled the overcoat from her shoulders, "Damn, I'll have to give him this back …"

But the man had followed them, standing looking down, one hand outstretched for his coat, a faint smile of concession on his face.

He looked at Alex, his English faultless, "You are fortunate in your friends, Monsieur the Frenchman. I will give you some advice. Keep your passport as a souvenir. Take it home with you to London. Explain to your superiors that France is not a playground for the English, do you understand? I will not apologise for your discomfort - you brought it on yourself. Go home."

Slipping his arms into the coat, looking at Justine, his expression was impossible to read, "Go home both of you. You do no good here." Turning back inside, he called over his shoulder, "Perhaps you will be good enough to explain, Madame."

At the corner of the street a battered lorry waited, a young man pulling at a starting handle, trying to get the engine to catch. The two women stopped talking as it exploded into life, watching them squeeze three abreast onto the dusty leather seat. At the crossroads they veered onto a narrow clay track, an impossible gradient, the engine screaming in first gear, climbing to a ridge high against the dawn sky beyond.

The driver barely stopped at the summit, circling a patch of open ground, nodding for them to jump. They stood listening as the sound retreated back into the valley below, Justine smiling at last.

"God, *Madame*. He's never called me that. A right old slap in the face."

Four

"Captain Vere sir, Captain Vere," Mother shaking him. No, somebody else shaking him. Wide awake now in his chair by the bed. He'd been dreaming. The same fetid smell everywhere.
It was too hot in here – you never get used to that.

"You've a visitor, sir. And why are you sitting out like that without your cover? You'll catch your death." She means well, this one. It would offend her to say he'd already caught it – but she wouldn't understand anyway. How she does rattle on.

"You don't get all that many visitors. Out of hours as well, but this one's got a chit. Top Brass I'd say, this chap, you can tell, little rose in his buttonhole an' all. I can ask Alfred to pop along and give you a shave if you like. He's busy this morning with the new lot, but just for you. Shall I do that? He'll wait, your visitor … ever so keen to see you. Important looking. I've to give you his card. Now … what about that shave? Spruce you up a bit."

This nurse was called Cecily. He'd always thought of her as his, she seemed to spend so long tending to him. Before Alex worked out where he was – and that took a long time – Cecily had been his only way of staying sane. Although that had been part of the problem – he couldn't be sure any more that he *was* sane: not exactly.

She used to live at Epsom with an invalid mother before they moved here. Away from the bombs, she said, although that was a joke because the bombs followed them. She had a boyfriend, Arthur, although that couldn't go very far - *you know what I mean* - because he'd been called up. Likely to go to Egypt or some such, so he said.

Alex liked listening to Cecily talking about moving here because eventually he found out where *here* was. Southampton. A hospital, although God alone knew why he was in a hospital in Southampton.

When he'd woken up he thought at first he must have been injured because there was a war on. Some battle or other. Shot perhaps? You get shot at in wars: he knew all about the war. But he didn't seem to be injured, certainly not shot.

He spent one whole morning indulgently working his way up from his toes to his eyelids, inch by inch and everything seemed to work. True there was a moment's panic remembering people with no legs think they are there all the same. But no, his legs had not been cut off. He could touch them. If the sheets hadn't been so tight across his chest, he could have looked at them. He had only the headache to concern him: an endless dull pain squeezing thought out of his head.

He knew it was a hospital because Cecily was a nurse. Netley hospital, she called it, *and a right old dump*. That made him smile: talking about how the nurses had only cold water to wash in, *and wasn't that a crime*? *And the lavvies ... well, you wouldn't want to know about them.*

That first night she'd spent befuddled hours with him, pushing him back into bed when he'd tried to get free of the sheets, when he'd asked where Justine was, when he'd tried to go home. Not that he knew where home was. That was when he decided she was nice, trotting off every few minutes in her starched white cap to attend to some other bed, always coming back.

That was the other thing, the place was full of beds, hundreds of them, row upon row. You're in Netley she said, as if he'd understand, although he didn't. *Block D, but don't you go making anything of that. Lots of the new ones come in here first. No call to go making anything of that.*

But he wasn't making anything of it. He just wanted the headache to go away and was too tired to ask. All he could remember was something about mice and it didn't seem reasonable to trouble her with that.

Of course, he did understand eventually. Block D was where they put the mad ones. Although Dr Hoffmann had explained he was no longer mad, which was to imply that he had been. Dr Hoffmann did not elaborate. Simply pronounced in her matter-of-fact way that he appeared to be suffering from a psychological reaction to some extreme event. And the fractured skull – there was that as well, of course. Severe trauma was the term she used, explaining she was a psychiatrist and it was her job to uncover it.

It would be hard to think of anything more pointless. Alex was surprised to realise he knew about psychoanalysis: a weird Viennese cult best practised in church, or synagogue, if you wanted to be precise. As scientifically legitimate as phrenology and about as much use. Talking about uncovering when there was nothing covered in the first place, patently the good doctor Hoffmann was happy to waste her time. Alex was hiding nothing. After all, he had nothing to hide.

Since there was nothing to recollect, their encounters seemed entirely futile: him sitting in front of her, staring into space, trying to be polite, she leaning back looking at him, a little like his mother, a kindly serious expression on her face, breaking the silence now and then to ask if there was anything he wanted to say.

They filled the time with games. She would say a word and he was to reply with what it reminded him of. It seemed he knew all about that as well, had read the books. She would write down his answers and often the following day they would talk about them, an activity that slowly became not completely uninteresting.

Alex grew to look forward to these daily sessions with Dr Hoffmann. Gradually, they took on a different character, the two of them slipping into a kind of complicity, as if they shared some unspoken common purpose.

Imperceptibly, he came to believe there were three people present: obviously, Dr Hoffmann and himself, but also someone else. Not entirely nice this other chap, shifty, devious, wriggling, cleverly shying away when things closed in on him, when things got too close.

It was one Saturday morning that the two of them finally pinned him down. It was a kind of trick. There were never sessions at the weekend and Alex had protested when the escort arrived, but Dr Hoffmann had come in specially that Saturday. Perhaps she had hoped to take this other person by surprise: her way of cornering this absent presence. The trick worked.

For the first time, he let them into a little part of his secret. Of a sudden, he remembered Justine, dear familiar Justine, shouldering open the battered door of a derelict stone hut overgrown with brambles, his memory charged with the smell of the animals that had invaded the place.

It belonged to Claude Barte, she said, the man who ran the local circuit. He had olives up here years ago but it got to be too much trouble. They were to stay until dark. Turning to him then, looking tired, but somehow triumphant, her question quite casual. *That WT, Simone, wasn't it? Where have they got her, do you know?* And he did know, this wily secretive chap, although the words wouldn't come, apart from I'm going to be sick, Justine grabbing his arm, shouting, no way, you can't be sick here. And you should take those trousers off, clean yourself up. They smell like you've pissed yourself.

Dr Hoffmann was smiling at Alex like Mother smiled long ago when he'd been particularly good, when he'd come home with a gold star. So he smiled back, a little crooked, but it seemed churlish not to. Both of them quietly smiling because they'd tricked it out of him. Pleased the two of them were getting somewhere, Dr Hoffmann leaning back in her comfortable chair, waiting for more. Now he'd started they both knew there would be more. And true enough the other chap remembered. Saying she's dead if you must know. Simone's dead. Swallowed that bloody pill thing. Remembered Justine saying hell, we could have got her out.

He could not remember how the session ended. There seemed to be a gap. Sometimes Dr Hoffmann would give him an injection, something to make him sleep, an odd sort of dreamless sleep with a sweet chemical taste all of its own.

It was Sunday before he woke to the familiar headache, that same taste in his mouth. The ward was always quiet on Sunday. Those allowed to, had gone to the chapel, a red-brick barracks of a place incongruously topped off with a florid green dome. Not Alex. He was in no need of prayer that day.

He would lie on his back, remembering Justine.

"Are you going to tell me how ..."

"How I turned up with the rescue party, you mean? You poor Guffin. You looked a mournful sight I must say."

She was rummaging inside a khaki rucksack left on the table. "God bless him, Claude's left us a bottle of wine. Shall I open it? We can drink it outside. It stinks in here." She turned to look at him, suddenly serious," I saw that car before you did – that's all there is to it. I cut and ran. Scarpered. Ran like hell. Until I realised I was making too much noise and nobody was coming after me. By the time I'd crept back, you were being bundled into the car by your German friend. Then you drove off, the lot of you."

They sat on damp grass under a plantation of umbrella pines. In the valley below mist still wrapped itself round tiny stone houses. Endless ripples of wooded hills stretched to the horizon, steel-grey in faint sunlight. She let her hand rest on his arm, holding him there. Although he surely had nowhere else to go.

It was an age before she spoke.

"I told you I used to live here. In the village. You won't like this. Hear me out. That man. The one all dressed up who made the little speech – slapped me in the face with Madame. He had a little house the other side of that wood. A sort of cabin. He used to call it our love nest. Something he'd read in a book, silly chap. I doubt I was the first girl he'd taken there."

As she felt him free his hand she sprang up, "Don't you look at me like that! Don't you dare! What the hell gives you the right to look at me like that? Stop gawping Alex. It was years ago. I was very young. It was flattering if you want to know. He said he loved me. He even gave me a ring. You've seen it. Mind you, he'd already given one to his wife ... that was a disappointment. Hotel decoration he called it. Alright, I know it sounds cheap ..."

"You don't have to tell me any of this. I've no right to hear it."

"You mean you don't want to hear – I'm not sure I think well of you for that. Listen. I joined SOE in thirty-nine. What was the chance of me ending up in this place? Seriously. Quite a coincidence, wouldn't you say?"

"You said you lived here. They must have known that."

"Oh, they knew alright. Why send women on missions at all? Why do you think they do that? No, don't look away. Don't tell me the thought never crossed your mind. Why send me? I guess there's a Pascal Renault lying in wait for all of us. What else do you think I was supposed to do? Can you seriously ask? And that stupid expression on your face. What's that supposed to mean? That I'm yours now? How do you think I feel about it, gold ring and all? I'll tell you how I feel – angry."

Alex walked to the edge of the clearing. The faint scent of woodsmoke rose from a chimney far below. A cock was still crowing.

Justine's voice drew him back.

"Once you'd been arrested Pascal was our only hope."

"But who the devil is he?"

"Who? He's a Colonel in the Gendarmerie. He used to be a big fish in the Deuxième Bureau. Now he's in something called the Office for Anti-National Affairs. Counterespionage. Gathering information on German infiltration of the Vichy setup. He knows your SS chum is spying on him. The hunter hunted – he was the target. Pascal loathes him. He told me once his job was to stop them infiltrating our networks. I never dared ask who *our* was. My first real mission was here – after those two trips to Fauquembergues I told you about. When I was settling in, the gossip among the girls in the village was all about Pascal. You're best to say yes when he asks, they said. I turned up to get my papers stamped and he couldn't believe his eyes. Went on and on about the old days. About how it had been a real coup de foudre, that there was nobody else and never could be. Very French – as if I cared who else he'd been bedding."

She reached out, taking his hand in her own, searching for his eyes. "But I said yes, Alex. You may as well know, so there's no misunderstanding. After that first time I realised he must have meant *some of the things he said. A week after I'd landed I was lying low. The telephone went. I knew the voice - it was Pascal – but all it said was clear out and put the receiver down. The apartment was raided later that morning. That wasn't the only time. I owe him my life several times over."*

"I owe you my life."

"Perhaps you do, but don't go calling it a trade, don't you dare. It was with Pascal. I was buying security and I knew what I was buying it with. There's a name for that, if you want to use it."

"You think you were sent here because they knew you had been … close? It sounds cynical enough."

"Not really. They don't care about the particulars. It's what women are for – that's what they think. I doubt anybody knows about Renault. For one thing, he doesn't like the English. Says Englishmen make him feel inferior – and they have humiliated France. It's just that he really hates your German. It's something personal."

"And you told him about me? He had no reason to let me walk away. Every reason to keep me, in fact."

"That was what he was going to do, believe me. He asked why the hell he should. Said he was damned if he would help my lovers – the French do make that plural sound so prurient. That's what he was screaming about when they brought you in. But I convinced him."

"I can't see how."

"Can't you? I'm afraid I told him there was no way you would hold out when that SS officer got back. Wimpish – that was you, I said. Given what he thinks about the English, he appreciated the irony. I told him they'd prise my name out of you, no trouble. No, Alex, don't get on your high horse. I happen to be right. You don't know that German. He has a reputation. He gets pleasure out of hurting people. I told Pascal that if they got me he couldn't expect me to hold out long. He would be next in line. God, he was furious. Saw what I was up to and went into one of those comic Gallic frenzies. Called me a little blackmailer, a bitch, a whore, and a good few other words he hadn't used in a while. But I'll give him this, he knows when he's cornered. You know, I've just realised he knew if he was arrested his wife would get to hear of his English mistress. I think that worried him as much as anything. Men

really are ridiculous."

"But that German will turn up this morning. He must be there already. It's us that's cornered."

"No. Both of them are at a conference all morning. Pascal arranged it. About clandestine operations, would you believe? He's left a warrant at the Gendarmerie to have you transferred to the special security prison in Limoges – with immediate effect. He has the authority to do that. They'll get back this afternoon to discover the place deserted, nothing about you in the Station log book, and the bird flown. If there ever was a bird."

"But they'll check with Limoges. They're bound to."

"And you won't have arrived, will you? Pascal will deny signing anything. He'll ask the desk Sergeant if he followed procedure and telephoned ahead for an escort. But warrants like that get forged all the time. I suppose the poor Sergeant will get it in the neck, but he's no option but to keep his mouth shut."

It was not until the following day that Dr Hoffmann heard this story, breaking her habitual silence to wonder aloud whether there might not still be something. Something more to fish for.

"That dream. I've been looking at my notes. You describe a dream you had on a flight. You say it was light, although it was night-time? That interests me. I am reminded of your description of the headlights of that car when you were arrested. In which case …"

"No, it was before I was arrested. I've had that dream since I was a child. A nightmare really, because it's always filled with feelings of dread."

"And you are always at a window in the dream?"

"Yes, in my bedroom. Looking down. And this woman's on the other side of the street. Do I have to talk about this?"

"I suppose not. You say the figure is a doctor? I did wonder about that. I am a doctor."

"When I was a child our doctor was a German woman."

"Hoffmann is a German name."

"She came to the house sometimes when we were sick ... she is just standing there, looking up at me."

“Looking at you?”

“It seems so. But I know this: the fear … dread really … was to do with the light.”

“And perhaps the fact she was German? You could say you were in the dark. Would you say that?”

Alex let out a sigh of exasperation, “If I was in the dark about something, I would know – isn’t that right? Why should I go to the trouble of dreaming, just to tell myself? It doesn’t make sense. It isn’t as if I was Joseph bringing news to the Pharaohs. D’you think we could stop? My headache’s worse.”

”But it means something to you – this light, this dark. Do you think it means nothing? Yes, I’m sorry, we should stop. If we had time …”

But they did not have time. Three days later a telephone call from the War Office persuaded Dr Hoffmann to sign his discharge papers. There was a war on, after all, and cases more pressing than unresolved childhood trauma: Alex could be returned to the world, if not completely whole, whole enough.

He was looking at the slip of embossed card Cecily had left on the bed - *Neville Archer, MC, Lieutenant Colonel* - when the man himself appeared in the ward, working his way from bed to bed, checking names. Alex half rose in his chair then sank back, clutching his blanket.

A stumpy barrel-chested old buffer from another age was eyeing him from the other side of the bed, breathing heavily as if the stairs had defeated him. Older than Alex expected, he seemed a relic of quite another war. This bloke properly needed a horse to sit on and a sabre.

Tiny black eyes peered out of a wide florid face with the astonished expression of a stunned ox, huge moustaches, their flaring days not quite over, jutting out like tufts of cotton wool making his square head look unnaturally big.

He was uncomfortably dressed in tweed civvies, a rosebud in his lapel. He extended a hand across the bed then, realising it was too far to reach, awkwardly withdrew it, sitting down heavily on the other side, looking for somewhere to put a pair of yellow kid gloves, finally placing them on the bed.

"Captain Vere? That's what it says, but always best to check. You don't know me. Name's Archer. Baker Street. I don't think our paths have crossed."

He started a condescending laugh then thought better of it, withdrawing it like the handshake.

Archer. Alex was sure he had heard the name somewhere. It wouldn't come. "No sir, I don't think we've met. I'm pleased to see someone from the unit. A few more days and I'll ..."

The glittering eyes were darting warily round the ward. "Not the best place to talk, here. About your last mission. I've read the report. It seems you were damnably unlucky. Damnably."

He lapsed into silence. He had found something on the ceiling and was staring at it disapprovingly, shuffling a little to get straight. The wooden chair seemed too small for him.

"And you ended up in this place?" It was a question, but Alex was lost for a reply. "I've not come to hear your story. Time enough for that."

"I don't think it could be much of a story, sir. I've suffered some memory loss. Still piecing things together. It was the immediacy of everything, I think. Barely time to bury the chutes and we're picked up." He managed an awkward laugh. "Still, better luck next time. Don't they say that, sir?"

"We can't send you back, Vere."

You could tell he rather enjoyed blurting things out. He had composed his face, trying to look serious, but you could see there was almost a smile behind it all. Perhaps he didn't even realise it himself – this ancient relic actually enjoyed bearing bad news. Perhaps it was the last bit of power left to him.

"You do know that? It's impossible."

"Because I've been taken? I know the rule, sir. It just seems arbitrary in this case. Given the circumstances."

The unfortunate secret smile escaped. Archer turning it into a half-hearted kind of laugh, no more than a little catch in his throat, trickling away to nothing.

"Can't change the rules just for you, you know." He leaned forward, tapping his nose in a strange conspiratorial gesture. "You don't realise what a rare bird you are, Captain Vere. Once an agent's taken they never come back. You appreciate that? Never come back. And here you are. You're the first."

"Meaning you can't trust me, sir? Is that what you mean?" Alex realised he was blushing. This old fool actually believed it. What made it worse, his protests would only confirm it.

Archer glanced round the deserted ward, picking up his gloves. "Don't be too hard on yourself. And don't be too hard on us. Let's just say we have to proceed on that basis. That's logical isn't it? Doesn't sound so bad put that way, does it? Who's to know whether somebody's been turned? Or what it means, come to think of it. The world's not black and white is it? You'll know more about that than me."

"But Mrs Perry's report. She must have explained ..."

"It's true we have a report. But ..."

"... I was only held overnight. A short night at that."

"There'll be time to go into this when we get you back to London. Tomorrow, isn't it? The point is you've been seen. Your papers have been seen ... "

"He said the passport was a bad forgery, by the way."

"Who did?"

"The German who arrested me. SS. A young chap but quite senior I think."

"They always say that – throws you off your stride. Your passport is perfectly sound. More so than the rest of the papers if it comes to that. People at Duke Street made it – even the ink's French. There's a point you're missing, Captain Vere, they've had it in their hands. You're *known*. I'm sorry to bear bad news, but you won't be going back. It can't be a surprise to you."

"I was thinking perhaps an exception, given the whole operation was a disaster: an utter shambles."

"You're bound to see it that way, but you don't get to see the whole picture. Overall, even taking your ..." he stopped, struggling to find the right word. The slightly supercilious smile seemed painted on his face. "... your *escapade* into account, overall, we were not dissatisfied. All in all, in terms of objectives, it went well. Hellish unfortunate for you, of course, but for the rest ... on the whole, a success. Yes, a success."

Five

At first, pleasure in being free of the smells and discomfort of Netley was enough and Archer's summons seemed suitably remote. But gradually Alex understood his discharge had been in a sense provisional: he had been left incomplete.

Each morning, he awoke to welcome the dull pain in his head like an old friend, lying for a few painful minutes sorting among scraps of remembered detail, checking what memories sleep had delivered back to him. The immediate past remained a once-familiar place, endlessly taunting him: he lived with his life on the tip of his tongue.

Archer's unit turned out to be an unprepossessing warren of dusty rooms over the Post Office in Bedford Square. A wooden plaque, newly-stencilled TPSU in white paint, army-style, had been screwed to the wall at the foot of a flight of tiled stairs.

Archer, in dress uniform, was standing at the banister rail, peering down beyond Alex into the gloom of the stairwell as if he expected someone else.

"Take the tube?"

"No sir, I walked. It's not that far for me. Dr Hoffmann says I need the exercise. To tell the truth I don't like being cooped up in the tube."

"Do I know this Dr Hoffmann?"

"Somebody at Netley, sir. Helped put some of the bits together. My bits, that is."

"Never met him. Go through," pointing to the door immediately behind him, "I'll be with you in a minute. We're only just getting settled in here. All a bit primitive, but it serves, it serves. You'll find a chair. The last lot left us that. They didn't leave much else. Park yourself, I won't be long. There's just the two of us so far."

When he bustled back he plonked a pile of brown manila folders onto a battered desk and stood leafing through the one on top, rustling pages, pursing his lips as though he was about to start whistling. Alex had stood up. He might as well have not been there.

Archer tossed the file down, slumping behind the desk.

"Right. You think you know why you're here. But you're wrong."

Alex recognised the familiar piece of yellow card clipped to the front of his Personnel file. He had last seen it at that final briefing at Tempsford, in the little back room with the Torridon Major. Before the drop. It seemed a lifetime ago.

"I've your file here, Vere. And it's not my intention to add to it. That surprise you?"

Alex found himself looking into the same glittering intense eyes he'd seen at Netley: the painfully puzzled stare of the slightly barmy, somebody always a step behind life, never quite getting the point.

But he was a Colonel, for heaven's sake – how had he wangled that? It must have been the MC - the reward for being brave. Or suicidally impetuous – sometimes that came to the same thing. Either way, this old boy's few mad seconds in the field had lifted him into command. It must have been in his sabre days. It seemed unfair.

"Never been very interested in files. Mostly lies. Here's a question – it says you speak French. How's that?"

"My mother worked in France after the war. In Paris. I picked it up at school there. And I still have an aunt there, my mother's sister. She keeps an art gallery."

"And your father?"

"No father, sir. He was killed in 1918. I don't really remember him.

It was a trench booby trap. His platoon walked into it. The war was over by then. They were just unlucky."

"It's no use going into all that now. We've work to do. We had WT confirmation you were captured, by the way. Although by the time the signal was decoded, you weren't, if you see what I mean." The sudden stare was unnerving, "Mrs Perry's account of how that trick was pulled off is … what's the word? … *vague*."

He raised a hand, "No, I'm not interested in your version until we can debrief the two of you. She's still in France."

He closed the folder and went on staring sightlessly through Alex, obviously miles away. "We can't send you back there, you know that. The MO says you're not fit yet anyway. You know the rule. Once they've clapped eyes on you you're out of the game. The question is what are we going to do with you?"

"I don't think I'm much use for anything …"

"Now that's defeatist talk. I don't like that, never have. Gets you nowhere," tapping the folder with the nail of his forefinger, "no, you'll be some use alright. That's what I want to talk about. It says here *Psychologist, Authority on Memory.* That right? Psychologist – that's some sort of medic?"

"Not exactly, sir. And, please, I'm not an authority on anything. I'd barely started my doctoral work. I was a year into it when I joined up."

"Alright, you were going to be a medic, let's not split hairs. It's the same thing. Honestly Vere, this mock modesty is girl's stuff. Drop it, we don't have time. It says authority here in black and white, that's good enough for me."

"I don't know who wrote that, sir. Was it Professor Burt? He hardly knows me. He probably thought he was doing me a favour, you know, putting me in a good light. We've only met a couple of times. He's not my supervisor."

"Who wrote it is not your business. And you shouldn't be fishing. You should know better. What's in here is secret. Stays that way. I need three things." He raised a huge blotched fist, clumsily extending one finger. "First, somebody who can keep his mouth shut. And we know you can do that."

The laugh, when it appeared, was a kind of bark, a sudden mirthless explosion, "Come to think of it, you seem an authority on that as well. Right? Right? You can keep your mouth shut, alright – we've not heard a peep about what you were doing after that miraculous escape."

"Dr Hoffmann says it may come back, but there's no knowing when, not with a blow to the head."

He managed another finger.

"Second. Somebody who understands the setup - how we work, what you can do, what you can't, and so on. We trained you, so you fit that bill. Trained you at some expense, I may add, so you meet that bill in spades."

A stubby final finger joined the others, making three, bound together with his other hand. "Third. Somebody who knows what makes people tick. And I don't want damned Intelligence people crawling over the operation … they're the last thing I want. Do you understand?" There was a peculiar defiant expression about his face, daring Alex to deny something. "I want somebody with a bit of imagination. Months, I've been looking, and then you turn up. A godsend. My own trick-cyclist. Isn't that the term?

"Well, that's a psychiatrist. I'm not a medic."

"Oh, for God's sake don't start quibbling again. Look here, I want somebody who knows what's true, what's a lie … that sort of thing. You're an authority on that. I may have prisoners for you to see."

It was impossible to see where all this was going.

"*Prisoners*?"

"That's right. Mind you, not your regular POWs," looking up at Alex, an odd ingratiating smile under the white fuzz, "think you can manage that?"

"Manage what, exactly, sir?"

"Sort out the truth, of course. Understand?"

"You mean interrogation? That's not really my …"

"You're not listening. Not interrogation. We've people for that. I want you to listen. Think you can do that?" A sudden panic flared his face, "God - should have asked. That comes of you raising objections ... lost my thread. You've signed, of course?"

"The Official Secrets Act? Yes. Before I …"

"No need to say when. Now …" He waved Alex back into his chair, leaning towards him across the desk.

"What I'm going to say stays in this room. Stays in your head. Understood? Nobody hears about it – that clear? Not your dear old Mum, not your girl, not your dog. Perfectly clear?"

"Perfectly clear, sir. And I don't have a dog."

"I'll make the jokes, alright? What do you know about Special Operations in Germany?"

"You mean the SOE German desk?"

"No I don't mean the bloody German desk. I mean Special Operations in Germany."

"But there aren't any, are there? I know something was tried in thirty-nine or forty. In Aachen wasn't it? I heard it was a complete flop. It must be completely impossible - that's what we were told at Torridon."

"Those chaps don't know everything. Good on theory, but life's not theory is it? Humour me."

He went across and closed the door, dragging his chair round the desk, sitting too close, eyes flicking to the closed door.

"What if I'm going to tell you there is organised resistance in Germany?" his voice was a kind of rasping whisper, "on German soil. Now, what can we offer them by way of support?"

"You mean if there was any? Supply drops, I suppose, that sort of stuff. But to tell the truth, if there was organised resistance on any scale, it wouldn't last half an hour. We'd be wasting resources. To say nothing of the risks of low level drops over enemy lines. We're not talking about occupied territory, are we? From what I understand, the regime is pretty well supported."

"Oh, absolutely," nodding a little too vigorously, the smile broadening, "we supported it ourselves until quite recently. I've seen some of the memos, joint action with the Abwehr against the commies. Not all that many moons ago either. Lots of red faces now among our Intelligence brethren down the road … damned embarrassing …"

"I'm sorry, perhaps I don't understand."

"Don't understand what?"

"About this organised resistance. Or are we talking about Austria? I suppose that's possible."

"No, I'm talking about the glorious Fatherland. Here's a question for you. What if I say I have the evidence? What if I show you documents, files, WT traffic, the lot. Would you believe me then?"

"We've really got this, sir? It seems incredible. No … I'm sorry … I'd still say it was more likely some kind of Jerry disinformation."

An oddly demonic grin appeared, "Good thought, Vere, excellent. What if I could do better?"

"You're telling me there really is organised resistance inside Germany. Do you mean civilian or military? Sorry … can I ask questions?"

"Of course, my dear chap. Which would you prefer?"

"No, thinking about it, it must be military. Military personnel. That might make sense. How long have we known? Can I ask who knows about this?"

"Ah, another excellent question. I knew you were my man. And the answer is, nobody." He leaned back, satisfied, enjoying the silence. "But you would believe me if I showed you evidence?"

"Of course, sir … I didn't intend to imply … what I mean is it's not that I'm questioning … I'm just not sure exactly where I come in. If it's signals evaluation, that sort of thing, I assume SIS is on top of it."

Archer was shaking his head, tipping back, blowing through the white of his moustaches, "To repeat myself, Captain Vere, our brothers in Secret Intelligence know nothing at all of this. And they will go on knowing nothing at all. This secret is ours, d'you understand? I specifically pressed you on this point and you agreed. You keep your mouth shut – that's an order."

He carried a chair back to his desk, dropping into it, his expression a kind of weary benevolence.

"Here's the point. Thought I'd never get to the point, didn't you? But I come to things my own way … always have done. You're the trick cyclist, the memory man. Given I have enough copperbottom information about this organised resistance, would it persuade you? Yes or no."

"Yes, sir."

"Well, that's what you're going to do, my boy. You're going to deliver me that information. You're going to copperbottom it."

He leaned forward, tapping his nose, rather spoiling the ancient conspiratorial gesture by changing hands in mid flow, "Check that door will you?"

Alex opened the door and looked down the dusty corridor, "Nobody aboard, sir."

"Come back in and keep your voice down. Now ... what I'm going to tell you stays between these walls, understood? Might give you an idea. I'm talking about the last war, you understand? Fighting Turks ... greasy devils. This chap leaves his kit in the desert. Looks for all the world like he's come up against it and fled the scene. Now ... what's inside his kit? Can you guess?"

"Sounds like Colonel Meinertzhagen, sir. False battle plans left for the enemy to discover – is that the idea? I think they call it The Haversack Ruse."

Archer's fixed stare was so unnerving, Alex found himself blushing. "Ah, you've heard something about it? But you don't know everything. He left his binoculars behind as well." He managed a triumphant snort, "Didn't know that, did you, eh? Not about the binoculars?"

Alex thought it best to shake his head.

"They clinched it ... that's my opinion. Crucial. Looked like he'd scooted in a hurry, you see. You don't go dropping your glasses like that. Clever."

He suddenly stood up, waiting until Alex had come to attention.

"Just an idea. Something to think about. Now ... you'd better get on, Captain."

So that was it. He was to exchange his one failed night of active service life for nothing much, see the war out accommodating to the dismal routine of a disinformation bureau. It seemed demeaning. Puzzling, what's more, given Archer's obsessive concern with secrecy. Disinformation and deceit were the stock in trade of SOE: it was why they existed. What was the point of trying to keep this ramshackle little enterprise a secret from the people best placed to do the job? It seemed inexplicable.

Two days later, the third and final member of Colonel Archer's miniature army arrived. John Cabot was a disappointment: short, bespectacled, running to fat, smooth face slightly puffy, large vacant eyes. Archer boasted he had recruited him in Oxford, adding proudly he could speak German like a native.

"Depends on the native, old man." Cabot had strolled into the room bearing a cup of coffee, looking for somewhere to place it on the desk in front of Alex. "Drink this. It may be a while before you taste its like. I got one of the servants in the Buttery to fill my thermos flask."

He settled himself into the chair by the window, already at ease. "Are we to be the sum of everything here? *We are but few* … I forget how the rest of it goes, that the idea? I volunteered, you know, but that doesn't mean I know what I'm supposed to do. any help on that front?"

"It's mad, I know, but I'm sworn to silence. I'm sorry – our leader's hot on secrecy. He'll spell it all out for you. I warn you, it's not very exciting. But written German's going to be an enormous help. Mine's pretty hopeless."

Feeling slightly ashamed, Alex tried to compose his face, "And you really volunteered to join this unit?"

"Well … not quite. I was called up, of course. Army. They booted me out in week one. Here … my secret shame," Cabot held out a pair of spectacles, pebble lenses set in heavy tortoiseshell frames, staring vacantly at Alex, blinking nervously. "The buggers wouldn't have me. I thought for a while I might wangle a job breaking enemy codes. That sounded fun. In fact our Bursar got me an interview. You know, I think he's a kind of spymaster. I was sent to some godforsaken place next to Bletchley railway station. Trouble is, arithmetic's not my strong suit. So here I am – blind as a bat, one more willing recruit to the service of the TPSU. What's that stand for, by the way? Nobody seems to know."

"I haven't a clue. I suppose Colonel Archer will tell us. He's not here today."

"A chap in my college knows a bit about your Colonel. I pumped him. You know he's Hungarian? So his name can't really be Archer. Odd choice, given the Arrow Party is a Hungarian version of the Nazis. He comes from Eger. I've been there. Lovely cathedral. Apparently, his parents were very well to do. *Stinking rich* was the phrase used.

The how and why of these great riches are a secret. I'm afraid that's Oxford code for Jewish. People in my college are like that, it's all they live for. Archer was shipped off to school in England. Never went back."

"He doesn't look Jewish. Wait till you meet him, I think all this is going to be a bit of a let-down for an Oxford Fellow."

"Steady on, nothing so grand. Junior Fellow, old boy. Even that may come to nothing. I'm working on a collected edition of Gotthold Lessing. Heard of him?" Alex shook his head. "No, few have. My contract here says *German Language Specialist*. I must bend my mind and accommodate to the new century. What do you do?"

"Archer insists I'm his Psychologist. But for heaven's sake don't go making a song and dance about it. You probably know more about Freud than me."

Colonel Archer arranged a surreal opening ceremony on Monday of the second week. By that time, telephones had been installed and there were sufficient desks and chairs to go round. He produced a bottle of Highland Park malt whisky, three assorted glasses and a plate of sandwiches bribed out of the charwoman.

That same afternoon, as a mark of good intent, and only slightly the worse for wear, Alex and Cabot began work on a list of imaginary dissident German officers.

Archer vetoed the suggestion that they simply obtain the current German staff lists from Records, forbidding any kind of direct approach to SOE in Baker Street. Cabot suggested they invent the necessary personnel, drawing on French and German newspapers for inspiration.

At that time the Paris newspapers were carrying reports of the recall of a German military attaché. There was even a blurred photograph. Alex drafted the first TPSU letter, addressed to Kommodore Ralf Spier at the Paris Embassy:

This comes to you from someone who shares your patriotic ambitions to warn you that others have become aware of your activities on our behalf and the Wehrmacht cell we are both concerned with. You will be aware of the appropriate action to take.

Cabot translated it, typing it himself on blank French stationery, adding a masterstroke of his own: *The meeting you had arranged for the 10th must be postponed.*

They hesitated over the question of a signature. It presented an opportunity to deploy one from their growing list of imaginary officers, but equally it would not take long to discover the person concerned did not exist. A compromise was found in the signature: *A brother officer.*

The letter was carried through one morning and laid with some ceremony on the polished surface of Archer's empty desk before his arrival. He was enormously proud of his first-born. He could only read restaurant German, but spent much of the day admiring the document. Ignoring SOE channels, he sought out a contact in Boodle's, to arrange for passage to a double agent in Lisbon. The letter was to be delivered, *strictly sealed*, to the unsuspecting Kommadore. The day Archer had confirmation the letter had been despatched he returned to the TPSU office in triumph.

"That Portuguese creep will open it, nothing's more certain. We'll just have to see how the information spreads. It's a first step, gentlemen. From small acorns, you understand. In six months we'll have our resistance cells functioning all over Germany. And we'll be pulling their strings."

His optimism was unwarranted. This first small step involving the unsuspecting naval attaché remained the only acorn actually planted.

Archer proposed an extension of the idea, using drops from low level flights to deposit briefcases containing the personal papers of selected members of the High Command. Mixed with genuine documents would be forged papers referring to resistance cells in Berlin, Hamburg and Munich. The plan was stillborn, stalling in the face of SIS opposition. It was at this point Alex realised how little operational authority the TPSU actually possessed. In particular, access to flights involved a sclerotic clearance procedure, permission invariably denied.

At one ill-tempered meeting an anonymous civilian appeared. Vaguely described as *Technical*, he pressed them to guarantee that objects thrown from a plane (and the question arose *by whom?*) would not be caught in the slipstream, with consequential damage? It was bad enough having to repair planes shot up by the *Luftwaffe*. Were we now expected to repair self-inflicted damage? Archer had stormed out of the room in a rage, slamming the door, the expression, *bloody civilians* floating up to them from the stairwell. He did not return for several days.

For Cabot at least, the fact he had time on his hands seemed not entirely disagreeable. He took to bringing notes to work from his Oxford days, working on the poems of Gotthold Lessing.

Watching him endlessly tinkering with translations, it was difficult to escape the conclusion that the TPSU would have little impact on the future conduct of the war. For Alex, at least, a conclusion tinged with the suspicion that the outcome had been intended. Even the unit's name, when eventually discovered, seemed demeaning. Rummaging in a drawer one day, Cabot pulled out a delivery notice for rubber date stamps (18s 6d) directed to *Third Party Supply Unit*.

Archer himself appeared to be waiting for some unspecified event to happen, unconcerned by the lack of concrete action. On occasion, he even spent a desultory afternoon with the two of them, working on the chain of command in the resistance movement, allocating duties, juggling the relative status of fictional German officers.

The telephone call came late one afternoon. They had spent much of that day discussing fish. Before leaving for his club, Archer had asked Cabot to concoct a rumour that two hundred man-eating sharks had been introduced into the English Channel. The rumour was to be spread within the *Luftwaffe*. Exactly how was left as a matter to be decided.

With Archer gone, Cabot sat in silence, doodling on a piece of paper.

"I know bugger all about sharks. It's not really what I joined up for. Would they survive in cold water, do you think? I thought they were tropical?"

"John, it's not going to matter much, is it? It's not as if they're actually going to exist. It's a mad idea. Who'd believe it? They'd attack our fliers as well. And where would you get two hundred sharks? He seems to have forgotten there's a war on."

Alex was consumed by a sense of frustrated anti-climax. Accepting the Torridon version of war was always slightly tainted, falling a little short of honourable, at least it was to have been fought on enemy soil. And he had come to believe the end truly did justify the means. But this? Stuck in a dusty room, unwashed teacups buried in piles of paper, old newspapers curling brown in sunlight. All the pointless detritus of a pointless office. He had hoped for something more.

Cabot was prodding his arm. "I'm walking across to the Museum. I'll see whether I can find you a shark that dines only on German flesh."

The telephone rang so rarely Alex was startled. He scraped it across the desk leaving a wake of crumpled paper and lifted the receiver.

"*Captain Vere?*"

"Yes."

"*Please hold.*"

Whoever it was disappeared with an abrupt click, leaving nothing more than a faint hum.

A second click.

"*Connecting you.*"

"Is that you Alex? I only have a second."

The voice close in his ear set his heart racing. "Justine! Is it really you? You've made my day. I was feeling a bit maudlin: this damned headache. Where are you? It's not late, we could …"

"Yes Guffin, let's take all that as read, I'm in a rush. Just wanted to pass on a friendly hello. How are things treating you? Getting enough to eat?"

"Eat? Yes, I'm fine. Look, I can get away, can we …"

"No, not right now, my dear. So long as you're getting your grub. Just wanted to say all's well. God bless."

The purr of the dialling tone left him feeling strangely bereft.

Six

The next day Alex was late for a meeting. He'd never been late before, but there's no accounting for a bomb. In this case, a thousand pounds of high explosive, a direct hit on the church at the corner of the street. He stopped for a second to look at the smoking hole, thinking how quickly you come to accept things; to adapt. A few years back the newspapers would have been full of this.

Of course, that had been a time when churches didn't explode. A time before German bombs thumped and crumped their indiscriminate way across London, night after night after night. Until you gave up flinching and became inured to the wantonness, even finding a kind of exhilaration in it. If you get the scale right, destruction has a certain majesty about it. You creep up from your burrow to smell the daylight, almost welcoming that sick lurch about the heart at the sight of what has gone. In the end you crave it, thinking of the things that are lost. Paper mostly - how easily paper burns.

The bombs stopped as abruptly as they started, German wrath turning to other targets. It was that had made Alex pause, because the blackened chunks of St Michael and All Angels distributed across the street that morning were out of the ordinary.

Unintentional, people had mumbled.

Everyone knew the story now: released by mistake on the way back from bombing Canterbury. Although what Canterbury had done to deserve a bomb was for God to know. Surely, there was nothing there but a cathedral? The thought was not consoling. It was our fault apparently. Some angry German thumbing through his Baedecker to find an English place pretty enough to bomb in revenge for Lübeck. Alex could only think that war deserved something more than revenge.

It was a lovely morning for December, cold, with a bracing wind chafing your face. A bright low sun glanced off a leather-bound booklet impaled on the railings, pristine blue, embossed *Order of Service*. A pity, prayer had come into its own recently.

He picked his way through the rubble, remembering Justine kneeling on the floor in that church at Torridon. Justine still alive: against all the odds, still alive. For weeks he had not allowed his mind to venture to that dark place, choosing to keep her alive. And the miracle was true, six weeks had not been enough for Justine.

At the corner, firemen wearily hauled at flattened canvas hoses sprawled over the pavement. The bitter smell of woodsmoke in the air reminded him of something not altogether disagreeable but the memory eluded him.

He followed the chalked sign past the silent queue at the temporary bus stop. It would have been comforting to see their wind-chilled faces as defiant, but they seemed merely resigned.

As he reached Bedford Square, a splash of reflected sunlight cast him instantly into his domestic prison in Saint Aunix. That memory, at least, was safe: Justine pushing him into fresh air, liberation filling his lungs, he would never forget that. But there was a gap, nonetheless, a soft patch where nothing held, where he could not go. How strange to know with absolute certainly that you didn't know something.

He stood immobile, the sun in his eyes bringing the forgotten something so close it was like a pain. Far away he was aware of a muffled squeal of brakes, someone shouting.

Bloody Fool! You want to kill yourself?

An unfamiliar army Sergeant stood at the top of the steps. He straightened up, stifling a grin. "You'll be Captain Vere? You're the last. Almost caught me there, sir. Me watching you dodge the traffic like that. Wouldn't do, me saluting you in civvies, like. Go along up, sir. They're all there."

"You mean I'm late. No need to be polite."

"Let's say just in time, sir. Quite a crowd today – that's why I'm here. Security. I suppose you heard about the bomb, sir?"

"Security for a bomb? But it was half a mile away. Security for what?"

"Really couldn't say, sir. Top of the stairs and on your right. Oh, sorry, you know the way, of course you do."

As he took the stairs two at a time he could already hear the drone of Archer's voice. He tapped and came in, resting for a second, back against the door, a little out of breath. The place was thick with smoke. The bewhiskered head behind its defensive wall of files paused just long enough to nod. Cabot looked up from his doodles, pursing his lips into a tiny moue, flicking a warning glance across the room.

So this morning it wasn't to be just the three of them. A thin-faced chap in smart Air Force blue had positioned himself at the other end of the table, poised to take over should Archer ever stop. Nobody ever sat there. As Alex dropped into his chair, a crisp blue sleeve was pushed aside, the glint of a steel watch.

There was somebody else.

Set a little apart, standing with his back to the window, the Torridon Major, smiling agreeably, lowering his head in mock-solemn greeting.

Archer caught the gesture, and managed a vague irritated nod of his own. "So you two know each other?"

"The Major briefed me at Tempsford, sir."

"But you don't know Connor here." He let Alex bob up, waiting while they shook hands. "I knew you'd be held up. Heard about the bomb, you see. A stray apparently. But we've not started. I was just filling in a few bits of background."

Connor's cadaverous liver-spotted face reared up, as if to say he'd come for more than background. He seemed about to speak then thought better of it, slumping back, letting Archer keep the floor.

"Wing Commander Connor's here because we need his take on things." Archer craned round awkwardly looking over his shoulder at the Major, "I don't know how long you two can stay ...?"

If it was a question, the Major, who had turned to stare down into the street below, didn't bother to reply.

There was a watery glint in Archer's eyes. Alex wondered, not for the first time, how on earth the old boy had engineered this job. Peering out over his barricade, puffy cheeks veined purple with too many late nights at Boodles, sagging eyelids little pools of tears, he was completely out of his depth. Emotionally labile, that was his problem. Perhaps his age, but in Archer's case he must have always been that way, always the tearful schoolboy.

Connor had opened a gold cigarette case to light a cigarette, the scrape of his match breaking the silence like a rebuke. Archer threw a resentful stare into space, pulling down a file, opening it, lost for words.

"Right … right. We're all here so we'll start. I'll skim through this – quicker that way. To put you in the picture, Alex, we're talking about an operation that took place a bit over a month ago. The morning of Tuesday the tenth of November, to be precise. At Saint Aunix. Columbine territory. A pickup for an agent called Perry. Alex knows Mrs Perry – that's right, isn't it, Alex?"

Cabot looked up, puzzled by the sudden tension in the room.

Alex was conscious of Archer's glittering eyes fixing him, daring him to deny something.

"The two of you were dropped earlier last year, that's right, isn't it?" Archer turned to Connor. "They were slated to join the Columbine circuit. That's the drop that went wrong, I assume you know about all that. Captain Vere and Mrs Perry got themselves into a bit of trouble. But we've got him back, at least." The smile for Alex was not friendly. "Bit of a miracle, Vere, but there you are. Anything new to add?"

"I wish I could, sir. I can't remember anything much after I was arrested. They tried to get what happened out of me at that hospital at Netley. No go, I'm afraid."

Connor continued looking at his cigarette end, picking off a loose strand. He seemed to be barely listening.

"It's alright Alex," Archer had left the smile where it was, "we're not here to talk about you. Now, where was I? This Perry woman was SOE from the start, one of the first to join. Effective, disciplined, no black marks." He prodded the file with a stubby finger, "*Fearless*, it says here. Sounds like a disadvantage to me, but who am I to say? Connor's people were to pick her up from the field at Saint Aunix."

He began furiously underlining something on the paper in front of him. "A point here, Connor. Probably nothing at all. Your Report has ETD – hard to keep up with all these acronyms. I assume that's estimated time of departure. It's down as eleven twenty. But that's the same as the ETA."

Connor looked up, suddenly grinning. In better times you could see him as good company. "Oh, you can take it they don't wait around, Colonel."

"Thought it would be that. Now … the complication. London Control …" He glanced nervously over his shoulder. "… I suppose it's alright to mention them?" The figure at the window continued staring impassively into nothing. "Right. London said they wanted somebody out of France pronto pronto, no questions asked. An artist woman who had got herself stranded after war broke out. *Celebrated*, it says here. I suppose they mean famous. I've never heard of her myself, but what would I know."

"Oh, she's celebrated alright, Colonel ..." For moment Archer could not place the voice, turning in his chair, puzzled. It was the Major, still staring out into the street, his words half lost against the muffled sound of traffic outside. "She's my sister. The French name's false, obviously. She'd been living there for years. sharing a house with Albert Bradley." Seeing Archer frown, he added, "Bradley celebrated enough for you?"

"*Bradley* ... yes, of course I know about him. It's just I thought he was dead."

"No, not dead at all, just old. As busy as ever, I gather. Until recently the Vichy lot left him alone. Too big to handle, I suppose. When the Germans moved South last November it became urgent to get them out."

"Too valuable to be left to the glorious Reich, you mean?" Archer was running to catch up, "Propaganda value, that sort of thing?"

"No, not really. We've been running the Bradley place as a safe house since the start. It was perfect cover."

"But we got your sister safely back. She's somewhere up North isn't she, John?"

"I gather she's in Scotland, sir. Dundee. It's on the East coast."

Archer had been pushing a bundle of paper back into its file. He tugged a sheet out, watching it tear, glaring up at Cabot, "I know where bloody Dundee is, just let me finish, for God's sake." He pieced the paper together, peering myopically at it. "I want to get the transport story straight, The local people in Saint Aunix had already teed up transport to the pick-up for Mrs Perry. when London ordered us to give her place in the car to your sister. Of course, I didn't know she was your sister. Nothing about Bradley, though."

The Major turned and smiled at Archer, "It's alright, you weren't to know. Bradley's still there. He said he wanted the arrangement with the house to stand if we needed it. Frankly, it's not an offer we can afford to pass up. Now ... about the transport for your Mrs Perry. The local people fixed something to get her to the field. Now, here's the point. The car they sent used was also carrying thirty pounds of TNT. Not that we knew …"

Connor threw his pencil down, grinding his cigarette into the ashtray, "Bloody Maquis. And they call it *resistance.* If I'd known it was going to be within fifty yards of one of my planes … Saints preserve us from amateurs."

"But you didn't know, Connor. None of us did." Archer raised a hand, glaring at Alex, "and that includes Mrs Perry, I imagine. Uncomfortable sort of thing to be travelling with. Of course, the damned thing went off. There wasn't much time to check, but it looked as if a grenade had been rigged up as the detonator, that and the usual alarm clock thing."

He ran his finger along a line of text, "Says here, *Yellow body fragments in the debris, almost certainly MK II TNT grenade*. You can see where this is leading, can't you Alex?" His stare was oppressive, false concern welling up into wet eyes, moustaches raised a little, a sadistic little twitch about his lips. "Are you with us, Alex? Are you alright?"

Alex felt sick. The answer was no, he wasn't alright, not alright at all. The bastard had orchestrated this whole recital simply to watch him discover Justine was dead. All this talk about debris was for his benefit. Perhaps the old fool thought his grotesque trick would trigger some lost memory. It would have triggered something alright - if he hadn't spoken to her yesterday he would have been out of the room by now, heaving his guts up in the corridor.

But she was not dead. That must be why she telephoned.

Images of Justine were sliding over each other in what was left of his memory, coloured with a sense of incredible relief. She was alive – somewhere, she was alive. That was all that mattered. And as the thought slipped back into the dark pool, a tiny focus of pain in his head flared like the sharp pierce of a needle. He felt hopelessly vulnerable, aware all the time of the Major's silent scrutiny.

Cabot retrieved Connor's pencil, placing it on the table in front of him, catching his eye, "We're not dealing with a regular army, are we, sir? They're just rural guerrillas. Not exactly your disciplined force. Chaps on the run from the call-up or forced labour in Poland, or Magna Germania, as they insist on calling it." A thought struck him, "I wonder how they got hold of TNT."

Archer shuffled through the papers, "Yes, good question. There's something about that in here. A quarry in the area with what you might call obliging security." He gave Alex a final vicious knowing look.

"While they were boarding the two women, somebody shifted the TNT from one car to the other. Tricky operation, given this was a daytime pickup. They must have bungled it, the car with the bomb had barely left the field when the whole lot went up. The chaps left behind did what they could, but it was hopeless. Just got themselves burned in the process. Hands too damaged to drive. They abandoned their own car, set fire to it, and made off on foot. Terrible business."

He closed the file, looking at Connor, "I think that's a good place for me to stop, Wing Commander, the point at which your plane took off. Can you take it from there?"

Connor was already making a fuss of reaching down into his briefcase: his little piece of theatre, dragging out a single slim file, posing it unopened in front of him, squaring it off with two hands. He let the silence run on.

"I'll give you our angle if you like. Not that we had much to do with it. Mind you, if there's SOE politics behind this, we're out of it, understand? We'd ferried your agent Perry before. We were just the transport, is that clear? We got the news about the extra passenger the day before – that would have been the Monday. Not entirely welcome news, people don't always understand you can't just add weight like that. But nothing to make a song and dance about. Anyway, the instruction was from the War Office."

He looked across at the Major and for the briefest of seconds they exchanged glances. "Of course, we know now why it was urgent – Jerry was about to move South in force. And so we have two passengers - your agent Perry and Mrs Beyrou. We'll stay with your sister's French name, that alright, Major? I'm afraid none of us knew anything about her."

Archer had settled himself complacently in his chair. The fact Justine had survived seemed of no interest at all. A surge of anger possessed Alex, leaving him blinking back tears. That single abortive solitary venture was going to be his all, Archer would see to that. Just one more bloody shambles to be picked over in a stuffy office in a back street in Bloomsbury. He could feel Connor looking at him, Eton and Cranwell exuding world-weary disdain. He was Air Intelligence, that much was obvious. Alex knew the type, always a little ahead of the game, knowing that little bit more than you. And his chum, the silent Major with a family interest, a black silhouette against the light of the window. What was he? Secret Intelligence Service, or worse. More to the point: why exactly was he here?

The ancient relic at the head of the table, was staring forlornly from one face to another, seeking reassurance. The deluded fool hadn't even the wit to see this secretive duo was playing him like a fish.

Alex found himself racing to catch Connor's words, blurting out, "Actually sir, not 'Mrs'. She's not married to anybody." He fell back into his seat feeling stupid, realising too late he'd got even that wrong. It was this artist they were talking about, he'd been thinking of Justine.

Connor's cool look rested on him a condescending beat too long, "Ah. Right you are then. So not *Mrs.*" He made to open his file then changed his mind, leaving his hand resting on it. He looked up to the ceiling, reciting from memory.

"We'd used that Saint Aunix strip before. Neat little place, tucked away. You can risk it in daylight. This was to be the last run for a while. The passengers were back at Northolt at seventeen hundred hours."

The glance at Alex seemed complicit, almost friendly, "We entrained Mrs ... I beg your pardon ... your other passenger later that evening. You won't want more on the artist angle, Colonel? The Major's sister was incidental to the operation, she's not really germane."

Not waiting for a reply he spread a sheaf of papers across the table. "Here's the tricky part – and I'm going to stick to the script if you don't mind. Your agent Perry had to get from Northolt to Randoph Square for debriefing – at least, that's what she said. Now, everybody accepts debriefing is not our pigeon, but we took the view *eventually* that somebody had to get her back and since nobody turned up for her, it seemed that fell to us. Rightly or wrongly."

He had saved a cold stare for Archer. "Wrongly, as it turned out. But there you are. One of our drivers took her." He had stopped. Obviously, that was all they were going to get. He allowed himself a little gesture of irritation, crumpling a sheet of paper into his case.

Alex glanced across to see Cabot roll his eyes.

Archer had discovered a fountain pen in his inside pocket and started screwing the top on and off, something to play with. "Connor, my dear chap, we're not here to squabble about who lost her. The fact is she's lost. Of course, if our people *had* collected her it might have been different. But they didn't, and we won't go into why. Water under the bridge. As I say, that's not why we're here."

This was too much for Connor. He scraped his chair back, barking across the table, "They didn't pick her up because they bloody well didn't turn up, that's why. You know that perfectly well. Two hours your Perry kept at it, belly-aching her life was in danger, she had to get back to London. We're an operational airfield, not a nursery. There was the hell of a flap on that night, a raid on the cards. She kept saying she had to get to London urgently. So we took her. There was a spare seat in the milk run car." He caught Cabot's glance and added, "The daily briefing papers – that's what we call it. Arrives with the milk."

"Can I check something with you, Connor?"

They had forgotten the Major. He had shifted to lean against the bit of wall next to the window. Connor shrugged, throwing Archer an insolent request for permission to speak, "Check away, old man. If I know the answer. I probably don't. This has nothing to do with me."

"I just wondered whether an SOE car ever did arrive. Perhaps you know, Colonel Archer?"

But it was Connor who answered. "The answer's no, Major. I asked. It never did. Right? Let me finish the story. Coming into London, Perry asked our driver to pull over outside Tufnell Park underground – the Tube station. Said she was nipping across to get some cigarettes. There's a kiosk there. That was the last we saw of her."

Cabot looked up, murmuring, "Clever choice."

"Why'd you say that?"

"No escalator. Just lifts down. Anybody following would have to wait for a lift to come back up."

"Why the hell would anybody follow her? We thought she was getting some fags. After five minutes the driver went across to see what was up. She'd gone, of course."

Archer turned to Cabot, "That's the Northern line, isn't it? Well, John, what do you think? Do we set the bloodhounds onto this trollop Perry? It's over a month she's been gone. We can't have that, you know. We've got to lay hands on her."

He tapped the file in front of him with the end of his pen, smirking, "Here's a thing – did you know she's called Justine – seems appropriate."

Connor looked blank.

"The lady Mr de Sade had his way with. Never read it? I asked for her file - our Justine, that is - all the operational stuff. I must say, there's enough to suggest we may have a problem. Let's say she's well informed. She was pretty central to the Columbine operation, responsible for liaison with the frogs."

He broke off, scooting the file across the table to Cabot, "John's done some research on the setup down there. Tell us what's afoot, John. It's your turn."

Cabot, his face shiny with a mist of moisture, pulled the back of one hand across his top lip, scrabbling at a spiral-bound notebook with the other. "Sorry, it's hot in here. I'll go back a bit, sir, if that's alright? For the benefit of the Wing Commander. And the Major. The Saint Aunix cell was set up in late forty. The leader's a chap called Claude

Barte. An accountant, incidentally. Not your typical left-wing rebel, inclined the other way, in fact. It must have beenBarte who drummed up the extra car for Mrs Perry." He glanced awkwardly at Alex, "So we have to assume the bomb idea was his as well. I can check the WT record if you like, sir. There may be something about that. He'd have needed our say-so."

Archer looked at Connor, "We've had a WT operator down there for a while. Very reliable. She was part of your drop, wasn't she, Alex? Name of Simone. No, John, I don't see we need that stuff. Just hurry on a bit. The point is he got our message about the passenger and did the necessary."

Alex was no longer listening. He was back in the draughty hanger at Tempsford, seeing the Major come out of the side door, a little mouse of a woman walking ahead of him. Simone: the curly-haired child with the woollen mittens. Simone: smashed up among bits of broken chair in the Gendarmerie, a sickly smell of cyanide everywhere. She was dead. You can't have your neck like that and be alive.

He found himself staring into the Major's eyes. Not friendly at all, that expression. The room was too hot. Too many sweating men suddenly tense with something.

"You with us, Alex?" Cabot had stuttered to a halt as Archer shouted down the table, "You seem miles away."

"This WT operator. Simone, sir."

"What about her?"

"She was arrested the same time as me. In fact, she …"

"That's nonsense, Alex. You're talking nonsense. And you're holding us up. You're getting muddled. My fault, I put things badly. She wasn't dropped with you. I meant she went on ahead."

He craned round, calling to the Major, "On ahead. That right?"

"Correct. She flew down in a Lysander ahead of the drop. She had her set with her."

"That clear things up, Alex? On you go, John."

"This is all I know about the extra car. Barte must have arranged it, plus driver, a chap called Scaffe. Declared unfit for active service. He had a terrible limp. Club foot. The Jerries didn't want him. It was

Scaffe who transferred the bomb from his car to the other one. That meant he survived, of course, lived to tell the tale. Although it didn't turn out that way."

As Connor leaned forward to speak, Archer had a smile waiting for him. He flapped a hand at Cabot, "A minute, John. Yes, Wing Commander, we wanted to discover what he had to say. But before you get too excited, we'll get nothing out of this man Scaffe. He's dead. Shot two days later. Trying to run away from an armed patrol. Not that he could run, of course. It was in a cake shop. He'd slipped inside hoping to use the back door. Apparently he'd used that way out often. So you could say there's something of interest here, because the door had been locked."

Cabot murmured, "Poor bugger."

"Alright John, spare us, we know there's a war on."

"You could question that in his case, sir. He was just a kid. I doubt he'd even handled a gun."

Connor was still leaning forward, looking at Cabot, the first real spark of interest he'd shown all morning, "Anything about why the door was locked?"

Archer conjured up the slightly unpleasant nervous smirk he had reserved for Connor, "Quite so: the pertinent question, Wing Commander. We shall have to discover. Go on Cabot, if you would."

"Not much more to say, sir. They must all have been very nervous on account of the daylight run. You can see the point – somebody is bound to hear the take-off even if they miss the landing. The car with the bomb exited in short order, leaving the others to follow. It exploded just past the gate."

Archer cleared his throat, fishing a sheet of paper out of the file in front of him, holding it by one corner, letting it hang down, looking like a man whose moment had arrived.

"This is the last wireless contact we had from Barte. It's been complete silence since. Concerns a young chap arrested for curfew violation. Nothing too much out of the ordinary. He'd been hanging around the local knocking shop. Sixteen – I ask you? Should have been in bed with a book. He had the misfortune to bump into a hard-bitten *SS-Rottenführer*, a squaddie. He hauled the kid off to the local police. I suppose they slapped him about a bit. Probably told him to run home and get his mother to sew his trousers up. But here's the point. On the way out, there's a door open. Barte reports this boy saw Mrs Perry in a side room sitting at a desk dictating something. Very much at home."

"When you say, *slapped him about a bit*?" There was a look of distaste on Connor's face. "What do you mean exactly?"

"You can only go by what these chaps say – they exaggerate. He'd be in trouble out after curfew. That would be for the French police, although the fact a German was involved could have made things worse. Apparently, the local station used to be a butcher's shop. Things still there, I suppose ... mincers … that sort of thing."

Connor was not going to let go.

"So he could be making this story up. He would be scared witless. Anyway, an agent hobnobbing with the local police – isn't that what they're supposed to do?"

"Except Perry doesn't work that way. She operates through the local Maquis. Cultivated them – kept them close, if you like. That bunch don't go in for subtleties. If they thought she was chatting to the wrong people she was not going to last long."

Archer stopped, holding on to the silence, enjoying himself. "My conclusion, gentlemen, is that the car Barte arranged to carry our Mrs Perry was never meant to arrive, it was meant to explode en route. The trip must have been faster than they expected."

Connor, head down, was making a pencil note on the corner of a file, "Then why transfer the thing to the other car?"

"I thought about that, of course I did. "Archer managed a smug little grin, "You'd have had to give the driver a reason for carrying it. They probably told him he was making a delivery. He just followed orders. They never imagined him delivering anything. He was going to be dead long before he got the chance – him and Mrs Perry. The damned thing went off ten minutes too late. My conclusion is Perry was the intended victim. The wrong people escaped."

"You mean the wrong people were killed, don't you?" For a second Alex could not place the voice. The Major had come up directly behind Archer, unaccountably angry.

Archer shrugged, pushing a bundle of papers into his folder, his tone mutinous, "I suppose you could to put it that way ... all the same …"

"Actually her driver didn't escape, sir," Cabot folded his book closed, trying to keep the peace. "If you think that locked door was no accident, Scaffe didn't escape. So there's really only Mrs Perry to account for."

Connor scraped his chair back, "Then you'd better find her, hadn't you?"

Seven

The Major was the first to leave. He stood silently in the doorway sheltering his shoes from a sudden shower until a grey staff car mounted the pavement, the driver struggling out with a vast umbrella. At the car door he distributed a perfunctory salute to the group left huddled on the stone steps.

Connor, bare-headed, let Alex wave down a taxi. They watched him disappear into the wintry gloom.

Archer stood for a second then took Alex's arm steering him back inside. "Got a minute? I'd like a word. Didn't get a chance before the meeting."

"If it's about sharks, sir, Cabot's on to that. He's gone back to work on it in the Museum. He's getting somewhere – I'd better leave him to say."

"Sharks?" He seemed lost. "Oh, yes, sharks. No, it's not that. we can leave all that to Mr Cabot. Something else. We'll go into Records if that's alright."

Records had been Archer's idea. It wasn't even a room, just the end of a corridor blocked off by a new door with an impressive security lock. The tiny space had been lined with filing cabinets, now awaiting something to put into them. It was airless and stifling hot. There was nowhere to hang a coat. Alex draped his over the top of a cabinet, shaking his head as Archer held out his cigarette case.

"Quite right. Shouldn't smoke in here." He lit a cigarette, elaborately perching a solitary spent match on top of a cabinet. "I want a straight answer. What do you know about this Perry business?"

"Apart from the operation we were involved in, I don't know anything, sir. She got me out, of course. I owe her that. It's quite a debt."

"You weren't in her debt at Torridon." He was smirking. "Got to know her well enough there, I gather."

It wasn't worth a reply. Alex felt himself reddening. Of course: the Training Report from Torridon. Some sweaty clerk blessed with a prurient imagination hearing tittle tattle from the maids who turned the beds down. He was damned if he was going to answer.

Archer was standing so close you could hear the breath wheezing in his barrel chest. "What you get up to is your business, Vere. I'm broad minded. But this chap Connor is Air Intelligence, hence no fool. And the other one, the one who barged in to tell us about his family. You weren't there, he doesn't seem to think it necessary to introduce himself. Just swept in with Connor. He's SIS alright. They're the bastards vetoing our every project. They want us closed down. He smells something about this Perry business, mark my words. I've been asking myself why he turned up at all. Why come knocking at my door? I'm asking why, Vere, because I think you may be the reason."

"You're talking about that explosion at the airfield, sir? Until this morning I knew nothing about it."

"Oh, I accept you *say* you know nothing. But that's the trouble, isn't it? And you know nothing about Perry's whereabouts either, I suppose? I notice you haven't said that."

Close to, there was something unsettling about Archer's eyes. Perhaps no more than the vanity of an old man in need of glasses but you could believe someone else behind them, someone else inside that huge whiskery head, peering out at you.

"I can certainly say it, sir, if you like. I don't know where she is. I haven't the faintest idea. But at least I knew she was not dead." No sooner had the words escaped than he regretted them. Never respond if someone goads you – it's a golden rule. As satisfaction mounted in Archer's face Alex could have hit him.

"Yes, I noticed that. You could ask how you came by that information. The way the story came out, it wasn't obvious she had survived, not obvious at all. Most people would have assumed she'd …"

"Perished? I'm aware of that, sir. It wasn't particularly kind."

"What the hell's *kind* got to do with it? You'll say I'm harping on about that remarkable operation of yours, but think about it. No sooner were the two of you dropped – you and Mrs Perry - but you get yourself arrested. Somehow they missed her, let's say they walked on by. Then by some miracle she plucks you from the jaws of death. I don't think miracle overstates it. And you can't remember much after that. Now we learn there's every likelihood the locals - her own people – are out to kill her. And she's upped and vanished. Are you surprised people are taking an interest? Where the hell's she got to? Look here Vere, I explained when I took you on I didn't want Intelligence crawling over our patch. I've got my reasons. And you've saddled me with exactly that."

He was standing so close that Alex could see tiny beads of sweat in the white fuzz of his moustache, a slight tremor working at the edge of his mouth, readying itself for something. "Just stop playing the innocent. You took a telephone call yesterday afternoon. Came through the Baker Street switchboard. Want to say anything about it? Want to tell me who called?"

"Evidently since somebody was listening, you'll know as much as me."

"Careful with your tone, Captain. I don't need to tell you we've just spent an hour talking about this woman. All that time you knew she had made a telephone call yesterday. She asked for you. And you didn't think to mention it? Thought nobody would be interested?"

"I apologise, sir. I took the view it was a personal matter. If you've seen a transcript, you will know that's the truth. It was a very brief conversation. You know she said nothing about an explosion. I think Mrs Perry wanted me to know she was safe and well. I don't need to explain why. But she didn't say where she was or where she was going. You know that."

"So I do. And no need to apologise to me. Just be aware if one or another of those two think you're playing games, they'll be back to roast you. That's your damned lookout, up to a point. *But I do not want them back here*, do you understand me?"

He was speaking in a ridiculous whispered shout, flecks of supressed fury spurting from his lips, Alex standing immobile.

Archer broke away, lighting another cigarette, turning aside to cough, prodding Alex in the chest, his oversized head nodding to the rhythm. Incredibly, there was a sly smile on his lips.

"Pull that door to, will you. This hole is virtually the only place I'm a hundred percent sure isn't *bugged* – that's the word isn't it? Ears everywhere." The stubby finger went on prodding. "I'm asking you to do something for me. Think you can do that?"

"Of course, sir."

"An end to secrets?"

"No secrets, sir"

"You won't know Abbott Court?" Alex shook his head. "It's a reception centre. Belongs to SOE, although I doubt you'll see that on the rent book. I want you to pay them a call. Collect a chit from my office before you go. It says you're our psychologist, alright? They're wary there, so watch what you say. And for God's sake don't start quibbling if anyone asks. They've got somebody there who might be exactly what I've been waiting for. A German. I want you to go and have a look at him. Let me know. Just me, you understand."

"Let you know what, sir?"

"He'll have a story to tell. They all do. He'll be telling lies, of course but it won't be all lies. That's where you come in. I want to know which bits to believe. You're the expert on lying. When I've had your opinion I might go and see him myself, find the best way to make him one of ours."

"You mean turn him, sir. With respect, I don't think that's a job for a psychologist."

"Who then? His mother? - if he's got one. His priest? I need to know what makes him tick. That's your job."

"I only saw interrogation from the other side, sir. That's what we were trained for – how to take it, not how to give it. Wouldn't someone from SIS ...?"

"How many times do I have to say it, Vere? No, you'll have to do the best you can. I want an opinion. That's all."

When he eventually found the place, it was to discover that Abbott Court had suffered the same fate as St Michael. The houses along the rest of the street, Edwardian villas that had seen better days, stood intact, a dreary subdivided warren of bedsitters. Abbott Court was a bomb site, the building cut off well below the waist, stone stumps black with smoke, its driveway blocked off with a high corrugated fence, newly erected, painted army green. A tiny door cut into the metal opened onto a gravelled courtyard and a large wooden hut.

Alex rang the bell and waited. It was getting dark, a frost setting in, his breath hanging in clouds of white mist. An army Sergeant snatched the chit from his hand and retreated inside, slamming the door, heavy boots clumping away on bare wooden boards. It was several minutes before lighter footsteps returned. An unsmiling WAAF led him along a narrow corridor running the length of the hut. The place was filled with a sharp antiseptic smell, the lights almost too bright.

She tapped on a door, pushed at it, and scuttled away. A man in a short white lab coat was getting up from behind a desk, the chit still in his hand. "This Colonel Archer, I'm afraid we didn't know him. Your outfit's new to me. Sorry to keep you. We had to check. Security is tight here. Your Colonel says he wants you to see our latest acquisition."

He grinned as he saw Alex trying to read the name plate on the open door, a varnished panel with MO/2 stencilled on it. "I'm afraid no names here. You can call me MO, that's what everybody does, although I'm not much of a medic. Not really the other thing either, more Gentleman than Officer, if you know what I mean. Hence the civvies." He was laughing, "Sorry to be mysterious. I'm showing off. It's what comes of being shut up in this place all hours God sends. The truth is I inherited the room and I've no idea what oblique two stands for – all I know is there isn't an oblique one." He glanced down at the chit in his hand, "Colonel Archer says you're his psychologist. Sounds impressive."

"He insists on putting it that way. I'm doing my doctorate – or I was before the call up. With Professor Campbell."

"You mean Campbell the Ganser man? I've met him. I've always thought the Ganser syndrome was just a fancy name for malingering, but I suppose I'm wrong."

"Professor Campbell has been working with prisoners of war. The Ganser syndrome's quite common in prisoners. I was going to work on it in the context of interrogation … but I'd barely got started."

"Sane people feigning madness. That what you think our latest's doing?"

"It's a possibility."

"Well you've come to the right place if you're looking for liars. What's special about this prisoner? We've not had him long. How did you know about him? No, sorry, I shouldn't ask …"

"I'm afraid I don't know. You're better asking Colonel Archer. But not long, I think. I only got the order today. Colonel Archer wants me to report back on this chap."

"I would have thought it was pretty obvious people will lie to get out of prison. Or lie not to get there in the first place. That's why I never believe a word they say."

"It's the *sort* of lie that's interesting, particularly with patients who might be pretending to be mad. It's not so easy to distinguish pretence from the real thing. My idea was that approximate answers might be the clue … then I got called up."

"Approximate answers?"

"Ganser called it *vorbeireden* – talking past the subject. You ask a patient how many fingers he has, and he says eighteen. Alright, it's a lie, it's nonsense, but it's only *approximately* wrong. It's a number, after all. It isn't as if he'd said *fish* or *custard*. There's the question - if you are pretending to be mad, which way do you jump? Do you have to be mad to make a really convincing madman?"

"That or a professional psychologist, I suppose." Suddenly embarrassed, he began laughing awkwardly, "Oops. Sorry – just my little joke. Your journey might be in vain, Captain. This chap's not pretending to be mad. Pretending lots else, but not that. Mind you, he's certainly lying, but then, that's true of all of them. He's as cocky as hell. Here's what we know about him. By the way, I wouldn't call him a patient if I were you – he's starting to get touchy, quoting his Geneva rights, you know. We've been using amylobarbitone on him ... to get a bit more than name and number. No, don't look like that, it's nothing to what they're using on our chaps. And we've got all the right consents, I assure you, given this chap's status."

"No, I wasn't doubting that ... of course not. It's just that I wonder about drugs, that's all. Professor Campbell says truth and drugs don't mix."

The MO shook his head, irritated. "Professor Campbell can afford his views ... scruples are a luxury for us. Tell him there's war on next time you see him."

He went back to his desk, scrabbling for a file. "Here's the background on this chap – it's all in here. The French Military Security Service delivered him. He'd been turning Jews in to the local SD. It's not his business and the French resent it. I don't think the Gestapo appreciated his efforts either. It's all got a bit delicate – on both sides if you know what I mean. I suppose you have to know when to look the other way. The Germans weren't that interested in Vichy Jews, so it's only recently they've realised the French enthusiasm for the business. It took them by surprise."

"The business? You mean rounding them up?"

"If you want to put it that way. There was already zero trust between the Germans and these Vichy people. With some cause I may add. Plenty of the French old guard still dream of the next uprising. Anyway, our prisoner got above himself and denounced the girlfriend of his local Gestapo chief, a man called Kloss. She was Jewish, although she hadn't registered. You realise that's a hellishly dangerous accusation. So the good Captain Kessler simply vanished, to general satisfaction, I gather. Spirited away on a dark night. The French arranged for it to look like he's gone AWOL. A bit hard on him, but no fear of reprisals that way. We squeezed him onto one of our flights coming back from near Poitiers. That was a few days back. Squeezed is the word, I gather; you wouldn't want to know the details. He didn't travel in comfort.

Arrived as slightly damaged goods, but we straightened him out. I'm not surprised he thinks he's in a hospital. But he's talking alright. One tall tale after another."

"It sounds interesting. If I can just see him …"

The MO was still holding Alex's chit. He waved it vaguely towards the door. "Your Colonel's SOE, isn't he? That's what Records came back with when we phoned about your pass. Alright, I shouldn't ask … I'll just say this … if you are one of that lot, you do need to hear what this man's saying. I don't think interesting quite cuts it - *startling* is more the word. Whether any of it is true is another matter ... but I suppose that's where you come in …"

Alex followed him down the corridor into a room without windows, its shiny linoleum freshly swabbed. This hot little room with its sickly smell of pear drops was not somewhere you would ask to be.

The Sergeant who had answered the door was standing next to a kind of operating table, glossy steel-framed lamps pulled down low, unlit.

A man in the crumpled dress uniform of a German officer was slumped in a wooden chair in the middle of the room, arms handcuffed from behind. He raised his head as they came in, sweat dripping from his chin, eyes dark with supressed fear. Alex looked away, remembering the Gendarmerie at Aste.

"What you are doing is … incorrect."

A dry croak of a voice, a crust of white round his lips, the German's breath was pungent even from across the room. An educated voice, the English correct, although the accent hard to discern, not completely German. Perhaps he'd spent too long speaking French.

"I am an Officer in the Wehrmacht … Hauptmann … you say Captain … My name is Kessler. Hauptmann Kessler. I offer my name and rank. You have my identity disk. Why have I been brought here? Is this a hospital? Why am I in a hospital? I am a prisoner of war."

"There are some problems with that, old boy." The MO had dragged two chairs across from the wall and slumped down on one, waving Alex into the other.

"You see, your colleagues - your colleagues in the French Service think you're a spy. That's the Bureau for Anti-National Affairs. You understand the term *Anti-National*? That would be their nation, not yours. They tell us you're a spy. That's why you're here. So no, you're not a prisoner of war unless we decide you are. In fact, you're not anything. You don't even exist until we find out what you were up to."

As Kessler leaned forward the sergeant stepped across and put a hand on his shoulder, almost affectionately, "You go easy mate, no point getting agitated."

The MO saw Kessler look at the hypodermic lying in the metal kidney bowl on the table. He leaned over to Alex, "Two and half percent. sodium amytal. A good response. Alright Sergeant, no need to stand over him. Take the cuffs off, would you, let him get comfortable. Hauptmann Kessler isn't going anywhere."

They watched the German wince as he eased his arms, rubbing his wrists, wiping the sweat from his face. Alex felt a sudden irrational surge of pity: we have you, and I know exactly how you feel. You feel death would be better than this.

He settled for the ritual packet of cigarettes, leaving them on the desk close enough to reach. Kessler shook his head. For a brief second their eyes met. How young he was. Not so long ago Herr Kessler had been sitting in a lecture room, perhaps taking notes on Schiller – *When we love we are as gods! We are dead matter when we hate.*

The MO suddenly got up, walking to the other side of the room spitting out brusque German as he went, "Our requirement, Captain Kessler, is you tell to this Officer what you told to me earlier. All details. If you refuse, we shall inject you and pose our questions again. Your complete cooperation will avoid that consideration."

The German strained forward, looking at Alex, replying in his own language, "I cooperate. I already explained."

"We wish you to speak English, if you can." The MO raised an eyebrow to Alex.

Kessler relaxed, the condescending nod almost insolent. "You are right. Denying me the liar's armoury: I would have made the same decision."

He continued in English, speaking quickly. "What I told you was this. The Officer leading your group – his name is Archer, his rank

Colonel. I can describe him for you, if you wish." He looked directly at Alex, "You are not he. I have already explained to this … what should I say? Is it *doctor*? I explained we have a chart of SOE, Section F. It is complete. That is your section, is it not?"

He was trying to take control of things. Alex raised a hand, slowing him down, "You say *we*. Who exactly do you mean by *we*?"

Kessler's frown suggested the question had revealed some unexpected level of ignorance, the frown of someone realising his advantage was greater than he had imagined. A tiny shake of the head wearily acknowledged he must be patient.

"The *Sicherheitsdienst*. Counter-intelligence Centre. Avenue Foch," the same lazy superior glance about the room, "in Paris … you would know that. Colonel Archer is head of your Work Group. It is called TSPU. We do not know what the letters mean."

He looked warily towards the MO, "You are going to ask for names again. I repeat, it was not my business to know names." He turned back to Alex, "But I believe you are Captain Vere. It is a guess, but you cannot be Herr Cabot because he wears the spectacles. You are the Captain Vere arrested at Saint Aunix last November."

The blow had been calculated. Alex saw the look of satisfaction as Kessler registered the shock in his face.

"If you're so well informed, Hauptmann Kessler, perhaps you can give us some names that are not in the Telephone Directory."

It was a brave effort, the best he could manage, although difficult to master the shake in his voice. Kessler's impassive face confirmed the damage had been done.

"There are so many names ..." He paused, head cocking up at the thump of passing boots in the corridor, shaking the floor. A distant door slammed. "English names are hard. *Patrick*? Is that a name? I recall a Patrick. He confessed to being a spy. He was shot. And a woman … you send women on such missions … no German would do that. We call them *Schmetterlinge*, you know. Fluttering into a net. We have them all. I remember one name: Simone. A French name, so I suppose I should say *papillon*. We stood in the field laughing while that butterfly looked for her wireless transmitter. On her knees … how you say it? … on her hand and knee. We had collected it for her.

She told us her name was Simone. She was persuaded to tell us her real name. Margaret. It is almost a German name. We had her. We have had all of them for months."

He was in his stride now, rattling on like some garrulous stranger in a railway carriage with a captive audience, "Since March is it? Perhaps earlier. It took time to get her transmitter to work. Ours are better. Your agents were cooperative. Even signal checks … your, how you say it? … your error bluffs. And these poem codes. A poor choice I must say, but we accommodated. We own your circuit, as you call it. For months you have been talking to us. Your orders come to us. And we obey them … in a certain sense. Your arms drops come to us. Your food drops come to us. Your money ..."

He had stopped, cunning eyes furtively assessing the effect of his story. A long way off, traffic sounds spilled in to fill the long silence: a whisper from a sane world somewhere else.

Alex remembered something, turning to the German, addressing him in his own language. "What circuit? This one you say you own. A name would be convincing."

"Someone – I forget who – told us the name."

"But you have unfortunately forgotten."

"No, I have not forgotten. The name is Columbine."

They stood outside in the cool of the corridor, the MO grinning at Alex. "See what I mean? Cocky bugger, isn't he? You're right of course. Most of that stuff is in Records. We've got their Staff Lists so what's to stop them having ours? You can't stop leaks. He's lying alright, here and there, I can see that. All the same, bits ring true. All that about drops."

"We don't make food drops any more. At least, I don't think so. I'll have to check. And money is never dropped … never … obviously," remembering that little room at Tempsford, waxed packages piled on the table, a single bulb swinging yellow overhead, everywhere the sharp smell of aviation fuel. *A bit sordid, things coming down to cash.* There had been an odd expression on the Major's face. Distaste? No, something else: the two of them complicit in something. Justine as well … Justine grinning, stuffing loot into her rucksack.

Alex realised the MO was waiting for him to go on, "No, money always goes by courier. Pretty well always, I think."

"What's this *bluff* stuff about? I was watching you. He seemed to score a hit there."

"Yes. He won't have got that from *Records*. I'm not sure I should say too much about it. There's a security check in the code protocol. We're still using poem codes – with double transposition it's just about adequate, because the traffic is always time critical. I imagine their code breakers have bigger fish to fry. Our WT people used to use Playfair code, can you believe it? You get sent out with a code a child can break, you could get angry about something like that. The security check is a deliberate coding error agreed with London. It lets us know you're captured – letters transposed, words of a given length … that sort of thing. It's not going to save anybody, but it does give you a last roll of the dice. Jerry spots it, of course …" Alex pointed to the hypodermic, "and uses that stuff if you're lucky ... or torture ..."

The MO looked away, suddenly embarrassed. "We've not gone that far. Not even cardiazol. You knew Jerry has started using cardiazol? You can control the convulsions, apparently … more or less. But the poor devils still end up frightened to death. Hellish stuff."

"You're trained to hold out as long as you can." Thinking of his cell in the Gendarmerie, Alex felt his face reddening, "… what I mean is … as long as you can ... depends how they go about it … but they'll get the error code out of you eventually. That's where the bluff comes in. When they fire up the WT and start transmitting, London checks for a second security check. There's always two, you see. If the second's missing ..."

"But this chap said *bluffs*. He's saying they've got both."

"I know, but he may have been fishing. It wasn't a point I wanted to pursue. His story does sound bad, but it's pretty well all circumstantial. If you think about it, he's actually told us nothing that confirms any sort of penetration, well, apart from the security check, and that may be a lucky guess. In fact, if I'd been briefed to give that impression, it's exactly how I would have played it. Can I ask who gave you this German?"

"The Free French people. The usual story. Violating the sacred soil of France. They're always ranting on about that, I suppose because they gave up the sacred soil a bit too easily. They saw a way of getting rid of this one and took it."

"So he might well be a plant?"

"Oh, almost certainly, my dear chap." The MO looked puzzled. "I thought you'd realised? We invariably work on that basis. Actually, in this case, you can't even trust the frogs not to be in on the act. You can get a bit incoherent with the amylobarbitone, but Kessler has already let slip more than he intended along those lines."

He gave a curious jerk of the head, pulling Alex away from the door, drawing closer, "You can't expect them to love us, can you … the French, I mean? Not with chaps like your Colonel fighting the last war. It's bad enough losing your fleet, but when it's your allies that sink it - I can see the way they feel. No, I'm going to assume this Hauptmann Kessler was intended to fall into our hands. He says he worked for Military Intelligence, the *Sicherheitsdienst.* I don't know if you read the stuff I see. They're a monstrous sinister crowd. If he's a plant, we have to assume he was sent to sell the story that they have turned the Columbine circuit. It's frightening how confident they are. We're expected to believe the whole rigmarole on his say-so."

"But he must know if this turns out to be just another disinformation stunt, he's had it. He can count his life in days. That would make our Fritz in there a very brave man."

"That's the point, he doesn't strike you as brave. Cocky, yes, but not brave. Not suicidal anyway. He knows we'll check."

"Well he's won a round whether we believe it or not. And here was Colonel Archer hoping to persuade him to our cause."

"Turn him, you mean? A double agent?"

"That was the idea. But I think you'd have to add one to the tally. Let's say triple."

Eight

When Alex got back to the TPSU, the only sign of Archer was an ashtray full of stubs on top of a cabinet in *Records*. Yellow light spilled out from the room at the end of the corridor.

Cabot was peering myopically at a large-scale map draped over his desk, humming to himself. He called out as Alex tapped his door.

"*Oceans of the Earth* – pretty isn't it? Got it on loan – chap at the British Museum. The things we're asked to do. But I've made a bit of progress. One snag, though, the Channel's far too cold. I did warn you. Why are you looking at me like that?"

"Sorry. I was lost for a minute. You're on about sharks?"

"What else? Come round here, I'll show you. Archer's not going to like it. He has a choice - sharks that might survive but wouldn't dream of biting anybody, or the reverse. The bloodthirsty sort are all tropical. A damned tricky question to pose, I can tell you. People kept asking why I wanted to know. What was I supposed to say? I bluffed it out as best I could. They said *Prionace glauca* might answer. The Blue Shark. Not really aggressive but it doesn't mind the cold. It turns up at what they called maritime disasters. It's all a bit grisly, but that should satisfy him."

"I'm sorry John – I think Archer will be giving sharks a rest for a while. Tell me, what do you know about Abbott Court? I have a story to tell."

By the time Alex had finished, it was late. Street sounds from beyond the blackout had long since ebbed away, London lapsing into dark. A distant random explosion from far across the river flexed the windowpanes, bringing a fleeting change of air to the tiny office.

Cabot sat thoughtfully running his finger along the contours of the map. "I can't work out how this Kessler chap knew about you being arrested. I don't want to be rude, Alex, but you're not that famous."

"I'm not famous, but I suppose my escape was. He would have got the story from the people at Saint Aunix."

"You realise he could fill in some missing bits for you – things you've forgotten. Did you ask him?"

"Of course not. You can't believe a word he says. These Abbott Court people have got themselves an expert at making a story out of nothing at all."

"Professional opinion?"

"If you like, yes, it is. Take the way he threw Archer's name at me. Impressive, until you think about it. Archer's signature was on a WT message this Gestapo chap was waving about. That's where he got it from."

"But your name? And mine? Where'd he get those? I know they intercept WT traffic but you won't get names that way." He shuffled awkwardly in his chair, "And you're ignoring the other possibility …"

"They weren't *my* orders, if that's what you're implying. Or Justine's, come to that. They could have got them off Simone at the Gendarmerie. It's a dreadful sin to fly with operational orders in your pack, but I suppose she was green enough – just a kid. The German that arrested me read bits of it out. It was authentic alright. The who, where, when and why of the whole damn operation. God, what a mess. You don't take your orders with you – I can't believe she did that. She'd have to be mad. Alright, an unfortunate turn of phrase, but let's get one thing straight. All these bloody hints. I am not mad."

"Calm down Alex, I'm hinting nothing. I can't help looking the way I do."

"I'm as sane as you. All I've lost is my memory. I can't remember what happened after Justine got me out. The people at Netley hospital say I got myself a knock to the head, I've still got a terrible headache most of the time. But that doesn't change the fact Jerry must have been waiting for Simone. I was taken back with her."

"Archer did rather stamp on that story this morning. Said you were muddled." Cabot started to roll up the map, "To tell the truth Alex, it did sound a little bit muddled."

"There's no muddle. We overshot the drop site and got picked up on the road half an hour afterwards. Well, I was picked up …"

"And Mrs Perry?"

"Got away. She was lucky."

Cabot looked down, frowning. He went on rolling the map.

"I know it sounds fishy, John. She was just lucky – it does happen."

"Why did Kessler say Simone was crawling about looking for her set? If she flew down in a Lysander it would have been in her pack. She'd have had it on her back. He tripped up there."

"Kessler wasn't part of the reception committee. It's something else he heard from the people at Saint Aunix. He just assumed she'd been dropped with us."

"And you're saying she was arrested?"

"I watched them drag her into the Gendarmerie. She looked like a frightened schoolgirl."

"And now this man Kessler's saying they got her working for them that same night. You can see why Archer's doubtful, Alex. Even if they scared the living daylights out of her …"

"Listen to me. You're not listening. She's not working for anybody. She's dead. I saw her after she'd swallowed her L tablet. You don't forget something like that."

Unconsciously inured to sounds of war, they were suddenly aware of complete silence outside. One of the periods of calm that punctuate larger raids had fallen on the city. Far away, a fire engine bell came funnelling in waves along deserted streets towards them.

"She can't be dead, Alex. Archer says she's sending. You heard him yourself."

"Whoever's using that set, it's not her. It can't be. She's dead."

Cabot sat aimlessly polishing his spectacles, staring sightlessly at Alex, the bell tearing past in the street outside. The room fell quiet.

"If you say so, old man."

"God, don't you go indulging me. She's dead, I tell you. And what if Kessler's right about all those agents? What if they've ended up on the Avenue Foch or in Frenses prison. Have you any idea what goes on in those places? What if we've been talking to the Germans for months?"

Cabot lit a cigarette, drawing hard, shaking his head.

"I'm sorry Alex. You've the field experience, I grant you, but honestly, I don't buy it, my dear chap. A couple of years ago you only had to telephone Baker Street, ask nicely, and you would get whatever you wanted. Security was a joke. It's not all that much better now."

"How would you know? Is that what Archer says?"

"I'm Archer's shark expert, remember? He doesn't talk to me – barks, but doesn't talk. No, security is what keeps my College high table entertained. That and the doings of our Colonel. They talk of little else."

"What about him?"

"Our little Hungarian was packed off to some dire English prep school and then to Rugby. An ancient don claims to have taught him. Eton wouldn't have him. The religion thing, you know. He turned himself into a proper little English gent. That's why his accent's so good. Mind you, I always find it a bit too perfect, if you know what I mean, as if he's still taking lessons. He picked up his MC in the retreat from Mons. Royal Warwickshires. Apparently led a platoon in a completely hopeless charge against a machine gun nest and found himself the only man standing when their gun jammed. Killed four and managed to blow himself up with his own grenade. Invalided out for best part of a year. It's hard to believe, but he actually went back. Wounded again at Arras."

"If he's Hungarian, he was fighting on the wrong side."

"I wouldn't mention that if you value your scalp. He's ended up more English than us. His family was wiped out by the end of the war. Every last stick gone. This war's personal for him. A word to the wise, by the way. Keep off Hungary – he doesn't appreciate it."

Cabot leaned back, exhaling smoke, grinning sheepishly, "Tutorial over. About your Kessler chap. You know who he reminds me of? It's us. He's here to sow disinformation. If you get too close to people like that you become blind to the obvious. You know that better than anybody."

"And the obvious is?"

"Come on! A whole circuit penetrated? I'm sure somebody hoped we'd believe it, but it's schoolboy stuff, Alex. History doesn't teach you much, but it certainly teaches you that the real world's too messy for secrets to hold. Think about it, every one of those agents has ways of signalling they've been captured. And it only takes one to get through. All of them operating under German orders? Do you seriously think we'd not know?"

"You weren't at Abbott Court."

"That's what I mean – you get sucked in. It's like one of Archer's insane schemes - Archer and his man-eating sharks."

Pushing the map across the desk, he failed to catch it as it fell, chasing after it across the floor like a plump puppy until it rolled itself up. He sat looking up at Alex, rubbing one knee, mild ingenuous face shiny with sweat.

"If you want my opinion, Kessler got his information about Columbine from loose talk. And the occasional leak. Sorry Alex, leaks do happen … I'm sorry, old man …"

"Why don't you spit it out? Feel free. Archer's already ahead of you, there's no need to hint. You think they got something out of me, don't you? When I was arrested. You think that's what I conveniently can't remember. Do you imagine I don't ask myself the same question?"

"Alex, Alex, I'm not hinting anything ..."

"How many times do I have to say it? You hand paperwork in after the briefing. Everything goes into the personal possessions box ..." Alex checked, suddenly leaning forward, tapping Cabot on the head.

"Christ - I've just realised - all that stuff must be logged. Why don't we ask? Go on. Just lift the telephone. That Air Intelligence chap. What's his name? Connor. Why don't we ask him?"

"No need to shout. You really want to bring him down on our head? You're forgetting something. If there's a leak, I'm in the spotlight as much as you."

"If you're a spy, John, England really should tremble. Without your specs I don't think you could find your way home. No, to state the obvious, a leak from this pathetic little crew would have to be me. Me or Justine Perry, I suppose."

"Archer? You could point the finger at him," Cabot was grinning.

Alex smiled back, "I'll let you do that bit of pointing, John."

Cabot struggled to his feet, looking at his watch, "D'you know what time it is? I don't think the haughty Connor would appreciate being dragged from his bed to attend our summons. It's Mrs Perry he wants. You can't deny it's awkward, her vanishing like that. No, Alex, no need to get on your high horse."

"Justine's no more a spy than I am. I owe her my life."

"I'm not sure I follow the logic there. And that business with the explosion - if she was the target, you have to ask why. *Why*?"

Alex sat silently rehearsing Justine's telephone call, a kind of weary depression seeping into his mind. What could he say? *Her lover was a Colonel working for French Intelligence.* What would Cabot make of that? What if Justine had joined the ranks of those judged too great a risk to leave alive?

The drone of a solitary engine far away brought a desultory bark of ack-ack. A single breathless thud from across the park rattled the fire-irons in the grate.

He would never see her again. It was almost a surprise to discover the bitter truth of this would end his life.

"You won't tell, will you John? Archer warned me off mentioning Abbott Court."

Cabot ran his hand across his throat, "Hope to die, old boy. Your secrets are safe with me. Not that I get much intercourse with the Great Man."

"Seriously … there's something else. Archer found out I took a telephone call from Justine Perry."

"God almighty, Alex! You're a deep one. Still waters and all that. Why on earth didn't you mention it at the meeting?"

"Honestly, I don't know. Professional instinct, I suppose. You get to hang on to secrets as a matter of course. And that man Connor got on my nerves. I'm sure he knew, anyway. It was all a sick game for him.

None of those toffee-nosed bastards care whether Justine is alive or dead. They just wanted to see how I took the news. You might as well ask why Archer didn't mention it. Anyway, she didn't say anything. Just that she was alright. And now I've got to tell him we'll never turn this chap Kessler."

Cabot had wandered over to the window pulling the blind open a crack, peering into the street below. "I'm going home. That name Kessler put me in mind of something. You don't think I could talk to him, do you? Would Archer let me, d'you think?"

Alex walked home, blind apart from his tiny torch, conscious of the plodding echo behind him. Whoever was tailing actually wanted to be heard or, at least, didn't care. As the thin penetrating rain unique to London started up, filming his face, he could only think *poor bugger*. Archer must have commandeered one of the SOE resident walkers. If he thought Alex was going to lead the way to Justine at half past two in the morning, it was one more proof the man was mad.

He hurried on, the feeble patch of torchlight bobbing ahead on the paving stones. Beyond the narrow circle of light, invisible masses of stone exhaled a faint warmth. The snort of a tug on the river was the only indication the road was opening out, the plodding echoes behind quickening pace.

At the corner, Alex was tempted to stop, let the chap catch up, tell him he hadn't the faintest idea where she was, tell him to go home, have a smoke, go to bed. Tell him, if he didn't know already, that he was employed by a lunatic. All he wanted was to get home and find something to eat – since he had started this job he was hungry all the time.

The thought struck so abruptly he instinctively stretched out a hand, finding the wet bevelled metal of a lamp post. How many times Archer must have combed through that grubby transcript of Justine's telephone call. Wasted effort, old man, because she knows her job, because she had worked out people like you years ago. He was smiling into the rain like an idiot. Archer could have read it for ever and still not understood. She had told Alex exactly nothing and told him exactly what he needed to know, because she had worked him out as well. All she had had to do was wait for the penny to drop.

He stood smiling into the dark, remembering how she called him *Guffin*. She had got into the habit and he treasured it, whatever it meant. Sometimes he would fall asleep remembering the husky fall of her voice: you take what comforts you can in a grim world. But, *my dear* - those listening ears in Baker Street were not to know she had never called him that. Not once. Not ever. They could not have known the lurch of his heart at the sweetness of it. A little boy home from school for the holidays, Mother pinching his ribs, *I'm sure you're not getting enough to eat*. Mother would always say that. And as the penny dropped, he realised Justine knew her job. She was something he would never be.

It had been two days before her last mission, just off the King's Cross sleeper, legs a little stiff, Justine looking for a telephone box that worked. Alex awake long since, waiting. Pushing the blinds aside to see into the street below, early sunshine falling yellow on his hand.

He remembered her voice soft in his ear, *It's me Guffin. Ready for breakfast? You little boys never get enough to eat. The usual place.*

An all-night café behind the station. Filled with weary ARP men delaying going home until the wife was up from the shelter; red-faced firemen smelling of smoke; a few women no better than they should be. Even if the food was awful – and it was – Alex thought it the most human place in London. He could have hugged the fat woman behind the tea urn, could have hugged Justine peering dubiously at her plate, the woman shouting *fried, missus ... all I can say is it's fried*. There was a dash of whisky in the tea. They had sat on opposite sides of the metal table, holding hands.

She would be waiting for him. Early. Sleeper time. She had told him as much and, miraculously, had allowed him to deny knowing for days.

When Alex reached his front door the footsteps behind had already stopped, the walker huddling into his habitual doorway. A match flared, the scent of fresh tobacco blowing past. He had a long night, poor bugger.

Nine

She was there. In the usual place, head bowed, idly pushing scraps of greasy food round her plate. She did not even seem surprised when he sat down opposite, fearful eyes dark from lack of sleep, warily checking the door.

Two women at a table turned long enough to size Alex up then resumed their conversation. Alex glanced at the clock over the counter and shrugged an apology.

"Hello Guffin. You're a welcome sight. I knew you'd be slow coming." Her hands were cold as she pulled him forward, "A day or two, I reckoned," leaning up, for a second her cheek touching his, almost a kiss. "Here's one hell of a mess. I'm scared. Never been frightened before ... should have known it would strike one fine day. Silly isn't it? There's me jumping out of aeroplanes, hardly a flutter. I didn't have a clue what it was all about. Do you know, Alex? Do you really?"

"All I know is thank God you made that telephone call. If you hadn't I would have probably killed somebody. Or myself. He had every intention of saying you were dead."

"Who did?"

"Archer. Vindictive bastard. They listened to your call, of course."

"Not much use if they didn't, that's the beauty of using the telephone. I knew you'd be fretting once that explosion story got out. I've been running like a rabbit ever since. Doesn't say much for Security. Nobody twigged where I'd got to."

"That includes me."

"Apart from the smell, those deep level stations are quite comfortable. Even camp beds if you get there early. I've spent a good few nights in one or another on the Northern Line. The only problem's eating. Not the weather for living on scraps, I can tell you. When I realised nobody was looking, I took the night train to Dundee ... it's alright, my love, I'm not mad. I wanted to find that woman on the flight back from Saint Aunix. The extra passenger. It's not impossible she had enemies."

"No, I don't think that's mad. I had the same idea. Apparently she's an artist. Famous according to the chap who turned up at the meeting this morning. The Major from Tempsford, would you believe it? He's her brother. Pulled strings to get her out."

"*Famous*? She didn't look all that famous in Dundee. In fact she looked half starved, but then who doesn't? All she would say was the people who drove her to the field had got themselves killed. That's the car that blew up. Kept saying she couldn't bear the thought they died just so she could escape. I felt like shouting at her you can't talk like that. It's not as if there were doing anything for her in particular - they were just doing what they had to. Talk like that diminishes what they did … why they did it. But what's the point? She wouldn't know what I was on about, so I kept my council. Actually she was very nice. Said she's never met anybody like me … whatever that means. She wanted me to stay, but Dundee is crawling with navy police. I wanted to get back to my burrow. It was a wasted journey, Alex. I got the impression she was holding something back, but I don't think she was any kind of target. She just got mixed up in something over her head. Unlucky."

"Look, about you going AWOL. You do realise you've precipitated the hell of a flap?"

"*Me*? Did they think I would just sit still waiting for the next lot to blow me up? Your six weeks are up, Mrs Perry, please go quietly. That the idea?"

"Archer brought the meeting down on himself. He's as stupid as they come. He'd convinced himself I knew where you were and set one of his old SOE minions to dog my every step. Now he's paid the price for his obsession. Crowds of Intelligence people fell on us, lured out of the woodwork."

She leaned forward, tugging at his arm, "God, you weren't followed here? You fool."

"Don't panic - credit me with some sense. I took my morning tail by surprise. He was half asleep. I don't think his heart's in the job. He didn't even see me until I was jumping onto a bus. Just stood watching me go. I think he was laughing. But there'll be hell to pay when the news gets back to the Colonel. I'm not his favourite son right now."

"Alex, can you sit quiet and don't ask questions. Please. It'll be quicker that way. I want to tell you what happened at Saint Aunix that morning. After we got you to the big house."

"What big house? I don't remember anything about a house. I can't very well sit quiet if I don't know what you're on about."

"The safe house. You must remember that. What d'you mean, *can't remember*?

"It's a long story. You don't know what happened after you left me. Did you leave me? I can't remember. I remember the little hut and going down a track. There was a lorry, I think. I can't remember anything after that. Nothing."

"I could see you were in a bad way. Reaction, I suppose. That and wine on an empty stomach. When the lorry came back for you we got you inside. D'you remember that?" Alex shook his head, acknowledging her persistence with a tiny smile. "You did seem in a daze, but you seemed alright. After the lorry took off I hung around for a bit, tidying the place up, listening for enemy feet. Then I walked back to the village to hand over the money."

Alex was barely listening, remembering the scent of woodsmoke drifting up through a canopy of green leaves, birds just starting, a low sun warm on his face, Justine shaking the hair out of her eyes, smiling as she tilted the bottle towards his glass. Barely listening to her urgent words, feasting on the recollection of that one sacred morning in his life when he had been completely happy. He reached out to take her hand.

"Yes, I remember the money now. At Tempsford. Loot, you called it."

"I knew Claude would have worked out something had gone wrong with our drop. The fallback rendezvous was the church. It was locked up, of course, you're not allowed church any more, some edict about mass gatherings, but Claude must have got there early – most unusual for him - and opened the place. He was waiting inside. And not alone. I'd never seen the other bloke before. I just assumed Claude had brought a new recruit along to show him the ropes. A tough looking character, the strong silent type. We exchanged nods and I handed over the cash. The usual litany of complaints while he counted it – it's not enough, why can't we bring smaller notes, and so on ..."

"The German stuff as well?"

"What German stuff?"

"Reichmarks. The Major said one of the packages was German currency. You didn't see them - that Corporal carried your pack to the plane, remember?"

"I'll lose the thread if you keep interrupting. I didn't see any German stuff, but Claude was making a mess of counting the notes, fumbling. I must have been really slow that morning. That business at the Gendarmerie had taken it out of me, and I'd had no sleep at all. Listening to Claude grousing I realised his heart wasn't in it. He just wanted to get it over as quick as possible. He was like a bad actor, incredibly nervous, voice trembling, hands shaking, sweating like a pig. It's stuffy in that church but it was quite cold. Usually he's the perfect little accountant - chop chop, even a receipt. He kept looking across to the side door. Obviously, I smelled a rat. I'd got myself into some sort of trap. On a hunch, I asked this other chap if he'd been with us long. Nice and friendly. He just mumbled *not long*, and walked off, lighting up. He'd had to risk saying something and must have hoped I wouldn't pick the German accent. He had his back turned for a second and Claude gave me this really desperate look. It was the cigarette that clinched it. The locals may be a tough bunch of atheistic commies, but they wouldn't dream of lighting up in the church."

"He was alone? Just the one?"

"In the church, yes. But I couldn't know who was outside waiting. I decided to bluff it out, I'd got nothing to lose anyway. Said I was in a hurry, shook his hand, gave Claude his usual little peck and trotted off. Not too fast, either. I'm no actor and I think our German friend was suspicious, but he let me go."

"No reception committee outside?"

"Nothing at all."

At first Alex thought she had finished. She had not released his hand, rising in her seat to look through the greasy window.

"No, it's alright. Somebody loitering across the street. It's nobody. I've got so I'm seeing ghosts. Where was I?"

"Nobody waiting outside."

"That's what I said. The place was deserted. Obviously Claude has been picked up. They'd sent this German chap to see what went on. Clever if you think about it. He was a witness. You know how they do love due process. Poor old Claude's going to end up against a wall and all they think about is their bit of legal paperwork to put him there."

"They just let you walk away?"

"I know how it sounds," she had dropped his hand, "I think they knew they could pick me up any time. I can only say what happened. Alex, don't look like that, it's the truth. That's exactly what happened. I was hooked, they were just letting out a bit of the line. God, and they wonder why people hate them."

A man in khaki uniform standing at the counter looked across. Alex shrugged. The shrug of a man with a hysterical woman on his hands. The wife, perhaps, determined to get something off her chest. The shrug of common cause. We all know who we hate, after all. The soldier looked away.

"Perhaps he thought I was armed. I was, of course, but it wasn't that. I was the mouse and the cat wasn't biting right then. I didn't rate my chances. All I could think was one more catastrophe of a mission. But I'd got you safe, at least. One of us was going to get back. Perhaps one out of three was enough. That's what I thought. It was a consolation."

"So you went back to that Renault chap. Is that what you did?"

"That look on your face, Alex. Honestly, it's the nicest thing I've seen in weeks. No, I couldn't do that. I'd be signing the poor man's death warrant. I'm not that selfish. I hid behind the wall until I heard them coming out of the church. I remember thinking that's the last time I'll see old Claude. Him and the money lost, and me as well from the look of things. I had thirty hours to get through before the flight out. All I could think of was going back to the church and locking myself in - the old tricks are the best, I suppose. I spent the next twenty-four hours behind some baskets in a sort of vestry, smelling of mothballs. Look, you'd better eat. Go and get something, they won't come to the table."

Alex shook his head, "I'm not hungry. This headache makes me feel sick. We can't stay much longer, we're getting looks."

"I've finished. You know the rest anyway. Next day I was out of the church miles too early for the pickup. It was still dark and perishing cold. The car was at the crossroads. Not the usual one, which made me panic a bit, but I knew the driver. He hangs about in the square all day, a young chap with a gammy leg, drives like a madman. When we got to the field it was deserted.

"About five minutes later this other car arrived. Delivering your artist woman. She was terrified, completely bewildered. I don't think she knew where she was or what day it was. She kept giving me this really desperate look as if I was going to tell her what to do. You remember, they don't turn the plane at Saint Aunix, there's room to run straight on. The damned thing barely stopped long enough to get us on board. Took off straight down the field and circled back quite low. I could see the cars on the field below. Then there was one hell of an explosion. We flew through a huge plume of black smoke, flames spurting up. That was when I knew why nobody had bothered to arrest me."

Alex was back in Archer's stifling office, fighting rising nausea. Watching the old fool stumbling over the words. *Yellow body fragments in the debris, almost certainly MK II TNT grenade.*

Justine leaned forward across the table, two hands gripping his, pulling him close. He had never seen tears welling into those dark eyes.

"God, Alex, would you believe it? I'm going to cry. I'm in a hell of a state. I can't manage much longer like this." She pulled away, pressing the back of her hand against her mouth. "It must have been our own people. Claude organised that car for me. Why would he do something like that?" She let her head drop forward, her hair covering her face. He could barely hear her. "What's the point, Alex? A bunch of homicidal thugs with a grudge against the English." When she looked up at him her cheeks were wet, "Remember what Pascal said at the Gendarmerie? Pascal Renault. *Go home bloody English* – something like that."

He waited while she fumbled for a handkerchief, watching her crumple it into a ball. He dared not find her eyes.

"Justine, listen to me. I don't understand it, but the locals think you're playing both sides, holding out on them ..."

"Don't be stupid ..."

"Alright, they're wrong, but that's what they think."

"Why the hell should they? No, you must be wrong. You've not tried to live there. They run your whole life – without them you wouldn't last a week. If they want me out of the way they can do it any time. God, why am I saying *them*? They're us: I'm one of them. There's no need for bombs, don't you see? I'm completely dependent on them. It only takes a word and I'm dead."

"Unless they wanted it to look like an accident ..."

"Who the hell's *they*?"

"How should I know? So long as it looks like your usual incompetant Maquisards blowing themselves up. The point is, that way, no reprisals."

She sat idly pushing the tip of a knife round an empty plate. It was a long time before she spoke, something cold in her voice setting his heart drumming. "What are you saying, Alex? Why would there be reprisals for killing me?"

Shutting up for the day soon, Miss. Can I have your plates?

Alex pushed his chair back, scooping things off the table, carrying them across to the woman wiping the counter. When he got back to the table, Justine was standing. She threaded her arm through his.

"And there was me thinking you were my rock." Somehow a brave little smile didn't suit her. "I usually go back to King's Cross when this place shuts. Every day bar Sunday. They have the fire lit in the waiting room and it's safe enough for a couple of hours."

On the way out he found her hand, praying she would yank it away. Praying she would shout, *for Christ's sake, what now*?

She clung on like a child.

The Waiting Room at King's Cross was packed with noisy sailors togged out in blue and white. With the arrival of two civilians the hubbub fell, only to rise again, the amorphous cacophony of children on a school trip. Most were little more than schoolboys, the old hands sitting apart in gloomy silence, crumpled uniforms not quite clean, a surreptitious silver flask doing the rounds.

Alex found a place on a draughty bench far from the fire.

"I'll tell you what came out of the meeting this morning. Not much really. One thing though: your runner boy was arrested. Picked up on the Friday night."

"Who told you that?"

"Who told me? Why d'you ask? I don't remember who. It was in some paperwork Archer was brandishing."

"René? Wasn't that his name?"

"Archer said his name was Rémy Bosquet. The point is, what could they have got out of him? What could he tell them about you?"

"Nothing. Really nothing. Poor little chap. He was carrying a message, but he didn't know what it was about. He knew it was a bit fishy because I paid him. Claude had asked for my code book. Poems. The sort of thing any schoolkid might have in his pocket. *Poems by Verlaine*. You know, *Il pleut sur les toits*. I put his girl's name in it. He hadn't the foggiest idea what it meant. Why are you asking?"

"It's not the poems. You knew he'd been arrested, didn't you?"

She had seen the trap spring too late, letting her eyes fall as she gave an imperceptible nod, barely whispering, "Yes" before rounding on him. "Is this you quizzing me? You mean I should feel bad using a kid? Of course I feel bad. Does that satisfy you? Don't play naïve Alex. What is it your lot call it? A proxy risk. Isn't that the phrase? But I ask you? Out after curfew? Half the kids in the town do it. It's not a hanging offence."

She shook a cigarette out of his packet, striking the match, drawing in hard, letting a tiny haze of smoke escape. "If you're going to say I should have been creeping around the place myself ..."

"Don't keep saying *your lot*. If you think I'm still in this game, I'm not. I'm nothing. I've been declared dead in the water. My effort's over. I harboured thoughts once I'd be fighting in a war, doing my bit. Maybe dying the best way I could for something ... something I believed in. I've ended up as a kind of second-grade clerk, working for a deranged Hungarian with peculiar obsessions. He's close to deciding I'm a traitor, by the way. He's sure they got things out of me when I was arrested."

"That's ridiculous."

Alex reached for her hand, abandoning the gesture as she leaned back, "At the meeting this morning he produced a message from your man Barte. Apparently, the last one he sent."

"And?"

"Well … according to him … and before you jump on me, I repeat it's his account, you were seen that Friday night. After the curfew."

"*Seen* – what's that mean?"

"Barte's version has you chatting to the local Gestapo chief. His story is the local Maquis didn't appreciate the company you were keeping."

"The night that kid made his delivery? That Friday I was in Toulouse. That's why I couldn't do it myself."

Alex leaned back, deflated, "Well, there you are. If that's right …"

"What do you mean *if*? There's no bloody if about it. And tell me: what exactly did this message say I was doing there?"

"I'm not sure … it was vague on that point."

"There's a surprise! Listen. On that Friday there was a functioning circuit in Saint Aunix, including Claude. The next Monday there was nobody. Even Claude was being led about on a lead. Well there was me, I suppose, but plainly that wasn't intended. I'm not a traitor, Alex, I'm a mistake. If the idiots had known how to set a timer I wouldn't be here talking to you. I'd be a few scraps of flesh in a field."

"We've got a German prisoner from Saint Aunix at an interrogation centre. The frogs let us have him. He was spying on them and got a bit too close. He's talking."

"Talking about me? And you believe him? You know better than anybody he'll say anything to save his skin."

"No, he's not talking about you, but he does seem to know a lot about Columbine. I didn't want to believe him but what he said confirms what you're saying."

"No point being coy is there? Isn't it obvious we've got a spy of our own? And no, I don't think it's you. I got you out of the Gendarmerie at

Saint Aunix, remember. Alright, you were in a mess, but I don't think anybody had laid a hand on you. And don't look at me – I skipped off because I was frightened, not because I was guilty. Every single operation has failed. Don't you think it strange they always seem to know in advance?"

"Who seem to know? French or German?"

"Both probably. Pascal Renault knows something, I'm sure. Bit it's your setup that's leaking. It's your lot need interrogating, not me."

"Justine, you're tired. This isn't some John Buchan story. There's only the three of us in the TPSU: Archer, Cabot and me. SOE pay us, but our boss spends his life ordering us to tell them nothing. To make sure we comply, he's ensured we have nothing to tell. We don't even have anybody to do the typing, just a WAAF every other afternoon. We don't plan missions, we don't select operatives, we don't order flights - in fact, SIS won't let us get near one. You think intelligence people are … what's the word? *Intelligent.* But they're not. They spend most of their time creeping round politicians hoping for a pat on the head. TPSU hasn't a clue. What are you saying? We haven't got anything to leak."

"What about your Colonel? You don't trust him."

"Only because he's pretty well gaga. I sometimes wonder whether he can find the way to his club. He's a nasty bit of work, but if he's a master spy, God save the Union."

"He's had you followed."

"Oh, he's done that alright. He doesn't trust me – of course he doesn't. He doesn't trust Cabot either. But only because we're cleverer than him. Believe me, that's not at all difficult. He's suspicious of us, but he's too stupid to know why. Most of the time he needs somebody to tell him what day it is. *Why?* What would be the point? Why in God's name would we send people and equipment to a godforsaken dead end like Saint Aunix simply for the local Gestapo to pick them up? It doesn't make sense."

Ten

Evening was closing in when Alex made the decision to find a hotel. Walking aimlessly through pelting rain, he had stifled Justine's protests, pointing to the vast terracotta palace sprawled along one side of Russell Square.

The one hotel in London that had inexplicably escaped the interest of the War Office had not completely escaped the interest of the *Luftwaffe*. Another unintentional bomb had left the entrance cluttered with broken glass and fire buckets. Improvised duckboards lay across the stone steps. A poster with a picture of Winston Churchill improbably declared the place open.

Alex paid in advance, the man at the desk insolently eyeing Justine, his smirk evaporating as Alex pushed their identity cards towards him.

"Oh, so you're Services?" There was something disturbing in Justine's eyes: something that made him look down, writing their numbers in his book. "I'll still need a ration card."

"We're not eating."

"All the same …"

Justine gave him hers and walked away, not bothering to reply to the question about luggage.

It was a long traipse along interminable dusty corridors, but the room turned out to be surprisingly clean, albeit smelling faintly of cordite.

Justine peered down into the Square below. “I think I’ve been here before. Years ago. I was a little girl. I remember how pretty it looked when the lights came on in the square.” She jerked the blackout curtain closed, turning towards him, “You were right, it beats sleeping in the underground. Reminds me of that gothic place at Torridon. But we’re taking a risk.”

“What risk? You’re not on the run from anybody. Not in England anyway. Neither am I for that matter. We can go where the hell we like. I’m damned if I’m going into hiding.”

Justine’s sudden smile turned his heart over. “Don’t look so *defiant*, Alex. It doesn’t suit. And it’s not convincing. You know you shouldn’t be with me. Even if I’m not fleeing your lot – sorry, I mean *them* - you should hand me in. I’d hand myself in if I wasn’t so scared. Two goes at killing me in as many days. I know they say it goes with the job, but it makes you wary when your own side starts on it. I’m sorry you’re dragged into the mess ...” She checked, “I was going to say my mess, but that’s not true. It’s nothing to do with me, things have been going wrong for ages. Speaking of mess, I wonder whether there’s hot water through there?”

“I doubt it. More to the point, do you think that ration book of yours runs to real food?”

She grinned at him, relaxing a little, “I haven’t done much shopping recently, if that’s what you’re asking. There’s a telephone in the corridor. See if it works. See whether they can make us some sandwiches. I’m going to inspect the bathroom.”

The corridor outside was lined with dark polished wood, windowless like the interior of some transatlantic liner. The telephone was perched on a spindly gilt table with matching chair. There was something absurd about the pretention of this little tableau, intended to preserve the dignity of the rich and important going about their communications. A single lugubrious electric lamp hung over it all.

Alex lifted the receiver, read the little card, and dialled the desk.

"Is it possible to make us some sandwiches? Anything … oh, no, not anything … not tinned fish. If you can? Room 208."

"Captain Vere, sir. I was just going to come and ask ..." The pause was too long. "About your Identity Card, sir."

There was something strange about the voice. This chap was rarely obsequious, you could tell that, but the insolence had evaporated.

"What about the card?"

"I didn't take the number down, sir."

Suddenly alert, heart pounding, "I'm sure you did. Alright, I'll come down."

"Don't you bother doing that, sir. I'll come up and see to it. With the sandwiches. We've got cheese, sir. Will that do? Anything to drink? There's only beer."

"Beer's alright. The number - I saw you write it down."

"No, it's not here, sir. There's no mistake. That must have been the other card."

When Alex got back to the room, Justine was lying on the bed, eyes closed.

"You were right. Cold water. It runs brown. As bad as the underground. Still, the bed's soft. Any luck with the food?"

"Cheese. I hope that'll do. That chap on the desk is up to something. I don't know what. Says he wants to check my ID again."

"You don't think …?"

"No. Not really. It's just that he sounded a bit off. We're alright here. At least you can get a bit of sleep. Then tomorrow … look, Justine, the best thing is you just turn up at the TPSU. My unit. I'll take you in. We'll brazen it out."

"Like hell I do. I'm not going near the place. My mind's made up. I'm going to write and tell them I'm un-volunteering. I can do that. I just have to tell them."

"They'll still have to debrief you. I don't mean SIS. I get the impression Archer wants to handle it. I know why. He wants to know about Aste – the bits I can't tell him. He's desperate to keep the SIS people out of it. He thinks he's got the advantage because it was Air Force Intelligence lost you."

"They hadn't captured me, for heaven's sake. I just got off. Quite a neat trick really."

"Archer's bound to pump you about me. He's not that interested in Columbine, he just wants to know what went on after you got me away."

"Alex, I thought you understood. I've done eight missions. Eight missions is impossible. Couriers last longer than WT people, I know that, but my six weeks were over long ago. I've changed from being a walking miracle to a walking embarrassment. By rights, I should be dead by now. The fact I'm not is going to kill me. The locals don't go in for finesse. Simone's arrested ..."

"Simone's dead. I told you. Swallowed her pill."

"Yes, I remember now. Poor kid. And Claude's probably in Paris already. Dead, if he's lucky, poor devil. That means there's nothing secure left of Columbine."

She was standing close to him now, her eyes blazing into his: "So why am I alive? That's what they're asking. Even you have doubts, don't you? Tiny little ones. You think perhaps she's up to something – nothing too serious, but *something*. I saw it in your face when I told you about Pascal. And in that café when you started quizzing me. Even you, Alex."

"I was trying to connect things. I can't see how you can even say that. If we start suspecting each other … no, I'd trust you with my life. In fact I have trusted you. I'd be lined up with Claude Barte if it wasn't for you. I could ask you the same question. Do you think I'm responsible? There, you looked away. You can't answer, can you? Because it's possible. Ask yourself what could have been prised out of me at Saint Aunix? Names. Contacts. That's what Archer believes. How do you know he's not right? How the hell do you think that makes me feel?"

She went on staring, silently waiting. She knew. She saw it in his face. Knew there was more to say. Knew he would never speak the words. And as the recollection of his sordid cell flooded his mind, Alex felt his face hot with the shame of it. Remembering *her name is Justine Perry,* he looked away.

He would recall that betrayal for the rest of his life, endlessly consoling himself that it is deeds that condemn, not intentions.

Confronted in reality by that thin-lipped monster, perhaps he would have kept silent. Torture is mostly in the anticipation after all. Confession is spawned by fear, not pain, he knew that well enough. He had read the books. The men in the Avenue Foch had read the books. He felt Justine's cool gaze on his face.

The sudden drone of an aircraft saved them, huge engines rattling the windowpanes, something monstrous, low in the sky, just beyond the blackout. Dangerously low. Alex dashed across, pushing heavy curtains aside, opening the tall window, stepping out onto the tiny balcony.

A rumble of heavy vehicles rose up from the vague blackness below, bells echoing between the chasms of distant buildings. There was a coarse stench of hot metal in the air.

Justine's voice from inside the room was muffled by the thick cloth: "I'm not going anywhere tomorrow. I've finished with it. All of it."

Alex looked down into the Square, feeling the muscles of his legs tense, his stomach turn. It was not so very far, that fall. Nothing compared to the drop at Ringway. It would be quick: over in no time at all. Then what? A finish to the lot of it. Would she mourn his loss? But the maudlin question answered itself – they had been bound together, Justine and he. Not by common cause, but by something more elusive. A sudden gust of icy air whipped his face, realisation flooding through him. It was not love holding them close but the certainty of death. How else interpret an insane enterprise destined to consume their last few weeks on earth?

This war – his war, Cabot's war, Justine's war – was surely lost. England's war, one catastrophe after another, all lost. London, above all, falling brick by blackened brick into ruin, had lost. German troops everywhere else would soon enough be here. What then? Only a fool would think that rumours planted in embassies were going to change anything. Faked letters would not mend a war. How could any sane man think they might? He was fighting a war with paperclips. A war that was lost long ago.

It was not just that the struggle seemed so unequal. At first he had shared the suicidal pride in certain defeat. No, it was the humiliating futility of his own part in it. What was left to him? Fighting bullets with lies, like some seedy crook in a back room. How many German fliers were going to turn back, repelled by thoughts of Cabot's sharks? If it were not so shameful it would be comic.

"Alex, that's the food at the door. Somebody's knocking."

As he pushed the curtain back, blinking against the light of the room, Justine was already opening the door.

Archer stood there, looking at her. Wearing his walking out uniform, a little swagger stick under his arm, immensely pleased with himself, moustaches rampant.

"Mrs Perry isn't it? I think we did meet some time ago," pulling off one glove, Justine took his outstretched hand, shaking it like an automaton, her face frozen. "At Baker Street, it must have been. Perhaps I can come in? You've led us a fair old dance, young woman."

He held up one hand in an impish little gesture to stop her speaking, turning back into the gloom of the corridor, "One moment."

Alex heard a quick tread of boots on the carpet. Archer returned, holding a tray, "I believe you ordered these sandwiches, Alex. It is you Alex, isn't it? Lurking behind the arras. And why not?" He turned to Justine, the smile luminous, "Bottled beer, I fear. Not ideal for the ladies, I am aware. Apparently it is all they can do within the law. There you are, how the law dogs us all."

He was playing the gallant old Colonel, playful with the little woman, even a trifle flirtatious. Incredibly, Alex watched Justine thaw as she settled deeper into her chair, shaking her head at the proffered sandwich, pulling back not quite enough as Archer leaned over to pat her knee.

He looked at Alex, his voice changing, "Chap downstairs was happy for me to bring them ... saved his legs, you see. I don't take to that sort. Chap like that should be serving his country. Left-handed, I dare say. Still, he telephoned the Unit, we should thank him for that. We're not idiots, Vere. Names are circulated, you knew that. After all, John keeps the list. Did you think Mrs Perry's name would be left off?"

The smile switched on like a lamp, its beam swivelling back to Justine, white teeth showing hints of gold, "John is a colleague of

Captain Vere, my dear. They work together. So don't blame John if hiding was your intent, he was only doing his job, his patriotic duty."

He perched himself on the edge of a chair, committee-style, leaning forward, suddenly serious, bringing the meeting to order. "Now. Mrs Perry. Justine. May I use your name? We have thought so much about you I feel I know you quite well. I assume you have explained all to Captain Vere? Lined up a story – that what you've done?" Justine remained silent, looking at her shoes. Alex realised she was thinking of Cabot's list, wondering how he could have forgotten that. "No, no, no, I'm not here to quiz you. Not now. We'll sort all that out tomorrow. Just one thing, though. I want you to promise me you won't run away again." The smile was back, Colonel Archer hiding inside a caricature of Santa Claus, "At least, not tonight, dear lady. You can do that for me, can't you?"

The sandwiches had rested untouched. Archer took one, waving it vaguely round the room, "Cheese. That's a comfort. This is a comfortable enough place. You won't run away, will you, because it would be irritating. I'm leaving somebody downstairs, but do us all a favour and stay put. Get some sleep. You look as if you could do with it."

He was standing now, jutting chest an inch too close to Alex, "That goes for you as well. Eight ack emma. Be there both. I've got news for you, Vere. About our good friend Captain Kessler. But it will keep, it will keep. No, don't get up, my dear. Enjoy your supper."

And he was gone.

Eleven

It was still pitch-black when they left the hotel, long before whatever might have been offered as breakfast. Last night she had kissed him like a little child and fallen asleep, her arms wrapped tight around him, mumbling something about Hansel and Gretel. Late in the night, she woke to find him standing at the curtain, looking out onto the Square and called him back like a patient wife.

The frozen streets were deserted, the air ahead hollow, footsteps a dull echo. Alex carried their only torch, his arm pulled tight round her waist, feeling her warmth, the flakes of snow tumbling through the narrow beam of light strangely consoling.

The familiar Sergeant was standing at the top of the steps, rifle shouldered. A shaded light directly above turned his face to a sculpted mask. A cigarette butt arced down onto the pavement as they fumbled their way across the road, the mask leaning back to call through the black of an open door. Two uniforms jostled out, the little group standing in barrier line on the steps, rifles awkwardly unslung, trying their best.

"It's you Captain Vere, isn't it? I do know you, sir, but I'll have to see your identity all the same. Yours too Miss. Orders today."

Justine mounted the steps, standing level with him. "So if I don't show it, you won't let me by?"

"Now I didn't say that, did I, Miss?" He took her card, stifling a grin, "Mrs Perry, you're expected, Miss. Orders were to escort you … if you don't know the way, that is."

"She knows the way." Alex took her arm barging through the blackout curtain into the hallway.

The TPSU had suffered a sea-change: two uniformed soldiers at the foot of the staircase stopped talking, straightening up. A desk had been dragged out onto the landing at the top of the stairs, accommodating a WAAF officer peering at the keys of a huge typewriter, clicking out letters one by one in the gloom. The Torridon Major stood behind her, looking down at them through the bannister rails.

"Captain Vere, how nice to see a familiar face." The same laconic drawl raised a trifle over the sound of the typewriter. "And Mrs Perry. Odysseus and Penelope all in one go – what a treat. Let them pass, Corporal. Come on up. I gather your Colonel's going to be a little late. We had to tee up transport for him. What a godforsaken hour this is. Who dreamt up summer time in mid-winter? Can I get you something hot to drink? Or something stronger?"

The curious proprietorial tone jarred. Alex could only wonder who on earth *we* were. Perhaps a coup had taken place overnight, some particularly flagrant misdemeanour finally dethroning Archer.

As they reached the top of the stairs, the Major wriggled round the desk to shake their hands, smiling broadly. "I must say I'm extremely pleased to see you Mrs Perry. And pleased you've come to no harm. I was worried."

Down the corridor, Cabot's door, invariably flung wide, was shut tight, a soldier slouched on a wooden chair outside, his rifle propped against the wall. Of Cabot himself there was no sign.

"It looks a little like an invasion, sir. I'm impressed somebody thinks we are so much in need of protection, armed protection at that."

The Major saw Alex glance at Archer's security lock and allowed himself a smile. The door to *Records* was wide open. "Not my doing. I'm only here on the off chance. I heard you would be coming. No, don't ask … I hear things. Why don't we find a quiet place somewhere? I'd so much like a few words with Mrs Perry."

As he started shepherding them through the open door to Archer's room, Justine stood her ground, resisting. "I thought it was arranged for Colonel Archer to debrief me." Hearing another woman's voice, the WAAF on the landing stopped typing, releasing a beat of silence into the cramped space. "I don't want to say everything twice. To tell the truth, I don't want to say anything once."

"It's actually only one thing. And this seems as good time as any. Colonel Archer can't be much longer."

He closed the door as they followed him inside, pausing with his back against it, listening to the murmur of voices in the corridor.

Justine crossed to the window, opening the curtain a crack, peering into the street below. "I've never seen where you work, Alex. So this is where you spend your days."

The Major gave Alex no time to reply. "I gather you've been in Dundee, Mrs Perry?"

"Yes, since you ask." She turned to face him. "There was somebody I wanted to see there. Can I ask precisely how you gathered that?"

"Ah, the *how* question. I'm always a little foxed by that. Actually, in this case I can honestly say I don't recall. Information comes my way, usually in a file – will that do?"

"I suppose it will have to. It's not pleasant knowing you are being spied on. But the answer is yes, I went to Dundee."

"To interview your fellow passenger from Saint Aunix?"

"I'd hardly say interview. If somebody tries to kill you, you comfort yourself with the thought that it might have been a mistake. Possibly I wasn't the target. The other passenger could well have been in the car that was blown up. I thought that perhaps …"

He was lost for a second, frowning. "Yes, that sounds logical. Perfectly reasonable. And?"

"Captain Vere told me she's your sister." She glanced Alex, "I wasn't aware of that. I'm afraid I didn't get far with her. She wasn't very forthcoming. She went on a bit about the people who were killed in the explosion, but ..."

The Major had raised one hand as if to slow her pace, his palm turned towards her, the gesture strangely diffident, the expression on his face hard to read – something not far from pain. "Forgive me, I was thinking of something else. Do please go on. About these people that were killed? You realise I have a personal interest in that? Any names?"

"Somebody close to her, I think, but she didn't say." Justine looked at him, her smile too bold. "Her man perhaps. You know how these things go … we women in far off places …" Staring at his bleak unsmiling face, Justine found herself stumbling, "What I mean is she didn't look as if …" She could find no way of finishing. "No … anyway she knew nothing about that operation. I think she'd just got herself mixed up in something. Which leaves me as your only witness. I'm afraid I may be all you've got."

"We'll have to see. Perhaps another Dundee visit? And Captain Vere is correct. Lucile Beyrou - I suppose we'd better stick with that name - is my sister. The people killed in that explosion - you're sure she didn't mention names?"

"None that I remember. Not anybody in Claude's circuit, anyway. I know them all."

"Let's leave it at that then." He seemed unaccountably relieved. "But you wouldn't be expected to know them all, would you? Not with cut-outs."

"God, is this you trying to trip me up? Listen, Major … I'm sorry … I didn't get your name … cut-outs might seem alright in your world, I dare say they do. I understand the logic. But you can't operate cut-outs in a tiny village. Just think about it, the idea's ridiculous."

"Justine's right, sir. In a tiny place like that, knowing other people's business is a way of life. You can't expect secrets to hold ..."

"Just a minute, Captain Vere. One at a time." The little gold-cased pad had reappeared, the Major peeling back pages, finding somewhere to write, keeping them waiting, an earnest expression on his face, finally snapping it closed, looking up.

"Interesting. Go on Mrs Perry."

"About the visit to Dundee you mean? When I was taken to her studio I remember she was mixing something up in a bottle. She didn't stop what she was doing. Scarcely looked at me. I don't think she meant to be rude ... perhaps *rude* isn't the right word ... I just got the impression she didn't want me there. She didn't want anybody there. And she certainly didn't want to talk. Then, when I …"

There was muffled rumpus outside, the sudden clatter of urgent boots on the stairs, the Sergeant's bleat, *No you can't sir … Please sir.* Archer's furious bellow echoed down the corridor, "*Hands off me, damn you.*"

The door burst open, Archer looking in at them, crimson with fury, moustaches flaring. He hung onto the back of a chair, his breath coming in gasps. "What the hell are you lot doing in my room? Who let you in?" He rounded on the Major, "Do you know that bloody fool down there asked me for my pass? A pass for God's sake! Why the hell would I have a pass? Is this tomfoolery your idea, Major? No, don't bother getting up, if you're comfortable sitting there. Was posting a sentry your idea? Was it?"

The major took his time standing, not bothering to supress a grin at *tomfoolery*, raising an eyebrow to Alex as Archer's expression hardened.

"That damn fool of a man went to lay hands on me? Is he under your orders, Major? Because …"

But they were never to learn the Major's fate. The Sergeant himself appeared at the open door, red-faced, torn between seizing his quarry and crossing the threshold.

Archer cast about for a suitable projectile, falling on Justine's handbag, stubby hands jerking it off the desk, hurling it across the room. The bag flopped limply against the Sergeant's chest, clung crab-like for a second, then fell to earth. Justine burst out laughing.

The Sergeant, at a loss, stooped down to pick it up.

"Leave it! Leave it where it is, God damn you. Step further in here and I'll have you court martialed. Do you understand? I'll not have it … I'll not have it. Insubordination. Never seen anything like it."

Realising he was still holding the chair he sank onto it, chest heaving, eyes raking the room, coming to rest on Justine, unforgivable laughter still on her face. It was enough to find his second wind, lumbering upright, grabbing a metal ashtray, beating it into the desk, punctuating his words: "Let's … have … some … order." The Sergeant moved warily back into the corridor.

"That's better. Now … who stationed you there? No, don't answer - I'm not interested. I don't want to know. Why the hell are you up here? Chasing after me like some damned shop girl. Why aren't you at your post?"

"Orders, sir. Orders not to let …"

"Don't you ask permission to speak any more? Get downstairs, Sergeant. Somebody asked you to stand guard. Bloody well go and do it. I'm in charge here. I give the orders."

He appeared to notice the line of pockmarks across the desktop, rubbing ineffectually at them with his fist, finally tossing the deformed ashtray into the wastepaper basket.

The Sergeant stayed swaying in the corridor outside, his face brick-red, his eyes swivelling helplessly between Alex and the Major.

Justine went to collect her bag but the Major beat her to it, scooping it up, letting their hands touch, tapping her wrist, murmuring, "A moment, Mrs Perry, I'll deal with this." He went across to the door. "It's alright, Sergeant. A misunderstanding. Get back to your post. We're expecting a visitor."

"Permission to speak, sir?" The Major nodded wearily. "A man under guard down there, sir," head rigid, eyes flicking dangerously close to Archer's, "arrived with the Colonel's party, sir … Corporal Wade's looking after him … with the other gent."

"Very well, I'll come down."

Archer pushed past, shouldering him aside, "The hell you will, Major. Misunderstanding my backside. Sergeant, escort them up here. Take them to Mr Cabot's room, they'll tell you where it is. Those are my orders. And if you ask any of them for a pass don't expect to keep those stripes. D'you follow me?"

With the Sergeant gone, silence fell on the room. Archer stationed himself in the doorway, his back to them, blocking the way. They could hear his breath wheezing. He did not turn round.

Eventually, the cheerful sound of men's voices floated up the stairwell. Alex made out Cabot's laugh. They were speaking German, apparently exchanging fragments of poetry, vying with each other, capping quotations.

As they passed the door, Archer joined them, calling over his shoulder, “You’ll have to tell your tale to the Major, Mrs Perry. I assume that’s what he’s here for. It may give the two of you something more to laugh over. Other business takes priority over SIS for me. I will eventually be favoured with a report, no doubt. You too, Vere, only don’t be too long about it, I shall want to see you. Ah, here you are at last, John. All safe and sound?”

Wedged against the doorframe he managed an awkward salute, “Hauptmann Kessler ... the room on your right. Mr Cabot will show you the way.”

Hauptmann Kessler shuffled past, glancing nervously into the room, his eyes meeting those of Alex, a faint nod of recognition.

Archer followed them, slamming the door behind him.

Twelve

It was left to the Major to break the silence. "Not SIS, in fact. I can't think where your Colonel got that idea. Never mind, it's a detail, it's the same war for all. You seem to lead a lively sort of life here, Captain Vere. Is it always like this? Perhaps you have your quieter days?"

"The Colonel was taken by surprise, sir. Armed men about the place … you know. And we are in his room ..."

"So we are. And you're right. Point taken. But the guard has absolutely nothing to do with me. Perhaps you could explain … at a suitable moment, of course. I believe the men are from Abbott Court. Part of the prisoner transfer routine. I'm afraid your Colonel jumped to the wrong conclusion."

"He does tend to, sir."

"But it seems he got his man. I'm intrigued."

"Hauptmann Kessler was at Abbott Court. Colonel Archer hopes there's a chance we can turn him."

The Major was checking his watch. "Not much time. My car will be here in half an hour. This debriefing, Mrs Perry, it looks as if Colonel Archer has other fish to fry. Perhaps we can find a convenient time. You as well, Captain."

He had installed himself in Archer's chair, drawing it up to the desk, pushing things about, looking for something to write on, glancing up at Justine, the expression suddenly disarming. "There is one thing you could help me with." He held out his cigarette case. "No, nothing to do with that trip back from Northolt. Frankly, I can't see why you shouldn't pop off and catch a tube if you feel like it. It's not as if you were a prisoner." He swivelled round to Alex. "A quick précis of the thereafter, as it were, would be helpful ... and we do have a few moments. When you were arrested after your drop, can I start there? I suppose no chance of running for it?"

"I'm sorry, Major, the situation was hopeless. I was in the middle of the road, a sitting target blinded in headlights. I wouldn't have got ten yards. There was an SS Officer in the car. He knew I was with somebody, but ..."

The raised hand again, palm forward, his signature gesture, "Just a second ... how could he know that?"

"Well, he had Mrs Perry's code name Marie. Perhaps they got it out of Simone at the Gendarmerie. I think they knocked her about looking for her L tablet, but she got to it first. I'm afraid she's dead. There's absolutely no doubt about it."

"No need to be so emphatic. I'm not arguing. I'm trying to keep up."

"The man who arrested me had a copy of Simone's orders, sir. Or rather, not a copy, he had the paper itself, the stuff she was supposed to leave behind at Tempsford. He must have got them from her."

"I can check. See what's missing. And you say she's dead? But you're not dead, you're here. As Colonel Archer said, captured agents never come back. You are unique. You can see why we want to know how that came about?"

"I was a month at Netley hospital. Nothing. I'm afraid it's all a complete blank. Perhaps it would be quicker to let Mrs Perry ..."

The Major sighed, ostentatiously folding the notepad closed, turning to Justine.

"Mrs Perry? I know you would have preferred to wait for Colonel Archer ..."

She was already speaking, "It may not be what you want to hear, Major. You want to know about the Columbine circuit?"

"That would be a start. Fire away. You don't mind if I jot down some notes?"

Justine nodded wearily, "What do you want to know precisely? There's barely a hundred people in Saint Aunix. All related to each other, more than they like to admit. It's best not to notice too much who looks like who. Good Catholics, though. Apart from siring children, all else they do is organise funerals. The idea an agent could *blend in*, as you put it, is nonsense."

"Not my words. It's horses for courses. In small rural communities … it's going to be different."

"You do realise *how* different, don't you, Major? Every single person knows you. Knows why you're there. Particularly kids. Children like oddities, don't they? If you want to talk about sides, some of the locals are with us. Most don't care. The choice between us and the Master Race is not that obvious. So *how do you survive*, Major? Any ideas? No need to look embarrassed. Isn't it obvious? If you're a woman you need protection. And I don't mean sturdy peasants singing the *Internationale*. The right people have to look the other way – and to get them to do that is an endless expense." She looked across at Alex, "Of money, of course. But mostly favours. You do understand what I mean, Major? Favours is how we stay alive. You do understand, don't you? You can witter on as long as you like about blending in with the natives, it's still favours that count."

She had talked herself to a standstill, hands resting calmly in her lap – SOE regulation pose – daring him to speak.

He sat, head bowed, the only sound the minute scratch of his pen, finally looking up.

"*Witter* – long time since I heard that word. Scottish isn't it? I had a nanny used it. Listen, Mrs Perry, I see what you're saying. I suggest …"

"I know, I know. You suggest I write a letter. You suggest I come across to Baker Street and give a talk. Explain how … despite everything … I end up still alive all these weeks later. Oh, I can explain that alright. Christ almighty, don't you think I've done enough?"

She went over to the window, pulling at the thick curtains, letting a little grey light seep into the room, waving a hand behind her back for a cigarette.

"Do have a seat, Mrs Perry. I can see you're exercised about this. Nobody is implying anything. We can stop if you like."

"I'll tell you a story, Major. About *blending*. My first operation, the briefing was at Castle Kennedy. Some chap gave a pep talk before the drop. *Your initial rendezvous*, he said. Smashing bit of French, nice accent. Your initial rendezvous is the bar in the square, that's what he said. I can tell you, by the way, that the bar's called *Le Sport*. Just go in, he said, order a coffee and wait, somebody will meet you. Sounds easy, doesn't it? Just a few snags. Biggest snag - that bar exists exclusively for the rugby club. The only woman in there is a tart called Nathalie or some such name, on a Saturday night. And you don't *order a coffee*, Major, for the simple reason there's been no bloody coffee anywhere in the South West for months. Alright - I admit I was met eventually, so you could say that part went to plan. And he got me out of *Le Sport* smartish. You could hear them laughing all down the street. I might as well have been wearing a placard saying *English Agent*."

"I do understand your point. Can we get back to Captain Vere? You were going to explain how he got out. How you managed that."

"The situation he was in looked worse than it was. For one thing, there is no official SS presence in that area. The local Vichy police are in charge and they're jealous of that. I happen to know an officer in the Gendarmerie, a man called Pascal Renault. He hates Germans treading on his toes. I have leverage with Renault."

"Blackmail?"

Justine looked at him, pondering her reply, glancing at Alex.

"Something like that. You can't keep captured agents in the local cop shop. They get sent on. Renault signed a chit for the prisoner to be transferred up the line. It was a bit unusual, him turning up to do the necessary at the crack of dawn, but there was only an old guy on duty and he did as he was told."

"No, I'm completely lost. How do you know all this?"

"Because I was there. Consider Renault as my captive, Major – it's not quite right, but it will do. I don't propose to elaborate. The paperwork said Alex was to be plucked from his dungeon and sent off under escort to Limoges. It was obvious to the old guy what was going on - he seemed to treat it as a bit of a joke. Everything was deniable. That Station is awash with forged papers. The SS officer had no business haring about chasing parachutes, he should have contacted his superiors. The whole arrest was irregular. I think he had a little free-lance torture in mind. He's a nasty piece of work, apparently, but he had no option but to go along with the daring rescue nonsense. If he didn't he was in deep trouble. So there's no story, really. Captain Vere just walked out. We sent him on his way to the safe house … I know it seems a miracle, but ..."

"It does, rather ..."

Alex broke in, "I'm not sure what you're implying, Major, but you should know something about Columbine. That prisoner Colonel Archer's interested in - the one down the corridor - confirms what Justine's saying. He claims the Gestapo own the whole of the Columbine circuit. All the WT traffic has been through captured sets. All of it. For months."

"A slight exaggeration, Captain Vere. I can see they would like us to believe that, but obviously they don't have the whole of the circuit. Mrs Perry is here, isn't she? Unless you're going to raise that business with the TNT?"

"Obviously that was intended to kill Justine. The thing went off too late."

"Intended by whom? I'm just asking. You need reasons to organise something elaborate like that."

Justine was glaring at him. "I haven't the faintest idea, Major. am I supposed to feel guilty I survived? How do you imagine I feel about that?"

"Can I ask about this report you were seen with the local Gestapo. Now, there may be a perfectly …"

"Not this so-called message from Claude Barte? When that was sent, Claude had already been arrested. Whoever sent it, it wasn't him. That Friday night I wasn't even there."

"Just to have something to write down, exactly where were you?"

"I was in Toulouse. If you think I'm in a position to go chatting to the Gestapo, you're gravely mistaken. For one thing I can't speak German …."

As Alex looked up, she grabbed his arm, "Ask Captain Vere here

- he knows. He was brought up in France as well. Schools didn't teach German. That Barte message stinks of dirty work. German dirty work. Or, more likely, English dirty work."

"I'm afraid I'm losing your thread, Mrs Perry."

"Really? Isn't it fairly obvious? If every member of a drop is picked up on arrival, how do you imagine that trick is played? Somebody is telling them, Major. Somebody at this end ... at our end. I can't believe you've not thought of that. You must be thinking of nothing else. Just don't think in my direction."

The Major had long since stopped writing, leaning back in Archer's chair, his expression thoughtful, calculating.

"I'll want to go through all this again. But let's see what we've got to be going on with. By way of concrete evidence, that is. A bit cold-blooded you'll say, but there you are – that's my job. First, we've got this WT operator Simone. Captain Vere claims she was captured and committed suicide. He was a witness to her death. Unfortunately, there are problems with this. First, there are things that Captain Vere can't remember at all. I'm not arbitrating – just playing devil's advocate. By his own account, his memory is unreliable. Now, taken along with the fact we've been receiving messages from Simone since the day she arrived … And yes, Captain Vere, all the necessary security checks are present. And no capture codes."

"She's dead, sir. My memory on that score is perfectly clear. She swallowed her tablet. She'd been sick … what more can I say?"

"As you say, Captain Vere, I think we've reached a stalemate on this point. Let's come to the message concerning Mrs Perry from the local Maquis chef." He flipped back through the pages of his tiny book. "Here it is. Claude Barte. Mrs Perry is certain this must be bogus because she is confident Monsieur Barte has been arrested. Let me put it crudely: the message concerns Mrs Perry and the evidence that it might be bogus has Mrs Perry as its only source. You see the problem?"

"I've had enough of this." Justine went to the window, pulling the curtains aside, rubbing at the grubby panes, seeking air. "If you're going to claim I'm in any way responsible, I'm resigning my commission." She went across to the door resting her hand on the knob, "You'll have to look elsewhere. Now I'm leaving."

His voice was so quiet she turned to catch his words, "No, you can't do that, can you, Mrs Perry? Do please sit down. It would embarrass the chaps in the corridor. They've orders no one's to leave. Frankly, don't you think they've had enough theatre today? Please do sit down, Mrs Perry. You were going to say something about that explosion."

Alex got up and led her to the chair, taking her arm. She was trembling.

"What about it? Am I supposed to be sorry I didn't die?"

His smile, when it finally came, was cautious, "I can understand why you interpret it that way. As your own lucky escape. Your driver was too quick and you arrived too soon, as it were. I realise that's what you think, but the truth might be simpler than that. I think the transfer of that bomb took place exactly as planned. The targets were exactly as intended. The targets were the occupants of the car that exploded. It had absolutely nothing to do with you."

Thirteen

Justine left with the Major. Getting into the car she had turned to look back, her face caught in sunlight filtering between the looming buildings. She looked frightened. As the car rumbled away Alex was consumed with the thought that her leaving was somehow irrevocable, that she was being taken from him, that things would never be the same again. He managed a half-hearted wave, conscious of the Sergeant behind rattling a rifle into place.

He walked inside, past the loafing soldiers, settling in his own room, waiting in silence for Archer's summons.

It was half an hour before Cabot tapped on his door. He was alone, looking excited. "Archer wants some time on his own with the prisoner."

"Why on earth? He can barely speak German."

"Kessler's English is alright. Anyway, who am I to ask? I've been banished. All a bit fishy if you ask me, secret communion with the prisoner. That's what we're to call him, by the way: *the prisoner*, except when addressing him. So we don't have to accord him a rank. Written orders to follow. I must say, only Archer would think of that. He's sent me to explain things to you. Has your Mrs P gone? I'd have liked to meet her."

"She volunteered to go back with the Major. In the sense it was that or being hauled off in chains. It's depressing. Punished for delivering a few home truths. He didn't appreciate it. She got the choice to share his car back or wait under guard for an escort. I'm to report to him tomorrow. Apparently nobody thinks I'll run away. What's afoot with this chap Kessler? And all these soldiers hanging about?"

"Archer's furious. He told them to clear off. He says it's perfectly acceptable for him to secure Kessler's parole and then for one of us to escort him back and forth. You wonder sometimes which war the old boy thinks he's fighting. The proposal was not well received. We either put up with the extra security or deal with Kessler at Abbott Court."

"But what's deal with him mean? Why's he here? What are we supposed to do with him?"

Cabot stationed himself in the only other chair, reaching across to ease a cigarette out of the packet open on the desk. "That's what I'm sent to explain. Incidentally, I was right about Herr Kessler being a student. Literature apparently. Half way through a degree when he was called up. I tried to talk to him about Gotthold Lessing. You know, *Nathan The Wise*, religious tolerance and all that, but he would have none of it. Said I was trying to trap him. It's peculiar – a couple of years ago I knew dozens of Germans. He's the first I've spoken to since they were all defined as the enemy. He seems quite a reasonable chap - not very well educated, but quite reasonable. There we were, chatting about Schiller, me wondering all the time whether he would think it his duty to brain me and jump out of the window."

"Quite a reasonable chap, apart from baiting the occasional Jew, you mean?"

"A bit harsh, Alex. Archer pressed him on his anti-Semitism. Kessler is hellish touchy about his background. I was right about that name Kessler, by the way. It was comical in a way, both of them pretending and both of them knowing perfectly well."

"You're losing me – what about his name?"

"I told you that name reminded me of something. It's Yiddish. It means coppersmith. Our Hauptmann Kessler is Jewish, that's why he kept shying away from the topic, trying to bamboozle us with legal niceties. He claims to be amazed at the French hostility to Jews, says it's irrational."

"Whereas German hostility is what precisely? But if he's Jewish … he's military …?"

"You surely don't suppose he's the only one?

"But he can't be Jewish, John. It's impossible. He's a serving officer in the Wehrmacht, for God's sake."

"This is Germany – how can you be German and not have Jewish ancestors? How the hell could you avoid it? Why do you think they invented insane rules about needing two Jewish grannies? One's enough in France, by the way – did you know?"

"He'll deny it. He'll know you're just guessing."

"No, I've seen the paperwork. Archer has his French Military Security file. Kessler comes from Breslau. His father had a business repairing violins in the Jewish Quarter. They all died when the shop caught fire. Certainly deliberate - the place had been boarded up. Not Kessler though, he'd left home by then. The French think he bought forged papers, got himself new parents after the fire. The odd missing baptismal certificate didn't matter too much. At university he became a good enough little Nazi to die for the Reich when he was called up. But it's not going to last. They're on to him. He must know he's not going to survive. No need to look that surprised - I doubt things will be all that different … when …"

"When they get here you mean? The ones without degrees in literature. Has it crossed your mind we may not live to find out, given our current occupation?"

"No, Alex, I'm being serious. People in my College are forever going on about the curse of all these cosmopolitan intellectuals. Did I ever pipe up and say, you mean the Jews don't you? I even catch myself nodding. I'm as guilty as Kessler: perhaps we all are."

"Come off it, John. You're not guilty of anything."

Cabot stared at him, the expression on his face difficult to read, almost embarrassment. He got up and walked to the window, standing looking down into the street. The silence between them stretched out until he turned to face Alex, shaking his head, "I think a lot about the invasion, you know. Do you? Mostly wondering how I'll bear up. It's different for you, I suppose, field agent and all that. The truth is,

I don't know how I'll face up to it. I suppose I won't know until … we're all cowards when it comes to the sticking point."

He had taken his spectacles off, wiping them on his handkerchief, weak rabbit eyes blinking. Alex was consumed by a kind of affectionate pity, lost for what to say. It was hardly a consolation to state the obvious: that this man with his gentle scholar's face was the sort you might torture to his grave before he would betray a friend. Surely he knew every martyr died believing himself weak?

And as images of the cell in Saint Aunix invaded his thoughts Alex saw Cabot look away, perhaps seeing too much, fumbling to fix his glasses in place, casting about for his cigarette.

"No need to look so tragic, Alex. Sufficient unto the day. I'm to tell you what the old man has in mind for Kessler. You remember Operation Briefcase? No, don't laugh, Archer thinks there's life in it yet."

"But we've been through all that. Even if there is life in it, SIS will veto the idea. And I can't see how a captured German helps."

"Ah, but you're missing a trick. The idea is that Kessler carries the briefcase. There's no question of dropping anything - he'll be jumping with it. We put him through the standard Ringway course then drop him as part of a scheduled run. Archer suggests Metz, which seems reasonable. He takes the local train, gets off on the French side of the border. Leaves the briefcase on the train. It's clever – the perfect plant."

"So clever he'll report the whole scheme to the local Gestapo. What then? Are we supposed to tick him off and make him have another go? For heaven's sake! He'll chuck the thing in the river and re-join his unit. What's to stop him? Really John, it's as barmy as the man-eating sharks. Let me tell you something. Before you got here, Archer had one of his temper tantrums – really spectacular. I thought he'd expire with rage. In front of the Major. Once that story gets around, God knows what'll happen to us. We're already a bit of a joke – they'll probably close us down."

"He seemed calm enough just now, talking to Kessler. Your trouble is you don't give Archer credit for low cunning. It's his speciality. He's desperate to keep the Intelligence chaps out of our hair and if he has to seem mad to achieve that, so be it – that's his philosophy. I thought fake madness was your subject. Can't you see what he's up to?"

"The people I was studying are seriously damaged … mentally ill."

"And it doesn't strike you Archer likes putting on a show? Honestly, Alex, he's not nice and he's not very clever, but he's exceeding crafty. Don't underestimate him. You know what he just told me? He said he'd been planning this drop for months. *Months.* Puffed his little chest out. He claims he planned the whole thing right from the start, including the phoney squabbles with SIS. He was perfectly happy for everything to be turned down because he was waiting for the right man to turn up. He's sure Kessler's his man."

"You realise that applies to us as well."

"I don't follow."

"He must have recruited us because we were right as well. What brought him to Netley looking for me? It's a long trip. Why me? I suppose it's because we're a couple of wounded ducks."

"You mean because I'm as blind as a bat and you're …"

"… not quite right in my cracked head. You may as well say it - no point being delicate. When I get a bad day, I can barely think straight."

"No, I didn't mean that. You're Archer's way into Abbott Court. Psychology and all that mumbo jumbo. Get's the old boy a free pass ..."

Cabot suddenly sprang up, noisily scraping his chair back, his plump face an unaccustomed pink. Archer had flung the door open without knocking. He stood looking into the room.

"Ah, both of you … good … why the startled looks? Just to tell you I've agreed that the prisoner's to be kept at Abbott Court. Not ideal, but we can't have this rigmarole every day. One good thing – we'll be rid of this damned WAAF woman kicking up that infernal row and hogging the lavatory. She's to go. All this affects you most, Cabot, because you'll be spending most time with him. You've briefed Vere, I take it? Now … I've talked with SIS and they agree we can do some initial planning. They were quite tickled I may say. It's to be *Operation Alathea* – what d'you think Cabot? Classical enough?"

"Goddess of truth, sir. Couldn't be better."

"You still in that hotel Vere? I'll drop you on the way. My driver's waiting."

Cabot glanced across, rapidly cancelling a puzzled look. They both knew Archer had made repeated requests for the allocation of a staff car suited to his status, all ignored. His response to this indignity had been to paste something cut from a War Office letterhead onto the windscreen of his own modest Austin 8.

Archer faced Cabot down, turning into the corridor, "Give me five minutes. Things to do. I'll leave you two to finish whatever you were up to." He left the door open.

"D'you think he heard?" Alex found himself whispering, feeling foolish. "Not that it matters. Alright, I'll sit quiet and keep the mumbo jumbo to myself. Convince me it could work."

Cabot went to close the door, changed his mind and pulled it wide.

"Start with the obvious objection. As you say, once Kessler's out of our hands he can simply ditch the whole thing. But here's the clever bit. By the time he jumps, that won't be an option. By then, Hauptmann Kessler will have a different identity altogether. A non-Jewish identity. We'll have him kitted out with all the right paperwork." He glanced across to the door, raising his voice.

"The Colonel suggests somebody exempted war service, a businessman, high level clerical maybe, somebody expected to be toting a briefcase. It won't be hard to persuade Kessler that his present identity would be a death sentence. Once he's convinced of that, we hold it over him indefinitely."

"We provide him with the identity that keeps him alive, and the quid pro quo is he's managed by SOE. Yes, I can see it's clever. So we've turned him, whether he's committed or not."

"Oh, he's certainly not, but that doesn't alter much. It's simpler in some ways, there are always layers below layers with double agents. Better to have somebody by the short hairs. Of course, he can refuse to go, but he knows we will turn him over to the French in Duke Street. They can probably justify shooting him for the spying. They've got the proof. He's dropping with a WT set, by the way. Instructions to report back once the briefcase is planted. If there's no corroboration it has actually been picked up, things will unravel for him fast. He'll be at the mercy of the local circuit."

"What if he simply reports in to his unit and confesses all? Explains the whole plot - how he was picked up and spirited here, his new identity, everything."

"An officer who's gone AWOL turns up with false papers? The only way he can get out of that is to come clean about who he really is. A Jewish run-away passing himself off as an officer. I imagine he'd be shot that night."

"Let me think . . . he joins the circuit at Metz. His French is alright, so that could work. He can come from Alsace, how about that? We've invented a few Alsatians, remember? I start to think it's not impossible."

They heard Archer's door slam. He stalked past. "Get a move on Vere. Trot, trot."

It was actually the Major's car. Archer installed himself, waiting for the driver to come round to close the door, leaning over towards Alex, eyes glistening, broken veins blotching his cheeks.

"I get the use of a car for Abbott Court if the prisoner's involved. That's where I'm going. You can get out there. Gives us time to talk a bit. It's not a long walk back."

As punishments went, it was not particularly severe. Alex was struck by the pettiness of the gesture: he was to be driven miles out of his way as Archer's response to some vaguely articulated grievance with Justine. She had laughed at him and for that he must walk back to the hotel. It would be getting dark soon. He remembered Justine had taken the torch with her.

Archer tapped the glass and they pulled away. He held out his cigarette case, running his other hand approvingly over the leather of the seat, "Superior sort of chap, Cabot. Always knows one better, don't you think?"

"He's very intelligent, sir. In fact he's the brightest person I've ever met."

"Brain's aren't everything, Vere."

He was looking through the side window, perhaps hoping to be noticed. He had kept his cap on, "In fact sometimes I think they're a hindrance. You know what Napoleon said? Spare me Generals with imagination. Knew a thing or two, that man. D'you know what I think?" Alex, starting to shake his head, thought better of it.

Archer was still staring through the window. "What I think is that German is playing us for fools. Those names he gave you, for example, including mine, the whole recital. He could have got all that information easily enough. Loose talk, that's the culprit."

"If you think it could have been Mrs Perry, I'm sure you're wrong ... is that what you're thinking, sir?"

"You're emotionally involved there, Vere. Doesn't do. But it doesn't matter what I think, does it? I intend to get the truth out of this German. We can do that, can't we? It's your pigeon."

"Truth's a funny thing, sir. If we start using Cardiazol on him, it's a sort of one-way road. Subjects usually end up so scared, they tell the truth alright, but it turns out to be false more often than not."

"Try to make sense, will you, I'm tired."

"I'm sorry sir. What I mean is extracting the truth is not like pulling teeth. It's the same with memories. Get somebody scared enough and they'll actually believe what they're saying – whether it's true or not. That's the trouble with drugs ... he'll say anything, and he'll believe it."

"Scared? Why scared?"

"Nobody knows. It's just the effect the stuff has. The books say it induces feelings of dread. There are cases where subjects fainted at the prospect of the injection. If we're going to be talking him into this Operation Briefcase, it will be better to forget drugs."

It was barely daylight outside, the weary fag end of another grey day, London drawing itself in to meet the night, trying its best not to flinch.

At Abbott Court the driver pulled over to let Alex out at the green metal gate. Abandoned, he stood for a second on the pavement, orienting himself, then turned and walked slowly back towards the city.

He had seen the other car pull up as Archer was making his perfunctory goodbyes. It had been behind them for most of the way. A decrepit Morris, headlamps painted over with black paint, creeping to a halt at the corner, reluctant to stop. The man must have waited until Archer's car masked the view then slipped out of the passenger seat.

They were not the same footsteps. After yesterday's lapse perhaps his allocated walker had been relieved. Then again, given that Justine was safely tucked up somewhere there seemed no point in following him at all.

Approaching a bookshop, Alex slowed to get a better look, peering down at a collection of yellowing pamphlets. Almost too soon, a reflected form loomed up huge behind him in the glass, feet pounding past. He watched the man hurry on down the street, wondering why, of a sudden, his heart was lurching. Days of benign surveillance must have tipped him into paranoia. For reasons beyond his power to fathom he now merited a professional. A surge of inexplicable fear invaded him, screaming alarm. This walker was not seeing him benevolently to his door, he was playing an altogether different game.

Well ahead now, walking fast, putting distance between them. You would say he was hurrying home to the wife, perhaps a little late for supper: a tall chap, long raincoat buckled tight at the waist, a vaguely continental look, trilby hat. At the corner of Clifford Street the man stopped to admire a tailor's dummy, tweed suiting long since unobtainable, letting Alex leapfrog past. The hat had been someone's mistake. The trilby didn't quite work. Plainly, this particular professional had never owned one in his life.

Half way along Saville Row he was in front again, chugging past Alex, metal toe-taps clicking on the pavement. A good ten yards ahead, perhaps more, he lolloped contentedly past two burnt-out shop fronts without a second look, before turning into New Burlington Street. So he knew where they were both going, his confidence on the point was infuriating.

When Alex reached the corner, the street was empty, the distant stream of evening traffic flowing right and left along Regent Street. He would be waiting there, Alex was sure of it – insolently waiting at the junction to fall in behind.

Perhaps it was a response to Archer's infantile spite. Certainly the response featured in no Training Manual yet written, but Alex found himself running. Running as he had not done since he was at school, legs drawing on some memory of their own, lifting him onto his toes, broken glass crunching beneath his feet, carving a suicidal path across Regent Street, threading between cars in a blaze of horns, hands arresting the polished bonnet of a car. By some miracle he was on the other side, weaving light-footed round startled pedestrians.

An awkward flying glance over his shoulder glimpsed a vague form rifling its way down the pavement opposite, head erect, checking to pick a time to cross. He was moving faster than Alex, the trilby hat fallen back giving him a vaguely Mexican look, the brim haloing a face red with sweat.

As they approached Hamleys, the revolving doors were disgorging a woman into the street. She stopped halfway round, tugging the chrome rail, crouching to settle a parcel under her arm. Alex threw himself at the other side of the door scooting it into her back, tipping her out in a confusion of parcels at the feet of the trilby hat.

Walk, don't run. How often had he parroted that injunction at Torridon? Easy to say, a damn sight harder to do. But he was safe enough here, safe enough to walk.

A hot oily smell hung about the place, last week's bomb leaving only half a shop. It was a miracle it was open at all. The girl behind the counter wore a tin hat. Somebody had written, *We never cl* in white paint round the brim, eventually running out of space.

Alex picked up a toy fire engine and stood looking at the ticket. He could see the man now, standing outside, nervously peering up the street, breathing hard. Alex handed the girl a ten shilling note. "Can you wrap this? It's for my little boy."

As she turned to close the drawer of the cash register he found himself locking eyes with someone along the other counter: someone who inexplicably looked away. God, there were two of them! How incredibly stupid not to realise. This ferrety bloke in the other queue had been waiting. That was why the trilby had risked going ahead, why he was content now to wait beyond the revolving doors. They were not following him at all. They were hunting him down.

He went on smiling at the girl as she looked for scissors under the counter. The little man with scruffy ginger hair jostled his way out of the other queue, nothing in his hands. He stationed himself at the only other door, brazenly watching Alex collect his change.

At least he knew what he was up against. If he left by that door he would only have this new man to contend with. Alex walked briskly out, turning into the jumble of streets behind the shop. *Walk, don't run.* Quiet footsteps, echoing his own, kept their distance.

They were in a narrow alley squeezed between the backs of buildings. A section of wall hung out across the footpath, casually remodelled by the bomb that had demolished half the shop, red security tape flapping loose across the path. Duckboards over a broken drain formed a narrow walkway between charred baulks of timber. Alex stopped to light a cigarette hearing the following steps falter.

He would take him as he squeezed past, he had nowhere else to go.

Along the street a daring splash of yellow light briefly framed two women in the doorway of a pub. The sound of a piano surged out.

As the man reached the duckboards Alex turned to give him room, realising in that second his mistake. He had a fleeting glimpse of bloodshot eyes. Surprisingly clean white hands stretched out towards him. He seemed insanely friendly, this ferrety stranger leaning forward to pinch your cheeks. Even intimate, you might say. And for a fatal second Alex let the thought cross his mind. It was a private enough place, after all. As the man let his hands drop an inch, Alex heard the sigh as if from someone else, realising too late it came from his own throat, the noise a girl might make. Too late. A face unnaturally close, stubble skin grazing his cheek.

"We're only doing our job, laddie …"

A surprisingly cultured voice. Funny how SOE always settled on that sort, whatever bit of grubby obscenity they had in hand. You could imagine this one giving lectures on something, *Pissaro and the Glasgow Boys* perhaps – there was something Scottish in the voice. Certainly happier in some college, this one. Happier, that is, than killing Alex in a dark alley behind a toy shop.

Something seemed to be pushing hard against his heart, the smell of stale tobacco everywhere as he caught his breath, knowing he had no breath to catch. Giddy now with the image in the Training Manual, his own manual, the one with the corner torn. Another remembered Scottish voice, impenetrable Highland accent: *Seven seconds ... maximum ... often found it less, gentlemen. Carotid Choke. Fast and painful, if you do it right. And you will do it right, won't you?*

Torridon flooding his mind like a consolation: Justine linking arms with a smiling policeman, the two pads of flesh in Alex's neck like radiating stars, a fearful darkness closing in. Sounds far off now: footsteps near his head. Lying down. Better lying down. Mother's voice: *time you were asleep young man.* Steps scampering away like mice. *Dame souris trotte.* Curious that it should be like this. *Do it right, he will be rendered unconscious in three to seven seconds. Unconscious or, if you prefer, dead.* And then the joke. The Scots like their joke: *You will usually prefer dead.*

Fourteen

They held the post-mortem that night in the hotel room: Justine grim-faced, staring out of the window, Alex sprawled on the bed.

"I shouldn't be in this trade, you know, it didn't even strike me. It was the classic move – one driving, the other waiting. And me thinking I was safe dodging inside that shop. If it hadn't been for the girl at the counter I would be dead now. The big toy shop on Regent Street. When I saw the other one waiting there I could have kicked myself. I picked up some toy or other, just to buy time, I must have left it on the counter. This girl came running after me just as he decided to move in. A little ferret of a man, you'd have thought he wasn't capable of much. I underestimated him – a big mistake: he had hands like steel and was as quick as a snake. He was going to kill me."

She was sitting on a cane chair, something not made for sitting, her pose upright, as if discomfort might somehow ward off the worst. When she spoke it was so quietly he could barely hear.

"Paying you back for giving them the slip. They hate being made to look stupid, you should know that. They were out to scare you."

"No. More than that. I know the difference. He was going to kill me. The bastard almost apologised for doing it. SOE-trained, that's for sure. You remember the carotid choke? I walked slap into it. He knew his stuff alright. I'm losing interest in an outfit full of thugs. I wanted to be a soldier – a soldier of sorts – not mixed up in a kind of gang warfare. What's the point? "

Justine turned and smiled at him. A smile so lovingly knowing that, for a moment her condescension seemed unbearable, almost he hated her for it. Why did he always end up thinking he knew less than he should, the schoolboy late for his lesson? The sad smile remained. She had nothing to say.

"This girl came running out of the shop. That's what saved me. I'd more or less passed out. I felt his hands relax, the relief was incredible. Then he let go. Next thing I know he's running hell for leather down the alley. She was wearing this stupid tin hat, you see. I suppose it was a sort of joke. There'd been a raid on the shop, mess everywhere. It was getting dark he must have thought she was ARP. He only had the silhouette to go by as she came round the corner. Thank God he didn't wait around to check. There I was, sitting in a pile of soot looking up at her, trying to speak and all I could do was croak. She didn't look much like a Warden with all those curls. The tin hat suited her. Reminded me of poor Simone. You could see she was wondering what the hell was going on, a bit scared. Shoved the packet in my hand and scooted."

Justine, still silent, sat on, impassive, waiting until she was sure he had finished. "How did they know you'd be anywhere near Abbott Court?"

"Archer had the use of a staff car. They followed it."

"But how did they know you'd be in it?"

"I suppose anybody could have known. Mind you, it was Archer insisted I came with him. Took me miles out of my way."

"So you know who's responsible, don't you?"

She came and sat next to him, struggling to loosen his collar stud, fingers gently exploring the bruise. He felt her hands trembling. She had drawn the blackout apart at the window and a pale trapezoid of light fell across the carpet.

A continuous low roar had started up over the river, distant clouds blossoming dull red like flowers, oddly disconnected from the hollow crump of bombs.

"It must be the docks again. That's two nights running."

She was staring out into the dark, her voice dead, looking past his reflection into nothing.

"Alex?" Turning aside as he sat up, "I have to tell you about this afternoon. Can you bear it?"

"Bear it? Why *bear it*? What did he say? If you told him you've had enough I can't see what he can do about it. You gave him a bad time, you know. I suppose he wanted his own back. Why the hell did you say you couldn't speak German? He'll have read your record."

"I wanted to jolt the bastard. Wipe that look off his face. Make him deny something. I really hate all these tricks. Men sometimes think they're so clever. You do it sometimes – it drives me mad."

"You realise he's probably jealous? There he is sitting in an office, filling out his forms, while you're ..."

"... Getting myself killed. Oh, yes, I can see it's not a fair trade. Actually, he didn't shout at all. He was quite nice. Look Alex, there's no easy way I can say this - they're sending me back. I'm to be dropped in two days."

"What d'you mean, *dropped*? That's insane! He can't make you do that. France would be suicide. You know that."

"If you'd only listen for once. I thought he was taking me to Baker Street. But it wasn't there. It was to some pokey little office down a side-street. I was left cooling my heels for about half an hour. Stuck in a room with paper pasted over the windows. Then he stalked back in with this big bundle of message decrypts. Chucked them down on the table in front of me. They were all from Simone."

"They couldn't be."

"He took me through them. Apart from the very first, they were all clean. No errors, no capture codes, nothing flagged at all."

"Apart from the first, you said it yourself."

"That doesn't mean much. The first message was incomplete, that's all. She forgot to send the header. There were only seconds before the allocated time ended on that frequency. She'd stopped after about ten groups. It wasn't that the checks were missing, the whole message was cut off. She must have panicked. It's her first mission, Alex. Everybody agrees she's green. I've seen her picture, she looks about seventeen.

Reality on the ground is never like the training, we've all had to learn that lesson ..."

"She's dead, I tell you."

"... And her French isn't wonderful. They assumed she had aborted the transmission to wait for the next scheduled time. That's correct procedure."

"*Assumed* isn't exactly convincing, is it?"

"There's more. He showed me the latest exchanges. That's after the meeting you lot had the other day. A whole series of questions. He said your chum Cabot wrote them. I can't remember them all: What car does Edith drive? How many windows in the Section F store? How tall are you? When's your mother's birthday? That sort of thing. Twenty or more. All the replies were perfect, even down to her asking if one was a trick question, because there are no windows in the store. There was one she said she couldn't answer, but that somehow made it more convincing, because it was a stupid question, something anybody might forget."

"What do you want me to say? I am certain somebody is working her set. She's dead. I was there. I saw her."

"And the Major is certain that's impossible. Alex, it does look impossible, unless they own someone who can provide all that personal detail. Some of the questions are things only Simone could know." She looked away, embarrassed, "That's why I have to go back."

"Don't be ridiculous, that's not a reason. It's insane. Remember Aste? You saw me being picked up. For God's sake, they were pretty well waiting for us. Kessler confirms it."

"Confirms what? Who's Kessler?"

"The German prisoner I told you about. He's talking."

She leaned forward, suddenly alight, "There you are. Ask him about Simone. Why don't you ask him?"

Alex sat rubbing his bruised hand.

"Alex, my dear. You did ask him, didn't you? What did he say?"

"He knew she was arrested the night she landed. With her WT set. He might be lying when he says he was actually there, but ...."

She took his hand, pulling at it, "That's not the point. Does he say she's dead? Does he?"

She heard his breath, a tiny release of exasperation into the silence. “No. But that’s no warrant for a suicidal operation. I’m going to see Archer. I’ll stop it. I can do that, at least.”

“Oh, my dear, you really can’t see, can you? If you keep on saying no like this, you’ll have me crying. Do I have to dot the i’s, cross the t’s for you?”

“Perhaps you do. Stop pretending you know best, that you always know that little bit more than me. If you go back there … you know how I feel ... if I lose you …”

“Poor Alex, my poor little Guffin, don’t start talking about love. Don’t you understand what comes first? What has to come before you can lose something?”

“I’ll tell you right now I don’t trust any of them. Not Archer, not even John Cabot altogether. Not now he’s best buddy with some SS creep, all because he can recite Schiller. Above all, I don’t trust your sainted Major.”

“Oh Alex, my dear, don’t you see it’s the other way round? It’s *you* that nobody trusts. There, I’ve said it. The Major’s convinced himself you spilled things when they had you at Aste. He thinks they did something to you. Either then, or sometime after. He says the circuit being rounded up is too much of a coincidence. Oh, he’s prepared to accept you can’t remember, but that doesn’t alter much, does it? Saying you can’t remember: it isn’t much of a defence is it?”

“*Defence*?”

“I have to go back because I’m the only person now standing between you and him.”

“What gives him … he has no right …”

“But he has. If they arrest you and all you can say is you can’t remember, it’s not going to wash. And it is all you can say, isn’t it?”

“Arrest me! Who’s talking about arrest? Don’t be ridiculous ...” He looked at her standing silent at the window, the distance suddenly a chasm between them, “… no, you’re serious aren’t you?”

“I told you they were sending me back. That isn’t quite true. I asked to go. I persuaded him I can settle the matter.”

“So nobody’s making you? Nobody’s blackmailing you? You’re

doing it to save my skin. Or rather to save my skin again. And you really think I'm going to let you do that?"

"Don't Alex, please don't. There's nothing you can do about it. In your position I'd resent it as well. They always talk about being stuck in a web – it sounds fanciful, but that's exactly how I feel. There's something rotten about this whole enterprise. You feel it and so do I. But do you think I'm going to let them shoot you?"

"Christ, I begin to wish that girl had arrived a few minutes later. That would have solved everything."

"Don't be melodramatic. It'll be alright. It's a perfectly practical plan. I can find out about Columbine. Discover who's still free, who's talking. I'm probably the only person who can. I know the place, I have the contacts, you know that. And, there's no question of dropping anywhere within miles of Saint Aunix. He's teeing up a drop somewhere East of Toulouse. I'm to make my way only when it's safe."

"God: two days."

"From Castle Kennedy. I leave tomorrow first thing. King's Cross."

He lay alongside Mrs Perry that night thinking, not for the first time, of husbands and wives, filled with a superstitious certainty that to touch her would be for her to die. She conceded with the familiar knowing smile, muttering she was dog tired anyway and he should have brought his sword if he was going to play Tristan, then fell asleep, her quiet breathing a gentle accompaniment to footfalls in the corridor, whispered voices beyond the door, closing doors, the distant drone of lifts: all the restless secret life of hotels.

Hours later, as he stood at the window staring blindly across the Square, he saw her reach out, paddling naked arms restlessly across the blank of the sheets, searching for his hand.

She would be gone in an hour or two, perhaps this was the last night they would spend together. How easily they had accepted that thought at Torridon. Drunk with the quixotic nobility of their enterprise it had seemed almost heroic. You would lay down your life for that: give yourself away without a second thought. They must have been mad.

What had she said? You have to possess something before you can lose it. But that was a symmetry that worked for things, not for souls.

Not for love. It was his turn to discover it didn't work like that. He would lose whether she thought herself his or not. In some ways, she didn't come into it at all.

"What time is it, Tristan?" He had not heard her get up, standing now behind him, pressing the warmth of her breasts against his back.

"*Grise dans le noir*," no more than a whisper, "a little Verlaine to get you into bed. I can tell you're having mournful thoughts just by the shape of your shoulders. You are, aren't you?"

"You should be asleep. You'll get cold like that. It's quiet now. The raid's over. Mournful doesn't do my thoughts justice. Suddenly everything seems dreadfully fragile. Like walking on ice. What will I do without you?"

"Is that what you plan? It's faith you lack, little mouse. Remember when you were captured? How the man in the white hat came riding in, just before scalping time? Well, this is going to be easier."

She put her arms round his shoulders, pulling him closer. "Come to bed with me. I'll tell you a story, if you're good."

What do you do when the person you love walks away? When the person you love, remembering she's English, straightens her gloves to shake your hand, not even skin to touch, a competent brittle smile, suited to outdoors. Justine gone. Striding along rows of swinging doors, peering up at paper labels, hers not properly stuck, climbing in, the slam of her door echoing along the empty platform.

They were dreadfully early, King's Cross, a cast iron cathedral, smelling of sulphur. What do you do? Alex held on to the latticed steel of the gate, the cold searing his hand, the man at the barrier prodding his arm, *Go in mate, if you like, there's plenty of time*. Too much bother to tell him he was wrong, this chap with his friendly Porter's cap. There was no time at all. Suddenly Alex felt tired beyond belief, felt he could not keep up, the world would have to go on ahead without him. He shuffled out into the first of the weary traffic.

When he reached the TPSU it was to discover his appointment with the Major had been cancelled: a polite note in his box, the signature illegible, suggested Wednesday.

Cabot looked as if he had been there all night. He was peeling papers out of last year's box files. "Here, I've found one. Colonel Steffle. Born Cologne. We did three letters denouncing him, remember? You did that one from a fellow student, how he drank too much and – oh the shame of it – criticised our beloved Führer. Surely you remember him? Alex? What's up old boy?"

"Nothing. I just saw Justine onto a train. Feeling a bit *distrait*, that's all. Life's a bugger, isn't it? What about your Colonel Steffle? Yes I remember. Happy days."

"I've a whole stack of his stuff here, Birth Certificate, Medical Records, Identity Card, Army Registration, Travel Pass, the lot. Some of it's first-rate. I was just starting to add a brother. We didn't think of it at the time, but he could easily have had a brother. What do you think of Stefan? Nice name. I'd just given birth to him when I heard you on the stairs. Shall we get him baptised? What d'you think? How about June 1912. Pick a date."

"This is to be wrapped round Captain Kessler, I assume. That would make him about thirty – push it on a bit, don't make him too old. He can't be military, you realise? Archer doesn't want that."

"Absolutely. No, he was a sickly child our Stefan. He's got a medical card as long as your arm. Serious stuff. Hospitals. I was thinking of St. Elisabeth Krankenhaus, but we need to find a Sanatorium for him. Somewhere residential because I'm striking him down with TB. Can you chase a place? Not too far from Cologne. He's a Tax Inspector in the *Gastarbeitnehmer* Guest Worker racket. Enough of those are French to explain all the border crossings. He'll be as popular as the plague with that job. Left strictly alone. Exempted military service on account of the TB - I've done a Certificate about that. And a letter from his brother on the subject. Quite stiff actually, hinting he's not pulling his weight. Full of harsh words about the Nazi project. I can't see Kessler complaining. I'll get a copy of the biography typed for him to memorise. I doubt he'll ever need it, but you never know. From this day forth he's Stefan Steffle. All those sibilants - what on earth was his mother thinking of?"

They worked all day, passing drafts across the desk. By the time the inventory was finished, it was hard not to believe in the consumptive brother of this delinquent officer. It would take no more than a few days for these fictions to take on life. In a week, perhaps less, a pile of dog-eared papers would return from the forgers of Portland Place bound in a thick rubber band.

Alex stared through the window, watching black plumes of chattering starlings in the winter sky. They always seemed to wait for evening. Another day gone. Justine would be there now. Jumping down from the train, letting someone catch her, remembering it's as well to look lively. What it was to be a women in a crowd of lecherous buggers. Squeezing a spot in some ancient jeep, sharing a cigarette, capping the worst of the dirty jokes. Fending off, she called it.

Fifteen

As Alex left for his Wednesday meeting he found Archer pacing the deserted hallway, waiting for the staff car. He barred the way, clutching him by the arm.

"I'm told you've an appointment at Baker Street. I'm off to see our Hauptmann Kessler. I'll drop you off."

"Happy to walk, sir, it's no distance."

"Ah, but you'd best not walk. Rumour has it you can't walk far without villains falling on you. What's the world coming to? In Hamleys of all places. Can that be right? What took you there? No, don't say. You'd best come with me. Fear not, you'll be in good time," the flash of a complacent smile, "best not be late for a roasting. I assume that's what's on offer?"

"I was followed all the way from Abbott Court. I must say it's a mystery how they knew I'd be there."

Archer showed no sign of taking the bait, shrugging incomprehension, striding out to meet the driver. "Trot on my boy, we've things to do."

"But you heard about the attack, sir?"

He affected not to hear, settling himself into the car, tossing his cap onto the leather shelf behind his head, tapping the glass as they pulled away.

"We'll call at Broadway Buildings first, Corporal."

They jolted to a halt, a bull neck craning round, “Beg pardon, sir, orders were to …”

“Switch the bloody engine off. Come round here.”

Archer leaned over to Alex patting his knee, “It’s a full time job taming these people. You’d think they had better things to do.”

He wound the window down as the driver appeared.

“What’s your name, Corporal?”

“Boxer, sir.”

“Ah, quite so. The pugilist or canine variety?

“Couldn’t say, sir.”

“And is there a Mrs Boxer?”

“Sir …”

“And little Boxers no doubt?”

“Blocking the road here, sir. Permission to move off.”

“Forgotten how to salute?”

“Beg pardon, sir. You having removed your cap, sir, I thought …”

“Given to thinking? Always a risk in the ranks, Corporal. You expect me to stand up in here?”

“Sir?”

“Orders in this car come from me, Corporal Boxer. Is that understood? Now move off, you’re blocking the road here. Broadway Buildings. I believe they call themselves the Fire Extinguisher Company.“

He leaned over to Alex, huge head close enough to smell something vaguely astringent on his skin, “You think anybody’s taken in by that sort of thing?”

His little theatre over, the car jerked forward, Archer smiling malevolently, clicking his cigarette case open and shut, humming to himself.

“You heard the good news, I suppose?”

“What in particular, sir?”

“We don’t have to put this chap Kessler through the jump course. He had ambitions to join a parachute regiment. Went through the full training at Wittstock. Got his parachute badge. So no need for Ringway. Avoids involving them.”

“He still won’t be familiar with our equipment …”

"God, Vere, you find a cloud in every silver lining. Don't you realise, man, he's trained. A parachute's a parachute."

"I think the German release system is different. We went into this at Ringway. I could check."

Archer sat silently for a moment winding his window up and down a few inches, assessing the mechanism, "Hot in here. Can't see the point of heating a car, one luxury we could do without."

He peered earnestly out as they weaved through the nightmare landscape, piles of sooty brick pushed to the margins of the road, everywhere the acrid smell of burnt cloth.

"That right? … about the release?"

"Their chutes are a bit different. Larger, I think. Not so manoeuvrable. I can work up a note on it if you like."

"Could you? Good man. Do that, will you? But I can't see it need hold us up."

"We could put it to Kessler himself, sir?"

"No. It's for us to take the decisions. Avoid complexities, that's my rule. Wait, we're here." He rapped ferociously on the glass with the metal ferule of his stick, "If this idiot can bring himself to stop. Off you go. Write me that note when you get back, will you?"

The Major was sitting at his desk, door wide open, sorting through piles of yellow signals traffic. He stared blankly at the figure in the doorway, recognition slow to come.

"Ah, yes, you're right. We've a meeting." He waved Alex to a chair, holding his place on the page in front of him with the tip of a pencil. "Sorry – slipped my mind. Still, you've picked a good time." When he finally looked up, the smile was genuine," Pull the door to, there's a good chap."

"There's very little I can add to my report, sir. If you've read it ..."

"I suppose you know we'd been thinking harsh things about you, Captain Vere. I imagine Mrs Perry told you?"

Alex started to speak, changing his mind, feeling like a tongue-tied schoolboy called in for a wigging. The Major pushed the pile of papers to one side, taking a slender file from a drawer.

"Do sit down, my dear chap. No need to look like that. It's my job to ask questions. That report … it was a bit vague, you know. I can see that's not your fault. Jumping to conclusions – we all do it. Always a hazard in this game."

"What conclusions, sir? If I'm to be accused of anything …"

"Nobody's accusing. It's good news for once. Mrs Perry has been on. We've got some first thoughts on your Columbine circuit. It doesn't look as dark as we thought."

Alex stared back, heart racing, lost for what to say, watching the Major idly tapping the pink folder with the end of his pencil. "You heard me, Captain? She's been in touch. Smart work, I must say. Look … I know some of the background, personal stuff. Can't help knowing. You'll be relieved."

"Relieved doesn't cut it, sir. Thank God. No problems with the drop?"

"Problems? No, nothing at all. And not entirely God's handiwork. A clockwork operation. They do happen, you know."

"You're saying you've heard from her already?"

"Right on cue, o-six-thirty. And no fumbles, either."

"Did she …?"

"Wait, I'll tell you what she says in a minute. It bears on these." He shoved a bundle of papers across the desk, "The people in Signals put them together. Have a gander. They're all from this Simone woman. They go back weeks. In reverse order, the first's at the bottom."

"I really don't think I need to, sir. Mrs Perry told me she was convinced. I don't think my reading them would advance matters."

"Fair enough. The problem is we've a report signed off by you, saying she perished resisting arrest. Swallowed her L-pill, wasn't that it? It looks like you're going to have to wind that back."

"I can't account for it, sir. Simone is dead. How can I be wrong about that?"

"I'm sorry … it's not easy to put this. I just wondered whether you could have got confused …we know you've not been well."

He opened the manila folder, handing Alex a single sheet torn from a message pad, "See what you make of this." A crisp sheet of yellow paper: strings of characters divided off into groups of five with slanted pencil strokes.

"Mrs Perry's, this morning. Wait a minute, I'll read you the decode: it's mercifully short. *Safe home. Claude asking cash urgent urgent. Simone safe and in good spirits. Expect reply 1325 apu. Arthur.*" Alex was staring blankly at the paper. "You see, *safe and in good spirits.* Rather settles it, doesn't it?"

Alex sat on in stunned silence, measuring Justine's words, the space around him dissolving. In some other world someone tapped the door, a face peering round, blue uniform, hands hanging onto the handle, "Sorry chief, didn't know you were occupied, I'll come back. Free later?" A subliminal nod towards Alex before the door closed.

"Can I ask, sir …"

"Error checks? Capture codes? That's what you're going to say, isn't it? Nothing. A hundred percent clean. By the way, Perry's Morse is surprisingly good."

"She did a special course at Torridon. When the idea was being floated that couriers and WT might double up. Didn't come to much."

"I remember now. It was on her record." He leaned back, shaking a cigarette from a packet, pushing it across to Alex, grinning, "Incidentally, along with the fact she speaks German fluently. I can see she likes to tease. You might mention that when next you see her. It's still a poem code, by the way. Nothing out of the ordinary."

"I know the poem, sir. Why *Arthur*?"

"Not my suggestion. The name's not currently assigned. After that business at Aste, Marie got dropped. Too strong a supposition that whoever arrested you got wind of it. More of *Captain Vere's Consequences*, I'm afraid."

"They got nothing from me, sir."

"Nobody's denying it."

"And *apu*?"

"Yes, you're right, it's not in the book. Signals suggested *As Per Usual*: seems right in the context, if less than elegant. He leaned across to retrieve the paper, frowning as Alex held on.

"If you've finished with it, Captain Vere … it has to go back. She seems in good spirits herself. There's a certain esprit about *urgent urgent,* isn't there? This chap Barte is always complaining about money." Alex felt him pull on the slip of paper.

"Sorry sir, all a bit overwhelming. Do you think I could see the decode?"

"Couldn't resist my little bit of theatre, reading it out. Here it is."

Someone had scrawled a line of text across the top of the page, *Noire dans le gris du soir Dame souris trotte*, a faint pencil line through the first repeated letter *e*. He saw Alex frown.

"Apparently she agreed that poem at Castle Kennedy before take-off. The book's in the Code Room."

But Alex was not listening. He had known what he would see before he took the slip of paper. Had known what he would not see. A kind of dumb horror consumed him. The room was stifling hot. How could anyone work in such a place? Ticking off the pencilled words, desperate, his heart booming in his ears. The Major was right: it was short. Short enough for there to be no doubt: no doubt at all.

It wasn't there.

Staring sightlessly at the scrap of paper, Alex was watching Justine against the pillows in Russell Square. Justine lighting two cigarettes, the match flaring yellow across her body. Justine's dark voice, as quiet as death. T*he word's WILL, Alex. Just right for a Guffin because that's what you need.* Him pushing her down at that, kissing her quiet, paddling the words into her flesh. *No, I'll think of Shakespeare. He's a Will.*

Staring sightlessly at the scrap of paper, Justine's sombre voice, hours later, drawing him out from sleep, his heart galloping. *You do understand, don't you, Alex? Forget error checks. Forget SOE. Forget SIS. Forget all that. If the word* will *isn't there, they'll have me, my love. And we're the only people in the world who know this.*

Staring sightlessly at the scrap of paper, little noises in the room filtered into his consciousness: the Major, rummaging in a drawer, pulling something out, suddenly impatient, "You seem very taken with that. Anything we haven't spotted?"

"Mrs Perry and I were very close, sir, I just ..."

"Why the past tense?" Alex felt the paper pulled free from between his grip, shrewd eyes searching his own, suddenly benign. "My dear chap, she'll be home before you know it."

"To be honest, sir, I'm not feeling particularly well. I'm not really over that crack on the head."

"We've asked her for a full report on Columbine. She'll need time to get around, of course." Scraping his chair back, the hint of a dismissal, "That Simone business, we can sort it out later. I'll get your Colonel in on it. Mend some fences – he's rather a character." He was standing now, lost for the words to speed Alex on his way, "Don't imagine we're not concerned about this memory thing. Is there nothing ...? Can you try ... rack your brains, as they say."

"It's not a case of trying, sir. But there are avenues, options. Things I've avoided so far. A doctor I knew in Netley hospital has a clinic in London. I've been considering going back."

"... Good chap. See what you can do. You'll see someone outside waiting. Ask him to come in, would you?"

In the event, neither avenues nor options were called for. Perhaps it had been thinking of Dr Hoffmann: more likely the terrifying certainty of Justine's loss diminished everything else. The persistent torment of inaccessible memory that had dogged his life for months quietly ended. Ceased without notice, a short walk from Broadway.

He recalled passing a worn wooden bench as it came to him, close to the gates of Paddington Street Gardens. Recalled noticing a carved rebate in the wood where a brass plaque must once have been. It was then his memory returned, thinking of memorials for dead husbands. Thinking with a certain nostalgic sadness how *Lovers Remember All* went well in Latin.

More than an hour he sat, a solitary hunched figure in the drizzle, watching a Mallard duck diving for weed.

No way would they take him to the safe house. This is as far as we go, the driver said. Braking hard where a narrow track branched off on the other side of the road, leaning over Alex, sweat smelling of garlic, pushing him out, Justine's rucksack bouncing on the hard clay next to his face.

He was lying on a trodden clay path. A stone hut was barely visible among lines of neglected vines, the ground draped thick with un-pruned cords. Lingering diesel fumes gave way to something permanent: the bitter scent of pine, a Torridon smell.

He sat at the roadside, feet dangling in a dry ditch, searching through Justine's pack: Model B tucked neatly down the side, combat knife in its leather sheath, powder compact, cigarette case. And a book - cheap blue fabric, ink-stained, the cover decorated with petal doodles - Le Nouveau Testament. Justine Perry, Ecole Sainte Marie, Caumont. *Round blue ink.*

The hut at the end of the path was shuttered. Let them come to you – that was the rule. You die for that mistake. He would wait. He took one of her cigarettes, leaning back against the wet grass to smoke, the exhilaration of escape fading. Time had somehow expanded, bringing a sense he had been here always. Although exactly why escaped him.

Voices were moving fast through the woods high above him, stones rattling onto the track. Men talking. Closer, it seemed only one man, an endless monologue, incomprehensible Basque echoing through the trees. Once, it stopped, replaced by some kind of drawn out whistle, as if to call a dog.

He appeared from nowhere. Leaning against a tree, very thin, deep lines etched black across his face. Breaking so abruptly from the trees Alex could do no more than roll into the ditch, Justine's rucksack open on the ground.

"If you want a password, wherever you are, I've forgotten it." The language was a kind of French, words buried in ferocious Basque.

Alex stood, holding his pistol, "Stay where you are, I have you covered," blushing at the words.

The man turned to spit into the undergrowth. "So you're going to shoot me, are you? Better get off this road to do it. People coming." He gazed past Alex, across to the hut, "You haven't been inside then. Very wise ... the place is full of snakes ... not so lively this time of year ..." Ignoring the pistol, he pushed past Alex, wading through a tangle of brambles, kicking at the door, Alex tagging breathless behind, scared he would fall and the pistol fire.

"What do you mean: people coming?"

A rank abandoned smell bowled out past them. It was dark inside, the floor piled with hurdles white with frost.

"What people coming?"

The man was picking up hurdles, stacking them, making room, holding one out to Alex straddling the outstretched pistol, a vicious grin cracking his face.

"Some bastard fascist informer. Action Française. *They bring them here. Your bad luck it's today." Standing at the door, looking across the banked curtain of pine, head cocked, listening.*

"We'll bury him over there,"

"What do you mean bury? Is he dead?"

The man threw a broken hurdle out of the door. As Alex turned, he felt the pistol eased from his hand, the man weighing it in his own, lodging it on a shelf over the door, changing his mind, wedging it in his belt.

"Dead? How would I know?"

They had cleared enough space to sit before they heard the first rough pinking noise of some machine painfully dragging itself up the track on the wrong fuel. A Citroen van, ribbed sides splattered with plaster, breasted the hill, barely slowing, someone pushing a large sack out of the back, jumping out alongside, thumping the side of the van.

Alex helped with the sack. Three men trailing a smear of something liquid to the crest of a bank. Soft underfoot, deep in pine needles. Ripping down the hessian, there was a sudden hot stench of faeces, head lolling out, the colour of ripe cheese, one unblinking eye suspended loose on milky threads of flesh. It seemed to be watching them.

No more than a boy, sixteen at most, nestling on his bed of needles. Fair hair, clotted threads, caked blood fashioning lips to a pout. Alex felt his gorge rise. If he was alive – could this thing be alive? The crotch of its trousers was an open mass of raw flesh and burnt cloth.

"You know, there's life in him. That's a wonder." Probing with his boot, he turned to Alex. "Here, you wanted something to shoot … he's best dead if we're to tip him out here." He pushed the pistol into his hand. "Head's best."

He scraped the sacking together with his foot, "Not that they'll find him. Nobody comes up here."

Sixteen

Walking through streets heaped with the blackened remnants of other people's lives Alex had been content to lose his way, content for a while to be going nowhere.

When he reached the TPSU, Cabot was crawling across a large-scale map of France spread out on the floor of his room.

"Well timed, I've just about finished. Thought I'd look at Metz: I wasn't sure where it was exactly." He leaned back on his heels, looking up. "I was starting to think you'd been clapped in irons. Was the gentle Major not so gentle after all?"

He scooted a bundle of papers towards Alex with his foot. "There you have it: Stefan's life from his mum's pregnancy bus pass to his inglorious present. You were right about his age, by the way. Our first go had his mother producing him when she was fifteen. We've shifted his date of birth. Nothing else drastic. Push that chair out of the way – it's easier on the floor."

"They made me shoot somebody." Alex realised his voice was not working properly. "Kill him, you understand? That's if he wasn't dead already. They made me. If I hadn't, I think I would have joined him down the bank. I'd forgotten all about it. Had it knocked out of me."

Cabot looked puzzled. "You're not making sense, old boy. Don't stare like that, it's unnerving. What's up?"

"You don't have a drink, do you? I've been wandering about for hours ... should have remembered you can't cut across that park any more. The streets on the other side have all gone, just dozens of little rabbit tracks through rubble. They don't seem to go anywhere. Just holes where the houses used to be, full of water, most of them. Where do you think the people are? Where've they all gone?"

Cabot had started rummaging inside a steel cupboard, pushing files aside. "That's the hell of a gloomy question, Alex. There's some whisky in here – my secret cache. I'll join you. Who shot who? You're being mysterious, it makes me nervous. And do stop pacing about. You're dripping on my map."

"John, you knew how my memory had gone? That there was something I'd forgotten?"

Cabot swung round, suddenly inquisitive, "My word ... you don't mean? Am I to know? You look alright. Wet, but not crushed. What's to tell?"

"I'm not sure it's a story you want to hear."

"Tell me all the same. And drink this - departmental contraband. Don't worry, we'll not see the old man again tonight. He's off to Boodles. The draw is fish pie, apparently – lucky devil. We're safe."

"No, John, we're not. Don't you ever start thinking we're safe."

"*Calme-toi, vieux pote*. Remember what Mother said - start at the beginning. I'll believe you whatever it is."

"Archer was so damned sure I had things tortured out of me. What I want to know is where did all those whispers come from? How do you think I felt about it? Why does everybody always believe the worst?"

"Not me, old lad, you know that."

"I suppose I do." Alex waited until their eyes met, Cabot painfully looking away. "All the same, the thought crossed your mind, didn't it? No need to shake your head, I know it did, because it crossed mine. I've never said this to a soul, but the truth is, when I was arrested, I knew I wasn't going to hold out long. The training just fell away, it seemed ridiculous. I'm not made of the hero kind of stuff. Why the hell didn't the people at Torridon discover that about me? It doesn't say much for psychology."

"Don't be so damned hard on yourself, Alex. You can't crucify yourself just because you imagine things. Most of us never get the chance to find out and thank God for that. I happen to think they got you about right, old man. Now … you were going to tell me. What was it you'd forgotten? Nothing so very vital, I'll bet."

"Well it wasn't war, John. Whatever else it was, it wasn't war."

"I still don't know what you're talking about."

As Alex described the body in the sack, Cabot seemed curiously unmoved, his expression no more than distaste. He got up, pulling the blackout across, pausing for a moment to look down into the street, resting with his back against the cloth. With the curtains drawn, the stuffy little room seemed to close in on them.

"I thought revenge killings had stopped. If this boy really was an informer, there'd be reprisals."

"You really think those people care about reprisals? So far as they're concerned, if you aren't fighting fascists you deserve everything you get. Anyway I only had their say-so he was an informer. He was just a boy. There were knife marks on him. Cuts. And he'd been shot to wound, not to kill."

"It's alright, Alex, *we know there's a war on*. I quote our leader. Of course, what Archer really means is we're not going to see any of it. The real stuff is somewhere else."

Alex reached down for the bundle of papers on the floor, snapping the rubber band against them. "This is our war, isn't it?"

They sat on, neither speaking, hearing a solitary car creep past in first gear, feeling its way round the square.

"Did I tell you they make you kill a sheep at Torridon?" Alex felt a sudden urge to shock. "So that you know what fresh blood is like on your hands." Cabot's impassive face was barely visible across the darkened room. "I managed it as well. I remember thinking it would be the real enemy next. The poor dumb brute wouldn't have died for nothing. But it wasn't the real enemy was it? Just some schoolboy who'd found himself the wrong friends." Cabot said nothing. "They kept shouting his father supported the chap who banned the Communist Party."

"Daladier."

"Like father like son, they said. That made him a collaborator. I don't think they knew what they were on about. They were laughing at me ... laughing at all of us, I suppose. The stupid bloody bourgeoisie ushering in their revolution."

Cabot walked into the light from the desk, "I'm not sure I want to hear about the politics of France, Alex. Not right now. Not after that story."

"Politics didn't come into it. They kept going on about how the rich bastards would get what was coming to them, how it was better in Russia. Why are we fighting their cause, John? Tell me, I've forgotten."

"Our enemy's enemy, isn't that it?" He shrugged, "I've always thought there was a flaw in that."

"I mean why's Justine fighting their battle? She doesn't want a revolution. I would have packed all this in, you know, if it wasn't for her. Joined a fighting unit, done something useful. I'd do it now if she wasn't … if they hadn't … Justine's worth more than this madness. Don't you realise, every single person we work for is crooked."

"You mean Archer? Cunning, maybe, I'm not sure about *crooked*."

"I wanted to go to war, John. That's what I thought at Torridon. Fight the good fight … like all those chaps getting killed right now. I've ended up in a kind of bureau of madness. Justine is the one island of sanity in all this."

Cabot reared back, tutting in mock indignation, "Not very friendly, old boy."

"And you, of course ... I meant you." Alex forced a smile, "You're sane. God be praised nobody's pressing you to go a-fighting. You're the only straight person in this damnable outfit."

"Nice of you to say it." Cabot slumped into the chair behind his desk, pulling his glasses off, shuffling papers to find a space for them. "Now look what you've gone and done? I'm embarrassed." He looked up, his face pink, "You're a nice chap, Alex. What made the good Lord wish that buffoon Archer on the likes of us? As for your French thugs, I'd put them right out of your mind ... sorry … unfortunate turn of phrase there. Honestly though, right now revolution's the last thing France wants."

"I'm ashamed to be part of it all the same. You know Justine's gone back?"

Cabot stared at him. "To France, you mean? No I didn't know. How's that? What about *Once captured never returned*? I thought that rule was infrangible?"

"It was me that was captured, she wasn't. They decided she was best placed to find out about Columbine. Who's *they*, John. Why don't we ever get told who *they* are?"

Cabot started folding up his map, stacking it alongside bundles of paper, yawning, "Never drink whisky after midnight. I have to go home. I'm done for. You know what I'd do in your place, Alex? Tell Archer what you've told me – the whole story. That'll put an end to his endless digs about you blabbing secrets. Anybody can see why you wouldn't want to remember something like that. I'd be the same. Worse actually, because I can't stand blood. You'd not get me killing sheep. That's what I'd do. Bamboozle him with how this psychology stuff works. No, don't look at me like that ..."

"Poor old Cabot. You think I've been suffering from psychological repression, don't you? Like some character in a Buñuel film. No such luck my dear chap. I was hit over the head. Probably a fracture. Don't look so crestfallen. I hadn't finished my story. You remember they were supposed to get me to a safe house?"

Cabot nodded wearily. "Yes, I think so ..."

"They refused to take me. I was left tied up in the hut while they stood outside arguing the toss whether to cut my throat or not."

"Why on earth?"

"The one who'd brought the sack knew I was connected in some way with *The Englishwoman*. He meant Justine. He said he knew she was a traitor. Then they started arguing. The last thing I remember was this big chap coming back into the hut. He had a rock in his hand."

Cabot winced, screwing his eyes up.

"Next thing, I'm lying on my back in a boggy field peering into the blue eyes of a Lysander pilot and wondering who I am. I was slipping in and out of consciousness. He got me on board somehow, bless him. That's how I ended up in Netley hospital with a cracked skull.

It's called anterograde amnesia - common enough. Don't go yet. Stay with me for a bit, will you, John?"

"Of course. You don't look too good, you know. A bit green about the gills."

Alex stared sightlessly through him, seeing only dawn bringing steel-grey light to the hotel room, the morning Justine confirmed their pact. Ever since, the certainty she was lost had tormented him like an untended wound.

"I have to go back, John. You don't understand. She wouldn't be there if it wasn't for me."

"Go back to France? You know that's impossible."

"I have to. I'll have to tell SIS she's been captured."

Cabot leaned forward, "*Captured?* Who said anything about captured? Are you sure you're alright, Alex?"

As Alex began to explain their secret pact, Cabot got up to close the door, shutting out the faint light from the corridor. The room was very still. "You can't tell them that, Alex. You know what they think about private codes. They'll say she forgot about it."

"No, you don't understand. It was something between the two of us. We …"

"Let me finish. Agents come up with private codes all the time."

"Do they?"

"It's common knowledge. Chaps hoping to get a message to the little woman back home, that sort of thing. Of course, once the mission's started they forget all about it. And Baker Street gets pestered by demented women convinced poor Jack's been captured. What evidence have you got she's captured? Hard evidence? Did she send a standard capture code?"

"No, no, nothing like that. That was the reason we agreed on something private. Hell, what can I say? The last thing I expected was you not believing me. I'm lost. She couldn't have forgotten. And don't look at me like that … I don't need your blasted sympathy."

Cabot stood polishing his spectacles, blinking vacantly into the darkened room, lips silently shaping something useful to say. "The trouble is it involves leaving something out ... there's no difference between her sending your code and forgetting to send it." He checked, looking hard at Alex, "You see what I mean?"

"Of course I see what you mean. D'you think we didn't realise that? You're forgetting her message. You're forgetting what she said. She said she'd seen Simone. That can't be true. That's why I'm sure."

"God almighty, Alex! What do you want me to say? You want to use the best evidence we have that Simone is alive as proof that she's dead. Don't you see the mess that will get you into? Me as well, if I start backing you up. We'll get ourselves arrested. Archer's capable."

"Justine went back on my account. She knew she was going to be betrayed and went all the same. For nothing. Have you any idea how that makes me feel? What can I do? I'll go mad if I don't do something. God, man, I love her …"

The telephone on the desk burst into life. Cabot turned aside, embarrassed. He let it ring, guiltily dropping the whisky bottle into the wastepaper basket, lifting the receiver, tracing damp lines with his fingertip where his glass had been.

A familiar tinny voice rattled into the quiet room, Cabot looked at Alex, steadying his voice. "No, he's not actually. Not now … I don't know … yes, tomorrow … yes, I'll tell him … righty-ho, let me get a pencil … go ahead …"

An impatient click cut across him as he finished scribbling.

"That was Signals at Baker Street. The Major left orders you were to be told when Mrs Perry acknowledged today's message. She did. Half an hour ago. He particularly wanted you to know."

"They gave you her message?"

"It's short. *Await silk delivery. Will confirm with Barte.* That's it, apart from headers. *Silk*? What's that about?" Not exactly loquacious, is she?"

Alex walked home in the rain, a single word drumming in his head. To fall into bed in a kind of feverish stupor, the night filled with restless dreams of Justine below his window, staring up, her expression indecipherable, an eternity of darkness behind him. He woke drenched in sweat, still hearing the echo of her voice.

He would not sleep again that night: heaving himself up in the bed for a better sight of nothing, praying she would sell his name cheap. Praying for the consolation of betrayal, the dark city beyond the window filled with intermittent sounds of war. It seemed unbearably alien. She had taken some indefinable part of him with her.

The next morning he picked a way to the TPSU through empty streets still dark, smelling of half-burnt gas.

The charwoman in Archer's room looked startled as he passed the door, hastily dropping a cigar back into its box, scuttling out.

He finished the report on German parachute design, one ear cocked for the thump of boots on the wooden stairs.

It was well past ten before Archer appeared, peering loftily through the open doorway, moustaches at the ready, immaculate in thornproof tweed, a tiny rosebud decorating his lapel. He carried a raincoat over his arm.

"Come along to my room, will you Vere. When you've a moment. Your chap Kessler's kicking up. What are you sitting there for? Chop chop. Things to do."

Alex followed him along the corridor. Handed the raincoat, he went to hang it on a hook, only to have it snatched away, Archer wielding a wooden coat hanger like a sabre. "Know what this is? Never use one? We'd best go to *Records*. Something I want to say."

He had a curious mincing gait, lifting each foot a little too high as if he might slip. He closed the door behind him, his voice adopting its confidential register, a kind of stentorian whisper. "The prisoner says he wants more time. He knows perfectly well we don't have more time: the moon's in two days. He thinks if he stalls, that's another month gone. I'm not having it." Bewildered watery eyes gazed round the tiny space, "Now … what are you here for?"

"You asked me to come, sir." Archer looked doubtful. "Although actually there was something I wanted to raise with you …"

"I remember now. I went through the briefcase. You two did a decent job. There you are, praise when it's due. A decent job, given the notice. You'll have more time with the next, of course." Alex winced as his arm was grabbed. "You were going to write something about parachutes. Where is it?"

"Done sir. I just need to tidy it up. But if Kessler completed the parachute course at Wittstock, he'll know about British designs. The Luftwaffe actually copied them: they thought ours were better. We used to sell them to the Germans before the war. Funny to think they're using our kit. But if he says he doesn't know, he's lying."

"The prisoner hasn't raised the matter. It was you started that particular hare."

"It was worth checking he could jump with our gear. And he can. The papers were ready yesterday, sir. There's just the border pass. It has to have a date stamp. If there's a delay …."

"There'll be no delay. He's going whether he likes it or not. Thinks he can play games. It's hot in here. Why did you bring me in here?" He pushed his way out, prancing along to his room, calling over his shoulder, "I'm going to Abbott Court when my car gets back. To tell him he'll go when I say. Now … what did you want? Can't it wait? I've a lot on at the moment."

Of course, the request to go back to France was dismissed. But in a minor key, merely a hint of impatience. Hurrying down the stairs, Archer listened to the story of the body in the sack, struggling into his overcoat, barely suppressing a smile, perhaps remembering some similar distant exploit of his own.

"These things happen." He held up a massive hand, hairs sprouting from stubby sausage fingers, "Changes nothing. Gratifying you've coughed it all up at last. We'd been wondering when you'd get round to that. Can't change the fact you were seen. Seen and docketed. Reason enough to keep you here."

He walked out onto the steps, shouting over his shoulder, "And you're wrong about that WT woman. She's alive and kicking. Alive and in good spirits."

"If you accept Mrs Perry's message at face value."

Archer skidded to a halt, turning back inside, breath hanging in clouds of mist, blurring his face. "You'd try the patience of Job, Vere. The answer's no. No today, and it'll be no tomorrow. Understood?"

"Have I your permission to ask the people at Broadway? They might take a different line … interpret the case differently …"

"No, you bloody well don't have my permission. Not that that will stop you. Come here."

Alex felt a finger stabbing his chest, orchestrating the words, "You go skulking round behind my back – *prod* - consorting with that SIS lot – *prod* - and you get no more favours from me."

The final prod met vacant air as Alex stepped back.

"Forget it Vere, you'll get nothing out of them except grief. They'd veto their own granny. You're needed here. Understood? And I want that bloody parachute report on my desk. Ah, there's my car."

Seventeen

Alex approached SIS about going back, any pleasure in this defiance of Archer blunted by the discovery that they already knew about his recovered memory. It was infuriating: some subterranean current seemed to flow through this shabby building, information materialising by a kind of osmosis.

The Major had heard about the body in the sack, even adding his own colourless recital of the event. How he had come by all this? Surely not Cabot? But if not Cabot there was only Archer, and informing his enemy, even to secure a petty advantage, breached every principle the old fool held dear.

The fact remained, the well had been poisoned long before Alex could drink at it, the futility of his request so plain he barely listened, mulishly staring at the wood-block pattern of the lino.

"Your Colonel didn't like it, you know that? You asking to see me."

"He knew I was making the request, sir."

"You make a decent spy, Captain Vere. Lying with the truth. Didn't someone tell me you were studying that? The psychology of lying. No, *lying's* a bit strong. How about *evading*?"

"I'm not sure I understand."

"I think you do. Did Colonel …" He scrabbled for a piece of paper on his desk, failing to unearth it, "Did Colonel what's-his-name …?"

"Archer, sir."

"Yes. Did Colonel Archer refuse you permission to return – yes or no?"

"Yes …" regretting the peevish tone, Alex felt like a schoolboy caught out in a lie, adding - because the Major's smile had not yet been completely withdrawn - "but he said he knew I'd ask."

The Major began pushing his pen across the desk in an unconscious gesture, releasing it to let the tilt of the surface roll it back to his hand. He must have done it a thousand times before. "D'you know what day it is?"

"Friday."

"No, not that. It's Christmas Day, can you believe it? Remember when that meant something?"

"I'm afraid it passed me by. Too many things on."

"I've a letter here from your Colonel. Alex recognised a sheet of TPSU letterhead under the Major's thumb, familiar purple scrawl filling the page. "He's in charge of your outfit, right? What makes you think it's for my lot to say yes? What makes you think we've the authority?"

"It was something the Colonel said about Intelligence a while ago ..." Too late to call the words back, Alex cursed himself.

"And what would that *something* be?" The Major's face was suddenly bleak, "There's a damn sight too much loose talk about. And your setup's the worst."

"I only meant he knew his refusal would not stop me asking. It seemed to me he was inviting … or at least not expressly forbidding. Perhaps I was reading too much into it."

The Major turned the sheet over, staring vacantly at it as if wondering how it came to be in his hand. It was the same curiously calculating expression that Alex had seen that day they had raided Archer's office.

Noises from elsewhere in the warren beyond the door filtered into the room: feet hurrying past in the corridor, muffled telephones, the hurried irregular clack of typewriters. Far away, the mechanical chatter of a teleprinter surged out as a door opened. All about them a steady hum of life, the murmur of bees. It seemed improbable, but this was what it came to - the prosecution of war. War on Christmas Day. The Major folded the letter, carefully sliding it back into its envelope. "He had rather decided views about your arrest in France, your Colonel. You knew that?"

Alex glanced at the envelope. "Yes sir."

The Major let the envelope fall, pushing at aside "Not altogether dispelled. I imagine you guessed that. But if it will relieve your mind, I can tell you we do want you to go back. God knows why that would be a relief to anybody. There's more risk than usual at the moment, as you're well aware. We've settled with Colonel Archer that you fly down as part of his *Operation Alathea*, that business with the briefcase. You can keep his prisoner company down to Metz. After that we'll take you West, drop you near Saint Aunix."

"Saint Aunix. We're sure that's secure, sir? I'm thinking of Kessler's story."

"Not dropping blind, of course not. They're laying on a reception committee. You're a land Surveyor, a local *arpenteur-géomètre* checking last year's crop records. Name, Georges Harcourt. Not much going on this time of the year, I doubt you'll have much talking to do. You won't be there long enough." He tapped Archer's envelope. "Your Colonel did agree, by the way. Can't say he's overjoyed, but he agreed ... eventually." He looked up, the expression suddenly friendly, "That's that then. Surprised?"

Alex was no longer listening. For days his every waking moment had been spent with Justine, watching her life trickle away alongside his own, his head filled with a mindless chatter of prayer. Godless prayers that she might live, knowing well enough it was better she should die. Knowing the best this venture could secure would be to die with her. Staring at the Major, he was overwhelmed by a sense of hypocritical betrayal. He wanted to scream, *She's captured, damn you. Don't you realise? She's a dead woman. Damn you all.*

"I fear you're not with me, Captain. I asked does the decision surprise you?"

For a second Alex could not place the voice against the blare of his thoughts, the Major leaning across the desk towards him, face lined with fatigue, glancing from his watch to the door, the rituals of dismissal.

Perhaps, after all, now was the time to confide? Explain his certainty that Justine was captured. Explain how the Major's acquiescence in his return sealed his own fate. He felt words spilling towards his lips.

"Sorry sir, I was thinking of something else. No, not surprised really. Obviously two would be better for a job like that. It's what I was briefed to do first time round ... when I was captured. We do need to get to the bottom of Hauptmann Kessler's story about Columbine … and Mrs Perry is alone."

"She's hardly alone, is she? She has her WT with her. I'm afraid this Simone is not going to forgive you, the way you insist on killing her off. You're still doing it."

He had returned to his pen: rolling it, catching it, rolling it, catching it, "But you're right, you'll have your work cut out. We need the full story, not Mrs Perry's enigmatic signals - understood? We'll get you back in a couple of days. You report direct to me."

Archer now spent his days at Abbott Court. He had taken over Kessler's interrogation, obsessively determined to sift the truth from the story of circuit penetration. The day after the decision to send Alex back, he burst into Cabot's room demanding to know which cabinet in *Records* was allocated to Captain Vere. Finding nothing more sinister than three French newspapers he ripped them into small pieces, leaving a heap of torn shreds on the floor. An angry monologue in what might have been Hungarian ended abruptly as Cabot came to investigate.

The following morning, as Alex arrived, Archer was descending the steps to the waiting car. He was cut dead. Thereafter, orders came through Cabot, although confirmation of his dismissal made further orders irrelevant. Delivered by dispatch rider from Abbott Court on TPSU notepaper: a transfer to Baker Street *pending operational duties.* A scrawled addendum in Archer's purple hand pointed out that access to the TPSU was strictly restricted to staff assigned duties in the building, the word *strictly* so heavily underlined it had punctured the paper.

Cabot helped Alex clear his desk then left for the British Library, saying he wanted to look at something – anything - that wasn't forged.

Alex had made no effort to put any kind of personal stamp on his allotted room. Divested of weeks of accumulated clutter it was returning to its aboriginal state. Even the original smell was creeping back: something dry and papery, like musty biscuits.

Since he had nowhere to go and time on his hands, he pulled a chair to the window and sat looking down into Bedford Square, forehead pressed against the glass. A grey staff car had drawn up, the Major emerging to help a young woman out of the passenger door. The two stood for a moment talking, then parted, exchanging a double kiss in the French manner.

She stood on the pavement looking tentatively into the dark of the stairwell directly below where he sat. Dressed in a long black raincoat, the belt fashionably tied round her waist in a knot. Realising she was overlooked, her face tipped up, large eyes meeting his own. She made no pretence of looking away, raising a gloved hand, almost a wave, as if to keep him at his station.

It was not long before light footsteps brought her to his door.

"Captain Vere? You are Captain Vere, aren't you? Can you spare me a few minutes? I was told I might find you."

He had forgotten about perfume. Justine rarely wore it. A dark musky scent had come into the room with this woman. She seemed to be in mourning: even her hat with its tiny silver pin was black. An aura of gaunt vulnerability surrounded her.

"I'm Lucile Beyrou." She was trying to catch his eyes. "Perhaps Mrs Perry mentioned me to you?" Disconcerted by his silence she paused awkwardly, searching his face. "Mrs Perry ... she came to Dundee to see me. I was hoping she might be here but I gather I'm out of luck."

Alex came across the room towards her, half barring the way, the gesture bringing a faint smile. As she shook his hand, he was conscious only of something cold, feather-light, barely touching his skin.

"How on earth did you find this place, Mrs Beyrou? Yes, I knew about her visit to Dundee. But I have to ask … this place, we're not exactly public … how did you find …?"

"Oh, I asked around. TPSU. Nobody knows what the letters mean."

"But asked around who? I'm not sure you should be here."

"I'm sorry. I'm being dreadfully rude." She smiled, knowing she had the better of him, "Perhaps I should have said. I know someone who told me where to come. He said I shouldn't tell, but you must have seen him. I saw you watching us."

"You mean the Major?"

"Is that what you call him? His name's Ian. He's my brother." Her eyes were unsettling, somehow belying her voice, challenging him to contradict her.

"Yes, I remember he said you were related. He organised your exfiltration last November, is that right?"

She stood looking at him, absorbing the word, finally offering a slight encouraging nod.

"And you're an artist ... he said you're an artist. You'll have to forgive me, I don't know much about your world."

"It's quite alright, you can say it: you've never heard of me." Laughing, she suddenly seemed years younger, almost pretty. "I'll tell you a secret - I've never heard of me either. Somebody suggested the name, but that's another story. Let's leave it that I'm incognito for the duration. Silly, I know, but there you are, I don't need to tell you about secrets, do I? The point is, I've found you, so not completely unlucky."

"You were luckier than you realise, this is my last day here." Alex pulled a chair out for her from behind the desk.

She shook her head. "No, I can't stay. It was just to deliver a message."

"For Justine? ... Mrs Perry. She told me about your pick-up. It must have been horrendous. You appreciate there's little I can say about that."

"Oh, I'm not here for secrets. I just wanted to tell her I knew I wasn't very helpful when she came to Dundee. It was ill-mannered of me and I'm sorry. She caught me at a bad time: that flight was the last thing I wanted to talk about. So I've come to make amends. Too late, I know. Funny, isn't it? Amends are always too late."

She looked at him then shrugged, turning towards the door, "It's alright, Ian said I wouldn't get far. Too many secrets. But at least give her my message, will you? Tell her that I came."

"I'm not sure I can."

She frowned, seeming to make her mind up about something, turning towards him, her expression suddenly defiant: "I knew she wanted to talk about that explosion. I couldn't bear it." Watching his expression tighten, she laid her hand lightly on his arm, "I can't talk about it either. Those men that came to get me back. All of them were killed. I feel responsible."

"You shouldn't. They were doing what they had to do."

"Yes, I realise that, but what you don't know is that one of them was my brother. He was killed fetching me home. How could you not feel responsible for that? I'll carry it to my grave …"

"I'm sorry ... I didn't know ... but your brother, you say?"

"I had two brothers. It was Ian's idea - that's your Major - to involve him. He thought I might need persuading. And he was right, I wanted to stay. France is my home, after all. I've not really lived anywhere else. So Ian wangled it that my brother would be the one to do the persuading. His name was Stuart. I'm the reason he ended up in that damned car. I'm the reason he's dead."

She turned to look through the window into the Square, tilting her head a little to check tears resting on her cheeks. As Alex came towards her, she pulled a cardboard box from her bag, pressing it in to his hand, keeping him at arm's length.

"That's where we've been, Ian and me. All morning. To a sort of ceremony. It's Stuart's medal. Would you like to see? You can open it."

The box was tiny, the lid embossed with a Fleur de Lys in lurid yellow. Alex prised it open. Something like a freshly minted copper penny lay inside on a bed of cotton wool.

"It was in a church off Leicester Square. Two French officers were there waiting for us, all dressed up. I'd never noticed that place before, jammed between shops. It's been bombed, but they're putting it to rights inside. Catholic. I suppose that's natural, being French."

She watched Alex struggling with the lid and retrieved the box.

"Ian said it was best I keep it. It's not much is it?" She dabbed her eyes with a tiny handkerchief. "He doesn't believe it was an accident. And yes, he told me not to talk about it, but why shouldn't I?" Her voice was breaking. "He's certain somebody intended to kill Stuart."

There was something shocking in her passivity, silently outstaring him, dark eyes welling tears. "Aren't artists supposed to understand? Well, I don't understand. War ought to be about more than things like that. When Mrs Perry came to Dundee she must have thought I'd been struck dumb. I just couldn't talk about it - it all seemed unreal, as if it couldn't really have happened. The truth sometimes sounds bigger than it should, don't you think? I mean when it comes to other people ... sorry ... I'm not making much sense."

"No, I understand perfectly." He sounded so vehement she leaned away. "You see, I know Justine Perry. I know her very well."

"I didn't recognise her. Not at first. I simply didn't know who she was. Then it all came flooding back. There was this woman standing in my studio looking at me and all I could think of was her on that aeroplane. She had that same look. It made me ashamed. I'd never been in an aeroplane before. I was terror-stricken. And she had been so perfectly calm in the middle of that hell. I remember thinking I'd never seen anything so brave."

"Oh, there are braver things than that."

Eighteen

Three days later, Alex walked from the station to the gates of Tempsford Airfield. He was directed to yet another stately home, operational briefings being now conducted at Hazells Hall, a damp Palladian country seat, an inconvenient distance from the airfield.

He was never to discover who had decided carved panelling, draughty bedrooms and alabaster cornices were adequate consolation for the certainty of death. Hazells Hall, being truly ancient, was inevitably less impressive than the fake Scottish pile at Torridon, but raw timber and new concrete walls served the same brutal purpose in both. It exuded a desperate air of make-do, a ramshackle conversion completed with almost vindictive incompetence, reeking of unsound drains. Dusty shrubs lined a driveway scored with lorry tracks. In the entrance, chequered marble was littered with the final stubbed cigarettes of numberless departing men.

It was a pity. For Alex, memories of Tempsford had been charged with a magical sense of high endeavour, one recollection above all: Justine stepping from her jeep, bringing a dissolution of dread. That single frosty moonlit night, filled with indefinable exultation, would determine the course of his life.

He spent the best part of a day pacing aimless corridors waiting for his briefing, the truth gradually dawning that he was so incidental to any operation, he had been overlooked. When finally called, the affair was scandalously perfunctory. Half expecting the Torridon Major, he found a flustered Captain from Signals hurriedly sent down from Donnington sitting alone in an empty room, spreading the contents of a briefcase across a dusty table like a salesman.

"Sorry, old man." He hardly dared look up, "Got drafted into this … not my usual game." He consulted a slip of paper like a prompt card, "Captain Vere, is it?"

"Actually I've been Georges Harcourt, since I reported. If you look at the log. Still …"

"Right-ho ... sorry. If you'll open your kit, I'm to give you your paperwork. There's a bundle of printed silks to be collected with your chute. You know about them - ready-made code keys? You've been told?"

"I was told I'd be carrying them. Nobody seemed all that interested. It's a change from when I was here last."

Relieved of the burden of explaining, the Captain relaxed, "Point is, you don't need to know. It's the WT needs to know."

He picked up a tiny paper package. "Here. To give you an idea of the size." He pulled a square of silk folded to a thumbnail of nothing from his pocket like an amateur conjuror.

"Neat, eh?" He unfolded it, picking the fold apart to reveal line after line of black print, letters, numbers, an exquisite calligraphic pattern.

"No more of your poem codes. That means no more undecipherables our end … or at least fewer of them. You've no idea the errors those poems throw up. All that transposition, I can't see how you put up with it."

Alex was about to say they hardly had a choice when he realised the Captain, head bowed, was already spreading the silk across his hand. "Here, I'll show you. You take your last line, cut it off and there's your key. Use it. Burn it. Bob's your uncle. Secure as a one-time pad." He pocketed it before Alex could say anything. "One thing, though. Mind you tell him to cut it carefully. It has to be scissors, you understand, otherwise the silk unthreads and you're in queer street. They're working on it."

Alex was thinking of an end to *Dame souris*, trying not to think of how you were supposed to conceal scissors. Perhaps that would be easier for a woman. "It's not a him, actually. The WT. It's a woman."

"Right … right you are. No, I didn't know that." His eyes were nervously raking the empty room as if he half expected her to appear.

"Well, she'll tell you all you need to know."

He shook a cigarette out and pushed the packet across to Alex, suddenly diving back into the briefcase, blushing scarlet. "There's this. I'm to give you this. They said you'd be *au fait*. There's a new one. It's blue. You're to keep it apart, but you'll know that. A quick-acting sedative. Poison at that dose. They said you'll know where to keep it. God, the world you chaps live in."

The tiny tin was flat as a button, the colour of lead. Alex squeezed it into his palm. "Yes, that's alright. *Au fait's* the word."

The Captain was already snapping the catch of his briefcase closed, pausing to look at tatty posters pinned to the walls, scraping his chair back, launching himself unsteadily upright.

"If the safe house is no go, you're to keep away from the church … it's not secure. If you need a last resort, make for … wait a sec, I need to check something." He retrieved the slip of card from his case, turning it over to read something written on the back, "The hotel in Saint Aunix. It says ask for Jules. That make any sense to you?"

"You mean *Le Sport*? You're not going to tell me to order a coffee?"

"Coffee?" He peered at the card, puzzled, shut out of a private joke. "No, nothing here about coffee." He looked up, suddenly grinning, "Caught me there, I'd forgotten how you fellows go on. Sorry to be slow … long day. No it just says make for the hotel, not the church. You're to ask to speak to Jules. Wait to be contacted. He ought to identify himself with a passphrase … it's in French, not my strong suit. Here, you read it."

Alex leaned across, "*Ô bruit doux de la pluie*. It's alright, it's somebody's idea of a joke."

"You're to exercise extreme caution - I don't imagine you'll have to. *Last Resort* - sounds a bit dramatic. I'll be off then. Your stuff's at the barn. The driver will take you."

"The barn?"

“Farm buildings. Gibraltar Farm they call it. Fake, of course, but damned convincing. I’ve seen the aerial shots.”

“I hope the plane’s not fake.”

“It’s where you’re kitted out … oh, right … sorry.” He had paused a beat too late, concocting a smile to catch up, he seemed irritated. “You’ll have to forgive me, I’ve not done one of these before. I suppose it shows. Bread and butter to you chaps, seen it all a dozen times I dare say. Now, is there more you need to know?”

Discovering he was staring at a poster about venereal disease, he scooped up his briefcase. The catch burst open, scattering papers across the floor. “What do I do now? What’s usual?”

Alex stooped to collect the debris, “Shake hands, I suppose. Wish me luck. That’s usual.”

Take-off twenty-three hundred - earlier than last time. Everything was filled with last time. No frost, though, just a chill settling clammy on your face. He stood in the hangar mouth looking at the phosphorescent blur of a full moon above the trees, risking a final cigarette, remembering Justine hugging him on this spot, stuffing her rucksack with loot, grinning like an excited schoolgirl.

It had started to rain, grey clouds bowling up from the West. As the first engine of the Hudson coughed painfully to life, faint streamers of yellow light came glinting across lying water on the grass.

Suddenly aware of someone behind him Alex turned, his heart jolting. But that was last time. This WAAF, awkwardly saluting, was not Justine.

“I’m your transport, sir. Jeep’s over there. Anything I can help with? You’re not to smoke here, sir. Although ….”

“No, you’re right.” He tossed it onto the grass, watching the red end refuse to die. “Just me in the jeep?”

“There’s a bit of a hitch with the others, sir. I’m to drive you across. Get you aboard the bus,” an embarrassed pause, “that’s what he said – the CO.”

“Things wouldn’t be normal without a hitch. How many others?”

Dumping his pack into the jeep, her glance back across the apron was oddly precise, the pause a fraction too long.

"Couldn't say, sir."

Alex followed her eyes, his hand wet on the handle of the door. A huddle of uniformed men was silhouetted in the mouth of the hangar. The Major – it could only be him – was stepping round puddles, sparing his shoes, pausing to stoop over things bundled on the ground.

Standing a little apart, huge in a calf-length greatcoat, another shadow loomed across the asphalt: barrel-chested, florid cheeks shaded white with protruding fuzz. Archer turned away as their eyes met.

"Wait a sec, will you? That's my Colonel."

"Orders were to …" but her voice was already blown away.

The Major shook his hand. "Came down to see you off, Vere." He was unaccountably lost for more to say, patting his pocket, a ritual search for cigarettes he could not smoke.

"We've had confirmation of your reception committee, by the way. But you'll get the gen on board." He looked across to the waiting jeep. "That your transport? Don't keep her waiting."

"If I'm to go down with Hauptmann Kessler, perhaps I'd better wait."

"No, no, you push on. We'll see to the prisoner. Best get you boarded. Get you settled. Flight will explain things."

"You're not flying, sir?"

"Me? God, no! But I wanted to be in on this." He let his voice rise to pull the sulking Archer in, "Something to remember, wouldn't you say, Colonel?"

Archer was not to be drawn. Ignoring the Major, he cast a full cigarette into the darkness, watching it arc down to the grass.

"Step aside Vere, would you?" Alex felt himself steered into the darkness, his elbow gripped, Archer's fingers squeezing hard, intending to hurt.

Away from shelter, rain fell in angled lines across the shaded lights at the hangar's rim.

"Got your own way, then?" Closer now, bringing the smell of whisky, chiselled English accent, always slightly phoney, hot in his ear. "What the hell makes you think you have special rights? Just asking. For my information, you understand."

As Alex tried to pull away the grip tightened above his elbow, fingers wriggling hard against the bone. "Stand still, man. Did you imagine I didn't know your game?"

For a fatal second Alex stiffened, thinking of Justine. How the hell could he know that? Archer sensed something, rearing back, mad ox eyes searching his face.

"You and that man Cabot, sneering all the time." He was speaking in a ferocious stage whisper, flecks of spittle on his breath. "Think I don't know?"

Alex wrenched his arm free. Hearing Archer grunt, the WAAF stepped back into the dark. "I understood you agreed this mission, sir. And with respect, I'm no longer attached to the TPSU. Your orders …"

"Respect! You don't know what respect is. Creeping about behind my back. I specifically ordered you … you're a bloody menace, Vere. If it had been my decision I'd have had you locked up, you understand? But … it's not ... it's not ..." Teetering absurdly on tiptoes, scouring the field beyond the jeep, Archer allowed his words to peter out. As Alex freed himself, backing away, a new grievance swept over him. "Don't walk off like that when I'm talking. Stay where you are. I'll just say this. Raise a finger against my operation and by God … by God …"

Exceeding crafty. Thinking of Cabot's phrase, Alex understood why this manic display left him unmoved. There was something absurd about passion bellowed out to no purpose. It was all he could do not to laugh in the old fool's face - the man really was ridiculous. Or was there, after all, a purpose? Alex had an uncomfortable feeling this display served some end, although God alone knew what or why.

For some time he had been dimly conscious of the group of men at the hangar piling gear into the back of a jeep on a kind of improvised litter. They had scrambled on board, the driver gunning the engine.

Archer watched the lights bounce over the field, tracing a pattern in the wet grass with his toe. He fumbled for his cigarette case, accepting the lighter Alex held out.

"About going behind your back, sir … "Archer blinked, puzzled to find him still there. "About SIS, sir …"

"You'll have to excuse me, Vere. I really can't stand about chewing the fat with you all night. That young woman's waiting. You do realise you're holding things up?"

He had already installed himself in the back seat of the jeep and was tapping the shoulder of the WAAF to move off. Alex scrambled onto the wet leather alongside, fumbling to close the door. Glancing across, he saw she was smiling.

At the waiting Hudson, two mechanics were abandoning efforts to push something at head height through the open door. Not an improvised litter, after all: a standard army stretcher tied with bands in three places down its length. It was hopelessly too wide for the door.

Keep back a minute if you would, sir. The Sergeant from Abbott Court moved across, barring the way. Beyond him, a tall figure in RAF uniform was staring at something on the ground: the MO from Abbott Court, it seemed, was a Wing Commander.

The Major called across, "Bear with us a moment, Vere." He sounded irritated, "Weren't you to be boarded first?"

"Can I help, sir? A medical case?"

"Not really," the ambiguity of his reply shutting Alex out.

Archer pushed past, staring defiantly at the Major. There was an unhealthy flush on his skin, the jutting face oddly demonic in the half-light. He seemed unfamiliar with embarrassment. This must have been the reason for the pantomime at the hangar. He had taken it on himself to hold Alex back until the stretcher was boarded; he had not considered the door.

Two sweating bearers finally yanked the stretcher out, the lights falling on a red blanket as it snagged back. Hauptmann Kessler, a waxy sheen on his face, lay peaceful in death, strangely impressive in uniform. An oval badge had been pinned to his lapel: a swooping eagle clutching a swastika, glinting yellow in the cabin lights. This German parachutist dressed for war was surely no tubercular clerk. His right arm had been braced under the top-most band, a briefcase chained to his wrist, the tiny handcuff an effeminate affair in mottled tortoiseshell.

They had him unstrapped at last, running the blanket underneath, shipping him easily into the waiting arms of the crew.

Alex turned to find the MO at his side. "Bad do." He glanced at Archer, receiving a savage glare in return. As the MO dropped his voice, Archer leaned closer. "And if you're going to ask, my advice is don't. About responsibility I mean. If you're going to ask who's to blame."

The Sergeant was steering Alex to the foot of the steps, the MO tugging at his sleeve. Shaking the Sergeant off, Alex turned to look back at a brief pinprick of light near the hanger, conscious of an inexplicable sense of menace. There was nothing but distant shapeless forms against a blur of rain.

"He bullied us into it … your Colonel." Rain on the MO's face fell like tears. "Mind you, written orders, full medical authority. I've kept them ... I've kept them alright! Kept saying he wanted the truth. All available means to be used."

"You're talking about Kessler?"

Alex saw the Sergeant stride across to Archer, watched him salute, erect in the pelting rain. "I helped plan this operation with Mr Cabot. The two of us did it all. Cabot's not here, but I can tell you there's something dreadfully wrong. Kessler can't drop like that. The paperwork for one thing … everything's wrong."

A man framed in the doorway of the plane was unhooking the emergency light, looking down at them.

"You know about those drugs," the MO's voice was an ingratiating whine in his ear, "that's what I couldn't get through to your Colonel. You know you can't just keep on upping the dose. You stop when there's nothing left to wring out of them. Stands to reason. The dose yesterday. I told him it was mad. The poor bugger's heart gave out. Nothing we could do about it."

He pulled out a cigarette case watching helplessly as rain beat down onto it. "How old was he? Seemed young. D'you know how old he was?"

"And did you get the truth?" Alex knew his voice carried. Archer stood huddled in his greatcoat, cupping his hands hopelessly round a flickering match, his face yellow in the flame. He abruptly turned away, striding into the darkness, rain bouncing off his shoulders.

"I asked did our sainted Colonel get his truth? Did he?" It seemed worthwhile screaming.

The MO stared. "What do you think?"

"What do I think?" Alex was howling like a madman at the distant greatcoat, already no more than a shadowy blur. "It's bloody obvious what I think. The operation must be aborted."

The MO had walked away. Alex cast round for the Major, finding the field strangely empty.

"We need to know what's going on. Cabot, he's involved as well. We're responsible ... responsible, do you understand?"

He did not hear the Sergeant. He came up fast, footfall hidden in a sudden bellow of engines. Arms stronger than his own wrapped Alex round, binding his chest, lifting him by the armpits like a child. Hands grasped his wrists from above, jerking him brutally over four metal steps onto the soaking sill of the open door. Rutted grass was running under his flailing legs, glinting in the cabin lights.

Nineteen

Darkness retreated to a green light, smooth and velvety, engines beating to some kind of harmonic of their own, felt more than heard, too slow to be safe.

"Channel coming up. About ten minutes." The voice was so close in his ear he thought at first it was his own. "Flak there most nights. Skip usually flies under it. Captain Vere - you alright?"

Rolling on his side, Alex stared into a child's face flushed with exertion. "Somebody pushed me."

No, two faces, looking down: schoolboys, dressed unaccountably in khaki flying suits.

"Nothing to do with us, old boy, blame Number Two. It was him saying get a move on or you'd miss your Toulouse rendezvous. All hell broke loose. Mind you, he has a point, we need the dark to get back."

The other schoolboy was nodding, straightening Alex up, his arms surprisingly strong, "Bit of a panic back there. Had to get you in."

This one had an earnest, spotty face, pocked with acne, unruly hair stuffed under his cap. There was the dark smudge of a moustache on his lip. He could not have been shaving long.

"Somebody pushed me."

"Right you are, squire. Heard you first time. Saw it myself. Wanted to get you aboard, pronto. Army type. Stepped up on the double. Orders, I suppose ... weird, all the same."

"Whose orders? You can't be ordered …"

"No point shouting. You'll end up hoarse. Take it up with teacher when you get back. Here, have something to drink," A metal bottle, strangely heavy, its stopper hanging loose, slopped warm liquid over his hand. "Only water. Careful where you sit. Some nights the floor in here … you wouldn't want to know."

Their metal prison was painted grey, punctured by tiny squares of sky, bright with stars. A ribbed metal floor sloped to a metal door swinging idly onto a metal oasis pinpricked with yellow lights; onto the backs of two men, leather helmets a little awry. A vast moon stared in through windows glazed like a greenhouse.

A distant sound, oddly festive, like corks popping, had the cabin suddenly tilting through a sea of bouncing air. *Pop … pop… pop … crump.* The last closer, its breath trailing smears of oily red past the greenhouse. *Crump … Crump.* Space itself lifted like a kite, heeling over tiny quartered fields, engines straining. Silver flashes of open water crossed the port window.

"Shouldn't be flak here," the voice was close again in his ear, "buggers keep moving … only light stuff. See if you can get some kip. It's alright, skip's got the orders about the passenger. Metz in about an hour."

Passenger Kessler lay quiet in the crook of the cabin wall, a red blanket for a catafalque, parachute backpack propping him forward. The handkerchief draped over his face had fallen away.

He was kitted out for rescue at sea, a distress flag stuffed into his boot, a circlet of flares clipped round one leg. He looked as if he was waiting for something.

Alex thought of the German's last days with Archer. Old soldier Archer running rampant in Abbott Court, believing there was more to know, certain he was being cheated. Old soldier Archer, who employed men to lie, searching for truth. What had he wished on this poor devil? Surely Kessler had expected to die, but not like that. Not lost in the endless fictions of sodium amytal, not swearing each lie truer than the last.

They must have used cardiazol at the end, persuading themselves that ill-defined urgency justified anything. After that, there would have been nothing but demented ramblings for Archer to pick over. The chap must have died of fear. Alex felt unaccountably complicit, ashamed.

At Torridon, Justine once had asked him to pray for her soul, taking him unawares, suddenly angry as he mumbled he didn't know how she could believe all that stuff. At least Catholics had it worked out, she said, none of the woolly graveyard claptrap his lot went in for. She would not let go, talking him into silence: *What if there were souls, Alex? What if there were? Have you thought?* And of course he'd thought, shouting there were some things God had no right forgiving, didn't she know that yet? That was when she had started to weep, her silent tears breaking his heart.

With Justine dead, prayer seemed too small a gesture, somehow demeaning. He had none of the words anyway. Surely there were special words? Would holy angels really bear your soul to paradise for the sake of a word or two? It seemed improbable.

Cabot was wrong. Justine would never in a thousand years have forgotten their pact. He would wager his life on it. That second message, with its reckless brazen *will,* was certain confirmation. She had wagered her life on this desperate trip, and lost.

It was staring into space, this Jewish Catholic corpse. Too late for Hauptmann Kessler to deliver his soul from the pains of hell. Perhaps in those final drugged hours he had forgiven himself. Kessler's impassive waxy face across the cabin gave nothing away.

Archer must have planned all this from the start. Archer and his pretend enemy, the cynical Major, snaring Cabot and Alex into a futile game of make-believe. They must always have intended Kessler's death, believing it served some warped view of a greater good. The creation of Herr Steffle had been no more than a convenient cover for murder, the two of them played for fools. Impossible to believe

John knew - it would take a consummate actor to fake that kind of obsessive dedication.

He should have felt angry at the thought of their eager, ingenuous, pointless work, at their infantile gullibility, at their betrayal. It was too late: the most he could summon was a kind of anaemic pity for the dead Kessler; for Justine's life thrown away; for himself, hurtling to the same end.

A pity he would never know who had brought them to this.

Approaching Metz, he watched them shuffle Kessler to the jump hole, limp legs dangling in a slipstream of mist, an awkward ventriloquist's dummy propped against their knees, head lolling back, dead eyes watching the drop light.

When they came to it, the affair was not unlike a burial at sea, Flight even managing a sort of tottering salute, shamefaced, but not wholly ironic. Below them through the hatch, the city spread out like a black stain against the lighter black of the forests to the West. Tiny farms, careless of the blackout, were pinpricks of gold.

There were shouted commands now between the leather helmets beyond the flailing metal door. The Hudson, impossibly low, swept over rail tracks, silver with frost, twisting along the glint of water. Far ahead, desultory fingers of tracer started up, raking the Eastern sky.

"On my go," he sounded like somebody's son, this pimply child, straining against his safety strop, shouting to make himself heard. A few months back this voice had been calling for a sneaked single in house cricket. It was cracking now, touched with fear.

"Christ we're low, bloody water everywhere … hold steady … steady … green … GO."

He was gone. Hauptmann Kessler sent to his rest, flailing chute a narrow cylinder of furled silk, tip flapping like a flag. To be discovered tomorrow, or next week, by some rambler. Snuffled over by hedgehogs, but nothing worse. Kessler, the first move in a chess game still in need of an opponent, briefcase stuffed with pointless artifice. Waiting in the mud.

The jump light off, Alex scrambled onto Kessler's blanket, thinking it somehow his proper place, the plane pulling up, sprawling him hard against the bulwark, thunder pulsing his chest, pain in his ears breaking only to hurt again. Puffs of icy cloud swirled free as they closed the jump hole. The next green would be his. Long before the lights of Toulouse those waiting on the ground would hear the engines delivering Alex to his death. It seemed somehow inconsequential.

In the cockpit the leather heads leaned together, calmer now, sharing a quiet joke. Gigantic towers of cloud parted briefly onto patterns of stars. Due West, engines settling to their beat, lumbering through a comforting cocoon of piled grey. They had lost the moon.

The cockpit door pushed back, Skip weaving an unsteady path to where Alex sat, shaking hands, accepting a cigarette, pulling hard on it. Tall, this one, almost gangly. You could hear his mother explaining how he had not quite grown into himself. Too young, this child pilot with the old man's smile. Three hours, he said, perhaps a little more, there was a head wind. He seemed proud, knowing a thing like that.

Three hours, and Alex would be perched like Kessler, legs dangling, Flight clipping his line to the rail. Three hours, and his turn to watch the red light with dead eyes.

The thought had lived with him ever since Archer's petty deception outside the hanger. When you collect your rig the thought is always there: was she paying attention, the WAAF who packed this one? If you ask for another the girls never mind. They know about accidents.

As he collected the bundled shute at the Barn, neatly tagged *Vere/ Harcourt,* a padded helmet perched on top, the WAAF standing guard, blushing, had offered a shy salute. How could he ask her whether the trailing cords had been cut?

Flight, propped against the bulwark opposite, his legs stretched out, ventured a timid grin. He was no Iago, this one: murder was far from his mind. He would dutifully clip the line, check it was secure, give that reassuring double tug, then shoulder tap, the squeak of *on my go.* All that. Before the fall.

Remembering those few seconds on the hotel balcony in Russell Square, Alex felt only an immense weariness. If oblivion was what they had arranged, so be it. It was too late anyway: with Justine gone, the whole damned thing was too late.

He woke to the sound of engines relaxing. Flight was up, stretching the stiffness out of his back, mouthing *descent* to Alex, flapping a hand to keep him in his place. A sudden rush of clean air had filled the cabin. Different air, smelling of land. Skip looped a gloved hand high in the air above his head. The jump light began pulsing red.

It was happening too fast, this business of joggling him to the hole, this business of falling to his death. One cheerful boy was clipping his line, the other tugging for good measure.

Low now, lower than Metz, the dull drone of engines drumming back from a sense of trees below his dangling feet, the hydraulics wheezing tiny nudges … down … down. He saw it then - a wavering triangle of lights rearing up dead ahead, three flaming points swaying against a vast purple sky, Flight's grip tightened on his arm, his head angled back to catch the jump light.

Down there upturned faces were already scanning for the billow of silk. He doubted they were French.

Thoughts of Justine ravelled themselves to a scream of hopeless rage, freeing the startled hands at his back. Alex wrenched away, tumbling desperately into the consuming black, his last sight a glimpse of frightened eyes. The jump light was red.

His chute deployed into a fierce up-draught, the triangle of flames jerking behind the crest of a wooded hill. Trees everywhere.

At Ringway there had been a session on trees.

I won't waste your time, Captain Vere, trees boil down to this. Avoid them. If you can't avoid them, come in face to wind, minimise speed over the ground. The theory is the canopy breaks the thinner branches, let's you down nice and gentle and Bob's your uncle. That's the theory. More likely you knock yourself out. Or to be really cheerful, you strangle yourself. The Manual says entangled more than eight feet up, wait for help. If no help comes, pray. Less than eight feet, I'd give it a go. Better than getting shot. Shoulder straps first, then legs, Face in crossed arms. Drop. I'd pray anyway.

It was on him before he could think: a huge cedar, rearing dead ahead. Face to wind ... face to wind ... where the hell was the bloody wind? Too late. Tight cones like lemons were banging his face, the silk above wrenching him round: holding, slipping, tearing, holding again, everywhere the cold resinous smell of Christmas. Mother hanging glass baubles, singing to herself. He wriggled to free his chest strap, taking the lash as his arm released a springing branch.

Eight feet? Didn't they know it would be dark? Somewhere below his dangling legs was the painful earth. Leg straps gone he leaned back into the sweet air, a sudden surge of liberty bringing thoughts of angels. The grunt as the breath thumped out of him seemed to come from someone else. He lay on his back in a bed of needles. He had forgotten to pray.

The dull rumble of the Hudson refused to wane, a huge shadow coming round, horribly close, shaking the trees, pounding the air. Straight and low: screaming into the night, pulling up steep.

Alex risked the torch. At Aste-sur-Torre they had overshot by miles; much closer this time. You could smell the target fires in the air. Half a mile, perhaps less. The go-around had given him a line due West, bless them for that. Somewhere ahead men were waiting, scanning for a chute. Puzzled by the second run, but waiting all the same. He hitched the pack onto his back. At least no swooping car this time to take him unawares.

The path was through an abandoned coppice of sweet chestnut, dense tufts of fresh growth covering lines of stumps. The going was easy: meandering woodcutters' tracks with only hanging ropes of spider web to contend with. He made for the faint cloud of blue smoke where the trees thinned against a lighter sky.

At the crest of a rise, the track dipped sharply down to meet a metalled road. They were closer than he had realised. Two fires still smouldered on the wet grass, a smell of petrol hanging in the air.

The drop site was on the other side of the road, hedged round on three sides by trees, a moon throwing the empty field into shade. A last few burning embers were blowing red in the wind.

Where were they?

They would know he was here, would sense something in the silence. No reception committee would seriously expect him to walk out. *Never show yourself first*: that was the rule. A faint scent of tobacco reached him on the wind. Far away, someone coughed.

A narrow beam of white light broke out of the woods, jerking across the grass to the centre of the field. A tall figure, torchlight catching the hem of a long raincoat. It swung round to signal the woods behind, receiving an answering flash. They were biding their time. Whoever it was had stopped no more than thirty yards from where he stood.

There was a whistle from the distant wood, like someone calling a dog. As if in response, a shaft of torchlight, glinting wet green, raked the leaves over his head. Alex held his station. It was flashing now, pulsing Long-Short-Long-Short-Long. The All-clear.

Where were they?

The torch flared again, held low against the waist, tilted up to throw a face into vivid relief. Justine, small against the expanse of dark, unbearably vulnerable, stark white face scanning the trees where he stood.

As he started forward, the torch swung back to the woods behind, a voice calling clear in the night, a voice he would die knowing: "*Es ist hoffnungslos ...Ich habe Ihnen gesagt, dass er nicht kommen würde.*"

German uniforms burst from the trees, lights bouncing across the grass. "*Ta guele, bordel!*" Justine's torch went spinning into the night, the blow felling her. She pulled herself up on one arm, grunting with pain as he kicked again.

Paralysed with the horror of it, Alex had not seen the trap. A third man was running from nowhere across the grass, pausing to ready his rifle. Boots were clicking fast on the metalled road below where he stood, the slam, slam, of car doors echoing. An engine coughed into life, then another. In a second he would be surrounded. Across the field, Justine was vomiting as a man in uniform hauled her to her feet, the white blotch of her face turned full into the moon.

Run!

Her cry collapsed into stifled silence as another blow fell.

Twenty

Some sixth sense kept him upright, barrelling between trees, leaping stumps, careless of bramble tearing at his legs. The cars would have to follow the sinuous road to the village. It was his only advantage: if he ran like hell he would get there first.

He stumbled out of the woods onto a clay track, houses closing in on either side. Rows of cabbages, tiny garden plots. To his left, a narrow cobbled lane squeezed against the side of a church ran directly to the square beyond. A stone colonnade stood in silent shade.

He climbed some steps into the dark of a shop doorway, bent double, an ugly cough racking his lungs. The square was deserted, the only light a single gas lamp hissing yellow green. He could see the battered menu board of *Le Sport* swinging drunkenly from an iron hook.

At Torridon in the session on the Last Resort some wag had called out, *What's the first then?* forcing a wintry retort from the solemn man tasked to explain to them what you do when there is nothing to be done. Most of them had skipped the session, Alex sharing their superstitious dread of last things.

Strange to think Justine had once been in that dingy hotel, standing at the bar, fending off. *You don't order a coffee, Major.* Alex pulled himself further into the shade, her voice vivid like a pain.

The church clock struck the half hour, the sound too loud for the empty square. Twenty yards of exposed pavement and he would reach the café. The following cars should have come by now. It was almost an irritation to realise he had not merited a chase. He stepped down onto glistening cobbles and padded softly across the square.

The bar was shuttered. Dusty curtains had been clumsily drawn across the glass door, the space inside dark. A metal gate at the side of the building led onto a tiny terrace set out with rickety tables, each with its metal ashtray. The back door, a little ajar, showed a line of feeble yellow light under the hem of the blackout.

Alex unhitched his rucksack and pushed through the curtain into a panelled vestibule smelling of pastis and stale smoke. The night porter had wedged his chair against the wall to get comfortable, feet cocked up on the counter. He was reading a newspaper.

"We're full." The accent was Basque. Black suspicious eyes lazily sizing him up. "Don't you know what time it is? You shouldn't be wandering about. Forget the curfew, did we?"

"Do you think I could have a word with Jules?"

The porter swung his feet down, sprawling forward over the counter for a better look. "I thought it might be something like that. D'you expect me to fetch somebody at this time of night? You're not from round here, are you?"

"Does that make a difference?"

"It might."

He went back to the newspaper, folding it over at the race results.

"I can pay in advance. Not a deposit – the lot."

"Oh, it's a room you're after. I thought you wanted to see Jules. I told you, we're full. Who sent you? Not Claude Barte?"

"Claude who?"

"Haven't seen our Claude for a while. What's he up to?"

"I told you, I don't know him. I don't think you're full. I just want a room. I can pay."

The man spun the register round. "It's five thousand for the night." He pulled his sleeve back, peering at his watch, an exaggerated gesture, enjoying his moment, "What's left of it. Another thousand and you can fill the book in tomorrow. That's a convenience, isn't it? Mind you, it's tomorrow now. I'll need your *Carte* in the morning. They'll likely come asking. If I don't have your papers that's going to be your look out. In advance, you say?"

"Here's the money. Nobody will be asking for me."

"Number 22. Top of the stairs, this end of the corridor. Second door. It's open. If you get visitors you'll hear them on the stairs."

A narrow wooden staircase opened onto a shadowy long corridor with doors along one side. The electric bulb had been removed, the only light coming from shafts of faint moonlight through two tiny windows.

The window in his room was open to rid the place of the smell of pipe tobacco and some kind of leathery hair pomade, reminders of the last occupant.

Alex locked the door, pocketing the key. He threw his rucksack on the bed, stretching out alongside it, staring vacantly up at a faint splash of sickly light on the ceiling from the street lamp outside.

The room was cold, but he was sweating from the run, his throat raw from coughing. He had not eaten since Tempsford and was desperately thirsty. There would be food in the pack - Belgian chocolate, far too sweet, but better than nothing. And water, you'd be mad to drink from the tap. With luck, there'd be a quarter bottle of cognac, the story at Hazells Hall was you got that on French drops.

He pulled at the straps of the rucksack, the packet of silks falling onto the bed. His mission. The waxed package rolled onto its side. He could barely remember what he was supposed to do with it. He began fumbling in the dark for the water flask. It was not there. No chocolate, either.

His heart unaccountably pounding, he got up and closed the curtains, turning on the tiny bedside lamp. The Model B was there, stubby suppressor screwed in. The ammunition clip had shaken down to the bottom of the pack. It was empty.

He remembered the Signals officer at Hazells Hall pushing a wallet with his papers into the side pouch of the pack. A brown leather thing, cracked with use. The one here was an inexplicable red. It seemed brand new.

He pulled it out, tearing it open. His *Carte d'Identie,* where the hell was it? He must have that *Carte* to survive. What would he do when that avaricious creep downstairs asked for his papers? It came to him that the porter had not offered the pass phrase. Georges Harcourt, travelling *Géomètre* with a Dutch accent, asking to see Jules - the pretence was absurd. Without papers he was dead.

There was no *Carte* in the wallet. No pass for the Gers border either. No train tickets. All the little bits of circumstantial colour – cinema ticket stubs, ration cards, the picture of his little boy – all gone. Yet he had watched that clumsy fool of an officer from Donnington pack them in his kit. Watched him carefully check them off against a list. Innocently watched the officer whose phoney incompetence had duped him like a child.

The wallet wasn't empty. A thick wad of papers was stuffed into a side pocket. He flattened one out. It was a chart. A stretch of coast past Le Havre, the tongue of the Seine snaking inland with hatched zones labelled *mined* in red ink. A small square marked *Artillery* had been crossed out, reinstated in a new location. It was headed: INFORMATION SHEET - NOT TO BE TAKEN INTO THE AIR.

There was a sheet of teleprinter paper, torn along a perforated edge, still crisp:

ETA 0245 STOP CONTACT ARTHUR AND SIMONE ST AUNIX EARLIEST STOP CONFIRM ARRIVAL 4.2 MHZ 1830 DAILY UNTIL ACK STOP ARCHER STOP END.

It was the signal confirming his drop, his own copy, the one he had handed over for destruction at the fake barn at Gibraltar Farm. He remembered the Donnington Captain taking it from him. The blundering Captain who wanted him dead. As a betrayal it seemed inexplicably vindictive. And to think he had felt sorry for him. How the bastard must have laughed at that. Laughed all the way home to his masters, whoever they were. Remembering Justine clubbed to her knees, that seemed the only question that mattered.

There was a greasy passport in the wallet. Issued in Paris to Adam

Walenski and dated March, 1935. The photograph, slightly blurred, showed a clean-shaven man with haunted eyes. At a pinch it could have been Alex. Much thumbed, it was empty apart from three Customs stamps for the crossing at Vogelbach dated January, February and March, 1938. He had never seen it before.

With the curtains drawn the room seemed unnaturally bright, his hands sticky with sweat. He filled the bowl, plunging his head into water smelling of sulphur. The face staring back at him from the tiny mirror over the sink was flushed, two spots of bright red high on his cheeks.

He switched off the light and drew back the curtain, cold air rushing past him into the room. The square below was wrapped in eerie silence, tiny houses on the other side above the colonnade shuttered and dark. A huge moon hung over the church steeple against a black sky.

Wait and you will be contacted. His instructions.

Pressed to say wait how long, the man in Torridon had turned away.

Alex undressed and lay on the narrow bed, pulling damp blankets round his shivering shoulders, an irresistible tide of tiredness sweeping him into a sleep as dark as death.

Always the same dream: the figure below his window looking up, light so bright it hurt his eyes. He sensed someone in the darkness behind him but could not turn to see. Someone waiting to push him through quartered panes of glass, splinters cold on his face like falling snow. Justine below his window, looking up, her mouth shaping a cry. Impotent, his arms pinioned by clinging cloth, he was conscious of a huge face, not his own, looming too close, stale tobacco breath, a booming whisper, filled with fear.

"For God's sake, quiet! If someone hears we're lost." The Parisian accent was subtlety coarser than last time. "You remember me?"

"Yes ... yes, I think so …" Alex struggled to sit up, the room unaccountably a misty blue. "The Gendarmerie. Last year. You're Colonel Renault. What time is it?"

Framed against the window there was something hallucinatory about the impassive figure stooping over him: stiff cap decked out with gold filigree, long polished boots, crisp purple piping buckling at his knees, a glint of gold epaulettes.

"It is a little before six o'clock."

"Dawn?"

"It is evening. I had to wake you, they would hear you downstairs. You were screaming. A fever, I think."

Filled with a sudden exultant recollection, Alex strained forward, hopelessly scanning the room. Renault followed his gaze, shaking his head. "I also remember our last encounter, Mr Englishman. No, she is not here. We are alone." Alex felt the bedclothes pulled away. "Can you stand? There is not much time."

"Am I to be arrested? Is that why you're here? To arrest me?"

"*Arrest*? Are you mad?" Renault sounded angry. "Incredible that you come to this place. I will do what I can to remove you, and do not thank me. I do it reluctantly."

"Justine?"

"She told me you might come here. If you were not arrested. Why here, in God's name? Only a madman walks into the same trap twice. Are you a madman?"

"I don't understand. When was this? How could she tell you? She wasn't dropped here. How did she get to this place?"

"You are wrong. Of course Madame Perry was dropped at Saint Aunix. And of course she was arrested. Like all the agents sent here." His hoarse whisper had a venomous edge: "You must know that your network - your ridiculous *Columbine* - is compromised? That your agents are captured? Yet every moon you send more. Are you all insane?"

A door slammed in the hotel vestibule below. Renault hurried to the window, tossing the end of his cigar into the fireplace.

"No, nothing. The night porter must not see us leave. You were never here, do you understand? This hotel is unsafe. It is used by SS officers. For … recreation. Yet you come here?"

Alex was barely listening, "But Justine. You know where she is? I saw her. Where are they holding her?"

"You really don't know?" He tossed his cap onto the table and bent close enough for his voice to carry, "She is in a prison block attached to the wireless station. Where the technicians operate your sets. How could you not know all this? The man in charge, I know him a little. His name is Gliess. He cannot believe his luck, his little army of puppet English agents. He owns them all."

"He doesn't own Justine, not that."

"Are you sure? I have the advantage over you – I have been there. Gliess has a chart in his room - the complete SOE command structure. Your agents have been purchased. Bribed, if you like, but I can see they had little option. They will be treated as prisoners of war ..." He stopped to light another cigar, walking across to listen at the door. He turned to look at Alex "… And they believe this."

"Justine wouldn't talk."

"You will think me insulting, Captain Vere, but I ask myself how you came to be selected for active service. When I arrive, for example, you are asleep. Is it not a symptom of hysteria? When the animal can no longer cope, it sleeps?"

He raised a hand as Alex started to speak, "No, you must listen to me. Reports come to my desk. I received one two days ago. *Captain Alex Vere, under the command of Colonel Archer of the TPSU.* How do you think it was obtained? Of course she talked. Would you want her to resist? Prisoners in the care of Major Gliess are not treated well. He looks the other way. Now get up. Collect your pack. You have very little time."

Alex stumbled about the room, gathering scattered things, aware of Renault's insistent quiet voice.

"The day before yesterday The Major invited me to the wireless station to deal with the accidental death of a prisoner. *Accidental* was the word he employed. Germans are not without a sense of humour. Such things are a matter for the French authorities. I was ordered to bring with me a doctor. One not too interested in the condition of the body."

"Why are you telling me this? To shock me?"

"Shock you?" Renault looked puzzled. "No. I am talking about Justine." Pronounced in the French manner, it seemed he claimed her for himself.

"You're lying. She's alive. I've seen her, I tell you."

"You misunderstand me. I meant I took the opportunity to bargain with Major Gliess, to plead for her life. I gave him reasons to keep her alive. You can imagine them if you wish. I am not proud of what I said. The Major found my request amusing. He said he had had much the same idea. Then he pointed to priorities between brother officers, explaining that a German Major had precedence over a French Colonel. *Precedence* was the word he used. Obviously, he was baiting me."

"I don't know what you're talking about." Alex crammed the waxed package of silk into his rucksack and tugged to pull the buckles tight. "Where are you going to take me? I'm sorry, I don't understand what you're talking about. *Precedence?*"

"Ah, perhaps because you think I am trying to shock you. I will explain. Major Gliess gives his prisoners little freedoms, secured against their parole. He is the psychologist, you see. He knows the English would not violate a promise if others risk execution. I suppose that is admirable."

"What freedoms? You said *little freedoms.*"

"Nothing much. An arrangement to bring them to the bar here."

Alex stared at him. "You mean Justine?"

"I will tell you something. Something you also may not find shocking. Shortly after we signed our armistice, I met with my opposite number in the Abwehr. He explained what was owing to an occupying power, making particular mention of women. *Our women*, is how he put it. He told me his men must have their fun, warned me against a hysterical reaction."

Renault had fallen silent. He released a haze of blue smoke into the cold air. Noises from the kitchens floated up the staircase outside. "The last woman to come the way of Major Gliess - do you remember?" Alex shook his head, bewildered. "She killed herself. He looked on that as an injustice. I believe Madame Perry does not have that option."

"She won't …" Alex checked himself, "…no."

"So you understand he sees her capture as a particular prize. That is the word he used. His French is not good. He said *prize.*"

He picked his cap up from the table and put it on, glancing in the mirror over the sink, turning finally to Alex. "He brings his prize here in the evening. There is a room commandeered for the purpose.

I imagine this will continue until she leaves. That is what he meant when he said he had another idea. It is a way of tormenting me. And now I torment you." He shrugged. "My regrets."

"What do you mean, *until she leaves*?"

"All the prisoners are to be shot. The executions are set for next week. I have been given orders to make the arrangements. There is paperwork to be completed. The promise they would be spared must be legally annulled, you understand. This is France, there are formalities, in so far as it was ever a French contract. The Germans have asked us to arrange this. As I said, they are not without a certain sense of humour."

"But Justine? You said a prisoner of war ..."

"She is not to be shot. I secured that much. She is to be sent to a camp. A place called Ravensbrook in the North of Germany. We arrange shipments every day now from Mont de Marsan. Two thousand at a time, mostly Jews. They are called *shipments*. There are even detailed manifests." For a moment, something broke in his voice, "It is a little like the movement of cattle."

"Do you know when?"

"I assume when Major Gliess can no longer think of an excuse to keep her here."

"At least she will be alive."

Renault looked at him, anger evaporating into a kind of exasperated pity. "They are freight waggons, Captain Vere. The French State is obliged to remove Jewish citizens … former citizens … as far as it is possible. But the rail company will only provide cattle trucks for the purpose. They say the risk is too great in a war zone. A journey of two thousand kilometres." Hearing Renault's voice thicken, Alex looked away. "There is only room to stand. No water. No sanitation. She may survive. I am told it is the young who are alive at the destination. They need the young - Ravensbrook is a work camp. For women."

"For pity's sake, this is France! Not some vassal state. You've got your damned armistice. You've kept your army. And you stand there looking sorry for yourself. You let this happen. You are as responsible as this man Gliess."

"You think I don't know that? Why do you think I am helping you?

And no, it has nothing to do with Justine. It is because I can. Do you understand? It is something in my power to do. Have you any idea what is happening in France? We are removing one hundred thousand. That is virtually all we do: count Jews."

"Then refuse."

"What – like some quixotic Englishman? You think that is an option? Listen. My service, the Gendarmerie, has no particular wish to refuse. Sometimes, quite the reverse. Since the summer fifteen thousand Jews have been arrested in Paris. Not by Germans, you understand. By my service. By us. No, *arrested* is not the word. Perhaps you would say *rounded up*. In any case that's what we do now. We round up women and children. We herded the first lot into the velodrome on the Boulevard de Grenelle. You know the place? I was there. It got out of hand – there were too many. Thousands and thousands. We crammed them in and left them to it. No food, no water. Nothing."

"They must have been released eventually."

"*Released*? No, not really. They were sent to special camps. There is one not far from here. They are to go to Poland, I believe. If there is still such a place." He was staring at Alex, "They will not be coming back. There is nothing I can do. So I do this."

"Look …" Alex was feverishly pulling open the buckles of his kit. "You can think what you like about me … I don't care. At least I can use a knife. You say Gliess comes here. What protection?"

Renault pulled the kit bag from his hands, threading the buckles closed.

"He has his driver. But Major Gliess needs no protection."

He fumbled in an inside pocket of his tunic, feeling for something, finally pulling out a folded sheet of typed paper. "I am unsure whether this is strictly legal … it is a matter under consideration. By a German tribunal, you understand. It is the proposed tariff of reprisals." He held it up to catch the light from the window, rattling through phrases at random, "*… intentional death of an ordinary soldier … five persons at the discretion of the Commune … Jews to be preferred … children and pregnant women excluded … junior officer … thirty, no exclusions …* Shall I go on?"

Standing very close, his voice was a desperate whisper, "I can tell you this, Mr Englishman, if there is even an attempt on the life of Major Gliess, Saint Aunix will be burnt to the ground. The whole commune, you understand? Every inhabitant will be shot where they stand. Or burnt alive."

He tossed the half-smoked cigar into the fireplace. "Here's your pack, Captain Vere, put your absurd knife away."

"You say he will be here? Here tonight?"

"It is not impossible. Long after you have gone. He is always very late."

"But you will see her? If she is with him."

"The bar is a public place until the curfew. I can buy a drink for whoever I like."

"Can you give her something?"

"A message? Impossible. Gliess knows my interest. We may exchange a greeting, but ..."

"No, not a message." Alex was pulling at the webbing at the bottom of the rucksack, tearing the fabric, feeling for its secret cache, his fingers closing round the tiny metal tin. "This. Find some way to give her this. It would be a kindness."

Renault took it, experimentally palming it from hand to hand, abandoning the gesture, pushing it into his pocket. He shook his head.

"Perhaps she no longer looks for kindness."

"Do it if you can. For her."

Renault checked the window again, turning to survey the room. "We must deal with you. I will wait here. Go downstairs. Walk through the vestibule. There is a road directly across the square. Three doors down, a cake shop." He looked at his watch, "You still have time. They will be closing, but you have time. Say you want directions to the church. Say, *perhaps there is a back way?* Exactly those words. They will show you."

"What if they don't?"

"There is only one kind of stranger that makes that request. Behind the shop, a little lane, at the bottom a wooden shed. Pass the night there. The police patrol will stay away. I will keep this passport. It may be possible to arrange for some papers … possibly not … the name is unfortunate. Early tomorrow morning, I will …"

The sound of wheels on the cobbles outside sent him hurrying back to the curtain. A car skidded noisily against the pavement under the window. Doors clicked open.

Renault stood, careless of being seen, muttering a stream of slow curses.

In the square below, a German officer was emerging from a polished staff car, finishing some fragment of conversation, adjusting his cap, calling out to someone, laughing.

Alex did not see her at first. Alone on the far side of the car, gloved hands resting on an open door, her face wore the faint uncomprehending look of someone not quite following a joke.

The man walked round, taking her arm as she seemed to stumble, dark eyes huge in the white of her face.

Renault closed the curtains, turning back into the room, switching off the light.

"If they find you here, we are both dead." He had picked up the rucksack and stood turning it over and over in his hands. "You bring your damned luck with you. He was not expected until after ten. Here, help me pull this bed away. Lie against the wall, I'll push it back. I must be downstairs when he arrives. I will leave the door open."

Twenty-One

A smell of cooking drifted through the open door: something frying, not altogether agreeable. Down the stairs there seemed too many people jammed into the vestibule, all talking, Renault made his entrance, greeting people from the car, managing a few stilted German phrases. A querulous reply, too loud for the space, demanded drinks. Gliess – it was surely Gliess – was speaking French, the accent impenetrable. He sounded like a thwarted child at a party. Desperate to catch her voice, Alex heard them move through to the bar, swing doors flapping.

A slow creak of leather boots made its way up the narrow staircase. Alex pressed his head against the dusty lino as torchlight flared wild across the ceiling in the corridor. Someone pushed at the door to the room with the tip of his boot. A beam of torchlight raked the bed, lingering a moment on the wall above where he lay. The man moved away, breathing heavily, tapping pointlessly at a door at the end of the corridor and pushing it open. It must be the guard for Gliess getting something to sit on. He was humming to himself.

At Torridon they had acted out situations like this, analysed their essential instability, the paramount necessity to kill before being killed. An alert guard always sensed a presence, however hidden you believed yourself, however still you might lie. No one knew how or why: perhaps some unconscious awareness of sound, more likely the scent of fear. Alex readied his hand to snatch his knife, remembering his kit was strapped tight. He would not stand a chance. A buckle on the rucksack had started to bite into his leg.

The soldier stopped humming, the sudden silence broken by the scrape of a match. Coarse cigarette smoke drifted down the corridor, hideous Russian stuff. Curious how soldiers always ended up preferring that brand. He seemed a restless chap, this sentry, idly scraping his boots on the floorboards, endlessly clearing his throat. How long before he decided to take another look at the room with the open door? How long before he wondered about the recent smell of expensive cigars?

The double doors from the bar flapped open, disgorging a babble of voices into the vestibule. Renault was complaining about something, his voice – perhaps a little too loud - reached Alex. He had paused to let the German labour over some elaborate parting formula in French. A burst of false laughter capped the joke.

Gliess was coming upstairs. Alex was sure it was him. He heard the sentry heave himself to attention, the floor under the bed shuddering. The peevish voice had stopped in the stairwell. It began again, struggling in mangled French as if speaking and walking together were too great an effort. He seemed determined to make his point, to get it right, fighting to catch his breath, wheezing like Archer the day he came to Netley. He sounded slightly drunk. A burst of officious German sent the guard thudding downstairs.

There was another voice. Alex had believed himself happy to die thinking of that voice. She was here. So close he could have reached out and touched her shadow darkening the doorway. She was speaking French, mumbled words that stopped his heart: *No, not here, Monsieur, the end of the corridor*, Gliess grunting an inarticulate reply.

He could see her shoes, black leather, a little masculine. She had perched on the edge of the bed putting them on, the morning she had left for King's Cross, a lifetime ago. *Sensible*, she'd said, as if answering a question.

They moved off, walking like furtive lovers. The faint rustle of cloth, Justine's dark voice again, *Not here, Monsieur,* Gliess laughing as he opened the door.

Braced against his wall, Alex cursed the tense silence that had fallen over the hotel. Cramp fluttering where the metal buckle pressed against his leg would sooner or later betray him.

In the room at the end of the corridor conversation had started up, the voices penetrating the flimsy walls: Justine talking about the dreadful wallpaper, switching to German to say she would pour him a drink, the other voice thicker, no more than a rumble, an oily teasing tone.

Justine again in French, telling him not to paw, protesting he would tear her dress, squeaking in mock alarm. A shoe fell to the floor. Gliess louder, importunate, Alex flooded his head with words: *Dame souris trotte, Dame souris trotte,* again and again and again - a pagan prayer. Sweet Jesus, anything not to hear.

They were quiet at last. The whole hotel party to the barely audible adjustment of bodies, tiny adhesive whispered moans, things he once believed his own. He sensed the presence of others waiting against the silence for some kind of end.

Gliess was calling out, untranslatable words rising above the rhythmical creak of the metal bed. Perhaps not words at all, thrusting, grunting, wresting a climax from pain. And threading through the hellish mix, burning his brain, Justine's voice - Justine liberated as Alex had never known.

The pain in his leg had become so much part of his impotent fury that for a second it seemed the muffled call had been his own.

A wooden chair clattered to the tiles downstairs, heavy feet stumbled up the staircase, thudding past his room. Justine's voice surged out of an open door, French, then German, her throat raw: *Fetch someone. Quick! What are you gawping at, man? Can't you see he's ill? Fetch someone. A doctor. I don't know. Only hurry!*

The swinging doors in the vestibule below clacked open onto bedlam: Renault ordering a press of voices back to the bar, taking the stairs two at a time, meeting the sentry running back, both speaking at once: *A doctor at this time of night ... What emergency? ... Are you mad?* Renault's voice again, shouting at a press of strangers on the stairs: *Get those people back! And shut up, for Christ's sake!*

Another voice. The night porter was half inside the room, whispering obsequious German. *I know where he lives, Herr Colonel Sir. The doctor. It's a fair way.* Renault barking in reply: *No ... telephone the Casserne ... Damn it, it's too late. Go with him. I'll deal with it. Get a move on.*

Voices surged into the square outside: shouts echoing clear in the frosty air. Someone conjured a reluctant engine to life. There was a skid of wheels, too fast on greasy cobbles.

Then they were gone.

Alex sensed he was not alone in the stunned silence. Someone was breathing, a shadow stretching across his patch of floor, Renault's polished boots silhouetted against a faint light.

"Captain Vere," the voice was low, almost conversational. "Nobody is here. Get up. I have to lock this door. Damnation! The fool of a porter's taken the key."

"No, I've got it," Alex had struggled to his knees, pushing the bed away. He fumbled desperately in his pocket. "No. Try another room, all the keys will be the same."

Alex pressed himself against the wall, his left leg too stiff to move. He watched Renault pull the curtains back, the sudden flare of orange light hurting his eyes. God, he was going to faint. Why was he talking about keys? Things were running away from him: his life lost, and all he could do was talk about keys.

"What do you mean, *Nobody here*? Has Gliess gone? Justine? Where is she?"

"Too many questions. Can you manage? Here, hold on to me."

The bedroom door at the end of the corridor was open wide. A wall of heat struck them as they went inside, logs still burning in a stone fireplace. The shade from the bedside lamp had been taken down, throwing sharp unnatural shadows high on the walls. The place was filled with the sweaty fetid scent of sex; it smelled vaguely unclean.

Justine's frock lay draped like a body along a brocade sofa, her other things scattered on the floor. Gliess had folded his clothes over a chair, his dress cap perched on top.

He lay face down, naked apart from grey stockings held by elastic suspenders. Slumped across Justine's body like some blasphemous *Pietà*, his buttocks, gelatinous blue mounds, rearing up. Patches of flaky skin showed through matted hair, his head nuzzling against her breasts. He was obviously dead.

"Get the bastard off me, will you?" Her look as Alex gripped Gliess by hairy shoulders was frigid, not yet recognition. As he rolled the body off, she pulled free, stifling a hysterical laugh, "God almighty! It only needed that."

Gliess lolled back onto the sheets, a grotesque priapic doll, penis stubbornly erect.

She struggled to the side of the bed fumbling with a gloved hand to find her blouse.

Alex leaned down to help.

"It's alright, I can manage." She winced as he took her wrist, "My hands hurt. Best not that one, the bastards did something. I've not dared look. I'm such a coward," dark eyes wide with pain. "Oh Alex, my dear, you look worse than me. Leave me be, I want to get straight."

"He's dead."

They had forgotten Renault. He was standing immobile in the doorway, his voice flat; it was not even a question.

"When that sentry came in, what did he see?"

Justine avoided his eyes. "What do you mean, *what did he see*? What do you think? You gave me the bloody pills." She raised a gloved hand in mute appeal to Alex, "I knew who they came from, it was knowing that kept me alive ... gave me some sort of hope."

"You don't understand. Did he touch him?" Something urgent in Renault's voice made her look at him, seeing him for the first time.

"Did the sentry touch him? Of course not. He didn't come in. Stood where you are. He was only interested in me. He couldn't take his eyes off me. You'd think he'd never seen a woman before. He stood in the doorway ogling like an idiot."

"But he knew he was dead?" He stepped into the room, moving towards her, "He could see that?"

She paused, weighing the question, "No. Why would he think that? I'm sure he thought Gliess had just passed out. He was trying not to laugh. He seemed very young. Fainted with passion, he must have thought. It was very hot in here."

Renault picked the glass up from the table. "The pills, tell me what you did."

"Only one pill. The new one. I put it in his brandy. He didn't drink it all. Too keen to get at me. They said it acted fast – that's a joke."

She stood unsteadily in front of the wardrobe mirror, straightening her dress. "Why do you want to know all this? I feel sick. I want to be sick. Hell! My coat. I just remembered, what's happened to my coat?"

"Your coat is in the bar downstairs. Listen to me, for God's sake. I have to think. When he drank the brandy, what then?"

"Nothing. Absolutely nothing. These trick things never work. But he was drunk anyway."

Renault kneeled at the side of the bed, gingerly straightening out the body, pushing the head back, examining the neck. "No mark … so far as I can see."

He stared up at Justine, some obscure embarrassment flushing his face, "The state he was in … I have seen it before. At Fresnes prison. Men when they are hanged." He waited for their eyes to meet.

"When he started to come off, my hands were round his neck. He asked me to ... begged me ... only so far, you know. He wanted pain … any pain. He was screaming, *Harder, harder.* You must have heard. The whole place must have heard. Pathetic bugger."

She raised her head to Alex, wide blue eyes embracing him, the first hint of a wounded smile, "Carotid choke."

"He didn't resist?" Renault let the head fall back onto the bed, "*Why?*"

"Oh, he resisted … he resisted like hell … but you can't resist that … you're always too late to resist. The way he looked when he realised - God, I'll always remember that. I made it ten seconds. I counted a bit fast I suppose. But he was dead long before ten." She extended a hand towards Alex, "I killed him."

Renault had pushed a pillow under the scrawny neck, allowing the head to sink into it, gesturing for Alex to look.

"He's older than I thought. I have a question. Perhaps you know. Can people die like that? Die of … how you say? *Congress?* Is it possible?"

Alex was raking his memory, dredging for details from the one undergraduate lecture nobody forgot. "Possible, yes. I believe it's a question of blood pressure. If it's high ... if there is a history. I'm not a doctor ... a doctor would know."

"This one they have gone for – I know him. He is a friend."

He stood up, turning to Justine, reaching out to touch her arm, his voice desperate.

"Tell me again. Our lives depend on it. More than our lives. Tell me the truth. When the sentry looked at Gliess, what would he have concluded?"

"I'm telling you the truth. Why should I lie? What do you conclude when you see your officer's backside like that? If you're asking did he think I'd killed him, I'm sure not. There was a bit of a smirk on his face. He drew the obvious conclusion – a climax of passion. It will be the talk of the barracks in a day or two. I told you he was young. Probably surprised to discover old men fuck at all."

Starting to say something, Renault stopped himself, opened the door and listened to the distant buzz of muffled sound below. He turned back inside, pushing the door closed.

"Captain Vere, the rendezvous for your return? It is when?"

"*Return*? There isn't one!" Justine blurted out a reply before Alex could speak. "You don't understand at all. We were never intended to. It's too late for all that, Pascal. You know it is. It's over. We're not going to get out. Can't you leave us here? For God's sake don't get involved, it's not worth your life as well."

Alex sat fiddling with the buckle of his kitbag, warding off rising claustrophobia, watching the two of them stare each other down. Justine had slumped back onto the sofa, grinding her nails into the pink brocade to control the trembling in her arms. She did not know who he was. This dreadful place would be his last sight of freedom. There wasn't room for four crammed into this stifling little space. No, not four – one was already dead.

"Leave her," Renault was pulling him aside. "It's a reaction. It will pass. She is wrong, the guard will tell no one about any of this. Now… your rendezvous?"

"I don't know how long Justine was meant to be here. Weeks, I think … on paper ... but we were betrayed. We were bound to be arrested. It happened before."

"My pickup would be Castelnaudary," Justine's voice was trembling. "That was my drop site. Except it wasn't. How do you imagine we get to Castelnaudary, Pascal? How do we manage that?"

Renault pulled closer to Alex, his back hard against the closed door, "She doesn't understand. It is your pickup I mean." He was whispering, "Obviously, one of your own betrayed you. That is your one advantage. Whoever it is still waits in London for news of your arrest. You see the consequence?"

"Frankly, no, I don't."

"It will be impossible to annul your return without news of your arrest. That was to be where?"

"Here, of course - the field at Saint Aunix. In two days' time. No, that's not right. Sorry … I've lost a day. Tomorrow. It was scheduled for tomorrow. Eleven hundred hours."

"To cancel the flight without knowing of your arrest would risk exposure. It is a risk he will not take … or *she*, I suppose, who knows? No, they will keep the rendezvous. Both of you will go. You will have to risk the patrols … but …"

Justine had started to laugh, "Do you believe all this nonsense, Alex? Alex, my love, look at me."

"Quiet!" Renault pushed the curtain aside, looking down into the empty square. "No … still nothing." He looked at his watch, "You have time. There are people down there. When I go downstairs I will take those in the vestibule with me into the bar. Wait until you hear the doors close, then make your way out into the square ..."

He took Justine's gloved hand letting it fall as she winced. "Can you walk?" His voice was suddenly softer, "Do you think you can get to the house at Aste? A long way, but not impossible. The house there is still safe. The owner is an artist … a painter, I think. He has been happy to accommodate fugitives … even Jews." He waited for her response, still staring at her gloved hand.

She struggled up, swaying slightly, clasping his arm for support. "Don't imagine things, Pascal. It's done now. Worse happens." She took a few uncertain steps into the room. "I'll manage. You mean the safe house? Of course. But there are Germans billeted there."

"Only one. And he is not there now, nobody is there, the place is empty. One thing, Captain Vere. Those papers you are carrying - they are a death warrant. Give them to me. You are better without them."

Justine supressed a choking kind of laugh, looking desperately at Alex, "What's he mean, a death warrant? God, my coat. It's in the bar."

"It will not be there tomorrow." Renault turned to Alex, "Wait at the house. I will bring a car. If I am late, wait." He shrugged, "If I am later than that, you will have to make your own way ..."

"And him?" Alex looked at the bed. Justine did not turn round.

"There is somebody in the bar. A girl. When you have gone I will talk to her. I think her name is Nathalie. She comes here on Saturdays. The German boys like her because she is willing to be friendly. They are happy enough to pay what she asks. It's little enough. We arrested her once for a moral offence. Her father complained. About Germans, you understand, not about her selling herself."

"You're going to mix her up in this?"

"When the doctor arrives, she will be detained. Not an arrest, after all it is hardly an offence. The sentry has no reason to involve himself further."

Alex looked down at the body of Gliess, no longer tumescent, its flesh already taking on the grey chalky bloom of death. "I recall that word now. The term is *coital death*."

"That is what the doctor will certify. I will contact Feldkommandant Kloss about the event. It will be very late. It is better to wake people up for this sort of thing, they rarely make sensible decisions. I will offer to intercede with the doctor to obtain a less specific certificate, for the sake of good relations. I will ask Kloss to suggest a more appropriate place to die and offer the services of the local Gendarmerie to transport the body. Kloss will tell the sentry how little he saw."

Twenty-Two

For the last mile Alex carried her, heavy in his arms like an injured child, finally persuading her onto his back, one gloved hand pressed into his neck. As she drifted into unconsciousness he stopped, bending gently forward, shaking her awake.

They found the house by the last of the setting moon, a blue shadow across lawns ragged with frosty thistles, dead leaves piled against double doors braced shut with an iron bar. The place looked abandoned.

Alex made for a pantiled building set apart from the house. He pushed at an unlocked door, the smell of turpentine rushing to meet him. The switch worked, a single bulb festooned with dangling spider webs throwing a feeble yellow light on paintings stacked three-deep against whitewashed walls. The polished reflector of a huge acetylene lamp faced a portrait clipped to an ancient easel with a wooden crank, the little tableau giving the room a curious arrested air.

The painting looked finished: an old man standing unnecessarily erect, jaw jutting forward, dark suit suggesting someone just back from church. It was a mean face, unused to concession, heavily lined. The German lodger, surely, with posterity in mind, imagining his warring days over. It was hard to believe the sitter would be all that pleased. Something disquieting about the vacant stare reminded Alex of Archer.

She had seemed conscious when they first arrived, able to stand.

Now, she slept in the chair where he had propped her, erect and silent, her bruised face in repose someone he had never known. She had stirred at the scent of smoke as he lit a few sticks in the fireplace. That had been half an hour ago. He sat watching. Her mouth a little open, a desperate beat to her breath, clinging to a kind of sleep.

There was a cardboard box of baking soda on a shelf over the sink, poked between empty paint tins. Alex stirred some into a glass of water and began easing off the glove. It was too big for her hand, white cotton, embroidered with flowers at the wrist. He had never seen her wear such a thing. As he pulled at it, a lump of bandage came away, caked black.

The nail on the little finger was gone. Raw flesh, horribly exposed, met the frayed remains of the cuticle, vivid lines running blue across her hand.

She gave a tiny instinctive flinch as he began sponging, the water in the glass darkening red. Reaching the open wound he realised he was weeping, tears blurring his view. Turning aside he met huge dark eyes close to his own, staring wide.

"Hello Guffin." She started coughing, pawing empty air with the wounded hand, "Hell, that stings. I'm done for. Did I pass out? How did we get in here?"

"The door was open. You keeled over in the woods, do you remember? I thought you'd tripped."

"Bloody shoes. No, all I remember is dogs. I thought they were following us with dogs. I do remember you carrying me piggyback … made me feel like a little girl." She turned to him, her face charged, "Can it be safe here? I don't think I can manage much more … I'm sorry, Alex, I'm done for."

"Renault said it was safe. It's quiet enough. Nobody's here, the big house is locked up."

Justine was looking at the portrait, "She lived in this house, did you know that? D'you think she painted it?"

"Who?"

"That artist, the Major's sister. The one in Dundee. She must have left from here the morning of that bomb. I was supposed to die that day, Alex. That bomb was meant for me, I'm sure of it." She seemed very close, searching his face, "Were there really dogs?"

"Not after us. Just strays. The woods are full of them. Try and get a bit of rest. There's some bandage in my kit."

She looked down at her hand as if she barely owned it. "You know, this is the first time I've looked. It had started hurting but even then I didn't want to." She stretched out her other hand, pressing it against his cheek, "No, no, my love, you did the right thing. It had to be … *cleaned* ... is that word?" He was winding bandage round her hand, the fabric crisp white against smudged bruises. "I knew you'd go crying on me. I didn't want you to look either."

"It all seems so senseless."

She let her finger ruffle through his hair. "I still can't believe you followed me here. I was in such a panic standing in that field, knowing you were there. With that go-around they'd figured out the drop had gone wrong somehow. Then one of them came up with the idea of using me as bait. He had a rifle. They knew I'd try to warn you, right enough. All he needed was a clear line of fire."

She snatched the glove off her lap. "Throw it on the fire, will you? Just get rid of it. Why on earth did you go to that hotel, Alex? I thank God you did, but … didn't you know it's not safe?"

"They told me to go there. The man who briefed me said to treat it as the Last Resort. He was lying."

"Gliess says it's a sort of brothel. Most nights it's full of Germans. When we went into the bar Pascal as good as said you were upstairs, lots of hand shaking, too much, really, but that's how I ended up with your little tin. In case I didn't cotton on, he started quoting bits of poetry, mice trotting about and all that. Gliess knew something was up, but he couldn't work out what. He put it down to gallantry. I think that's what they hate about the French: that gallantry comes natural."

"He doesn't think much of me either, your Renault chap. He thinks it's my fault you came back here." He had nestled the bandaged hand into his own, stroking it, "No, Justine, let me say it. You're keeping something back, aren't you? It's about London, isn't it? Renault knows who's behind all this, doesn't he? You as well."

"Oh, love, no. He knows nothing at all. He's angry he doesn't. He just thinks London is wilfully stupid. That's why he started helping. Until the rumours started about him. He knows his time's up. Getting us away might be the last thing he does. He told me once why he started playing a double game. You know what he said?"

"He told me it was about the Jews."

She nodded. "It got so much worse when the Germans moved South. It was as if we'd stopped playing at war. That's when this Vichy setup really changed. Pascal says it made him complicit. It's the way people accepted things, not just looking the other way, actually helping. He says he's ashamed. And it's true. Most of them aren't even particularly unhappy. You know the motto's *Work, Family, Fatherland* now? Poor Pascal, he just couldn't stomach the idea of a fatherland. He wants his Marianne back."

"Or his Justine?"

"No, Guffin, not that, he was ashamed of that as well. Don't think ill of him. He's making amends. But he doesn't know anything about London. Perhaps there's nothing to know, has that thought never struck you?"

"Oh, it's struck me alright. That's what we're all supposed to think. But somebody's behind it, right enough. That's how you get told your being sent to Castelnaudry."

"I'm sorry Alex, I'm too feeble to talk much. Is there anything to drink? I'm horribly thirsty. And something to eat? Can you look?"

Alex fetched a glass of water from the sink. He walked round the studio, opening cupboards, calling out over his shoulder: "There's a box here with biscuits. Very fancy. German. And brandy. Lots of brandy. Artists seem to live on the stuff."

As he turned towards her, holding out the bottle, he realised she was already speaking, almost to herself, a numb quiet voice he barely recognised.

"It was the Major told me the drop zone would be near Castelnaudary. Even showed me the spot on a map. Explained about the local reception committee, names, pass phrase, all the usual stuff. My orders were I was on no account to come scouting round Columbine until there was intelligence that it was safe to move."

"What was the pass phrase?"

"Why d'you want to know that?" The sweetness of her sudden smile stopped his heart, "Oh Alex, have we come to that? You don't think I'm lying to *you*, do you? It was *Fête Galante* if you must know. We were betrayed. Both of us. That's all it comes to."

"It's this Major I want to know about, not you. I don't trust him since he told me his brother was killed by that bomb. And *Fête Galante* was one of the Verlaine pass phrases - he told me once he didn't know anything about them. So if he teed up the drop for Castelnaudry, how did you end up here?"

"All I know is the flight down was a lot longer than I expected. I couldn't get a word out of the crew: they said they were under orders to keep mum. But as soon as they got the hole open I knew something was wrong. The Major had gone through the approach to Castelnaudry and it was nothing like it. For one thing we were miles lower than we should have been and there were no buildings, just trees. Then I realised the landing markers seemed familiar … the pattern. I had this weird feeling I'd seen it all before."

"You mean the Aste pattern?"

"Three times I'd been on that approach. I realised we were right over Aste-sur-Torre just before they shoved me out. When I hit the ground I knew exactly where I was. You've been there, it's where that car caught you."

"And this is supposed to be some kind of cock-up? I can't believe that, not complete with landing markers ..."

"It was exactly the same story. There were soldiers waiting on top of that little hill, above the road. They hadn't even bothered to cover their uniforms. There was nowhere to run, not with a harness pulling me. Gliess himself was in the car keeping out of the cold. He knew every last detail of the operation. It was all exactly like the last time."

"You think the local circuit …?"

"No, of course it can't be. They can't change a flight plan. They can't even ask. London orders all that."

She held out her glass, shaking her head as Alex went to add water, "You'll have to go easy with this stuff. It's a hell of a walk … if we have to."

"Not *we*, Alex, *you*. I'm not going to get out of this, am I? You realise I'm all in. I can't walk – are you proposing to carry me? It's miles."

"You won't have to walk anywhere."

"You still believe in Pascal and his car? I thought it was me that believed in miracles. Just listen: it's as quiet as the grave out there, we'd have heard a car by now. He's probably been arrested. Accept it, Alex, you'll have to leave me here. You'll make it alright walking on the road."

She reached out, pressing her finger against his lips. "Be kind, love. No quibbling. This is where my six weeks end."

"He'll come. You didn't see the look on his face. Your Renault will get you out of here if it's the last thing he does. Me too, but it's you he's thinking about."

"He's not my Renault. And it's nothing to do with me … except it was me that killed Gliess. With us out of the way, what he ought to do is get rid of the body, forget fancy stuff with the doctor, get the local Maquis to deal with the driver, then dump the two of them somewhere in the mountains. They do things like that if you pay them enough. A long way from Saint Aunix, anyway. Don't go thinking Pascal's doing anything for our sake. It's reprisals he's thinking about. You don't know what those bastards will do. But if you want me to say I shouldn't have … shouldn't have …"

She seemed unaware she had stopped speaking. Her head had slipped forward, eyes fluttering. He rested a hand on her shoulder, feeling it yield like a dead thing. She seemed already beyond waking.

"Justine. If we're going to get away you must try to keep awake. I need to know what happened after they arrested you. If only one of us makes it back …"

She started up, "Yes, you're right, you'll be going soon. Sensible. Pour me another glass of that stuff, will you. A shame Pascal took the pills off me. Benzedrine's what I need."

"Wait a minute …" Alex dragged a chair across to the open door and helped her onto it. Dawn had broken, feeble sunlight slanting across the lawns, turning the track to the house a dull red. He kneeled down at her side, "You'll breathe better here. And we'll have a couple of minutes to scram if it comes to it."

Justine downed the brandy. "They didn't take me to the Gendarmerie, if that's what you're thinking. No Pascal to the rescue this time. I got taken to some kind of barracks the other side of the village. It was dark, but the place is obviously a wireless station, masts everywhere. I was marched in behind this man Gliess. He was horribly polite, I think he believes that's what the English expect. He said he wouldn't bother interrogating me, he doubted I could add to what he already knew. His English is very good, but now he's got this wireless game going he fancies himself in French. He's a cocky bastard ... God, I've just realised he's dead."

"Renault said there were English agents there … prisoners. Is he right?"

"He gave me this lecture about how easy it was to cheat the stupid English WT people. Then he came on friendly, apologising that the English saw fit to employ women. I've seen friendly like that before, believe me. He said I was to operate under German orders, *like the others.*"

"But the other English agents: how many others?"

"I never saw them. I heard them talking the next morning. Five or six, I think, English alright. They sounded quite cheerful."

"Six? Renault said there were more."

"Gliess said I could be treated like the others … with my parole."

"He couldn't ask for that, could he? Not really ..."

"You mean given I'm not a fighting man? That didn't seem to worry him. He pulled this letter out of a drawer in a fancy desk. He's kitted the place out with bits of furniture, even carpets. Stuff looted from old grannies. Antiques. Pictures on the walls. It's a concrete air raid shelter, for God's sake! He treated this letter like it was the Magna Carta. Covered in signatures and red stamps. Told me it had been initialled by Adolf Hitler himself. He read bits of it out. Very florid German. In return for compliance, there was a guarantee of treatment as a POW. He called it a pact. He went on and on about how it was honourable, given we were under French jurisdiction and France was not at war."

"It's all nonsense. I heard about that letter. It has saved nobody. There's been an order that all irregular forces are to be shot. It's supposed to be secret but word gets round. Renault knows all about it. Agents are to be executed as spies. Gliess must have known his fancy letter was worthless."

She sat for a long time, looking at her bandaged hand, finally mumbling, "I guessed it was something like that. Everything's glued together with lies, isn't it? One lie on top of another. One thing's worth saying, though … after they'd finished with me … I must have said something they didn't know. I can't think what, but his tune changed. Everything changed. They started dismantling things. I knew I wasn't going to last long."

"You know that Renault went and pleaded for you to be spared."

"Oh, yes, it was the first thing Gliess told me. He thought it was funny. *Like an earnest schoolboy*, he said. I felt like killing him right there." She looked at him, the expression something he first saw in Torridon, defiant eyes daring him to pity her, "You surely know what *spared* means? Do you really think it needed any pleading to spare me?" She peeled his arm away, leaning back, waiting to catch her breath. "You don't have a cigarette? I'll be alright." She managed a tiny smile, "I'm sorry, my love, you're all I've got to shout at now."

Alex lit two cigarettes in his mouth, handing her one. She drew hard on it, "They'd got my set working. How could they have done that, Alex? Without the key? They had everything set up, times, frequencies, everything. I could have been in Baker Street."

"The Major showed me your first message, the one without the word *will*. With our word missing."

"I almost funked that. I'd never thought what it would do to you, getting that message. I suppose I'd been clinging to the notion I'd never need to send it. We never thought of that, did we? You'll have to forgive me. It was one thing we had between us, a sort of goodbye."

She lifted his head from her lap, cradling it, her eyes filled with tears. "I do love you, Guffin, despite your jealous looks. I suppose I always will now. In the end I sent it because I was so sure you could not come following. But you did. *Why?* No, that doesn't matter, but *how?* I thought it was impossible."

"The Major changed his mind. It was his decision. Archer was furious."

"The Major. It was not the only thing he changed his mind about.

Something really strange happened. In Baker Street he'd ordered me not to use standard capture codes, I was to send completely straight. They've got a machine now that can tell whether it's your fist that's sending. Then when I got to Castle Kennedy, it seemed he'd changed his mind. This urgent wire arrives with changed instructions - if I was sending under duress I was to use any non-standard abbreviation in the body of the message. That's why I came up with *apu*. The Jerry operator jumped on me about it, of course, but I told him it would look fishy if I spelled it out."

"I asked about *apu*. The Major just said you were always doing things like that. He said it was irritating."

"He knows that's not true, either. I've never sent anything at all before. That's why I did that course at Torridon."

"All he seemed interested in was you confirming that Simone was alive. He beat me over the head with how I'd got that wrong."

"It was Gliess who added that bit. Clever, really. He'd got one more WT operator on his books. A dead one was perfect."

"But why would the Major lie?"

"You said it yourself. He was hardly going to tell you the truth, given he wanted you out of the way as well."

"You weren't there, Justine. He was incredibly convincing. I know a bit about lying. I can't believe he was lying."

"Isn't that what you lot are paid for? No point being a bad liar, is there? But our code – the word *will* missing – he didn't know about that, did he? You didn't tell him?"

"I thought he'd veto the mission if I told him. Perhaps I was wrong … I still don't see him lying, nobody is that good."

"You haven't heard it all yet. *Lying* is too kind. After the message with *apu* had gone off, they bundled me into a little cubbyhole next to the wireless room. I guessed they were waiting for the acknowledgement from London. You know that comes back in seconds, but they took the hell of a time about it. After about a quarter of an hour, I was hauled back in. There were three of them, German WT operators, all looking at this bit of paper, a horrible tense silence in the room. Then Gliess himself came rushing in. In a dressing gown. Face like thunder, really angry, asking to look at it. He shoved it in front of me. It was *en clair*, from London, on the same frequency. Asking for confirmation *apu* signified *as per usual.* And would Arthur please avoid non-standard abbreviations."

"God almighty!"

"After that, Gliess had me back in his office. He'd got dressed. He was so deadly calm it was terrifying. The man's not normal … I think he's really insane." She stopped, suddenly solemn. "I'll tell you something: some people do deserve punishment … I really believe that. The world's better off without people like him in it. He was pacing about, cursing God and the devil, saying he couldn't believe a woman would try to trick him. Then he started pawing me, pulling at my dress. Was I real woman? A German woman would never do such a thing … and so on. As they were taking me away he called after me. Said he wasn't responsible if others were less tolerant. I knew what he meant. I could see it in his face. I was so frightened, Alex. It's my problem. I know I look solid … but all the time I'm scared stiff inside. It's been eating me away ever since I joined up."

"I'm the coward – I know what you're going to say and I want to stop you. I don't want to know."

"It's best I tell you. It's not so terrible. That way you won't go imagining. They took me to a cell downstairs. The place was just like they said it would be at Torridon – horribly dirty and cold, concrete floor. It smelled like a sewer. There was a bucket, but the floor round it was slimy with shit. A grubby little light bulb in the ceiling. No window. A sort of mattress – really filthy - on a wooden bench. I remember standing there, knowing I couldn't sleep on that thing."

Thinking of the hopeless hours in his cell in Aste, Alex felt her hand move on his head. "You remember what it's like, don't you? I don't know how long I stood like that. I began to think I was paralysed. Then I heard them coming. Two men chatting along the corridor. I thought they were bringing something to eat. They left the door open so there was light. One of them was carrying a metal cup. They weren't in uniform. They'd brought this weird smell in with them – methylated spirits, I think. This big fat bloke suddenly got his arm round me and shoved my hand down on the mattress. The other one had a pair of pliers. They were in the cup. I remember they were dripping … and this meths smell was everywhere."

As Alex raised his head she pressed him down, his face buried in her lap. "He did it so quick, Alex. As if it was nothing. Gripped the end of my nail and snapped it back. I couldn't believe it had happened. I was watching blood bubbling out of my finger and it didn't even hurt. No pain at all, just this hot feeling down my back. Then something bigger than pain. I didn't think you could hurt that much and stay alive. I was jumping up and down, trying to get out of myself. Howling. They just stood there watching me skidding about in all that slime, waving my hand, praying the bloody thing would drop off. Then the bloke with the pliers put them back in the cup and they walked out." He could feel her breath coming fast. "I'll have to stop … I'm not sure I can explain the rest."

"It's alright, Justine, it's alright. Stop. There's no need …"

"No, I've started. You haven't heard what I want to say. After they locked the door I think I fainted. Gliess must have come down later and had the cell opened. I was lying on my side across this bench thing looking up. I remember seeing him there in his shiny uniform, with a handkerchief over his face, like I was something in a dog kennel. I was taken back to his room. Propped up in front of his desk. He apologised for the injury – that's how he put it, *the injury*. Then he said the business with the transmission was a shooting offence."

As Alex lifted his head she raised her bandaged hand, arresting him. "I know what you're going to say. *Make silence your only goal.* All that Torridon stuff. That book wasn't written for me, I know that now. Stuck there with Gliess in his horrible little fake *salon* it didn't make sense. I felt sick. Then I really did throw up, all over his carpet. I think I fainted again. Crumpled up. Nothing in the book about that."

"It's the book that's wrong."

"When I came round, some poor Corporal with a bucket was wiping up sick. They'd put a sheet over a chair and got me into it. Gliess was mauling me about, slapping me, not hard, more like I was a naughty little girl. On my backside. There was this excited look on his face … aroused … you know. He kept saying I must do what he wanted. A horrible sing-song Daddy voice. I didn't understand what he was on about at first, whispering in my ear I was going to obey or a nail would be removed from my hands. One every ten minutes. He made it sound like some kind of medical operation. Something he could watch. The ten minute interval was because I might die of shock. Then these same men came in again, and that awful antiseptic smell."

"Barbaric stupidity. There's no need … Christ, there's drugs … you can get information. You can get anything you want. They know that."

"Of course there's no need. That's what he wanted."

"Hurting, you mean?"

"It's more complicated than that. He wanted to deal with the aftermath. I knew what was at the end of that road."

"Your L tablet, Justine. Didn't you …?"

"You know why. I left it at Castle Kennedy. It's funny – even when I was praying they'd do me in, I knew I couldn't have done it myself. I left it behind, all the same. To be on the safe side. It's a mortal sin, Alex, don't you know that? No … you don't know, do you? Eternal death. Better be punished here than face that. It's alright, my love, you don't have to understand. I don't understand myself – that's why I left it behind."

She had stopped. A small bird had started up somewhere near the door, an echoing wintry song. He strained to listen for the sound of a car. Renault was dreadfully late. For the first time in many months Alex felt at peace. He would not be leaving her here. She surely knew that. It was enough to be together. *Faithful unto death*, was that not the phrase? Enough to be together, watching the dark line of the woods.

"What makes us so sure we'd never betray a friend, Alex?" She was weeping, tears falling openly across her face. "It's the easiest thing in the world. I suppose that was my punishment. *The punishment of Judas* – you see? One kiss too many … you never understand that until it's your turn to do the kissing. You're not going to make me explain, are you? It's too hard to say ... about us. Once I'd started, even Gliess seemed surprised. I told him everything."

"It's not betrayal if he already knew it. You said that yourself. You can't call that betrayal."

"That's your friend Cabot talking. Saying clever things doesn't alter anything, Alex. I told him all I knew. I let him kill me inside because I was terrified of being hurt again."

Remembering *her name is Justine Perry*, Alex felt her tears running unheeded down her face. He drew her close against him.

"Stop now. Please stop. Please don't go on. Stop for us, please."

"But that's what I'm saying. I gave them us. My poor little Guffin. I gave them you. Gave them our pathetic little code … the word *will* … everything. Colonel Archer, Captain Vere, Mr Cabot, and so on. When I said your name I thought of that hotel. You talking about love. And now every time I kiss you … I was starting to believe in the future … stupid … but I really did believe. It was like killing us, both of us. Killing everybody I'd ever known. Killing the children I'll never have. God knows how long I went on for. I was desperate not to forget something, leave somebody out. Gliess had to stop me. He told them to take me to the ablution block and put me in a hot bath. I was to be put in a room in the Officers' Block. A room with a bed."

They sat for a long time huddled together, staring through the open door, a violet sky hanging low over the line of the trees. A light rain had started up, pattering on the leaves, nothing very much. Somewhere far away, dogs were barking. Alex looked at his watch thinking it a mercy that hopes faded so gently. Renault was not coming: certainty slipping away like a retreating tide.

"I know why you were sent here, Justine. Why we both ended up here. If you were captured, they had all the proof they needed that the Columbine circuit really was dead. And that's all they wanted to know. You're a justified sacrifice. I once heard Archer use that term."

"*They*? Who's they?"

"Does it matter? Perhaps that's what always happens when you start calling people agents. We're just proxy people. Once they have you, you're not really a person any more. That code the Major gave you was always going to be one-way. The message told him all he needed to know. You're a sacrifice worth paying. I can just hear somebody saying it at one of those interminable meetings. Pompous statements of regret for the necessary deception. Somebody will come up with *brave young woman* or some such pious claptrap. They might all stand up for a minute looking solemn. They do that sometimes if it's a woman. Then that's it, back to their war. God, I despise the lot of them! As for me - getting me back here was the surest way of never seeing me again, short of murdering me - and they weren't going to risk that again. Anyway, *killed in action* is a neater way of closing the account. I might have got a medal."

"But you're not dead, are you Alex? Pascal is right, you've not called in and the men in the wireless station don't know your call sign and won't risk faking it, not with Gliess out of the way. Pascal is right, the RAF will run your pickup. They will have had the order days ago and there's been no reason to cancel it." She tried to look at his watch, "You'd better get going."

"D'you know what my orders were? *Make contact with Simone.* Cynical bastards."

"What time is it, my love?"

He put his arm round her, pulling her close,

"He's a bit late. Nothing serious. The French are always late."

Twenty-Three

They let themselves be herded through sheeting rain to a broad arch of corrugated steel. Animated clumps of men in blue were sheltering in the mouth of the hanger around trestle tables, trading jokes like schoolboys.

At the desk in the far corner Alex faced a pair of dead eyes: civilian clothes, steel-rimmed glasses. "Mrs Perry here needs somewhere to rest, can you fix that? She's not too good."

The spectacles turned to Justine, perhaps hoping for some response, they didn't get many women here. Something in the expression that met his own made him look away.

"They put fighters up over the coast." Alex remembered a stream of obscenities as the pilot corkscrewed blindly into cloud, thick cords of rain whipping the cockpit. He tried to master the tremble in his voice: "Ours, thank God. I don't think they knew who the hell we were."

"Christ! You were on that Lysander? Landed crab fashion. Still you were lucky to have the rain ... nothing but bloody rain here."

Alex thought it better not to speak, his jaw frozen. There was something wrong with his left arm, rattling against the wooden ledge of the counter. "*Lucky*," he got the word out, "yes, I suppose so."

A hideous stink of burnt rubber had blown into the hangar. Justine at his side retching, murmuring, "God, I'm going to be sick."

"We were to be met."

The man strained forward to catch the words, "*Met?* What name?"

Alex glanced at the soaked trousers wrapped round his legs, knowing this interrogation would draw him back into a hopeless world of paper. He felt unbearably vulnerable.

"Archer, I would think." If anyone was to meet them, it would surely be Archer. You couldn't see Cabot finding his way past the gate. "Yes, Colonel Archer. It'll be him."

"Unit?"

"You can hardly miss him, he stands out, rather. He'll have come down this morning."

"That narrows it down nicely, squire. Do you have any idea how many …? No, you don't, do you?" He threw a weary grimace to draw Justine in, "You alright Miss? Sit down over there, take the weight off. A unit really would help, sir."

Alex looked past him to a varnished wooden door incongruously bolted into the metalwork, "Perhaps if you asked …"

"Archer, you say? We don't go by names. Mostly it's numbers. But we've logged the flight in. I don't suppose …?" A slow shake of the head, "No, I suppose you don't. What name?"

"I just told you, Archer."

"No, your name. And you're together?"

"This is Mrs Perry. I'm Alex Vere. Captain Vere. Our pickup must have been logged out."

The man shook his head, "*Pickup*? Not from here it wasn't. Not that Lysander."

"No, you could be right. Perhaps it wasn't. My unit's TPSU. I'm attached to that. No, that's not quite right." There was an exasperated release of breath, as the man let his pencil fall. "I mean, I'm not currently with the TPSU. Okay, forget all that. I'm part of Colonel Archer's outfit, that should do the trick."

"Archer … Archer …" He pulled a thick sheaf of stapled papers from a drawer, and started running a pencil slowly down a column on the first page.

"Nothing issued to an Archer ... No, sorry, I'm a liar ... correction, what about this one? *Lt Colonel Neville Archer, MC*. That him?" He frowned at the paper as Alex nodded. “It says *Second Directorate.* What’s that when it’s at home?”

“I’m sorry. I can’t help you.”

“No contact details. Nothing. There wouldn’t be.” He dismissed the pile of paper. “And you’re to be with him? That’s the two of you?”

“I’m being transferred. Is all this necessary? If you’ll just find him ...”

“Right-ho, old boy. Homing in on that task.” He began pulling sheets of yellow paper from a spike. “That’s back to yesterday. Your Archer’s not logged in, meaning he’s not here. He can’t be. We do know who’s here, you understand?”

Something indefinable in the taut expression facing him made him relent, “Okey-dokey, I’ll see whether the Winco is free.” He waved an arm into the blue haze of empty air, “Park yourselves over there, I’ll go looking.”

They sat together on a battered sofa pushed against the wall, leatherette arms punctured with cigarette burns like black wounds. Justine slumped back, her body flaccid, eyes closed. Since the landing something seemed to have snapped inside her: something had gone. She seemed barely alive.

There was a Christmas copy of *The Beano* on the seat. Alex had watched a man in uniform abandon it, hurrying off to join the voices echoing down the distant metal corridors. He picked it up. A picture of kids dancing round a huge flaming plum pudding, a girl in a brown dress, the edges snipped to make her look vaguely elfin.

A tiny plane screamed past the mouth of the hangar, teetering against the wind. The rain had stopped. On the far side of the field a little bleak sunlight sparkled through wet leaves. The plane gone, the place was eerily quiet: apparently no war today.

A door behind the desk pushed open, a man in uniform leaning out. He seemed disappointed they were still there.

“Sorry to keep you.” He came round the counter, hand outstretched, “It’s Captain Vere, isn’t it? We watched you in. The Wing Commander’s apologies. He doesn’t know your Colonel. TPSU was new to us. Bedford Square, that right? He says there’s a story about that, but you’ll know, of course. Yes, we can lay on some transport. There’s a car going in about an hour.” He glanced down at Justine asleep, cradling the grubby bandage in her other hand, his voice suddenly softer, "She won't mind sharing with RAF types, will she?"

After he'd gone, Alex walked to the mouth of the hanger, feeble sunlight throwing long shadows across the grass. A row of red fire buckets hung under a *No Smoking* sign. He lit a cigarette.

Justine's head had fallen onto the pock-marked arm of the sofa. She was breathing quietly, drawing in the tainted air that had defined her life for more months than he could remember. Marking her out for death in a cause neither of them would ever be permitted to know. He walked to stand over her, keeping guard, wondering whether she was dreaming of liberation.

Liberation, when it arrived, was predictably banal: a gleaming Citroen hearse progressing majestically up the drive to the safe house, like God's last joke. Pascal Renault, newly shaved, eased himself out of the driver's seat, pausing to light a cigar, standing a moment to survey the house.

He helped Justine onto the polished leather, answering the question on her desperate face with a single laconic, "As you see."

He stayed with them after they reached the field, scanning the sky, waiting on the narrow path, thin rain dripping through bare trees.

It took them unawares: the cough of an engine like the sound of a shotgun in the trees, feathered props fluttering suddenly too close, a humming suck of air, wings dropping to the grass.

Renault watched Alex clamber awkwardly aboard, peeling off his gloves to take Justine's hand. She let him slip her arms into his overcoat, rising tiptoe to brush a kiss against his face as he leaned close to catch her words.

The Lysander was already moving as Renault strode back to the hearse.

It was late afternoon when the promised transport reached the TPSU. Milky white water smelling of Dettol puddled down the steps onto the pavement. Four neat holes in the brickwork was all that remained of the plaque at the foot of the stairwell. A man in uniform at the top of the stairs stopped whistling. Khaki puttees over huge spit-polished ammunition boots clumping heavily down to meet them.

"Can I come up?" Alex had never seen him before.

"I'm not sure as you can. There's nobody here. You're not the van, are you? I'm waiting for a van."

"Removal van, you mean? What's all this about? Is Mr Cabot in?"

"Nobody in, mate. His room was done yesterday. The amount of stuff ... books … like a bloody library. Anyway, he's not here."

"Colonel Archer then. I won't be long."

"Take as long as you like, he's not here either. Like I keep telling you, nobody's here. They've all gone. And don't ask where. I haven't the foggiest."

Alex peered up into the stairwell, nodding for Justine to stay where she was. "I'm Captain Vere. I work here."

"Sir ..." The voice was suddenly resentful, "Sorry, sir … didn't appreciate … you not being in uniform. Well, you'll know then …"

"Alright, Corporal. Look, there's your van. I'll just have a quick look round."

Alex shouldered past him, running up the stairs.

Cabot's room smelled of damp and old tobacco. The familiar battered desk had been left sizing up the narrow doorframe, its drawers, stripped of linings and stacked in towers on the floor. Everything else had gone. There was something obsessive about the depredation: even scraps of newspaper had been torn from their pins. Cinders lay scattered over the floor where the fireplace had been raked out.

At the end of the corridor, the door to *Records* had been taken off, square patterns in the dust all that remained of the line of cabinets. There was a pile of spent matches on the floor.

Odd to think he had been standing in this cramped little space, when was it …? Not so many days past, a tide of Archer's fury sweeping over him. Archer, the old soldier playing spies, not knowing his adversary had written the rules of the game.

Perhaps old soldier's games always ended like that, with nothing much to show for the effort. Certainly there was nothing to show here: everything gone. Not that *everything* had ever amounted to much.

How easily they had been duped, even Cabot, for all his intelligence. Tricking out this dusty corridor said all you needed to know. How many agents had ended up in a stinking cell in Auch at the whim of old soldier Archer? Would they have thought it worthwhile? How could anyone in their right mind have been deceived by all this ham-fisted nonsense?

The Corporal, banging along the bare floor, seemed startled by the sudden flush of anger as Alex turned to face him.

"Beg pardon, sir, they say as how they have to dismantle the desk … if you don't mind. And I ought to get your names, sir. The lady downstairs as well. If you would …"

"Do you know where this stuff is going?"

The guileless face turned towards him had seen off better than Alex.

"I can't say as I do, sir." He gave a little deprecatory shrug, "Orders are to secure the place once cleared. Lock up, you know."

"Where are you to take the key?"

He grinned. "No key, sir. I'm to slam the front door."

Alex returned the smile, starting off down the staircase, calling back: "The name's Captain Vere, Corporal. You'd better write it down. For when you report back."

"That's alright, sir. I'll remember."

"Report back where, exactly?"

"Couldn't really say, sir, I'm to go with the van." He tossed Alex a final bone, "Not far, though, I wouldn't think, not at this time of day. I reckon we'll be settled before the blackout."

It took all night to reach Oxford, the last train from Paddington moving in spasmodic jerks, finally coming to rest in open country. Justine had slipped into a deep sleep, passengers leaning over her crumpled body to watch the undersides of clouds flaring dull red in the distant sky.

They were shunted into Oxford station at first light on Sunday morning. The Refreshment Room was closed.

Not so The Queen's College, its huge oak gates pushed in to offer a cold glimpse of immemorial grass, less trim than usual, a grudging concession to a war that had otherwise passed it by. A board leaned against a trestle outside the vacant Porter's Lodge, the time of Morning Eucharist scrawled in chalk.

Justine stood in the stone tunnel letting a biting wind catch her hair. "I think I'll go. I suppose I'm allowed? Would you mind?"

"Go where? We only have to find his staircase."

"You can go looking, he's your friend. I'm going to the service. Ages since I went to church."

"You'll be awfully early."

"I'll wait." She squeezed his arm, "It's alright Alex, I'm not running away. If you can't find your chum, come and sit next to me. We'll listen to the sermon together. It'll do you good."

He found Cabot bent over a tea chest just inside his room, fishing books out, mumbling titles, adding them to towers ranged behind him across the floor. His door was flung back. Hearing the timid tap, he looked up, darting a glance beyond Alex into the darkened hallway, the smile a little awkward.

"Alex! My dear chap! Like the proverbial bad penny. I was just thinking about you. I knew you'd end up here. Late, of course, but then, you're always late."

"You don't know the half of it. I've been searching for a familiar face ever since we got back. What on earth's going on? I'm so pleased you're here. Well, aren't you going to ask me in? It's alright, I can jump over."

Cabot, stepped back to make room. He seemed vaguely embarrassed, "Of course. In you come. My humble abode."

"I was beginning to think I was a character in one of those stupid modern plays – you know, that I'd invented everybody and now they'd started to slip my mind and disappear."

Cabot managed a half-smile, shaking his head, "No, Alex, you didn't invent me, perish the thought. Find yourself a chair, old man.

I'm unpacking … hateful task … almost finished. Make yourself comfortable."

Alex made his way to the window, looking down onto the grass.

"You knew I'd be coming? How's that? I mean, how could you know?"

Cabot was dipping low into the tea chest, his voice muffled, "Oh, I got wind you were on your way."

"But got wind how?"

He stood up, easing his back, his face flushed from stooping, "How did I hear, you mean? Oh, the usual tom-toms. Drums along the river." The smile, always a little uncertain, had evaporated, "Forgive me Alex, I'd better not say. You know how it is?" He glanced at the open door, "Mrs Perry? She with you?"

"Justine? No secret about that. She's in your Chapel. Morning Service."

"My word …" inexplicably relieved, Cabot pushed the door to, turning a long silent scrutiny onto Alex, warily seeing the place through his visitor's eyes, gauging an opening gambit.

Junior Fellows seemed to do themselves surprisingly well: Cabot's rooms were furnished in bachelor style, overstuffed armchairs on either side of an unlit fire. Faded Persian rugs showed just enough of wide polished floorboards. Heavy figured panelling was picked out in black and gold, paintings hung against the wood - uncomfortable modern things he felt he should recognise. The desk faced a window, deep stone mullions framing diamonds of thick glass. The surface was empty apart from a pile of unopened letters and a tall bottle, uncorked. Three glasses were set out on a silver tray.

Cabot stayed with his back to the door. "About Kessler …" immediately changing tack and walking to the desk, "rude of me, I should have asked. I've opened a bottle, something to drink the New Year in. To think, it's 1943 tomorrow. Anyway, a homecoming for me … and you, of course. Hock. Would you like some? Or fake coffee? I'll have to make it, but I don't mind. Sorry it's so cold in here, my devout scout's idea, apparently the Almighty has set his canon against fires on Sunday. The things you learn in Oxford. Do sit down, old man, you're looming rather."

He poured the drinks, taking his own back to the window, staring into the quadrangle, a beam of dusty sunlight catching his face, softening it. He held up a hand as if he had somehow conjured the deep diapason of the organ from the distant chapel.

"He must be rehearsing. It's Buxtehude, I think. Majestic stuff. I rather envy Mrs Perry."

"I'm sorry. I didn't think. Do go if you want to. I'll come as well."

"Not me, old boy. I've a superstitious horror of sacred places, always have had. I think it's the idea of being secretly watched."

He seemed to make his mind up to something, turning to face Alex. "Yes, Kessler. Funny how all that business turned out."

"Because he ended up dead, you mean? Not all that funny for him."

"You know what I mean."

"Actually, I don't, not really. It's why I'm here. We have to talk. I feel complicit in that Kessler affair. I don't know how much you know, but we've been taken for fools. I know it's hard to credit, but *Operation Alathea* was changed at the last minute. God knows who by, but whoever it was decided we didn't deserve to know. Archer is nowhere to be found. He's vanished. Shut up shop. I'm not going to drop it, you know. I'll go over his head if I need to. We don't owe him anything."

The sunlight framing Cabot against the window had converted him to a black silhouette, patiently sipping wine, the rim of his glass twinkling yellow, waiting for Alex to finish. A clock outside in the quadrangle began to beat slow asynchronous chimes, the order not quite right.

"The plan wasn't changed, Alex." He was tracing patterns on the misted window with his fingertip, his voice barely audible, "This operation you talk about. At least, not in essence. I thought you knew. The idea was that his parachute would fail. That was always the plan. Surely you realised? Kessler did."

"The thought crossed my mind. Archer's insane enough to think of something like that. But that would have been murder."

"You're sounding a trifle gothic this morning. We're soldiers aren't we? Well, you certainly are. And I suppose I am, in a manner of speaking. Soldiers kill people on their field of battle – it's what they're for. Anyway, the failing parachute is academic. The problem went away."

"That's a bit cold blooded. I thought you liked Kessler. And you're suddenly sounding very well informed. You're not suggesting his dying was intentional?"

"Drug overdose wasn't it? Not my ticket, old man, more your province. I suppose accidents happen. All I'm saying is, given it was deemed Kessler had to arrive dead, somebody brought his death about. Let's be grateful for small mercies. If that's cold blooded, so be it."

He stood holding his glass by its foot, idly gazing through the window, letting a long embarrassed silence fall into the room. It came to Alex how much he resented this violation of his private world. Apparently the camaraderie of the TPSU, always a little asymmetric, did not travel as far as Oxford.

He came across to where Alex sat, standing over him, an irritated edge to his voice. "I'll tell you what he was carrying, if you like. Is that what you came to hear? Incidentally, why *did* you come? It's early for a social call."

"What d'you mean, *tell me?* I know perfectly well what he was carrying: all that fake junk about German resistance. You can hardly make a mystery of what we were up to. You know, it came to me coming down here on the train today. What we we've been up to. You only have to get away a bit to see it in perspective. None of it would fool a child."

Cabot had slipped into the other armchair, friendly at last. "You're a nice chap Alex. You know, I didn't realise until this minute, just how nice. Scout's honour, I really did think you knew. And now I'm going to feel bad, because apparently not so. Kessler didn't take our Steffle stuff. That was all smoke for prying eyes. Honestly, I thought you knew. The operation involved something altogether different."

"*Different?* How different? And how come John Cabot knew? How come you, and not me? How do you imagine that makes me feel?"

"Left out?" A yelp of a laugh was instantly cancelled. He took his spectacles off, polishing them with a handkerchief, a tiny apologetic gesture.

"Sorry, Alex, that was a low blow. This place makes one waspish. It was unworthy. I take it back. *Betrayed*, I suppose. Then again, that's an ugly word. Let's settle for *let down*. But we've all been let down one way or another in this business, haven't we? Look at Archer, not a clue, poor devil. All those blind rages wasted on the desert air. Incidentally, I haven't the faintest idea where he's got to."

"You were right first time - *left out* will do perfectly well. And the TPSU? I was there yesterday."

Cabot said nothing.

"I was with Kessler – his body - on the flight down to Metz. Since you seem to know everything, I suppose you heard they got us out of France, I mean both of us. The situation there is unbelievable. D'you know what's going on?"

"Rather a generalisation, old chap. Can you be a bit more specific?"

"Sorry, I'm fagged out. Bear with me. I mean who changed the plan? Is that specific enough?"

"*Changed* – that's a loaded word, Alex. What our lawyer friends call leading. I'm not talking about changing things, you are."

He was back at the window, looking down into the quadrangle. "When they recruited us I was given orders to divulge nothing to a living soul." He whirled round, "The same for you - correct?"

Alex returned his stare, "I suppose so. No need to make a drama out of it. I suppose it would have mattered if we'd had anything to divulge in the first place."

"I'm serious, Alex, deadly serious. I do as I'm told. Didn't you notice that trait? Until a few minutes ago I thought we'd both been playing the same game, neither of us letting on. You were so damned good at it. All that world-weary stuff about being left out of the scheme of things … I thought it was for my benefit. I was quite jealous. You and your lost memory! Priceless. Alright, I was wrong ..."

"*They* recruited us. Who's *they*? You mean Archer? I was recruited by Archer."

"So you were, Alex … in a manner of speaking … so you were. And you never thought to ask who recruited Archer?"

"No I didn't. Is that such a lapse? Archer's bad enough. Are you going to explain? Or would that be breaking another sacred oath?"

"And now you're getting angry with me. Please don't. The whole operation's probably dead anyway, thanks to you. Or thanks to the indestructible Mrs Perry at her prayers.

He crossed the room and went out into the hallway, standing head cocked, in the panelled gloom of the corridor, listening. Finally satisfied, he stepped back inside, pulling the outer oak closed, his expression a kind of harassed embarrassment, the eternally gracious host saddled with the wrong sort of guest. Finding his way barred by an open tea chest he plucked a book out, turning it over and over in his hands, sensing the tension in the room.

"Alright, I'll explain, if you insist."

Twenty-Four

"You won't believe me, old man, but I'm at a loss as to where to start. For heaven's sake, why the long face? We're still friends, aren't we? Let's not fall out over this. About this war we're all fighting, as good a place to start as any. Haven't you noticed it's pretty well lost, Alex?"

Cabot had always been a little inclined to talk down. It was worse now: he had taken on a strange air of proprietorial superiority. Alex wondered whether he had always been beaten over the head with his own name like this. He could not remember.

"No, I haven't noticed, John, old man." He watched Cabot's eyes widen, "High strategy's a bit out of our league isn't it? If you learn one thing in Bedford Square it's that this war isn't really our affair. We'll have to wait to see who wins, if they bother to tell us. Meanwhile, we do what we're ordered."

"There, you put your finger on it." Cabot perched himself warily on the edge of a hard chair by the desk, keeping his distance. "We're ordered to tell lies. You can't be selective about lies: *Lie to one, lie to all*, as the saying goes." "People are going to look back and say that was the defining spirit of our age, our *Zeitgeist* - a time to tell lies. Take that cover story for Kessler, his sickly childhood and so on. You knew it was nonsense right off, didn't you. I remember you had dozens of reasons it couldn't work. What changed your mind?"

"Actually, you did."

"Are you sure, Alex? Perhaps you didn't want to face the truth. Didn't inventing Herr Steffle take your mind off what you knew was really going to happen to Hauptmann Kessler? Or is that me playing the psychologist?" He checked, frowning slightly, lips silently rehearsing a phrase. Words, when they finally arrived, spilled out in a rush, "Truth is, Alex, we planned for Kessler to be carrying maps."

"And who's this *we* you keep on about? This isn't about us, is it? You've been playing some kind of double game on the side. Deceiving me - is that what you're saying?"

Alex knew the question was idle. That morning, walking alongside Justine through echoing Oxford streets, a prayer had been beating in his head: *Let it not be Cabot. Not the only one I trusted. Let it not be him.* In truth, he was here only for confirmation.

Cabot solemnly regarded him: the gentle perfect scholar, smooth ingenuous face, the expression no more than a little awry. "Deceiving you? Well, you could put it that way. Mind you, deceiving Alex Vere isn't exactly the alpha and omega of the business. Why the resentful tone? You said it yourself – we're under orders."

He seemed to make up his mind about something, lowering himself deeper into the chair, leaning forward. "I'll be perfectly frank ... well, as frank as I can be. The plan was that maps would be planted on Kessler's body. Maps. Nothing else."

"*Maps*? What maps? No, wait a minute, how could you know it was going to be a body? That Kessler would be dead?"

"How you do harp on about that. It's tiresome, you're beginning to sound like Miss Marple. All I was told was that the matter would be arranged. And it was arranged. As for the maps ..." His face suddenly dissolved into a curious tentative smile, the proud schoolboy up for his prize, "The landing site for an eventual invasion of Northern France. Disposition of forces, lines of supply, the lot. The best I've seen Portland Place come up with. An incredible job."

Cabot smiled, opening his hands, a weary little *nothing to declare* gesture: "So there you are, now you know."

It was difficult not to return the smile. Alex felt a surge of embarrassed relief, blushing for Cabot's naiveté. "Come on, John, don't tell me Archer sold you his version of the Haversack Ruse? He tried it on with me. He's at least one war too late for that game."

"Colonel Meinertzhagen and his devilishly cunning deception. Interesting chap. I've met him. I wonder whether he really did it. Perhaps it doesn't matter, it's such a good story."

"Well nobody's going to fall for it twice, that's obvious. Honestly, you let Archer get to you. Too many hours in the museum, that's your problem ..."

Alex found his effort at a conciliatory laugh turning false. There was something unsettling about Cabot's impassive calm. "I'm sorry, I'm not mocking, really - it's just that for a minute I thought you were serious. It won't be the quality of the printing Jerry will be thinking about when they find Kessler. The idea's typical Archer - barking mad. Only an idiot would be taken in."

Cabot waited with exaggerated patience for Alex to finish, staring into the fireplace, perhaps wondering whether to put a match to it. When he looked up, his expression was a kind of bleak exasperation, honed through numberless hours with struggling undergraduates. He glanced at the place on his sleeve where his watch might have been visible.

"Not *completely* mad, Alex. But you do put it awfully well. As you say, only an idiot ..." He reached out to gather the empty glasses. "You know, I think this stuff is rather good. Would you like some more?"

Alex stared dumbly at the convoluted pattern of the rug at his feet, feeling strangely outmanoeuvred. "But you do see it's completely barmy? A German officer kitted out for a landing at sea in the middle of a field."

Footsteps clattered along the corridor outside, loitering at the door, apparently drawn to the sound of their voices. Cabot raised one hand, waiting long seconds until someone shuffled noisily away. The bang of a heavy distant door echoed shut.

"My shadow ... I do wish it would desist." He grimaced. "Speaking of idiots, Alex, that was your definition of Colonel Archer if I recall correctly."

"The man's a fool."

"No, *idiot* does perfectly well. Our flamboyant Colonel provides an endless source of merriment for spies from Whitechapel to Mayfair. All those watching eyes."

He settled into the armchair opposite Alex, patience finally exhausted. "For heaven's sake, you're not usually so slow. For months the German High Command has been asking why we're still hanging on. We do read their signals traffic, you know." He tapped Alex on the knee, harder than necessary, beating the words as he spoke, "You understand? You understand?"

Alex wriggled back, "Understand what, for heaven's sake?"

"Their Intelligence people have concluded we really are irredeemably stupid. You understand the consequences?"

His puffy face was tight with satisfaction, a slight sheen on his skin: the tutor giving the struggling pupil one final chance to leap the humiliating gap. Alex felt sick.

"You could have explained without all that rigmarole. And I'm not slow, just bloody tired. I've been on a train all night. Yes, I see what you're getting at. Whatever arrives in the briefcase defines itself as false – is that the idea? Not deception - cover."

"Hole in one, old man! I knew you'd get there. Here, I'll top you up."

"And this was really Archer's idea? It sounds too clever-clever for him."

"Nothing to do with Archer," Cabot sounded irritated, "and it is clever. It's given us the perfect channel."

"*Us* again?"

"Sorry, you know I can't say who. I've already said far too much. You can't expect me to be entirely frank."

"You never have been, have you? All that stuff about the short-sighted German scholar. What else isn't true? Look at this place. Is this how Junior Fellows live?"

"Well I *am* short-sighted." Cabot allowed himself a faint self-deprecating smile, "And I do claim to be a German scholar, you know. Quite a sound one, as a matter of fact. Did you never think to check?"

He was leaning forward now, the flowery scent of hock on his breath, his tone curiously intense. "We've another drop next moon.

Same idea. French maps this time. And it's going to work. They'll think they know what we want them to believe …"

"And flag it as disinformation?"

"Of course! The most cack-handed transparent disinformation you can imagine. Irredeemably stupid. If the claim is we're landing for certain at a certain place, the only sensible conclusion is *anywhere but there*. We've had the army types on it. It could be worth a Division if Jerry swallows the bait. That's ten thousand men in the wrong place. Gold, Alex, pure gold. And he will swallow it, he will."

You could almost smell the triumph on his skin.

Alex got up, feeling like a cheated lover. From now on, humiliation was always going to have the cold foxy smell of this room about it. He looked round, wondering whether he'd brought anything with him.

"I think I'll be off. See whether Justine's service has finished."

"But you can't go, you've barely arrived. Stay for lunch. Oxford's safe enough. I heard the other day that the Führer intends to settle here. He says he won't bomb us if we won't bomb Heidleburg. He gets the better of that deal, I must say."

"I suppose I shouldn't ask who told you. I shouldn't have come, I can see that. I thought you could help with something. One more thing I was wrong about."

Cabot followed him across to the window, standing alongside, peering down into the quadrangle. "Bear up, Alex. It doesn't suit you, all this hurt pride. What do you want me to say? That I'm sorry we misled you? Well, I'm damned if I will. It wasn't in my power to disabuse you, you know that perfectly well. Do stay. Can't have you standing outside in the rain nursing your grievances. The Service hasn't even started. You're perfectly safe here. Mrs P knows where you are."

When he grinned like that he was the old Cabot again. Alex remembered watching him on all fours like a plump baby crawling across his giant map. Feeling a condescending arm on his shoulder he flinched away.

"I'll stand in the rain if I feel like it. And why *safe*? Why shouldn't I be safe? You surely don't think I'm going to give your game away? Not everyone's made that way, you know." Intending to sound angry, Alex realised he sounded merely infantile. "I'd better go, I wouldn't want to be in your way. You have your next drop to think about. Another prisoner, is it? How are you going to arrange for this one to be dead?"

Cabot stared at him, rabbit eyes blinking behind heavy lenses. "It's unfortunate, you taking it this way. I didn't appreciate you were so touchy. What can I say? The other briefcases won't involve personnel if that's what's pricking your conscience."

"Nothing to do with *my* conscience. How am I supposed to take it? Months and months we worked together on one insane project after another, all the time you going behind my back, knowing I was wasting my time."

"And now you really are angry. But it's not true you were wasting your time. The TPSU will get the credit, after all. In as much as you were - how shall I put this? - a necessary decoy, not wasted at all."

"I'm meant to be consoled by that?" Alex heard his voice fail to echo from book-lined walls. He felt impotent. "A bloody *decoy*!"

"A little humiliating I grant - not a role I'd like myself - but not wasted effort. That French setup in Duke Street is riddled with German spies. You've been watched ever since Archer brought you back from that hospital."

"But you're not working for Archer, are you? Who *are* you working for? Can't you say? That's surely not a state secret."

"Isn't it?"

"Oh, it's not so hard to guess. Isn't it obvious? The Major …"

The laugh, when it came, was an infuriated bark. "I know damn-all about your Major. Apart from the fact he's an infernal nuisance and has some weird personal agenda of his own. You know he's chased me down here? Keeps leaving his card at the lodge like some Victorian suitor. That was him at the door just now. Thank God for the porter - I am resolved to be not at home. I suppose he's found out I organised that damned explosion. The one that went wrong."

Standing close, Alex could see a purple smudge of tiny broken veins under his eyes. He looked desperately tired.

"I'm employed to deceive people. Apparently I'm good at it, that's why I was picked. Rather wounding, as a matter of fact – it makes me feel cheap. Go if you want to. Please yourself. What did you come for, anyway? What do you want?"

"That explosion. It was meant for Justine, wasn't it?"

Cabot stepped back. "Not you as well? People endlessly going on about one little pop in a field. For God's sake, *yes*. The answer's yes. Are you satisfied now? And what's more, the local people had good reasons for doing it."

"Good, but completely false. She would have died for nothing at all. For a lie."

"The fog of war, Alex, the fog of war. Why go on about it? As I said, she's a lucky woman."

"I suppose you know the Major's brother was killed in that car?"

Cabot stared at him, startled, "No … no, I didn't know that ... His brother, you say? How did that come about? No, I didn't know. How could I know that? Now that is unfortunate ..."

Alex followed him as he retreated to his armchair, standing over him. "*Unfortunate.* Is that all you can say? It's bad enough you're responsible, do you have to humiliate the poor devil into the bargain?"

"That's nonsense."

"Is it? How do you think you'll feel when you discover somebody's been pulling *your* strings? It's always somebody like you, isn't it? Always some bastard who knows better. You know why I came here, don't you?"

Cabot gave a momentary flinch of distaste as a fleck of spittle caught his cheek. "My dear chap, of course I know. You wanted to play catch-the-spy. You had your doubts about the good Major and now I've dispelled them, all at once he's a poor devil. So you turn to me. I'm right aren't I? Do you really think this is a job for a psychologist? Not exactly your *metier* is it?"

"There's no need to sneer. You don't know bloody everything. You deserve a few home truths. Other people have died on account of your pathetic cack-handed meddling in the Columbine circuit. Real people. And for nothing. You realise they could have killed Justine for no reason at all? I'm not surprised the Major's looking for you. How long do you think you can avoid him? I know what I'd do in his shoes."

"Oh, I think I'll survive." Cabot leaned back, hands steepled, "You were going to explain what I don't know? These home truths. Do tell.

Is it a long story? Are you cold? Shall I light the fire? I can make an exception."

Alex ignored him, "Do you know how many missions we've deployed in the South West?"

"Missions? Are we to talk about missions? No, I don't know that. Twenty perhaps."

"What you don't know is that while you've been going behind my back playing with briefcases, every mission has failed. Agents dropped to reception committees have been arrested on the spot. Even those dropped blind have been picked up in a matter of hours. The last was Justine. She was arrested at the drop site. I was intended for the same trap."

"Yet you say she is here in the Chapel. And you are here with her. You do both seem to lead charmed lives. But yes, of course I know some agents are sending under duress. It's unavoidable. Why do you think we spend so much effort detecting it? You're not saying I'm responsible?"

"Of course you're not responsible. You have no idea what's been going on. And it's not *some* agents, the Gestapo are working all our sets in Saint Aunix. There's a WT station there doing nothing else. And I'll tell you something else you don't know. The resistance groups we've been supplying in the South West are fakes. They don't exist. We've been dropping supplies straight into German hands for months. It's a catastrophe."

"Alex, my dear chap, captured agents have been turned for years."

"I'm not talking about that. Somebody's been helping them on their way. When Justine Perry was arrested she transmitted a capture code, one she was expressly ordered to use if she was sending under duress. You know what London did? Queried the code over an insecure channel, *en clair.* Whoever did that signed her death warrant. What name would you use for whoever did that?"

"What do you mean, *expressly ordered*?"

"She got an order about the code by wire just before take-off. From the Major."

"You know, Alex, I find that rather hard to believe. Are you sure the Major sent it? Are you really sure?"

Cabot left the question lying in the silence between them, the faint smile on his earnest face striking Alex like a blow. For a moment the room appeared smaller than it should be, tumbled piles of books leering at him. Suddenly, it seemed there was not enough air in this cold place for both of them.

Twenty-Five

It was some time before Cabot spoke, leaning his head back against the leather of the armchair, head cocked to one side, the familiar moue almost an apology. "Why do you think I was against Mrs Perry going back to France, Alex?"

His name again, mutating into an assurance that he was wrong about something. Had always been wrong, fatally wrong.

"Justine? Were you against her going? Perhaps you were, I don't remember. What's it to do with you, anyway?" Annoyed at the slight quaver in his voice, Alex felt something in his chest scudding too fast, something drumming in his neck. "All I know is she was betrayed."

"You do keep using that word. Let me tell you why I was opposed. She could have done immense damage to a vital operation." There was a slight hoarseness about his voice, as if words could not do justice to the immensity of his thoughts, as if speech somehow demeaned them.

"What vital operation? Justine didn't even know about Kessler. How could she possibly damage your precious plan? Alright, it's a clever idea, but aren't you getting things out of proportion?"

Cabot batted the objection away, suddenly impatient. "Remember that day you went to Abbott Court and came back with Kessler's story about captured WT operators? That was the day I realised you weren't just pretending you knew nothing. You really did know nothing. Mrs

Perry as well. The two of you blundering about in the forest like bloody Hansel and Gretel. Look at your face now, you still don't know what I'm on about, do you?"

Alex got up and walked over to the window. Gusts of wind had streaked the glass with rain. Cabot continued, coldly addressing some invisible audience of his own.

"There we were, about to launch the biggest disinformation project ever undertaken – really huge - and by some stupid mischance two agents were risking the whole thing."

Alex rounded on him, "This is mad, John. It's the TPSU you're on about. You worked there. It couldn't launch a teapot."

Cabot ignored him. The tone of his dry recital changed, his voice more reflective. "The first WT operator we dropped into France lasted quite a long time, a couple of months, I think. His codename was Patrick."

"That's field stuff. How could you possibly know that? What the hell did it have to do with you?"

Cabot paused, looking up, irritated, "I'm afraid I wasn't entirely frank about what I was up to before Archer's TPSU business. I spent most of last year designing protocols for the code room at Baker Street. I'm attached to another unit now. No reason you should know more. Now … do you want me to go on or not?" He sat in composed silence, waiting until Alex reluctantly nodded. He barely recognised him.

"One day, Patrick came on out of hours with news his courier had been arrested. Nothing after that for several days. The next message came with both capture codes. Both - the bluff and the second."

"He'd been arrested … of course ..."

Cabot, swept the words away with an irritated gesture, "For God's sake Alex, will you pay attention for once in your life. Do you want to discover what perfidy is? Shall I tell you about perfidious Albion, Alex? I really wonder if you deserve to know."

"I do know who I am, if that's your concern – there's really no need to remind me. And yes, I know what capture means. You forget I've experienced it. You're aware that agent must have been tortured to get that second code. That's what it cost."

A curious expression, not quite pain, fleetingly crossed Cabot's face.

"You really are infuriating you know. Why won't you sit down? Do you think you're intimidating me pacing about like that? You're missing the most obvious point. Capture codes are completely worthless? *Completely*. There is literally nothing anyone can do with them."

"You don't think it's important to know an agent's been captured?"

Another weary shake of the head. "No, not really. Not from the agent himself, anyway. Not a reliable source, is it? How can it be? Capture codes as such are pointless. And that includes the one I arranged for Mrs Perry to send, by the way. I sent her that wire, it had nothing at all to do with your obtrusive Major scuttling about in the corridor outside. It was our one last effort to make them believe we thought her safe. Futile, of course, given she was bound to talk. Alas."

"I'm getting tired of *we*, you know. This unit you work for? Are you going to say?"

Cabot bowed his head, a kind of mock apology, "Can't, old boy, and that's that. Let me go on. The substance of Patrick's message was a request for the coordinates of a drop. I suggested we reply, saying his Morse was garbled, asking for a re-send. Mrs Perry would recognise the tactic. Two days later we went ahead with the requested drop. Exactly as if he was safe and sound tucked up in bed."

"Dropping what?"

"God almighty! Ever the irrelevant question. What on earth does that matter? Small arms, I think, ammunition, explosives. All in perfect order. Over the next month, three more drop requests, obviously sent to dictation. With capture codes, of course, but we bounced those. Went ahead with the drops. It served as a trial run."

"Trial for what?"

Cabot blinked at the question, the first slight hint of a smile, "I'm coming to that, old man. Patience. The fourth time he came on, he included the letters CAPT in plain English mixed in with the cipher. I admit that was unexpected. It was his last transmission. I'm afraid it has to be assumed he perished. Of course, he was a dead man from the moment he was arrested. But we had turned his capture into something really significant."

"Can you imagine how he must have felt, thinking he was betraying the circuit?"

"You're being sentimental, Alex, let me finish. By then, we had intercepted a message to Berlin from a Major Gliess, the lucky communications officer. Excitable chap. Crowing that he was working a fake agent trusted completely by the fools in London. In other words, his very own golden goose. He had his proofs - arms drops, food drops, explosives, medical supplies and so forth. Of course, they were not going to buy that. After all, perfidious Englanders play games - I'm sure Berlin has read about *haversacks*. But this time Berlin already had the crucial bit of additional proof. You know who, of course?"

"You mean that poor fool Archer?"

"Exactly. Transparent Colonel Archer, busy fighting a war in which the Hun is even more stupid than he was last time. Archer and his pathetic briefcases. Beyond belief, the English had put this lunatic in charge. They couldn't believe their luck."

He reached out for his glass, taking a sip, a long theatrical pause. "All we had to do was give Archer his head. Soon enough Gliess was boasting he had information about drop sites, circuits, safe houses, contacts, cut-outs, everything. We have all the signals traffic. He believed he was pulling the strings for a whole circuit. In fact, you know its name. With Patrick dead, Gliess could barely wait for the next arrest."

"If you're going to say what I think you're going to say, perhaps you shouldn't."

"Oh, for God's sake, man. He believed he'd got himself a completely reliable source. Can't you see what that's worth? Gliess was a godsend."

"Not any more. He's dead."

Cabot looked up, surprised. "Yes ... I heard. A heart attack apparently. Visiting an ack-ack battery near Auch. In the middle of the night. I wouldn't have thought that was his sort of thing." He smiled, as if remembering something, "Odd you knowing that."

"Even odder, you knowing. Friends in high places?"

"You're a rum character Alex. Maybe you really do know something. Why don't you sit down? Finish your wine. I'll tell you about the first story we planted through Patrick. A planned raid on the harbour at Toulon."

"You never considered Patrick's part in this? What he thought? Poor devil."

"On the contrary, we thought about little else. It was crucial that he would deny everything, throw sand, anything to convince us that something was wrong. They would take all that as confirmation, of course. The High Command swallowed the Toulon raid story, by the way. They still have a sizeable force waiting for it. Gliess has never once smelled a rat. We've been feeding him for months. They've swallowed every single story. It's close to a miracle."

"But it wasn't just Patrick, was it?"

"You want to talk about that WT? Simone wasn't it? Yes, she was *enrolled* - I suppose that's the word. At least, we flagged her arrival with Columbine."

"You might as well have posted it to German Intelligence. In fact, that's precisely what you were doing."

Cabot shook his head, "Arrested WT operators are well-treated ..."

"You really believe that? Have you any idea …"

"… accorded POW status if they cooperate. Frankly, it's more use having Gliess think they're working for him than …"

"Than have them think they're working for us. Than have them carry out their mission? Is that what you're saying? God almighty! I don't believe I'm hearing this."

"Even if you're right, Alex – and you're not - Simone was bound to be captured. It's part of the deal. I've never understood how you people blind yourself to the truth of that. Feelings of invulnerability, something like that, or is that me playing the psychologist? It's just a matter of time. Six weeks, isn't that what they say? You know perfectly well that's an overestimate. The German Direction Finding is now so good, operators are refusing to transmit. You can't blame them, but what use is that? The truth is we thought she'd be a useful addition to the Gliess setup because her Morse was so error prone. Nobody expected her to take her own life."

"Now I know why they were waiting for Justine and me at Aste. If it hadn't been for a cock-up at the drop zone …"

"But you came back to us, Alex. And Mrs Perry." He looked up, eyebrows raised, "Obviously she has somebody protecting her. We'd give a lot to know *who*? Any help in that direction?"

Alex stared him down, feeling the blood rise in his face, "How could she possibly be protected? Who would risk that?"

"Well, some other time then." The familiar grin had returned. "You're a dreadful liar, Alex, it's endearing. I really can't fathom why you're in this trade. You see now why it was quite impossible for Mrs Perry to go back. She only had to let slip we knew agents were acting under duress and Gliess would realise how completely he was being fooled. And she did know, Alex ..." He leaned across to empty the fag end of the bottle into his glass, settling back into his chair. "She did know. Because Alex Vere told her."

"What's this really about John? Am I supposed to be impressed by little anaesthetic phrases like *under duress*. Do you know what Justine risked, going back to France? Have you any idea?"

"Mrs Perry? I told you I vetoed her drop. I'm afraid telling Archer I had the authority to do that precipitated another bout of wrath. I was cursed in purple for five minutes then told to go to hell. You have to admire him, don't you? I smiled sweetly, explained I was already well on the way there and would shortly be leaving his employ. But it was all too late. Your damned Major decided to send her back before we could do anything about it."

"Apart from changing the drop zone, you mean? Apart from sending her to certain capture? You do know she was tortured?" Alex found himself shouting: "Tortured, John. Do you want to know about that? You couldn't wait for more arrests could you? You've been hurrying things along. It's not much of a step from waiting for an arrest, to ensuring one takes place. I'm right, aren't I? At least fifteen times right, all told. And one of those was intended to be me."

Cabot looked away, spinning the empty glass round and round in his hand. "I didn't know you when that drop was planned. That's the truth. At least believe that."

"Oh, I believe you, alright. What are friends for, after all? And what was to happen to me? Am I allowed to know?"

"It's in your Torridon Report, Alex. They thought you would break under interrogation ... do you really want to hear all this? If you must know, we thought you would talk yourself into a hole. Something about your interest in the Ganser Effect. It's all in the Report …"

"And John Cabot saw my Torridon Report, did he? Go on, finish your sordid little story. What else?"

"You were to believe you were carrying forged currency. I think the idea was if you were captured … and yes, Alex, it's *if* … they would be holding a senior intelligence officer. Under interrogation they'd discover a plot to flood the French market with forged Reichmarks. Then you had to embarrass us all, turning up alive and kicking. Obviously, once you'd met Kessler you couldn't be allowed back. Fortunately, Archer was only too willing to believe you'd talked."

"I asked what was to *become* of me? What if I'd not come back? Or isn't that consideration part of the equation?"

"I didn't make you expendable, Alex, you made yourself. You were expendable as soon as you signed on. I'll ask you a question: do you really believe dropping rifles to disaffected farmers is going to win this war?"

"Bugger your sophistry. Dropping agents to certain capture. There's a name for that."

"Not certain capture, Alex, not certain. Take you, for instance. And not murder, if that's what you're implying. Perhaps a kind of suicide, I admit. But volunteering for your business is already a kind of suicide, isn't it? Part of your equipment is the means to commit suicide, is that not so? Operational life measured in weeks. I've never understood how you people can do that."

Alex came to sit in the chair opposite Cabot, waiting for their eyes to meet. "Would you like to know how Patrick died, John? Don't ask how - just accept that I know this chap whose name you can't quite recall. Do you want to know exactly how he died? No, I thought not. I'm going to tell you all the same, and you're going to listen. Then you will have to hope I can bring myself to walk out of here without wringing your superior neck."

Cabot drew his legs in, feeling in a pocket for his case, half rising to light a cigarette. Alex put a hand on his shoulder, "No, stay there. I want you where I can see you. Patrick was taken to a house in Saint Aunix. I think you know the place. It used to be a butchers shop. He was hoisted up onto a meat hook in the cellar. Did you know there's a way of piercing the wrists?" Cabot looked away. "No? Surprisingly, it takes the weight."

"Look, Alex, I know what you're trying to do. Really, you're wasting your time. I don't live in your world, don't you understand that? You're embarrassing yourself."

"You're going to hear anyway. Perhaps I can live with being embarrassed. For God's sake! Do you think that matters?" Alex leaned across, their faces inches apart, "They beat him with a length of electric cable. Nothing very sophisticated. What came to hand, you might say. Other things as well. Cigarette burns - heard about those? Worse things than anything we could even begin to imagine. There's a mincing machine in that shop. Frankly, you don't deserve knowing – he's worth better than that."

Cabot had taken his spectacles off, mechanically polishing them, weary red eyes blinking in cigarette smoke. He seemed to be curled into himself, waiting. Alex broke away, leaning back.

"And do you know why they did all this? What all your lies bought you? I'll tell you. They wanted the code he used to assert that his messages were secure. They didn't get it. Oh, not because he held out. People don't hold out, virtually never. *You will succumb* is the first thing you learn in this business. It's our motto. No, they didn't get it, because there wasn't one. There was nothing to give. After a few hours they took him down. They managed to put some clothes on him. Not shoes - you need complete feet for shoes. Then he was shot. In the yard at the back of the Gendarmerie. Executed. You're not allowed to beat people to death in France, it's an orderly place, there's due process."

Alex stopped, aware his voice was shaking, the pain behind his eyes beyond bearing, squeezing them closed. Tears ran hot across his cheek.

Cabot went on looking at the end of his cigarette like a man forced to hear a tiresome story he'd heard before. "We're in too far, Alex, all of us. Too far in blood, don't you see? Maybe your precious Mrs Perry can ask her priest who she can kill, who she can't."

"So you were lying when you said you didn't know about Gliess? Of course you were."

"Tell me this, Alex. What if the Gliess bluff got us into Africa? All things considered, that was a miracle. Don't you think that was worth the life of a soldier?"

"Oh, no, no, that's *your* cheap little comfort, not mine, you're not getting away with that. And if you're talking about Patrick, you have your answer. Justine as well, Simone, all of them, God knows how many - they didn't volunteer to be deceived. To be lied to. It's as simple as that."

"That's an absurd thing to say. You always were slightly absurd, Alex." He looked at his watch, frowning in mock disbelief, "I think I'll forego lunch and get away myself. It was interesting meeting up again. There's an earlier train. At least I'll miss the customary New Year hoards of drunken Scotsmen. It's only a walk to the station."

As he struggled up Alex prodded him in the chest, feeling plump flesh yield to his finger. Cabot registered the indignity with an expression of pained distaste. Watching him fall back, bouncing slightly, it seemed to Alex his whole life had been contingent on the indulgence of people like this – people who knew better, people one crucial step ahead. The noble cause for which he would have given his life no more than a grotesque charade designed to deliver him hog-tied to his enemy, reality itself predicated on lies.

Cabot sat on, lips nervously forming silent words, oblivious of that part of his web of betrayal that was truly unforgiveable. The justified sacrifice: Justine's future casually snuffed out. No, worse than that - casually consigned to hell. Alex felt nails bite deep into his bunched fists, an emotion he had never known before consuming him. Torridon had schooled him in the precision of violence, where a blow must fall for maximum harm. Had schooled him how to sidestep the inevitable spurt of blood that would blind his adversary, the nose crushed to a broken mass of flesh and mucus. It seemed he almost felt the initial blow jarring his wrist as Cabot's upturned face registered sudden alarm. And in that instant, Alex realised a single blow could never be contained, would spawn a hellish frenzy of others, until all that remained of that gentle scholar's face pressed back against the chair would be a single filmy eye hanging loose.

"You really don't know what you've done, do you? You don't have the faintest idea. Don't you know what you did to her? You and your kind. Our masters, that's what you think, isn't it? God damn you ... God damn you to hell." Clotted with impotent rage, Alex heard his voice lost in the dead book-lined space. "You're no better than a snivelling little cunt. That's the word. You want to know how I feel knowing I've been mixed up with a cunt like you? Ashamed for the whole bloody human race. No, don't turn away. You made a mistake telling me that story, Cabot. I could beat the life out of you right now ... God knows why I don't … for Justine's sake … Justine."

As Alex stepped back, Cabot eased himself warily out of his chair, slipping past to pull at the door of a panelled wardrobe, reaching inside for a raincoat. When finally he turned to speak, his voice was steady.

"Odd word that …" He was balancing a coat hanger in his hands. "*Cunt.* As a term of abuse, I mean. You get it in Catullus … about a mule, I think. I always found Catullus slightly obvious - you know … gross. As for your threat. It was a threat, wasn't it, Alex? Mixed in with that extraordinary little scatological outburst. Why do you think I told you?"

"I've been wondering. I suppose treachery needs a knowing victim. Dante worked that out, if I recall, and by God there's a circle in hell for friends like you. You had to tell somebody – that's the liar's flaw. You couldn't resist boasting, could you?"

"Resist? Oh, I think I could do that alright. Not everybody is worth boasting to, Alex, not even you." He glanced at his watch, showing a flash of starched cuff, "In a little over two hours I shall be explaining how Captain Vere has come into possession of a significant state secret. *Unauthorised* knowledge of one of our most secret operations. Why don't you think of it as an infection? You're infected with knowledge. Knowledge you really shouldn't have. What do you imagine the remedy will be?"

"You mean somebody strangling me in a dark alley?"

Cabot looked pained. "I'm a back room man, you know that." He folded the raincoat over his arm. "But I suppose you do need to take care, old man. Precautions, you know. Now … where did I put my briefcase? You're an incredibly lucky chap, Alex, it's enough to get one believing in angels. I really must go. Pull the door to, if you would.

We don't shake hands in this College, did you know that? As well, really, avoids any last minute unpleasantness."

Outside in the quadrangle it was raining, lines of black running down buttressed stone walls. The Chapel was dark, hazy blue light from tall stained glass windows reminding Alex vaguely of the interrogation room at Abbot Court. The place seemed empty, a single candle in a stand on the chancel steps struggling restlessly to stay alight. The organ was still playing. He walked a little way along the central aisle and stood leaning against one of the wooden stalls to listen. Bach: one of the trio sonatas, counterpoint like a relentless argument that would never reach a resolution.

He was about to leave when a figure in a stall near the altar rail struggled to its feet, sensible shoes clicking towards him on the wide stone flags. She was smiling.

"Hello Guffin. There, you've caught me about my secret rites. Would you believe it? There wasn't a single soul for the service. Well, I suppose two souls if you count me and the vicar or Dean or whatever he's called. He seemed nice. Very old. I was his congregation. Really shocking hearing it all in English, though. Had me blushing when he came to the *Dearly beloved* bit. I didn't go up, of course … what's the matter? You look bad."

Alex frowned, "Go up where?"

"It's a Mass. I didn't take it … couldn't really … of course I couldn't."

She took his arm, drawing him in close, her face tipping up to his. "Don't you bother your heathen head about all that, not now. How did it go with Cabot? Did you get what you wanted?" He felt her lips brush his cheek, "You've been drinking."

"Oh, it went well enough."

The music ended abruptly in mid-course, echoing briefly in the stifled space. Justine pulled him aside into a stall, sliding along to make room.

"Here's as good as anywhere now that racket's ended. There's something I want to tell you. You remember how I was miles early for the service? I was sitting quietly up there when I heard somebody come in. In a stall behind me. He wouldn't have known I was there. Over there. D'you know who?"

Alex shook his head, finding the musty-sweet silence of the place vaguely menacing. He glanced vacantly at Justine at his side, her face turned to his.

"It was the Major. What on earth was he doing here?"

"Same as us. Looking for Cabot. There was somebody in the corridor outside the room, I guessed it was him. He must have heard our voices – anyway, he went away."

"He saw me when I turned round. I sort of waved and he walked along the side there until he was quite close. It was then I saw. He looked terrible."

"You mean ill?"

"No, not ill." She checked, suddenly embarrassed, "I almost feel I shouldn't say. Completely distraught. Rubbing at his face like mad. I know that look, you can't fool a woman about secret tears. He came up, all fake friendly, went to shake hands, then saw this bandage thing. The way he looked at me ... I don't think I'll ever forget it. He just turned tail and walked out. Didn't say a word. Why would he do a thing like that? I can't understand."

"I think he'd just realised his whole life this past year has been a kind of fiction. I know how he feels: your whole existence suddenly defined as a show put on for other people. A pathetic bloody humiliating pantomime."

"What other people?" She squeezed his arm. "No, you don't need to talk about it if you don't want. I knew as soon as I saw you. It's that Cabot chap, isn't it? He's not right, is he?"

Twenty-Six

They spent the weeks after Oxford in a flat Alex barely remembered as his own, venturing out like fugitives after dark to eat at a tiny restaurant, the cellar of some long-abandoned town house, neither willing to assign any concrete form to Cabot's nebulous threat. Uneasily marking time.

At the end of the first week in January Justine returned from Baker Street clutching a bunch of tulips.

"It was a woman. A nice old biddy dragooned in to wish me well. Said all the right things. She gave me these. Apparently they were in Amsterdam a few days ago. I'd rather not have known that."

Alex filled a vase with water, passing it to her, "Don't tulips mean eternal love? I think I read that somewhere."

She took the vase from him, avoiding his eyes, and began to strip away some of the waxy leaves, forcing the stems down into the water. She suddenly stopped, laying the flowers on the table. As she turned to walk away, mumbling, "I think I'll do this later," he realised she was weeping.

Orders for Alex arrived on Wednesday morning the following week. It had been snowing heavily and the embossed envelope shoved under the door was already limp with damp. He took it into the bedroom to read. Marked *secret* in superfluous red ink, the letter was headed, *War Cabinet Office, London Controlling Section.* Three lines of laconic prose informed him that a car would collect him the following day at eleven hundred hours.

That night she kissed him on the lips, which was rare, pulling him close, protesting when he tried to speak, murmuring, *Time's up for us, Guffin,* a crushed teasing tone he did not like, tears wet against his face. Later, when she thought him asleep, whispering *One kiss too many*, clinging to him like a child.

The summons had been to an address in Whitehall, an anonymous stone portico shored up with sandbags. There was barely room for two in a tiny panelled room, dense with smoke, a man in civilian blue, almost a uniform, standing far too close, craggy face walnut brown like a piece of carved wood.

"No need to sir me. You don't know me, after all. That correct?" Alex had the wit to nod, conscious of sharp blue eyes sizing him up. "Your Colonel said it might be otherwise." He pointed at Alex with a bundle of limp paper covered in florid purple ink. "*Psychologist* it says here. Make a speciality of lying, that right?" His expression was a kind of controlled distaste. Alex found surprisingly firm hands pushing him down into a hard chair in front of the desk. "Don't misunderstand me, Vere, I'm not saying all that's a waste of time. This Unit of yours."

"You mean the TPSU, sir? With respect I don't think Mr Cabot would agree with you about that."

"*Cabot*? He's out of it now. Anyway, what d'you know about him?" He leaned down, his face suddenly very close, "No … what I mean is you chaps get things out of proportion. Just that."

He broke away, walking across to the window, rubbing at the grimy glass, peering through it. Apparently finding nothing to see, he turned back to Alex. "D'you want to know how wars are won, Captain Vere? I'll tell you. High explosive - the rest's just decoration."

He sat down at the desk, pushing papers aside to clear a space, quietly staring at Alex. When it seemed nothing would break the silence he suddenly barked: "Stalingrad – heard the news?"

"Not very much, sir. Apart that the Russians seem to be holding out."

"*Holding out.* Is that what you heard? No, you're wrong there, it's more than that. He's lost Stalingrad, certainly lost it, a matter of days I'd say."

"*Lost*? You mean …"

"I mean Corporal Hitler didn't get his way … the German offensive … it's lost. The master strategist has seen the whole of his sixth army wiped out. I didn't imagine we'd have to watch all that again. Do you have the faintest idea how many men? Hundreds of thousands ... more possibly. We'll never know how many. You can ask me why I'm not smiling if you like."

"I'd rather not do that, sir."

"No, perhaps not ... perhaps not. But it means you've won your war, young man. Or rather somebody has lost it for you."

He scraped up a sheaf of papers from the desk, rifling through it, searching for something. "Now … your orders, Vere. You're to go back to Torridon. You know the place?"

"Of course, sir. I spent a few weeks there. You mean training? Colonel Archer said …"

"No, not training. You're doing the training this time. That's what we want you to do. Keep you out of mischief. You can tell the buggers about lying. That's what you know about, right? Tell them all you know about that."

"But if I did, sir, perhaps there'd be fewer of us."

Too late to call the words back, they produced no more than a weary nod of acknowledgement. "Spotted that, did you? Pick up a travel warrant on the way out. The desk at the end of the corridor."

Alex walked home, spoiling his shoes on pavements lined with low walls of snow. Content to be lost again. Hoarding the minutes he could still believe Justine might be there to greet him.

She had left her ring on the breakfast table in the empty flat, lying among the wilted pile of tulips. There was no note: nothing to decipher.

The man at the desk in Boodles directed him to a private clinic in St John's Wood. Archer had been taken ill making a speech at a dinner to celebrate Allied victories against Rommel. Needing to read something out, he had failed to lay hands on his spectacles. Apparently, he had fainted. Perhaps Alex could tell them how the old Colonel was doing. You couldn't deny he was an awkward customer, but then, the club had lots like that and not all of them were MC.

It was a cottage hospital, set back from the road. They had given Archer a private room, less on account of his status, more that he had begun calling the others in his tiny ward to order in the middle of the night. He seemed quiet enough now, sitting erect against pillows, beady magpie eyes feverishly popping from object to object in the room. He had not been shaved for several days, untidy grey stubble competing with the white fluff of his moustaches.

He looked up as Alex closed the door. A large illustrated book lay open across his legs. "Says here there were tigers in Hungary. Didn't know that." He seemed suddenly angry. "But who's to say different? Who the hell are you?"

"I'm Captain Vere, sir, do you remember? I heard you'd been unwell."

"Well you heard wrong there. And I remember you perfectly well, just couldn't put a face to the name." He glanced at the door, leaning forward, suddenly conspiratorial, "Do you know the people here? I can't seem to get out."

"You mean a nurse? I'm sure …"

"Sure, are you? That's more than I am. Don't bloody well patronise me." A sudden spasm produced a grimace of pain. He shifted awkwardly on the sheets, craning to look beyond Alex at shapes flickering white against the beaded glass. "Look here, can you fetch somebody?"

"I wondered whether I could ask you something, sir? Only if you feel up to it … it won't take a minute."

"Why shouldn't I feel up to it? I feel fine. Ask about what?"

"I worked at the TPSU …"

A faint wrinkle of distress creased Archer's forehead, the look defiant, "And?"

"With Mr Cabot, sir. John Cabot. We worked under your command."

"I remember Cabot. Slippery chap. Wouldn't trust him as far as I could throw him. Wouldn't trust him with my spoons. Always sloping off to the museum. Even when it was shut. Thought I didn't know. Can't stand that sneering type. What about him?"

"It's not him. I wanted to ask you about a German prisoner, a Captain Kessler."

Archer looked offended. "Didn't take too many prisoners in my day. Nowhere to put them. What is it you want to know about him?" His face suddenly brightened, "I remember now. Weren't you with that woman? Set yourself up in that hotel in Russell Square?" He closed his eyes, nestling back into the pillows, a slight smirk on his lips, "Can't say I blame you. Nice little thing ..." A single alligator eye blinked open, "Gone missing again, that your problem?" The familiar sadistic smirk seemed oddly lop-sided. "*Perry*, that's the name. Knew it would come to me. Left you in the lurch, has she? Gone to ground, has she? I remember your friend Cabot had something to say about that, insolent beggar."

"I've been assigned new duties, sir. I think it was your suggestion."

"*Me*? What's it to do with me? Taking her with you?"

"Mrs Perry is not involved. She has resigned her commission."

"Looked like you wanted her, all the same. You want to marry her? Got that in mind? And you can't find her … that your problem?"

Alex had forgotten Archer's need to hurt. "I'm not sure where Mrs Perry is."

"Ah, but I knew where to look. Something else you forgot. I found her, you see."

"I can come back later if you prefer, sir. If you're tired …"

"*If you prefer* – too bloody polite for your own good. You'd be tired cooped up in here."

Archer wriggled restlessly under the book on his lap, handing it to Alex, "Here, put it where I can get it, there's a good chap." The weight off his legs, he seemed more alert. "Kessler – what about him?"

"You interrogated him at Abbott Court. There doesn't seem to be any record."

"Writing things down, you mean? Why would I do that? I'm not a clerk. I don't write things down."

"No, no, of course not. I wondered what he said about our Columbine circuit. About it being played back to us under Jerry control. Do you recall that?"

"He's dead, you know. Damned unfortunate business." Archer's expression was comically wary. "That what you're here about?" Watching the huge be-whiskered head slowly oscillate, Alex realised he had, long since, lost his audience. Fatigue, or something far worse, had consumed what was left of Colonel Archer.

"Did he ever mention someone called Gliess, sir? A Major Gliess?"

"Name rings a bell. Who is he? Look here, can't you fetch somebody?"

It seemed futile to press on. "You mean a nurse. Sorry … I'll call one … are you alright?"

"Of course I'm alright. I need my pot if you must know."

Alex stood with the MO from Abbott Court in the corridor, the two of them side by side at a window, staring out over a patch of turned earth that might once have been intended as flowerbeds.

"I didn't think anyone knew he was here. How did you track him down? You'll need to go easy on him. He's very ill, you realise?"

"No, I didn't know he'd been ill. I didn't even know he was here until I asked at his club. He doesn't seem too bad now. A bit confused. But he can always put that act on, the old devil."

The MO did not return the smile, "It's not an act. He's had a stroke. A bad one. Lost his temper once too often, I suppose, old chaps and their blood pressure. A curse for me, I've orders to keep an eye on him. Have they got you on the same game?"

"Me? No. I found out he was here, that's all. There was something I wanted to check with him. But surely the people here can keep an eye on him?"

The MO shrugged, "Not that sort of an eye. I'm here to stop him blabbing. You get a bit garrulous in his state. Walls have ears, to coin a cliché. Got myself saddled with the job. I think they imagined I wouldn't stick out too much, being an MO."

Alex wondered who *they* might be. The MO seemed to sense the question coming and steered away, "As if I didn't have better things to do." He leaned forward, beating his forehead against the glass in a comic display, "What's the old chap supposed to know that's so important? Any idea? Or shouldn't I ask?"

"All I can say is our unit's closed now. There were only the three of us and I've been posted away. Now with Archer out of action, it would have left Cabot on his own."

The MO stepped back, conjuring a curious solemn expression onto his face, "Yes, dreadful business, that."

"Oh, not so dreadful. I#m sure Mr Cabot is happy enough. Oxford's his world really."

The MO seemed suddenly embarrassed, "Hell. There's me talking out of turn again. You don't know then?" His face had flushed with irritation, as if Alex had somehow tricked him, "How can you not know?"

"Know what"

"That chap Cabot. I should have kept my trap shut, I was sure you'd know about the accident. I'm afraid Mr Cabot's dead." He sounded aggrieved, "I can't understand you not knowing. Mind you, I know nothing about it."

"*Dead*? No, you've got the wrong chap. He was perfectly well when I saw him last. We're talking about the same person?"

"Worked for Colonel Archer. German specialist. Was some sort of don at Oxford."

"Yes, that's him. But …"

"Mixed up with London Controlling Section, the wallahs running your show."

Alex felt his colour rise. "Colonel Archer ran the TPSU. I don't know anything about a London Controlling thing."

"Well, that's me shot then." The MO grabbed his arm, giggling, "It's alright, I'm not always like this. I do know about denial. We're all in the same damned boat ... why d'you think I'm stuck here? Utterly ridiculous."

Alex stood looking across the wasteland to the silent flow of distant traffic, a surge of guilty relief giving way almost instantly to something else. Sudden death was commonplace enough these days: somehow, death didn't suit Cabot.

"*Accident*? You mean a raid? I thought Oxford was pretty safe. When was this?"

"New Year's Eve. At the train station. But it wasn't a raid." The MO struggled on, Alex staring through the window, silent, immobile. "There's a through train before the London one … it belts right through the station. This Cabot chap was trying to get to the other end of the platform. That's where first class on the London train ends up. The place was jam-packed. People said he seemed to be looking for somebody … kept turning round … he lost his footing. Ended up on the track."

"You mean somebody pushed him? Is that what you're saying?"

"What an extraordinary notion." He glanced nervously at Alex, instantly looking away, "Why would you say that? No, the police said it was an accident, pure and simple. He fell. You knew him, of course?"

Alex reached for his cigarette case, opening it out for the MO. "Well if the police ruled on it, that's settled. Mind you, Cabot was not without enemies. You may number me among them." The MO looked puzzled. Alex squeezed his arm. "It's alright, I've an alibi. I've been a bit out of circulation, that's why I hadn't heard this tale. How did you hear it, by the way?"

"That Major chap told me – the one at Tempsford the night you nearly missed your flight. I bumped into him in Baker Street and he gave me the whole story. He was there when it happened. The two of them were waiting for the same train." He broke away, "If I'm saying more than I should … I'm sorry if it was a shock. I know nothing about it. I'm going in search of tea. If you want time with Archer you'd better catch him now. He tires quickly. Don't leave him on his own when you're finished. Get them to come and fetch me."

"It's really bad?"

"It's not just the stroke. His heart's in terrible shape. In fact, the drugs are the only thing keeping it going. If they go on with them, he'll have another stroke. Not much they can do. If you ask me, he's unlikely to see the week out. Don't quote me, I'm not treating him."

"I didn't appreciate that. I'm sorry." To his surprise, Alex found he meant it. There was something reassuring about Archer's bovine stupidity. “He seemed lucid enough, a bit aggressive, but no change there. I had been hoping to get some information from him. I won’t press.”

“Ask away. Mind you, I won’t guarantee you’ll get the truth. Lying’s second nature. He’s as crafty as a cage of monkeys. Drives the nurses barmy. But at least while you’re quizzing him we’ll all get a bit of peace. Just go easy. By the way, he breaks into a foreign lingo when he’s really steamed up. That’s the sign you’re best to stop. Possibly Hungarian. Nobody here has a clue. Not Polish, anyway.”

“He’s Hungarian. I know a few words, I’ll see if I can make it out. I suppose it’s the stroke … you know, drawing on what resources he’s got left.”

“What is it you want to know? Can I ask? Or is it a secret?”

“Actually I don’t want to know anything. I want to be sure he doesn’t know something.”

“Best of luck with that.”

W hen Alex went back into the room, the book had been restored to Archer’s lap. He was mechanically turning pages, devoting a brief inspection to each. It was hard to believe he saw what he was looking at. He turned in the bed as the door opened, leaning on one elbow.

“Wondered whether you’d come back. Vere, isn’t it? I remember you perfectly well. You’re the chap who spilled the beans, had things squeezed out of you. You’ve a cheek coming here pestering me. No, damn it … don’t flounce off like a girl. Come here. Fetch that chair. That name - what was it again?”

“Kessler, sir.“

“No, not him. The other one.”

“Gliess, sir. Major Gliess.”

“What about him?”

“Nothing specific. I just wondered whether you knew anything about him.”

“Fishing, are you? Well, you’re not going to hook me.”

“But you do know of him?”

“I can do better than that.” The beady eyes were suddenly cunning, “It won’t be what you want, but it’s all you’re going to get.”

He stretched painfully across to a tiny table by the bed, tugging at a knob, the effort eventually defeating him, "It's in here. Can't reach. Get it, will you. My wallet."

Alex swung open the little door. A flat leather wallet lay alongside a metal urine bottle.

Archer took his time peeling papers out one by one, opening each, pressing them flat, folding them back. Finally, a familiar yellow sheet torn from a decrypt pad.

"Got this from your chap Gliess." He flapped the paper, teasing Alex with it, "Shan't tell you how, so don't ask."

"May I?"

Alex caught it as it dropped to the bedspread. Someone had written in ink under the message header, *Arrived en clair - English language as original.* It was dated the day after Justine's capture.

FOR THE KIND ATTENTION OF COLONEL ARCHER STOP TPSU STOP GRATEFUL THANKS FOR YOUR MANY GIFTS STOP REGRETS OUR GAME IS OVER STOP PERHAPS WE SHARE A CIGAR IN PARIS IN BETTER DAYS STOP HERMANN GLIESS STOP HEIL HITLER STOP END

"I won't ask *how*, sir. But it would be helpful to know *where*? Can I know that?"

"You mean where did I see it? Where d'you think? Baker Street, of course, can't you see who it's addressed to? *Kind attention*. Impertinent bastard."

"This word *game*?"

"Nothing to do with me. I don't play games."

"But what do you make of it, sir?"

"Make of it? Boasting he'd got our men, I suppose. Ask your friend the Major. Not that you can. Somebody in Boodles said he'd gone to America. Here give it me." He clutched the wallet to his chest, vulnerable eyes suddenly darting round the room. "Bad do, that man dying."

"You mean Kessler, sir?"

"Pour me some of that water, will you." As Alex handed him the glass he found his wrist wrapped in a dry hand, the grip transferring a subterranean tremor to his own.

"Come closer," hot sickly breath smelling of chocolate, "that's why they put me here. Out of the way, you know. Because I killed him."

"You mean Captain Kessler?"

"You know what?" His glittering filmy eyes seemed to know more than their owner, "You know what? I'd do it again." The lop-sided smile still sadistic, still triumphant, "Can't let them get away with that … won't do."

Alex stood up, "I've a message from your club, sir. To pass on."

"The Boodle Boys?"

"For a speedy recovery. For a speedy return."

Archer looked thoughtful. "They said that? Must think I'm here for good. *Return*, eh?"

"It must have been around the New Year?"

"Fishing again, Vere?"

"No sir, not really, I just wondered …"

"Operation Torch. Heard of it?"

"Of course, sir. The North African campaign."

"It was a little dinner, that's all. Got myself too hot. Here, read this." He opened the wallet, tugging at a folded slip of paper, "Read it out if you like. Remind me. I needed my glasses. Can't see so well."

It was a letter, very short, apparently unsigned: *Dear Colonel Arthur, General Eisenhower has asked me to convey his thanks for the invaluable contribution of TSPU to recent operations.*

Alex read it out, correcting the errors. Archer had closed his eyes. He seemed content.

The MO had slipped back into the room.

Alex looked up, feeling like the fretful spouse at a deathbed. "It was something he wanted to hear. He just fell asleep."

The MO leaned over, taking Archer's wrist. Each inhalation of breath came separated by a pause so extended it seemed certainly his last.

Alex prised the wallet from Archer's grip, pushing the letter back inside. Bending down to the little cupboard he found huge sightless eyes close to his own, fetid breath unnaturally hot.

Jó hogy itt vagy, Fanni.

The MO looked at him, eyebrows raised. “Like I said. When he gets worked up. Make anything of it?”

“Just some girl called Fanny. He thinks she’s holding his hand.”

“Some people get all the luck.”

“Is he alright?”

“He’s not dead, if that’s what you mean. Just tired. It takes you like that. Did you get what you wanted? Come again tomorrow, if you like. He’ll perk up again.”

A little thin sunshine was waiting for him outside, casting long shadows, the afternoon drawing in that imperceptible fraction later, a tiny presage of spring. Alex decided to walk. Aimlessly at first, then with resolution as his destination seemed more certain, the Russell Hotel sprawling greedily across one end of the square, layered nine storeys high like some vast wedding confection. A terracotta palace, Venetian colonnades glowing pink, row on row of silent windows watching as he crossed the square, fluttering pigeons rising at his feet to fall again like restless waves.

Part 2: The Things that are Lost

Albert Bradley (1881-)
"Girl in Straw Hat"
signed 'Bradley' (lower right)
dated 'Mai 18.' (on the reverse)
oil on canvas 242 x 339.2 cm.

Twenty-Seven

Saturday June 10 1944
Inverness

Alex pulled the jeep into the kerb and killed the engine, suddenly aware he had not the faintest idea what came next. If this was what escape felt like, the sentiment was overrated. He'd imagined exhilaration would come into it, and maybe it had, at least at the start, driving too fast, checking the mirror like some demented getaway man. All that had gone now, drained away. Nothing left but the damp quiet of a deserted street and a curious furtive feeling: the delinquent boy who'd run away from school wondering what the Headmaster would say when he came skulking back.

Somebody had left a packet of Players under the dashboard. He shook one out and lit it, letting a plume of smoke hang thick between his lips, staring into blackout Inverness. A dreary line of cramped stone houses dissolved into a grey pall of coal smoke, everywhere the smell of tar. The place wore its silence like a shroud.

The pub at the end of the road was filled with the dull murmur of massive soldiers smelling of wet cloth, shoulder to shoulder at a mahogany bar crowded with glasses. Green tooried bonnets added an air of threatening gaiety to khaki uniforms.

As Alex came in, wary eyes fixed him in the huge mirror behind the bar, gilt letters emblazoned *Dewar's Whisky*. A resentful ripple of soft voices fluttered round the room. He ordered brandy, embarrassed by the sound of his own voice, the man behind the bar pretending to search for the bottle, smirking at the others as he poured the measure.

That had been four drinks ago. Or was it five? He'd forgotten.

He had been vaguely aware of the woman at the other end of the table, inconsequential words washing over him in a soft highland accent. Now and then a tiny face would thrust itself forward to peer at him, sharp features, black hair combed to a severe white line across her scalp. She seemed a restless soul, forever fishing for the bag at her feet, fumbling inside for cigarettes. She stood up resting a hand on the table to steady herself as Alex reached mechanically for his case.

"What's that stuff you're drinking? Can I get you another?" She was smiling.

"Brandy." Adding, because she seemed offended he had not returned the smile, "You know. Artists drink it."

"You can have it on me. I've never met an artist. I dare say I can run to it. What brings you here? Torridon now, that's miles away."

"*Torridon*. What the hell d'you mean? How …?"

"No need to bite my head off. The jeep down the road. It's yours isn't it? It's always here. At least, it used to be. Nice boys, as well ... polite …" She glanced across to the bar, dropping her voice, "There was one … Donald he said his name was … a right joker. You wouldn't know him I suppose? He was the same. No uniform, I mean."

Alex shook his head, "Best not ask that. I'd be careful if I were you."

"If you say so, Mr Artist. You've chosen your night, though, haven't you?" Reading the look on his face, she jerked her head to the men at the bar. "They're always going on about it. Uniform. It's the look of it, I suppose. Can't say it bothers me, it's just clothes when it comes to it. That boy Donald. Him with the jeep, he was English as well. They pick on that if there's nothing else." She scooped up the two empty glasses, one finger in each, "I'm right, aren't I? You're from there. You've that same look. Half starved. You a spy then?"

It was difficult not to smile at this tiny figure defiantly trying to stare him down, patches of red high on each cheek. Alex abandoned the effort to prise his glass from her hand, "You know where talk like that lands you, don't you?"

She started to speak, changing her mind, settling to something else, suddenly timid: "I could if you like ... you know … *pose*. Posing you call it. Not for nothing, mind you."

Alex closed his eyes, struggling to remember a Donald among an indefinite sea of faces. Nothing came, other than the weary certainty Donald would be dead by now. Perhaps he should explain that her lovely boy had been shot. They all had that in common, even the jokers. They were all dead.

"No, I'm not an artist." He looked up into the woman's guileless face, its baffled expression a little pained. "You're mistaken on that score, nothing further from the truth."

He watched her walk away, her skirt too tight, pushing an awkward way through the blue haze to the bar. She stopped to share a joke with someone he could not quite make out, standing tip-toe, hanging onto stiff khaki to keep her balance.

As she pushed his glass across the table she let a drop jerk out across the back of her hand, licking it away, pulling a face. "That's fierce stuff, that is." She prodded his arm, suddenly familiar, "What d'you do, then, if you're not an artist? D'you have a name?"

The smell of brandy fresh on her breath overwhelmed him, squeezing his eyes closed, remembering the safe house a lifetime ago, a desperate grudging dawn coloured red, rain coming on, Justine barely alive. They had been drinking brandy then. He sensed the woman searching his face, puzzled his eyes were closed, shoving hard against his arm.

"I said have you got a name, then?"

Another memory spiralled from nowhere: Justine drawing him close, her hair across his eyes, the sun breaking through pine trees, the bitter scent of woodsmoke on the chilly air. Justine resting her lips on his, barely a kiss, two hands behind his head.

Alex flinched alive as something prodded him again, hearing his own voice strangely distant, "Your pack, Justine, where's your pack?"

He found himself staring into two startled eyes. "No … thinking of someone else. Bit addled. Got you muddled there ... mea culpa."

"*Culpa*? Your girl? Or wife is it?"

"No girl. No wife."

"Go on … you say that."

"And it's bloody true."

The man behind the bar stopped polishing a glass to look across.

"No need to shout. You'll have us chucked out. Donny doesn't like shouting."

"No, you're right. Sorry … sorry. Look, best leave me to myself. Thanks for the drink. Things to think about. Another time …"

She scraped her chair back, pressing one hand on the table to hold herself erect. "Suit yourself, I'm sure." She cast a half-hearted look about the room and slumped back down onto the chair, her bag clasped tight against her knees. "Looks like you'll have to put up with me. There's only here to sit." Suddenly conspiratorial, her voice fell to a whisper, "It's Sheila, if you're interested. I never liked the name, but my mother must have. So there you are, Mr Mysterious."

He felt a hand feebly pecking at the cloth of his sleeve. "You can buy me another if you like. He'll be at the bell in a minute, but you've time. That's six of those you've had, mind."

Alex reached out, eyes closed, taking her arm into both hands, feeling bone through the fabric of her coat, this foreign wrist strangely too frail. "Yes, get me another Justine. Here … wait … take this ..."

"Sheila. The name's Sheila. You've had too much. He won't take a fiver."

"Yes he will, Sheila. Get me another, Sheila … if you would."

She had dissolved to a blur of creased khaki, small bloodshot eyes staring into his own, a belch bearing the raw smell of hot beer. A beefy man in uniform was perched on the edge of her seat, too close, the red pom-pom of his bonnet absurdly alien. Why the hell would anyone wear such a thing?

"Go on Shirl, you heard what the wee man said." He had clenched an arm round her legs, pulling tight, squeezing skinny thighs. Glasgow accent, hoarse with the smoke, ominously soft. Alex had known voices like that before. Known too many. These were voices to end your life.

He felt his heart jerk, the throb of something urgent in his neck, a sickening weariness, knowing what came next.

The soldier pushed the woman on her way, letting his hand ride up with her skirt. "You heard what the wee gadgie said - he wants another. *If you would.*"

Alex leaned across the table, close enough to feel the heat off the man, knowing already where all this must end. "Beetle off, will you, there's a good chap. Three's a crowd."

"*Good chap* is it? Well I'm no' all that good. An' she's no' your Justine, see?"

"Leave him, Jimmy, you can see how he is. The boy's drunk. He's mad wae it."

"Oh, aye, he's that. What's he to you?"

"Nothing ... nobody. I dinna know him. And you know Donny won't have it. Not fighting."

"Who's fighting? Away and look for his bevvy." He pulled the five-pound note from her hand, stuffing it in her blouse, "An' you're no' his bloody Justine, mind. Tak a wee minute getting back."

A sudden stink of sweat jerked Alex up, a blotchy face close to his own. "*Justine*, what sort o' name's that, then?"

Twenty-Eight

The interview had been Major Elton's idea, calling, "D'you have a minute, Alex?" as they finished dinner in the emptying mess. He was waiting in his office. Stationed safely behind his desk, back to the window, silhouetted in Scottish sunlight. Uniform a little too crisp. The dark blue corpse of an Inverness Burgh Police Report lay splayed on the desk in front of him like a sacrifice, its back broken. Alex burst out laughing.

"You'll never pull this off, Maurice. Honestly, what's it all about? Am I called in for a wigging? The Third Degree? Called to account? Come on."

A clock ticking somewhere in the room measured out an awkward silence. Not long in the job, Major Elton was the last in a succession of passed-over military to command *Station 402 Signals Torridon.* Alex had known them all - the not-quite brigade. Mostly, they had run away, abandoning a shadow war to join a real one, while there was some of it left. Torridon had lost its point.

Elton folded the Report closed, pressing it face down as if to make it disappear, struggling for an authority that had somehow escaped him. Alex was the first to speak.

"I suppose this is about Inverness? I don't usually get that drunk, Maurice. Never, really. You don't know me very well, but that's the truth. It's just that things finally got to me. You're surely not going to ask what things?"

Elton turned to gaze through the window to a landscape of black rock, waves of heather not yet in bloom. "No, I'll give that a pass."

"It was the news about the landings. I'm sorry ... that's how it was. Not a hanging offence. Have you any idea how long I've been stuck in this blighted place, kicking my heels?" Alex heard the petulance in his voice and tried to soften it, "I know it's no defence, but ..."

Elton thought of something, suddenly reaching inside a wooden file tray at the head of the desk, scraping out a sheaf of notes clamped in a giant bulldog clip. He freed a few sheets from the jaws, fanning them out.

"No, we'd better leave *defence* out of it ... complicates things. Listen to this. Chap on the South Gate. *Captain Vere failed to stop when signalled to do so. Uncertain whether unable or unwilling. Driving erratically.*" The recital petered out. "Don't laugh, Alex. It's not bloody funny."

"Oh, isn't it? What else is it? *Unable or unwilling.* Some of these blokes have a nice literary touch."

"And what if some of these blokes had opened fire?"

"Don't be ridiculous. Old Wrigley wouldn't shoot me, I bought his kid a spitfire last Christmas. Anyway, you know that gate is always open. Not to me, of course, but always open."

Elton wriggled round in his chair, changing tack. "What was wrong with the pub in Torridon? You could have got drunk there if you had to."

"Are you sure? Not on Saturdays I couldn't. Weekdays only, remember? Weekends I need an escort."

"If you'd just waited a couple of days. Couldn't you have done that? You brought this bloody nonsense down on us all for the sake of a couple of days. It's not as if the place is even going to endure much longer. It's perverse. D'you think you could sit down for a minute."

He opened a cigarette box, pushing it across. "Want a smoke? I don't myself. That's why it's full. Came with the desk. Inherited, you might say."

He began tapping the Report with his finger, forgetting to stop. "It's alright, I grant you that. Inverness police won't make a fuss about the fight. We're all agreed nothing happened. That's going to be the line."

"Nothing did happen. And it wasn't a fight … alright, perhaps it was, but I didn't start it. Great big chap, very aggressive. I'm allergic to Scottish drunks. He went for me. What was I supposed to do? I had to defend myself."

"Oh, you managed that alright. If the chaps in the bar hadn't got to him. For God's sake, Alex, you half killed him."

"Yes … I'm sorry. He was trying to choke me. Not very professionally, but once somebody has his hands on your throat, the training kicks in. It's automatic."

"That's not the point. You turn up out of the blue like that. Peaceful pub ... I suppose it was peaceful, wasn't it? Inverness is always bloody peaceful. You turn up in civvies, the place full of soldiers. I don't want to be rude, Alex, but you look like you couldn't swat a fly. Then what happens? Up you get and fell a great ox of a man. People are going to put two and two together and get five. We have to think about security."

"He wasn't that much of an ox. As for security, you're joking. You know what some woman in the bar asked me? Whether I was a spy? She'd recognised the jeep. If you think this place is secure … well …"

"You nearly killed the chap."

"I nearly died myself that way once. Paid the price for being careless. When I was operational."

Elton stopped tapping the cover, his expression unfathomable.

"Somebody should have told me. I didn't appreciate … not until I looked you up." He let the pause run on. "This soldier - Second Camerons, wasn't it?"

"Yes. The place was full of them."

"That's a Highland regiment. Not given to playing pat-a-cake with civilians. Mind you, brawling in uniform, he'll be in trouble for that." He stuffed the Report into a drawer. "When he recovers, that is. No, the Regiment won't come back at us … thinking about it, I don't think we need worry about the fight … or whatever you want to call it …"

They sat in silence on opposite sides of the desk, listening to the tick of the clock. Outside, a low sun stubbornly refused to set, changing the light to a kind of milky opalescence.

Alex crushed his cigarette out, rising to leave.

Elton leaned forward. "Don't go yet, Alex. You're not in a rush, are you? There was something else." He was struggling with another drawer, tight against his stomach, finally pulling something out. Alex recognised the bulging manila folder. *VERE, A, CAPT.* Faded black stencil, army style. Unaccountably, he felt his heart-rate rise. The file had gained something on its journey to Torridon: a stapled docket on the cover, War Office pink, *SECRET.*

Elton got up to switch the light on at the door, lingering with his back to the room before switching it off again. He stared out into the gleaming landscape, "Can't get used to the light here. Never seems to get dark. What time do you make it?" There seemed something vaguely menacing about his indecision.

Alex looked at his watch, "Ten. Your clock's slow. What's this you want to say, then?"

Elton came back to the desk, twisting a feeble circle of light from the lamp down onto the manila folder. "I hadn't realised you were trained here. You must have been one of the first. SOE days, wasn't it?"

"Yes, the very first. Career cut mercifully short."

"No, Alex, you can't get away with that. What's in here is pretty impressive ... I mean what you did. More than most of us managed. More than me, at any rate."

He had run out of words again, staring down at his finger ends, picking at the edge of the pink docket where it was peeling away, settling his mind to something. He shoved the folder a few inches forward on the desk as if the action might summon up the right words.

"You trained alongside an agent called Perry. No, don't get agitated. She was in that same first crop. No need to say anything. Just so you know I know."

Aware of what Elton was bracing himself to say Alex felt his stomach clench. *She's dead.* He felt like screaming it at the poor fool doing his pathetic best to find a way of putting it. One that might not hurt too much. Hurt Major Elton, that is, spare him the awkwardness of someone else's grief. How long had he dreaded this interview? She was dead: the certainty of it fell on him like a blow. Alex felt his face stiffen as confirmation erased two pointless years of numb uncertainty.

Elton was struggling to find the best phrase, "What I mean is, she was the *why* of your peculiar escapade in Inverness, wasn't she? When London Control salted you away up here, they forgot about Mrs Perry, isn't that it?"

"*I* didn't forget about her, if that's what you want to talk about. What is it you want to tell me, get it over with.

"I mean you knew her very well."

"I'm sure it's all spelled out in there. Is it anybody's business now? Why the *secret* docket?" Hearing the shake in his voice, Elton looked away.

"Alex, you're making this difficult. I was coming to Mrs Perry. The last time you saw her, when was that?"

"The day I was dispatched to this place. Good word that - *dispatched.* She told me she'd resigned her commission. I haven't seen her since. Or heard. Nothing."

He watched Elton register the shake in his hand as he reached across to stub his cigarette out, "It's alright, Maurice. I'll put you out of your misery. She's dead, isn't she?"

Elton frowned at him, unlacing the folder, extracting a single sheet of paper. "*Dead*? Not so far as I know. There's nothing here that says that ..."

"But, you said …" Relief had left him suddenly light-headed, vulnerable. "But I thought that was what you wanted to tell me."

"No. I just wanted to get to the bottom of this Inverness business. Go through the orders covering your time here. I thought we should talk ..."

"About keeping me out of harm's way? I know who thought it up, but …"

"Did you ever see the orders? I've been going through them. Did anybody ever show them to you?"

"Of course not. I was posted here as an instructor, you know that. I never imagined they'd keep it going this long. I'm hardly all that important in the great scheme of things."

"Oh, you're important enough, Alex. When I got here they flew a chap up from London just to brief me about Captain Vere. From Baker Street I assume – they never tell you." He waved a page of War

Office notepaper. "Brought this letter with him. The last CO had exactly the same."

"Written orders about me? Mad."

Elton didn't reply. There was something calculating in his expression as he searched for the right words. "Actually, it wasn't all written ... one bit wasn't. I was told to deal with the situation as best I could. That's what he said. And I did, you know I did ... I mean, not knowing what was going on." He was searching Alex's eyes, looking for something he could not find.

"Oh, I absolve you, if that's your concern. No complaints from me."

"I'll read you the orders if you like. Can't see it matters now. This bit: *Captain Vere must be kept on site as far as is practicable.*" He let the paper drop onto the desk.

Alex stared back: "If you're looking for illumination, I can't provide it. You know, one of your predecessors … I forget the name. Colonel somebody or other. Asked whether I was willing to be honour bound not to stray, in the interests of operational security. Quoted Geneva Article 21 at me. I remember I asked him whether he was aware the Geneva Convention related to prisoners of war. He got shirty and said he only meant it by way of example. All the same, it's been interesting to be a prisoner of the wrong war." Watching Elton fidgeting with the folder, Alex leaned forward. "There is one thing you could tell me, though. I suppose there's no point asking who signed these famous orders?"

"They came right from the top, believe me. War Cabinet Office. All a bit heavy handed."

"But the name. Can't you tell me? I've been kept under a kind of house arrest for months on the say-so of somebody ..."

"All signed off, Alex."

"Oh, I'm not questioning the legality. I'm not that stupid. But it would be nice to know at whose behest. It's a reasonable question."

"You mean who actually signed the orders? God, how the hell would I know? What's that matter? I can't see why you're worked up about it."

"I don't suppose the name Cabot features?"

"*Cabot*? I've no idea. You really want to know?" Almost angry, Elton began pecking through the folder, snatching pages apart, stopping now and then to peer down.

"It's here I think. Yes, it does look like *Cabot.* Some kind of Under Secretary. Cabinet Office. I don't move in those elevated circles. You've heard of him? You know who he is?"

"Enough to know he's dead. There isn't a date there, I suppose?"

"The date he signed it? Of course - December twenty-five. You got your marching orders on Christmas Day."

"Not exactly. That was the day I was sent back to France. I can't imagine I was expected back. It's as well he signed it then. Not long after that he was dead."

Seeing Elton's puzzled stare, Alex made to get up. "In fact, well and truly dead by the time those orders brought me to this place."

"*Dead*? What d'you mean, dead?"

"I'm told it was a train accident. Mr Cabot fell under a train."

"You mean he was pushed?"

"Interesting you should say that. I thought the same myself. But no, apparently a completely regular accident. In another life I worked with him in a disinformation outfit. If you want to know why I managed to get myself cooped up in this place, how about a little bit of vengeance. Posthumous orders from a supercilious bastard who pushed people around like chess pieces, who didn't live to see the consequences of what he was up to. Look, Maurice, I'd better take myself off. Thinking about Mr Cabot is bad for my soul. I've a sermon to write for tomorrow's lot. Can't let the chaps down."

"No, wait a minute, there's no hurry, I want to get this straight. What had this man Cabot got against you?"

"It started when one of our agents was captured. The Jerries started working him back to us. Cabot decided to play along."

"Yes … I see." He was looking hard at Alex, "A bit cold blooded … but it happens. You have to take what chances you get. This agent? Someone you knew? I'm sorry ..."

"No, I didn't know the chap. And you don't see at all. Once Cabot saw it was working, he started feeding agents into the Jerry network."

"*Feeding*? I'm not following you. Or perhaps I am. But you can't mean …"

"That's exactly what I do mean. He ended up dropping agents to certain capture - twenty or more. All for the advantage of Jerry thinking they owned them. One of those agents was me, by the way. The really perverse thing is, it damn well worked. Against all the odds, it came off perfectly. It became a textbook disinformation operation - helped get us back into France. Jerry never believed their own intelligence about the landings, even when it was staring them in the face for months on end. They swallowed every crafty lie Cabot fed through his army of fictitious doubles. It was incredible."

"But nobody in their right mind could authorise an operation like that. It would be calculated murder. A war crime." Elton sat staring sightlessly down at the open folder waiting for Alex to say something.

"Obviously, you're right. Nobody could possibly authorise that. So nobody did. You will be discouraged from asking who teed up all those drops. Quite right, too. More convenient if the man responsible is dead. Mr Cabot must have known a train accident was on the cards. *Allegedly*, as the newspapers have it. I might have ended up feeling sorry for him if he hadn't been so damned superior - you're hellishly exposed when you're deniable. All the agents were shot, of course, when the game was up, but that was for his conscience to deal with.

"Who else knows about this? I mean of those out of the SOE loop?"

"I'm sorry, you're missing the point. Nobody knows. There's nothing to know. Mind you, Mrs Perry probably guessed."

"There are orders about her as well, you realise that? That's what I wanted to talk about."

"*Justine*? What orders? Why the hell wasn't I told?"

"Calm down, Alex. I didn't even know who Mrs Perry was. Still don't for that matter. The orders are nothing out of the ordinary. In no circumstances were you to contact her." He shrugged, spreading his hands in a mock hopeless gesture. "That's how it was. Perfectly routine. The usual guff about all best efforts to be employed and so forth, but no detail."

"And Cabot signed that as well, I suppose? Amazing what you can manage when you're dead. Christ, how bloody obedient you all were."

"You're not seeing things straight Alex. You know we get orders like that every day. Standard instructions for dealing with doubles, absentees, rogue agents, you know ..."

"*Rogue agents.* Christ almighty! Do you know what they did to her? Do you have any idea? She was tortured. Some bastard raped her. She killed the man involved - an Intelligence officer called Gliess. Is that in your damned file?"

Elton turned to look through the window, a slight flush rising to his face. "I'm sorry, Alex ... very sorry. Nobody here knew anything about her until your file was sent up last week. And no, that's not in the file, nothing like that."

"We got her out but that was the end of her service, her active service. Obviously."

"No you're wrong about that, she's still listed as active. Section F, the French Desk."

"Something else they've got wrong. How could she be? You know the rule. Once captured there's no going back. Think about it, how long d'you think she'd last? An agent who'd assassinated a Wehrmacht officer."

"I'd better not say any more. Until this week I'd have been court-martialed for even mentioning her. That's the truth."

"*This week*? You mean the landings?"

Elton laced the folder up, patting it like a dog, "You've got it. *Until such time as the Allied invasion is underway.*"

As Alex stood up to go, Elton fished in a drawer, pulling out a box file bound with two rubber bands. He tipped out an untidy pile of torn envelopes. Alex recognised his own handwriting.

"My bloody letters ... I knew it … bastards."

"You may as well have them back. It's that or having them burned." Elton's face was flushed with a kind of embarrassed pity. "God, Alex, what were we supposed to do? Letters meet the definition of *contact.* Obviously they do. They're all there."

"Not all of them. You'll have missed the stuff I got the chaps in the guardhouse to post. And don't make anything of that. I ordered them."

Elton pushed the box across the desk, avoiding Alex's eyes. "Those as well. They're all in there. You'd better take them."

Twenty-Nine

An end to the humiliation of his benign imprisonment was ludicrously inconsequential: a letter in the *Cpt Vere* mail box acknowledging he existed, listing his pay and declaring him on indefinite leave.

Major Elton was nowhere to be found. For some days rumour had it he had wangled a posting to London and would not be returning. He would have had little to return to in any case, Station 402, having outlived its time, was to be abandoned to the sheep.

An invitation card was among the heap of post awaiting Alex. Deckle-edged in gilt, a little vulgar, it was addressed *as from* Boodles Club, announcing a Service of Thanksgiving to commemorate the life and work of Colonel Archer.

It did not say when the be-whiskered Colonel had finally relinquished his grip on life. It would have been some time ago: a foolish old man left over from the wrong war. In the great calculus of things, Colonel Archer's tiny contribution to Normandy had been entirely accidental – indeed, it had been planned that way – nonetheless, the ceremony coming so close on the landings, it was difficult not to smile. Perhaps he had bequeathed the funds himself, paying for people to praise his corpse, he was just about conceited enough. *Thanksgiving.* Who on earth had Archer to thank for anything?

All the same, Alex did not throw the card away, propping it up against the looking glass, alongside his forlorn pile of letters to Justine. Something to glance at now and then. As the days passed he would take the card down to look at, reluctant to admit that he would accept, after all. It was not impossible - not entirely impossible – that Justine would be there. Archer once had tracked her down to the Russell Hotel. In his dying hours it had been her name he had conjured up to taunt Alex. It was not impossible.

In the lost days after Torridon, life had become no more than a search for Justine. It was all he did. Endless sallies against an unyielding officialdom, each more futile than the last. Walking the burnt streets of London he became aware that his absence had somehow converted the world to couples. He would sat alone in restaurants, eating too quickly, a book propped open at the side of his plate, conscious that people now came in pairs. Every woman of a certain build, perhaps reflected in some shop window, appeared like a reproachful ghost jolting his heart.

Sometimes he would return, to hear her voice beyond the locked door of his flat, only for whatever sounds had deceived him to be absorbed into the silence of an empty room. Imperceptibly, their brief time together condensed into little more than a handful of vivid recollections suspended like crystals in the denser fluid of his memory. Terrified he might forget, he clung to tiny fragments of their past like scenes in some shadowy inconsequential film looping forever in his mind.

One scene above all others filled his sleepless nights. The Russell Hotel. Turning to the sound of the opening door, affecting surprise. Justine slipping off her blouse, her eyes on his, laughing: *It's usual to take your clothes off. Here, shall I make a start? Time you were abed, young man.* Justine leaning over him, her breasts against his mouth. Justine's dark voice, suddenly gentle. An awareness of what it might be to be happy.

Notre Dame de France the card said. Somewhere off Leicester Square.

It seemed he knew the church, but could not remember why. Catholic, for sure. Another reason she might be there. It was not impossible. He would wander from room to room in the echoing empty flat, mumbling the phrase until it became a kind of maudlin emotional tic that set his heart pounding. *The simple lack of her is more than others' presence* - where had he read that? He could not remember. It seemed right enough. After Torridon he had believed he was coming home. To discover that, without Justine, he had nowhere to come home to.

Picking a way through the maze of demolished buildings behind Leicester Square, he had got hopelessly lost. As he pushed at the heavy felt-lined door of the church, clammy ecclesiastical waves of candle heat met him. The service was already underway, the church packed. At the distant altar an ancient priest intoned preliminary words in impenetrable Hungarian, *Archer* the only recognisable word. Alex stood alone at the back, hypnotic Latin echoing from the fluted dome, children's voices improbably floating above dark ranks of sober suited men. Justine was not among them.

The service over, they shambled out, blinking into pale sunshine. A field of rosebay willow herb swayed like purple corn in the gap across the road where the cinema had been. Hoards of scruffy urchins crawled among the stalks. *Fireweed* they called it, not unreasonably.

Carried by the crowd Alex found himself snaking single file down a flight of steps past heaps of blackened brickwork, all that was left of a town house. Trying to break away, he pushed up from the area yard, fighting to reach the pavement, hoping for a taxi. Someone grabbed his arm, steering him towards an open door, alcohol and cigarette smoke surging out in hot waves.

"I do believe you were thinking of running away. Won't do, old chap."

Seeing Alex's expression, the tall figure at his side seemed offended.

"No, you don't know me from Adam, do you? Tempsford Airfield … that poor German chap ... you remember …"

Too late, Alex acknowledged the face. The MO from the Interrogation

Centre at Abbott Court standing guard over Archer's dying days. He had not worn well: a sallow cadaverous face, the colour of war, seemed unhappy in the open air. There were dark purple smudges under his watery eyes. Untidy greyish hair had been pushed under an Air Force cap. The uniform was blue, not completely clean. His rank was lost beneath a long coat, but there was a kind of easy authority about the grip on Alex's arm.

"That's two of these things this month. Good enough show, I suppose. Apart from the Latin, can't abide Latin, reminds me of school. You worked for the old boy, didn't you? I suppose you knew he was Hungarian? Hence the priest they dug up to do the necessary. Do you go for all this Catholic stuff? You that way inclined?"

Watching the MO's incurious face, Alex looked away. *No, but Justine was. The only woman I'll ever love. She was. That's why I came. It was not impossible. She might have been mad enough to come.* He let the words echo in his mind, pondering escape.

The MO leaned over him, mock-conspiratorial, "Formidable chap, old Colonel Archer. I got to know him quite well. Of course he was hardly *compos mentis* on account of the stroke. But you worked for him didn't you?"

"I was in his unit, if you can call that work. I think formidable will do. You realise I wasn't his favourite son?"

"I guessed as much. You chaps were always at each other's throats those days. Some kind of cloak and dagger outfit, wasn't it? It's alright, you needn't agree."

"The TPSU? More dagger than cloak at the end, mind you, quite effective, as things turned out." He was talking too much. Alex stared round a roomful of strangers. "I'd better not say any more. It's not over yet – isn't that how it goes?"

The MO tugged encouragingly on Alex's arm, "Don't mind me, my boy, when you reach my age, the less you know, the better. It's a wicked world."

Shouldering a way through the crowd, he found a chair for Alex, perching himself uncomfortably on a window sill. "God, the noise in here. How d'you think we get a drink? I don't know why I bother. I keep saying this'll be the last. Then again, I suppose you can't help thinking it's your turn next." He barked out a laugh, "Not you, of course. You're just an infant." He squeezed Alex's shoulder, "But I'm glad we've met up. Knew we would sooner or later. Something that's been exercising me. D'you mind if I ask you something?"

"Ask away. Sorry, I must have seemed a bit rude when you grabbed me up there. You took me by surprise. To tell you the truth, I didn't intend coming to this bit of the do. I felt I was barging in, rather. I'm amazed the old boy had so many friends. Frankly, I'm surprised he had any."

"*Friends*? Here for the drink more like. Speaking of which ..." The MO launched himself forward, reaching over Alex's head, grabbing two glasses from a tray carried past by someone in a white coat. "God, whisky. Somebody's stumping up. Mind you, Boodles isn't short of a bob or two. Can you see any water?"

Alex shook his head, watching the MO lean back on his perch, gingerly testing the weight of one shoulder against a leaded windowpane. This makeshift bar must once have been the housemaid's quarters.

"What was it you wanted to ask me? Nothing complicated, I hope. You can't hear yourself think in here."

"No, it's more by way of an apology. Perhaps I should have looked you up at the time, but I was stuck in that hospital in St John's Wood keeping tabs on the old chap. He expired on my watch, of course. That's why I thought I ought to turn up to see him off." He stopped, peering awkwardly into his glass, working himself up to say something and changing his mind. "Weird place, that hospital. Bars on the windows, that sort of thing. You remember? A bit demeaning for me, I can tell you, treated like a sort of hired nursemaid."

"I suppose I can say it now. Colonel Archer didn't have anything he could blab about. No secrets. He was a remarkably simple chap."

"Funny job to be in, if that's right."

"Oh, I don't know. Sometimes it serves to have an idiot in charge. What's this you want to ask about?"

"Nothing to do with Colonel Archer, God rest his soul. It's a bit awkward. It's about a colleague of yours. A Mr Cabot. I forget his other name, but you will remember him."

"Of course. His name's John. John Cabot. We worked together

for months, right up until his accident. I remember you telling me he fell onto the tracks at Oxford station – wasn't that it? It's funny, accidents shouldn't happen in wartime, don't you think? It seems excessive somehow. There's more than enough death to go round in a war without accidents."

Seeing the MO grimace, Alex tried to smile. "Sorry. Not in the best of taste. Silly idea anyway. Cabot's dead enough."

"Yes, that was the word they used - *accident*."

The MO had barked the word out as if Alex had denied something. Pressing one hand into his eyes as if the smoke was annoying him. He stared intently into Alex's face, as if hoping for something, finally turning away to wave his glass at the crush of sweating men. "You think that's all we're going to get?"

"Seems that way. About John Cabot. If he was a friend of yours I'd better be careful what I say. He was no friend of mine. In fact, he was the bastard who managed to get me locked up. I think that's the word."

"Come again."

"John Cabot had me posted to this sort of training centre in the wilds of Scotland. When I got there I ended up like Archer in your hospital, more or less for the same reason - I found I couldn't get out. I'd better be careful what I say, but I knew things about Cabot I wasn't supposed to know. You follow me? It was decided I was best out of the way. Permanently, if possible."

"Steady on, that's going it a bit, old man."

"You think I'm joking? I'm sure they considered the option of polishing me off. All things considered, in the end it was decided I was better buried until D-Day. Deliverance Day, I call it. Of course Archer solved the problem by obligingly dying."

"What d'you mean, *decided*? Who thought that one up? And who the hell's *they* anyway?"

"That crowd at the London Controlling Section can do what they like ... no, it's alright, you don't need to agree. But you know it's true. We've got to win the war, one way or another. Best not to stand in the way. John Cabot was one of them."

"And you say he had you locked away. *Why*, for God's sake?

Alex stared at him.

"Okay, shouldn't ask." He looked mildly aggrieved, his face suddenly pink, "Fair enough ... right you are."

Alex relented, "I'll tell you this much. Cabot spent his time concocting stories, mostly for the enemy to swallow. He was extremely good at it, but not all that discriminating. He ended up lying to everybody. It was his speciality. I've thought since how best to describe him. The best I can come up with is *deformed*. People like him are hellishly dangerous, not properly human. It's a hard thing to say, but I'm not sorry he's dead. That train did the world a favour."

The MO looked unhappily round the room, vainly searching for rescue, lost for how best to put something, "You appreciate, I didn't like it." Alex could barely hear him, "Being used that way. You know what I mean?"

"*Used*? This is Cabot we're talking about? I thought you said you didn't know him. Yes, you're right, he used people, rode roughshod if he got half a chance. A devious character. Do we have to talk about him?"

"I suppose not. Well … in a way, yes, we do. I never knew him, nothing like that, but what I'm saying is I resented being drawn into a put up job like that. Then finding he was behind it." Unaccountably embarrassed, the MO fumbled awkwardly in an inside pocket for his cigarette case, opening it for Alex, suddenly defiant. "Because that's what it was - a put-up job."

Alex took a cigarette, waiting for the match, suddenly uneasy,

"What d'you mean, a put-up job? I'm not with you."

"I mean whoever spun that yarn to me about the train accident knew I'd pass it on. People know I'm a talkative sort of chap. Can't be helped, that's the way I am. Makes me feel used, all the same."

Alex laughed, "God, you're not going to tell me it wasn't an accident after all? So somebody pushed him. I can't say I'm surprised."

"You're not following me. I mean the people running this show … the people in London Controlling Section, don't you see? They were lying. Your Mr Cabot is alive and well. I saw him myself a few days after Colonel Archer died. I had a few days leave after that bloody hospital and who would come trotting down Baker Street, fine and dandy, but your Mr Cabot. Tipped his bowler at me. A bit shame-faced, now I think about it, but he didn't stop. That was when I realised I'd been taken for a mug. As I say, I was used. Didn't like it."

He seemed relieved to have got something off his chest, looking down, spinning the last of the drink in his glass.

"No, like I say, your Mr Cabot is no more dead than I am."

Thirty

The room was quieter now, people drifting away into the afternoon. Alex sat on in silence, revising his world, painfully aware the task was beyond him, tangled threads breaking in his hands. He had never really believed in Cabot's accident, certain that someone had pushed him, content to leave it at that. It hardly mattered: the man was gone. Dead was dead.

But dead was not dead. *Dead* was very much alive.

And remembering the pile of letters on his mantelpiece, Alex flushed with sudden panic. *Gullible* - hadn't Cabot called him that in their dreadful quarrel in Oxford? It had seemed almost a compliment at the time, a kind of exoneration, purchasing no more than a modest sense of shame, excusing him from the sordid truth of a life built on lies. Thoughts of Justine flooded his mind, thoughts he dared not pursue. All those intercepted letters, dozens of them. With Cabot alive, his futile cries had not simply been witness to his sense of loss - each word had risked Justine's death. God, what would be made of all those incautious, stupid, poisoned words? Reaching out to her may have been the surest way of ensuring she would never be found.

At the far end of the room, a group of men wearing the Boodles tie had crowded round an ancient tinny piano, vainly trying to remember the words of some music hall song. The MO looked nostalgically across, lips mumbling half remembered words. Seeing Alex's face he shook his head apologetically. "I'm sorry. More of a shock than I'd imagined, I can see that. And there was me thinking it wasn't all that important." He fixed Alex's face, a show of fake contrition, "Look here, I'd have told you at the time if I'd known where you were. That was the trouble. Incidentally, where were you?"

"Scotland."

"Rather you than me. Too bloody cold."

"That was not the only reason to avoid the place, believe me." Alex pulled back his sleeve, throwing a ritual glance at his watch, "I'd better be off. Some things I need to look through. God … all that time. I thought he was dead. Sure of it." He nodded towards the open door, "I'll just slip out. It's alright, don't blame yourself. Nobody's fault. Well, mine, I suppose. It's not even that I was taken in, I took myself in. I was so damned sure." He flinched as the MO lunged past his head, clutching the sleeve of a reluctant waiter, bringing him up short, liberating two more drinks. "Alright, just this one, then I do need to get back. Things to think about ... to read. Homework. *Revision* we used to call it. Plenty of that now, given your so-called accident."

The MO looked pained. "It wasn't *so-called* when I passed that message on. You believe what you're told, don't you? Well, I do. Alright, it wasn't true, I know that now, but how the devil are you supposed to arm yourself against bare-faced lies?"

Alex took pity on him, a defeated man, old before his time, blinking into a whisky glass. "Oh, that's easy. *Assume everybody is lying.* Of course, it ruins your social life, but it gets you by. John Cabot taught me that rule, he just forgot to explain it applied to him. To tell you the truth – that's a joke, by the way – I convinced myself he'd been pushed. I should have thought about it. People like Cabot don't just die. The fact is, at that time accidents were easy to arrange. Still are probably. You learn to look the other way." He perched his glass, still full, on the windowsill next to the MO's. "Now I'm off. I won't thank you for the news, but I'll try to accommodate to it. Mind you, should I believe it? Bearing in mind Mr Cabot's famous rule."

The MO managed a nervous laugh, "Now you're teasing me. It's true alright. I saw him as close as you are now, scout's honour." He raised himself up on his perch, scanning the emptying room. "Actually, it crossed my mind he might have been at this do. Archer was his boss, after all."

"He wouldn't have put it that way. But that's a story for another time."

Alex followed the MO's gaze through the blue haze of smoke, the crowd a little thinner, those left behind determined to see the afternoon out, knots of men standing too close, capping each other's jokes with sudden bursts of barking laughter. Resolutely masculine, all of it. If women had played any part in Archer's life it had been a secret he took with him. Stupid to imagine Justine walking into an affair like this, she had more sense.

The MO jumped down from his perch, standing almost too close, earnestly searching Alex's face. "You were miles away there, old chap. I could see it in your eyes. I know exactly what you're thinking. No women. That's what you were thinking, isn't it? I'm the same. I hate these men-only things."

"Actually, it was not completely impossible someone might have been …"

"… At the service? No, there's never women … well, the odd widow, but not otherwise. You'd be out of luck there. None at this one, anyway, not so much *rara avis* as *avis invisibilia*. God, all that Latin must have got to me." Starting a choking laugh, he checked himself, his head rearing back, as if seeing Alex for the first time. "Damned silly rule, this not exchanging names. Who dreams them up? Y'know your name's just come to me. I remember now." He lowered his voice to a theatrical whisper, "You're Captain Vere, aren't you? It's just clicked. Been plaguing me ever since I saw you outside the church. I remember you coming out to the hospital to see the old Colonel."

"Better late than never for introductions: Alex Vere. I doubt I'll be shot for telling you …"

The MO ignored the outstretched hand, raising his own instead, palm forward as if stopping traffic. "No, wait ... what you don't know is after you left, Archer went on endlessly about you. For days on end. *Gone missing*, he kept saying. You and some missing woman. Y'know what he did then?" Alex shook his head, suddenly alert, "Ordered the nurses to phone the Russell Hotel, of all places. Said he knew she was there. He was really agitated."

"Oh, that old story." Hearing the disappointment in Alex's voice, the MO looked puzzled. "I thought for a minute it was something else. That's an ancient story. When Colonel Archer was in charge of the TPSU, he tracked down an agent to the Russell Hotel. She'd gone AWOL. The old boy was incredibly pleased with himself, fancied himself as Hercule Poirot. He must have been thinking about that."

"You may be right. All the same, he talked me into traipsing across the town with a letter."

"What? To the Russell Hotel? But that business was ages ago …"

"I could have been in trouble for leaving my patient, but he was so worked up it seemed best to humour him. I sorted out a nurse to cover for me very early one morning. The Colonel was always asleep then. To tell you the honest truth, we made sure he was asleep."

"But there would be nobody there. There couldn't be. At the hotel, I mean ..."

The sudden urgency in Alex's voice brought an odd cautious look to the MO's face, realising he was trespassing. "Well, there was actually. It was hellishly early and the woman on the desk made me wait, but eventually she came down."

"Who came down? Not Justine Perry?"

"Mrs Perry. That's it, the name on the letter."

"You actually met her?"

"Had breakfast together. All very civilised, very pleasant. I remember she said she'd stayed there when she was a kid. I suppose that was why she'd picked the place."

Rescuing his whisky Alex watched the glass trembling, gripping it hard in two hands, pressing it into his chest. "And this letter of Archer's?"

"*Letter*? Oh, yes, what about it? I gave it to her and she read it right there in front of me. Stuffed it in her bag. Nothing else."

"Exactly when was all this? No … sorry … I shouldn't press you. But it means the hell of a lot to me. D'you remember when exactly?"

"When Archer sent me off on this errand, you mean? You could work it out for yourself. Around the time you came out to see him at the hospital. It was about then. Is it important? I wouldn't make too much of that letter if I were you. He was very muddled at the end ... dying, you know. Strokes take people like that. They get an idea into their head and ruminate on it endlessly. Probably decided to send her something he'd cut out of a newspaper, something like that. You say he'd traced somebody to that hotel before, well, there you are. He couldn't shake it out of his head. I think that waiter's avoiding us, if we want a drink I think we'll have to find somewhere else."

"No, thanks all the same. I'm off. All this has been a bit of a shock. I should have explained, I've been looking for Justine Perry ever since I got out of Torridon."

The MO clambered back onto his windowsill, steadying himself against Alex's shoulder.

"I think I'll stay on a bit. Nothing else to do. I've gone and stirred things up, haven't I? I'm always doing it. Comes from living on my own. You get out of the way of talking to people, and then when you do ... seems I'm saying sorry again … talking out of turn." He had summoned up an expression of ritual concern, not entirely convincing.

"So you've not found her?"

"No. Hearing you just then, I felt cheated. I spend pretty well my whole time looking for her, while you just walk into the Russell on the off chance and meet her pat like that. I tried there myself, but she wasn't there. She'd gone."

The MO rested his hand on Alex's arm, "Actually, I did see her again in a manner of speaking. Steady on, old chap, don't jump on me. Only in a manner of speaking."

"What the hell's that mean? Sorry … sorry. *In a manner of speaking*? What's that mean?"

"I saw a painting of her. If you give me a sec I'll remember where. I'm certain it's her. Not somebody you forget, is she?" He started tapping his cheek, mumbling to himself, "Where was it? Where was it?"

"*A painting*? Of Justine? No, you must be wrong."

"I'm right, I tell you. It was the woman I met. Look, d'you want to know or don't you?" He screwed his face into a laboured frown, "I'll have to think. It was a long time ago. Now where the hell was it?"

"I wasn't doubting you. I just can't understand. A *painting*? And you're sure it's her?"

"Got it! *Carters*, that's the place. New Bond Street. I used to pass it every day. And yes it's her. The woman I had breakfast with."

"Justine Perry?"

"If that's her name. I'd stake my life on it."

"A portrait?"

"That's right. A bit modern for my taste, but it's her alright. All on its own in the window, I remember. No price ticket on it. That means too pricey for the hoi polloi, doesn't it? Now you're going to ask who painted it. The artist and all that. Not a clue, old boy. Pictures aren't my cup of tea. But I remember the title. I stood looking at it because the title seemed a bit obvious. She'd been got up in a straw hat, you see."

"And the title?"

"*Fille au Chapeau de Paille*. Sorry for the accent. Carters, New Bond Street. Why don't you go and ask about a girl in a straw hat?"

Thirty-One

Dundee. A weird little place clinging to the banks of the river Tay, its only easy access the flimsy lattice of an iron bridge. The second bridge, to be precise: the rusty stumps of the last effort still visible.

Alex tottered into the corridor to watch the train launch itself improbably above the river, riveted columns of red metal grinding past. Far below, trails of creamy spume swirled in with the tide, seals fighting for space on shrinking sandbanks. The sun had gone, leaving a vast luminous vapour the colour of blood hanging over the city.

The station was a grubby warren of gas-lit passageways leading up to air smelling of the sea. Twin slate towers to his left reared over the town like some strange Assyrian monument, a white arc of letters plastered to its side: *The Queen's Hotel.*

Her letter was waiting for him at the desk:

Dear Captain Vere,

Of course, I remember you. It seems a long time ago. Carters said you would write, so you have not really taken me by surprise. Yes, I can tell you something about that painting. We can meet at almost any time – my hours are my own, although I have things to do tomorrow morning. The big store opposite the City Churches has a tea room. I will try to be there at noon. Bear with me if I am a little late.

Lucile Beyrou

The following morning he walked to Draffen's Store, stationing himself in sight of the double doors to watch her come. He would wait a little then follow her inside. Or *them*. Surely that was the word? Why else would she say she had things to do? He had feasted on that thought through a troubled night, waking to the certainty of it: she would be bringing Justine with her.

He stood for half an hour in a chill wind, hardly knowing what he would say, simply aware she would ease the passage; Justine was like that. She would mock him just a little. He could hear her now, laughing at his earnest wind-pinched face, hear her dark voice, teasing him for standing in the cold.

The church clock at his back forced him into the heat of the shop, feeling foolish, taking the stairs two at a time, bursting breathless into the panelled tea room on the floor above. The place seemed empty, no sound but the echo of Justine's remembered voice. Then he saw. Not empty. Lucile Beyrou sat alone at the far end by a window, a paper parcel tied with string at her feet. She must have been here long before he arrived, watching him in the street.

She stood up as he reached the table, letting him shake her hand.

"Captain Vere. I was worried I wouldn't recognise you. Thank goodness you've not changed." Her voice was oddly familiar, hesitant, like her letter. She seemed nervous, darting eyes taking in his uniform. "I'm afraid it's just tea. I've ordered."

"Tea is welcome. I've been standing in the cold. You must have seen me. I got here early. Hoping to beat you to it."

"I was thinking about that day we met." She waited to let a tram grind past outside. "Bedford Square. The day of Stuart's medal. All I remember is a flight of dark stairs." She was fussing with the lid of a metal teapot, pushing a tiny milk jug towards him. "I didn't ask for sugar ... forgot the coupons …" She had stopped speaking, idly turning the tiny spoon round and round, watching the spinning circle in her cup.

Thinner than when she had climbed those stairs at the TPSU in search of Justine. She looked vaguely unwell, her forehead misted with sweat although the room was cool. Her smile when it finally touched him was friendly, a tiny apologetic moue, confirming what he had known since he saw that she was alone: she bore news he would not want to hear.

"I didn't mean to spy on you. You looked cold standing in the wind like that. Dundee's never really warm, you know." She stopped again, rubbing at a tiny fleck of something red on the heel of her thumb, peering down into her cup, her voice suddenly tense: "I would have come down, but I saw it wasn't me you were looking for. She's not here. Did you think she might be? I'm sorry if I led you to think that."

The place was filling up, a chatter of lunch-time voices, women mostly, wrapping itself round the awkward silence.

"No, no, you didn't lead me to think anything. I was deceiving myself. I deceive myself a lot, it's become a habit lately. Keeps my spirits up. Looking for someone is such a dispiriting business. After a while ... I mean … I have days when I know I'll never find her. You won't know what it's like. I wouldn't wish it on anybody. Sometimes you think you're going a little mad. I find myself recognising complete strangers, it's humiliating …"

She paced out a beat, measuring the seconds, staring quietly at his face, perhaps hoping to read something there. "Oh, I know all about that. More than you might think. I know exactly how you feel. I just feel responsible, bringing you all this way on a false prospectus, you thinking she might be here."

She finished her tea, carefully settling the cup in its saucer, frowning vaguely at the mass of faces around them, as if wondering how they came to be there. Alex had the impression she had forgotten he was there; she seemed to be talking to herself. "Hope's miserable stuff, isn't it? I quite wore myself out with it once. A long time ago. There was somebody on the wireless the other day. He said it was our duty to hope for the best. I'm not sure about that." She looked up at him, gathering her thoughts, managing the brief flash of a smile, "Well, here you are anyway. To talk about a painting. You haven't said why."

"Sheer chance really. Funny how things are always like that. You remember askingabout Justine Perry that day you came to see me at Bedford Square? And please don't worry about my coming all this way. It means a lot to me just to meet somebody who knew her. Well, there was this extraordinary coincidence. I met somebody who said he'd seen a portrait of her. That's how I tracked you down - I winkled your address out of the people at the gallery. They weren't all that keen, but when I told them about my Justine they relented."

Hearing the name she seemed to remember something, shaking her head. "I seem fated to disappoint you, Captain Vere. The painting isn't here either. Did Carters not tell you that story?"

"That it wasn't intended for sale but somebody bought it all the same? Yes, they told me that. They said you weren't at all happy."

"They were right about that! But is that all they said? Didn't they tell you who bought it?"

"No, they didn't say. Confidential, I suppose. They didn't tell me anything, actually. The chap could see I was only there to get your address. I thought he was going to throw me out."

"But didn't they know who you were? Didn't you say?"

"We tend not to volunteer names. It's something that comes with the job, I'm afraid. Regulations. And I was in uniform. That always seems to induce deference, God knows why."

"So you don't know who bought it?"

Alex shook his head, reaching for his cigarette case, puzzled by the sudden intensity in her voice.

"It was you! Carters wrote to me saying it had been bought by someone called Alex Vere. A cash sale. And yes, you're right. I was irritated they'd let it go. Then I worked it out. I could see why you might want to buy it."

"But it's not true. It's complete nonsense."

"Please don't look so worried, Captain Vere, I knew at once it wasn't you."

"Somebody must have used my name. Are you sure it wasn't Justine herself? Perhaps she got somebody to buy it."

"No, it wasn't that." Her voice was suddenly flat. "It couldn't have been that. The people at Carters remembered him well enough. When they started to do the paperwork it turned out the address he'd given was somewhere bombed out years ago. They said it was a tubby chap, *tubby*, that was the word." She glanced at his uniform, the expression embracing him suddenly warm, "Now nobody would call you tubby, would they? Short sighted with big pebble lens glasses, that was the description. Oxford accent. Well turned out, sporting a rolled umbrella. Impressively up to speed on modern painting. Carters assumed he was from a gallery. Actually impersonation happens quite a bit in the art world. Disreputable people looking for ways of getting a better price. It sounds like a mystery, but …" Seeing something in his face her voice petered out.

For a few seconds, before reality imposed itself, it had seemed to Alex that he must embrace contradictory truths: Cabot laid to rest in some Oxford churchyard, long dead; Cabot very much alive, haunting Bond Street galleries. He felt suddenly lightheaded, thoughts of Justine's vulnerability engulfing him. "I'm sorry, what were you saying? Getting a better price … yes, I can see that. I was thinking about something else. And this tubby chap. Did he give a name?"

"But I told you, your name." She reached across, briefly resting her hand on his, pressing it against the tablecloth. "It's alright, obviously it had nothing to do with you."

"I'm not so sure about that. It had to be somebody who knew me to use my name. In fact, I know this man very well, very well indeed."

"Oh, I didn't realise ..." Her face had closed on him, suddenly wary, "So you know who he is. I'm sorry, I don't understand."

"He's from my world, not yours. My former world, I should say. He worked in that unit in Bedford Square you visited."

"But why would he buy my painting?"

Alex turned his head away, mumbling to himself, "Cabot has a reason for everything ... he must have had a reason. No, not *had* … I mean *has*. That's what frightens me. Sorry … just give me a minute,

I have to think. Why is he interested in this painting? He must have a reason. *Why*?"

The silence between them became infectious, women at the next table glancing nervously across. On the other side of the road a knot a people huddled at the tram-stop were unfurling umbrellas.

"I don't sign paintings *Beyrou*. Perhaps that's relevant ..." She was struggling for his attention. "That was the only time. What I mean is, he can't have wanted it for my name." She was blushing, "People did, you know, when I used my own name. It's the only painting I've ever signed that way. That's why Carters got mixed up. Perhaps he knows it's an assumed name, that there's no such artist."

It was some time before Alex spoke, his face clearing. He had barely been listening to her. "No, it's not the signature. He knew he wasn't the only person looking for her. Buying it meant one less chance of finding her. But why didn't he come looking here, that's what I don't understand. He knows she must have been in Dundee because you painted her. Look, it would be easier if I knew what brought her here. Can you tell me that?"

She shifted to the edge of her chair, reaching down to the parcel at her feet. "I went to get some sketches this morning. I'd lent them to somebody. They're of Justine. Do you have time to come to the College? It's coming on to rain, but if we run, it's not very far. I'll tell you what I know. Then you can tell me all about Paris. I never imagined I'd miss France so much. I'm greedy for news."

"*Paris?* What about Paris?"

But she was already standing at the little counter by the door, shaking coins out of her purse to settle the bill.

The walk to Bell Street took them through the old Houff graveyard. The rain eased off a little as they pushed through the iron gates. She walked ahead, pausing to wait for him, resting her parcel on a gravestone set back a little from the gravel path, a single chiselled skull over crossed bones, cavernous eyes widened by centuries of rain staring past the brown paper to the sky.

"I wanted to show you this. It looks best when the weather's grey. I used to come here with Justine. We'd talk about the day of that flight, the day your people got me out of France."

"Not really my people. It was her mission, not mine. All I know about it is that it was vital we got you away from that place. Did you realise how dangerous the house you were living in had become?"

She perched one shoe on the edge of the stone. "I did know … later … after I got here. Justine explained to me about that damned explosion that killed my brother. I think that's how this got into my work. Come here, look at this." She tugged at his sleeve, pulling him to the foot of the gravestone, "They were monks. Franciscans. Crossed arms was their sign: did you know that? I'd always imagined it meant peace, fellowship, love, something like that." She waited until Alex looked down at the huge triangular slab of grey stone. "They're not arms at all if you look, they're bones, it's all a sick kind of joke about death."

She had already set off towards the other gate, calling back to him, her voice a little unsteady. "Dundee is full of graveyards. Perhaps that's why I ended up here. The place is made of bodies: I hate it."

Thirty-Two

A huge cranked easel draped in a piece of blue cloth stood in the centre of her studio, next to a pine table piled with crushed tubes of paint. The place was much larger than he expected; and colder, the smell of turpentine barely defeating the pervading damp. Two tall windows looked across to a forlorn cliff of red stone tenements on the other side of the road. It must have been a classroom once, tucked away on the fourth floor of the college, little used, its bare wooden boards now stained with paint. Unframed canvasses were stacked three deep next to a white china sink. Whatever mysteries were created in this chill place must surely have been hard won.

She dragged out two wooden chairs, waving him into one, standing for a moment alongside him, scanning the room. "I'm used to that look, Captain Vere. Immune to it, you might say. I'm afraid I can't satisfy your curiosity, I'm superstitious about showing work in progress." She was laughing, "Anyway, it's one of a series, you'd have to see all of them and I couldn't do that to anyone." The warmth evaporated, "But that's not why we're here, is it?"

"I had just realised why everything seems so familiar. I've been in your studio before. With Justine, the last time. In France. Did she tell you? Was that why you brought me here?"

"I suppose so … partly. I thought if you're going to quiz me, I'd better be on my own ground." She continued to stare round the studio, letting one hand vaguely follow her gaze. "But you're right, I've made the place a kind of shrine, a *momento*, like those bones out there. To tell you the truth, remembering I once lived in France has been the only way I#ve been able to stay sane in this place. Albert Bradley's house was my home. I worked with him there for years."

"But you knew the place was more than just his house, didn't you? You knew it was our safe house."

She pursed her lips, "That was one of Albert's better secrets, I don't think well of him for that. Mind you, people were always coming and going and I never asked. Perhaps the truth is I didn't want to know."

"After forty-two his house was the only really safe place in the Gers. Eccentric artist, as rich as Croesus, living like a hermit miles from anywhere - it was a godsend. I was there with Justine the night before the RAF managed to get us home. She'd managed it on foot from Saint Aunix, God knows how, she was in a bad way. I think the house had been abandoned by then but we got into this little stone building next to it. Justine said it must have been your studio. It was set out just like this. Even the blue cover."

"No, it's not abandoned, I'm sure Albert is still there. His kind of fame is its own protection. It's funny, he never seemed to believe in your war. There were Germans billeted on him after you got me away. I was relieved - I thought at least he'll be able to work. I heard he's been working in Paris recently, I suppose that makes sense. Perhaps you came across him? Albert Bradley, I mean ..."

"Paris? I'm sorry, why are you asking me about Paris?"

She was blushing, a faint pink alteration to the pale of her cheeks.

"God, another thing Justine said I wasn't supposed to know. Now you'll think me a complete fool. I confess, she told me. She said you were stationed there."

"Justine told you I was in Paris? But it's not true. How could it be? I've been locked away in Torridon. I haven't been in Paris since before the war. Look, forget about Paris for a minute, just tell me about when she came here."

"The second time, you mean? It must have been more than a year ago. March, I think. There's never a proper spring here, that's the first thing you learn about Dundee. I remember it was so cold that night I was working in gloves. It was very late. I paint a lot at night. A porter came up to the studio, banging on the door. I thought he'd come to complain about seeing the lights, but it wasn't that. He said there was a woman asking for me downstairs. That was a time they had to leave the main doors open in case of a raid."

"And it was Justine?" Alex realised his heart was drumming. "Is that what you're saying?"

"Well, yes, but I didn't recognise her at first. She'd been here once before, but it was dark with the blackout. There was just this dim figure standing in the hall looking up the stairs. Anyway being pregnant changes the line of the body, the posture. Of course, when she spoke I remembered the voice ..."

"Pregnant."

"… She said she'd been on a train all day. Got diverted somewhere. It's a hellish journey at the best of times. She was very tired, completely lost. This place was all she could think of. She asked about somewhere to stay. It was the middle of the night …"

"What are you saying? You're saying she's pregnant? You mean Justine?"

"It was over a year ago."

"I didn't know." He stretched one hand out towards her as if pushing her words away. "I didn't know. She'd said nothing about that. No … stop a minute … I want to think."

She let him sit, silently searching his profile, finally murmuring, "I'm very sorry, that was clumsy. You mean she hadn't ... yes, I can see why she wouldn't ..."

Alex went across to the window, staring blindly into the street below, trying to catch a little air. "Still, why come here? *Why*? I don't understand." He turned to face her. "I'm sorry, tell me again. When was all this? I mean when exactly?"

"I told you, March. I'm not sure of the date. But I can tell you *why* easily enough: she was looking for you. There was a rumour you'd been posted to somewhere in Scotland. She'd been here before, it was all she could think of. I don't think she was thinking very clearly. She seemed desperate, demented almost. I can only tell you what she said. She said you'd vanished." She was searching his face for some kind of reassurance. "And now here you are saying exactly the same thing - that's she's vanished."

Outside, the rain had come on again, slanting against the windows in gusts. Alex watched a couple of students run for shelter. The girl let the boy pull her into a doorway. They stood close, their heads touching.

When Elton had handed him that pile of letters it had seemed the final move in a grubby game that had ended with Cabot dead on Oxford station, an end to something. It had seemed he could take up a kind of life, re-set things, find what remained of a war to fight, find Justine. Whatever the reasons that had kept them apart, they were surely spent. It only remained to somehow untangle the threads. Cabot dead, they could start again.

Except Cabot was not dead, not dead at all.

The sound of pattering rain insistent against the windowpanes filled the silence in the studio. She sat immobile alongside her secret canvas, hands posed calmly in her lap. There was a steady pulse to a blue vein in her neck. How many lonely hours must she have spent in this desolate place? She was waiting for him to say something.

"The last time I saw her ..." He could think of no other place to start. "We were in the flat in London. We'd been staying there after France. Waiting. I spend a lot of my life waiting. I remember I'd been summoned to a meeting that morning. We both guessed it was about my posting. When I got back, Justine had gone. She'd taken her things, not that there was very much to take - a suitcase, I think. I've not seen her since. That's how I lost her."

"*Lost*?"

"There was no note, nothing. I left for the posting in Torridon the next day." He came and sat next to her, finding the eyes meeting his own suddenly less certain. "So yes, the rumour she heard was correct, Torridon is in Scotland."

"But why do you say *lost*? It's not quite lost, the way you tell it. Perhaps your going away made it the wrong time to tell you about the baby. She would surely have thought that. Why make it sound so irrevocable?"

It was the question that had haunted him for weeks. A question to which there was no rational response, other than the overwhelming sense of loss that consumed his life. He heard himself mumbling, "She left her ring on the table," the words so inadequate he looked away. "I wrote to her from Torridon trying to explain. Love letters I suppose. The censors impounded them. She never saw them."

"*Ring*?" Madeleine seemed suddenly confused, "Then you're married? I'm sorry, Justine didn't tell me."

"No, no. Not married. What I'm trying to say is that day everything that happened seemed to have some special meaning, some special significance. I can't explain. I'm sure Justine felt the same. I remember her arranging this bunch of flowers in a vase. She was standing at the table with her back to me. They were tulips. She suddenly seemed to change her mind and went into the other room. As she walked away I could tell she was crying. She left the flowers scattered all over the table. They were still like that when I got back from the meeting that evening. That was where I found the ring, mixed up with the flowers."

"But not a wedding ring?"

"No, it was something she always wore. Somebody she'd known a long time ago gave it her. A man. I'd better not start explaining, I'd only make a hash of it. You could guess the story, anyway. The hours I've spent trying to make sense of that ring."

"When I painted her she didn't wear a ring … if that's what you want to know."

"No, not that at all. I'm putting this very badly. Can we talk about the painting? This man who bought it …"

"Oh, him - he doesn't matter. What mattered was doing it." She shook the hair out of her eyes, a tiny gesture of concession, "I admit I was angry Carters sold it - I wanted Justine to have it. But the man doesn't matter really."

"Oh, I think he does matter. He matters a great deal."

Thirty-Three

Outside, the rain seemed to have stopped, a clearing sky filling the studio with brittle watery light. Across the road a little weak sunlight coloured the buildings red. She walked over to the other side of the room, taking a tiny framed photograph down from a shelf, holding it out to him. A line of children seated awkwardly on a lawn, a sepia echo of a time long ago, untouched by war. The shadow of a white parasol suggested a sun too high for England, the bulky form of whoever was holding the camera reaching out across the grass. In the distance, geraniums trailed from the windows of a stone house. A boy holding a tennis racquet stood a little apart from the others, his shoulders lost against the edge of the silver frame.

"Yes, I recognise the place. That's the safe house. Better days ..."

"That's my brother Stuart on the left. He'd been playing tennis. Sorry, it's not much of a snap ..." She seemed reluctant to let go, "I wasn't to know this was all I'd have left of him."

Glancing up at the pale face brooding over him Alex wondered where he was being led. "And the prudent one who'd remembered her sun hat. Was she always so solemn?"

"My sister? You're right about the prudent bit. She eased the frame from his hands, her voice harder, "We haven't spoken for years. She never forgave me for staying behind in France. It was as if I'd betrayed her, betrayed the whole country." There was something burnt-out about her voice. "I suppose she's right. I only think about my work. I sometimes think I'm rather a feeble soul. All I can do is paint. Yes, I know I'm good at it, but it's not enough, is it? Not now the world's the way it is. I think Justine realised this."

"Did she tell you about that last mission? About Saint Aunix? About why she resigned her commission?"

"She said she couldn't talk about missions. I know she was arrested in France, she told me that much. I think she was going to tell me what they did to her, but I got too upset. I'm just not strong enough for that. I'll never forget Justine in that aeroplane, she was strong enough for both of us. I suppose that's what makes her who she is. Her life seems utterly unimaginable to me."

"When you're captured strength doesn't come into it. It makes no difference, the outcome is inevitable. That's why you have to define the end point as suicide. Not Justine, though."

"You mean because of her religion? I told her I wouldn't talk about suicide. Believe me, I keep that subject strictly at bay. She said it wasn't a case of *wouldn't* for her – it was that she *couldn't*. I didn't understood the difference. I still don't."

"I think it's why they tortured her. There was no other reason. She had no information of value, nothing they didn't already know. She had to be diminished ..." Alex left the tiny silence lying between them, both acutely aware of unsayable words.

When she eventually spoke her voice was dangerously quiet, "You don't have to explain. She told me about that man ... what he did ... she told me everything. How do people like that come to exist? I think about that question all the time."

Oh, for people like Major Gliess torture is incidental. People like him don't torture people, nothing so vulgar, his kind find the sight of blood upsetting, they have other ..."

Hearing the anger in his voice she stretched out her hand, placing it on his. "The man who raped her? We talked about that." Feeling Alex ease his hand away, she held on, "No, you need to hear this. You need to know what she said about that dreadful man. It was the only time I saw her cry. But not for herself, *for you*, do you understand?

She kept saying she knew what it would do to you, all the things you would imagine. Said it meant nothing ... nothing at all."

"How can it mean nothing? You say she was pregnant."

"I didn't understand either. It used to drive me mad. She seemed so … I'm not sure of the word … so *accepting.* I thought, if she won't take revenge, I'll damn well take it for her. That's why I painted that portrait. I can't do much in this miserable world, but I've got my work. God almighty, are you surprised I wanted to paint her, after hearing what she had to say?"

She sat restlessly running her thumb against the material of her dress, staring at the covered easel, letting tears well into her eyes. "We used to tell each other things about ourselves. It was a consolation talking about love like that, like a couple of schoolgirls. That's when we settled she would stay until her baby."

Alex leaned forward taking her arm, his voice suddenly urgent. "You mean it's here? The baby?"

Seeing the pain in his face she looked away, struggling to find words,

"I'm getting things out of order. No, she was only here for a few weeks. I finished her painting quite quickly. Sometimes things are like that. I sent it off with some other stuff to Carters for framing. That was when there was that mix-up and they told me they'd sold it. It was about then these two men came to the College asking to see Justine. Something complicated to do with her Identity Card. They sounded French, very polite, I assumed they were from the Embassy. I let the three of them have this studio to talk. I went shopping that morning and I remember they were still at it when I got back. That evening, Justine was in a strange mood, she wouldn't settle to anything, pacing about. Eventually, she made her mind up to something and asked me not to breathe a word to a soul, but that she'd found you. Then she blurted it out - you were in Paris: alive, safe and well in Paris."

"*Paris!* But how could I be? You said yourself she thought I was in Scotland - and I was. When did all this happen? Are you sure you've got this straight?"

She ignored the question, pained eyes far away, struggling to recollect something. "Looking back I realise it all seemed wrong. She should have been happy finding out where you were. Well, relieved, at least. But she wasn't. That night over dinner she seemed almost sullen. Then she came out with this kind of announcement, that she expected to be leaving soon. It was such a funny way of putting it, as if she had nothing to do with it."

"You mean leaving because of these men?"

"I suppose so, but I'm not sure. All I remember is she seemed angry about something." She took the brown paper parcel from the table, pressing it into his hand. "That was the night I did these sketches. Here, take them, they're yours. No, not now, open it when you find her, you'll see the way she looked. Like some kind of avenging fury."

Alex stared at the flat package on his lap, remembering an ice-cold morning, years ago, Justine tugging at a carriage door on King's Cross station, an iron face fleetingly turned to his. "And did she? I mean, did she leave? When was this? Please, the date's important: do you know exactly when?"

"She left in May. I remember they came back … the same men … and everything suddenly became urgent. That afternoon she came here to the studio to say goodbye. It was all terribly abrupt. It's strange how war makes things like that seem normal."

"Leaving where to?"

"It seemed mad but I remember asking her whether she was going to Paris and she didn't completely deny it. All I remember is she seemed furious."

"Furious at leaving?"

"It seemed more than that. She left that evening. In a big car. It looked official. I remember I felt very let down, angry. It's shameful, but all I could think was I'd not get that portrait back. I'm ashamed of myself, but I'd had them put the title on the frame. I had so much wanted her to have it. I knew what it would mean to her. Trying to be clever, I suppose."

"Something about a straw hat, wasn't it?"

"*Fille au Chapeau de Paille*. It's the title of a painting by Albert Bradley, something he did for his dead lover. I knew Justine would understand."

"I'm not sure I do …"

"You will if you ever see it. I was thinking about the years I'd spent working with Albert … and about her baby, of course. That's why I painted it. Just so you know."

She stood up, collecting empty cups, carrying them to the sink, turning to look through the window, putting an end to something.

"There, the rain's stopped. I was bothered you'd have to walk in the rain." She seemed puzzled he made no effort to move. "I still feel guilty letting you come all this way. It was selfish. The truth is I wanted to talk about Justine. And all I've done is talk about myself. Apart from telling you something you probably didn't want to know, I've been no help at all."

"You've been more help than you realise. Can you give me a few more minutes?"

She came back to him, sitting down, leaning towards him. "Of course, of course, I'm not pushing you out. It's just that I honestly think I've told you all I know."

"I was going to tell you about the man who bought the picture."

"Oh, him. What about him?"

"When I was posted to Scotland I found myself in a kind of benign captivity. The man responsible for putting me there was called John Cabot. He was the man who bought your painting."

"How strange. So you must know him quite well?"

"I worked with him. Secret work. I stumbled on something by accident and ended up knowing too much for my own good. Mr Cabot decided I was best kept out of harm's way. Actually, I should count myself lucky. His usual method was more radical."

She frowned. "I'm not sure I understand ..."

"What do you imagine happens to people who end up knowing too much? When what they know might imperil the war effort? Justine must have talked a bit about the world we work in. It's pretty brutal."

She stood up, awkwardly looking about her, glancing at the door. "Justine told me nothing about her work, if that's where you're leading me, Captain Vere. Nothing at all about secrets."

"I'm sorry, you misunderstand me. I didn't want to alarm you. It's just that you need to know that this man Cabot is dangerous. I think

I'd better try and explain how he works. One of his tricks. He used to boast he got it out of *Hamlet.* You send your victim on an operation with instructions that pretty well guarantee their capture. That way you get the enemy to do the work."

She sat silent for a long time, immobile, pressing one hand to her cheek, her eyes dark against the sudden pallor of her face. When she spoke, her voice was a whisper, "I'm so slow. You're talking about Justine, aren't you?"

"My operational days were over. I was simply put away. It's more effective than you might think."

"But Justine ..." Her voice was breaking, "What about her? What are you saying? What had Justine done? God, you're not going to say you can't tell me ..."

"What had she done? Nothing at all. It's what *I* did. Those letters I wrote while I was in Torridon - dozens of them. Perhaps there was enough in them for people to assume I had talked."

"*Perhaps*? You mean you don't know? And what people? You mean this Cabot person?"

"I told Justine nothing. But it hardly matters. You can always find things between the lines. In our world you're as likely to die for a supposition as for the truth."

She stared at him, her eyes wide, "I'm not sure I understand what you're saying. You're saying she's dead? That Justine is dead."

"No, not that. I'm saying I can explain why she was so angry … furious, you said."

"This story about you being in Paris. You mean it was a trap?"

"A trap, of course it was trap. She would have seen that at once. But a trap needs bait. In this case, the bait was *what if it's true?* Or even, *what if it's half true?* You see why she was so angry?"

"You mean …?"

"If John Cabot thought he had hooked another of his gullible Guildensterns in Justine, he had another think coming. She was one of the best agents SOE ever recruited. She's his match - that's what I'm clinging to. As you say, hope is wretched stuff. Look, I'd better go. I need to think about all this. If somebody wanted rid of Justine, why the elaborate plot? God knows, disposing of people is easy enough. Accidents happen all the time. And why Paris?"

He stood up, looking for where he'd left his cap. "There is one thing I wanted to ask. This portrait of Justine. Is it a likeness?"

She seemed startled by the question. "*Likeness?* I suppose it is. Why d'you ask? I don't paint portraits. But yes, in a sense … yes it is. Oh, I understand, you mean would you know her from it?"

"I needn't have asked. Somebody did know her from it. Two somebodies in fact. And one of them was John Cabot." He stretched out his hand, "I'm off. I'll write to you if I have news."

"But what are you going to do?"

"*Do*? I don't think I need do anything. You didn't hear me say this, of course, but I think I may be going to Paris." He realised he had not smiled for many months, the experience was oddly invigorating. "Quite soon, I imagine."

She smiled hesitantly back, like someone not quite understanding a joke. "Of course I'll keep all this to myself. I see very few people here. But Paris? Is that even possible?"

"Well, it's true they don't send played out agents like me back into the field. But I'll lay odds an exception will be made. When I get back to London there'll be a letter waiting. No, come to think of it, more likely a telephone call."

"Now you're teasing me."

He took her hand, holding until she pulled gently away.

"I'll set your mind at rest about one thing. Justine is alive. I'm sure of it."

Thirty-Four

Paris. The concourse at the Gare du Nord was strangely silent. The same smell, of course: warm garlic breath mingled with Gauloises cigarettes, but echoing only to the click of footsteps. Otherwise completely quiet. Alex stood looking round, the reason dawning. The endless feverish rattle of engines was missing. There were no taxis.

Mounted on the pavements outside were sad lines of bicycle dogcarts touting for trade. Alex picked a contraption like a motorcycle sidecar, daringly displaying the words *Herr Himler's Stagecoach,* and lowered himself gingerly onto dirty plush cushions. Asking for the rue Albéric Magnard, the man on the bicycle turned and shouted, *nice day for a joker.*

He made him get out at the corner, pointing ostentatiously up the steep hill. Alex paid him off and stood for a moment, unsettled by a sense of pervasive familiarity. Paris had surely changed, but everything here was dreadfully familiar. Even the battered drainpipes against the red brickwork seemed simply to have been waiting for his return.

Tuesdays and Thursdays this was his route back from school. Every week, regular as a clock. Further to walk, but he could watch the girls playing tennis in the Park. Those were the Aunt Madeleine days, when she would greet him with soup and salad in her apartment on the Faubourg Saint Honoré.

Rue de Franquville stared down at him, its blue and white cartouche lower on the wall than he recalled, the battered enamel reassuringly unaltered.

Less reassuring were the new fingerposts: black metal brazenly concreted into the pavement. The closest redundantly pointed to the gates of the Ranelagh Gardens across the road, Gothic script, black on white, oddly alien. It seemed typography had secured an occupation more potent than any number of grey uniforms.

He paused for a moment at the iron gates of the park. Twenty years ago a man sold ice cream here, little boys crowding round a painted box fixed to the front of his bicycle.

A notice in German had been screwed to the metal bars: *Jews Unwanted*. The squeamish French translation underneath - *Jews are Not Admitted Here* - seemed somehow worse.

The wooden benches at the end of the gravel drive were empty. He chose one half-hidden behind a statue of a man pulling something from an elaborate marble lake. It was a terrible place for a rendezvous, the gates at the other end of the path too far for a safe escape. What sort of madman would select a place fenced on four sides? Any of a dozen windows in buildings across the road overlooked the park. Even now, someone on a tiny balcony stood looking down.

Apart from a desultory group of children sitting on the grass, the place seemed deserted. Two women pushing prams came through the gate at the apex of the long triangular walk. They seemed to be arguing. It was too far away to hear.

Alex shook a cigarette from a packet of Gitanes, idly picking at threads of tobacco, leaning forward, listening. Footsteps scrunching the gravel directly behind him changed to a softer sound as someone stepped onto the grass. Someone walking fast, too close to make it safe to turn. A man tapped his shoulder, pressing lightly as Alex made to rise, holding him in his place, walking round, hand outstretched, smiling.

Younger than Alex had imagined, a thin lugubrious face, unshaven, his suit a wide pinstripe that had seen better days. The sort you saw haunting the market, selling watches. The wire-framed spectacles could not have been his own.

"It is a fisherman." Paris accent. He slumped down next to Alex, legs stretched out, breathing heavily. "It's supposed to be a fisherman catching the head of Orpheus in his net. There's a description on the other side." He tugged at Alex's arm, trying to pull him up, the gesture too friendly. "D'you want to see?"

Freeing himself, Alex walked to where the flowerbeds were set off with little metal hoops. Things had not started well. The place was bad enough, but pointless familiarity was going to kill them both. He turned to face the man, speaking quietly into his face. "You are Jules, right? *Jules*?"

The grin was not pleasant, a kind of sneering concession. "Ah yes, of course. I was told." He gave a weary little bow. "The Captain Vere will be formal, they said." He scraped a line in the gravel with one foot, darting behind it like a fencer, a childish comic gesture. "*And you, Alexandre*? I am correct, eh? Or do we fight?"

Alex stepped back, feeling foolish. A German soldier in dress uniform had turned in through the gate. He seemed too fat for the girl at his side, one chubby arm barely stretching round her waist. Seeing men standing at the statue, the girl pulled away, the two of them taking the other path, talking quietly together, her head tipped up to his. They seemed an unlikely couple.

The voice of the man at Alex's side merged with their distant whispered conversation: "Paris is for lovers, is it not?" You could smell tobacco on his breath. "Best not to look. We will startle them. Let's sit. We are quite safe. Rue Saint André des Arts. You know it?"

"In the sixth? Vaguely. I can find it."

"Come through the Place Saint-Michel. The house is Number 32, it's on the left. Eight o'clock tonight. Paris keeps Berlin time now - you will remember that?" He reached for Alex's hand, "Eight precise. You understand the word *precise*?"

Alex jerked his hand away, "For Christ's sake …"

"The time is important."

"I'll be there."

But the man was already walking away, pausing only to light a cigarette at the gates.

The absurd charade in the Ranelagh Gardens had been Major Elton's idea. Maurice Elton, his Torridon rank unchanged, flexing London muscles, settled behind the final utility desk of his career. A modest adjustment to his security clearance had served only to change the colour of files that filled his days.

Two nondescript men in raincoats had met Alex off the night train from Dundee at King's Cross. Standing next to the newspaper stand, inquisitive eyes had settled on him even before he reached the barrier. They waited as he searched for his ticket, standing politely to one side while he read their warrant cards.

A car was waiting outside. You would hardly call it an arrest.

The meeting in Coram Street later that morning brought memories of endless Torridon days spent with Cabot, manufacturing lies for the TPSU. Yet another requisitioned room in some anonymous Bloomsbury flat smelling of cats. The windows were pasted over with strips of paper throwing faint bars of sunlight across the wallpaper. Perhaps England's war was always going to be like this: sweating, anxious men crammed into unsuitable places. Improvising.

They were three: a silent anonymous man perched next to Alex, his massive shoes spoiling someone's abandoned carpets, the two of them on borrowed chairs, their knees almost touching. And Elton safely behind his desk, curiously emboldened by a new London veneer. Elton playing spies, there to do his masters' bidding, whether he knew it or not.

During those interminable months at Torridon, Alex had dispensed only one certain truth to the agents in his command: *Gullible people for the most part know they are gullible.* He considered it a personal discovery. Certainly, psychology offered no explanation for the strange social alchemy that obliges the gulled to acquiesce in their own downfall. It was obvious to all three that Alex was being set up, and equally obvious that he would acquiesce. Watching Elton's mouth move, Alex had the impression he was attending a kind of demonstration. He heard him out in rising fury, barely bothering to listen to the stream of disingenuous velvet words, thinking of Justine's Dundee visitors, thinking only how puerile it all sounded.

"It's too complicated." He had become conscious Elton was waiting for a response. The words were blurted out, they were the best he could do. "Complicate things you end up with a cockup. I should know, I've been in enough."

Elton looked pained, "I can't agree. This is Paris we're talking about, not your rural stomping ground. It's all a question of allegiances. In Paris they shift by the hour, if half of what I hear is true." He leaned forward, "We're not all that sure whose side this Cabot chap thinks he's on."

He tapped a bulky anonymous folder as if Cabot himself might be folded inside, "You'll need to tread carefully if you're to trace him. But you know him. Canny's the word."

"Oh, that's the word, alright. Cabot runs rings round most people."

Watching Elton's face, unwisely confident, even smug, Alex finally understood what he was up to. The fool must have chased up Cabot's name after that interview in Torridon. He must have discovered Cabot was alive, after all. Incredibly, he'd set himself to second guess somebody who'd outsmarted the counter-intelligence service of the Abwehr. Knowing the inevitable outcome one could only wish him the best of luck. Demeaning, all the same, to be played by someone like Elton. The hell of it was it was not impossible Justine might be in Paris – not completely impossible. Elton was staring at him, trying to read his expression. Alex smiled back: "What's dear John supposed to have done? I'm tempted to say, *what else*? He's bound to ask if I'm to haul him back to mother in chains."

Elton's laugh, when it came, was not particularly convincing. "You aren't listening, Alex. No question of chains, or hauling for that matter. We just want you to find him. You're a godsend in that department. Nobody in Paris knows him from Adam. He was a civil servant, not a field agent and you know him by sight. That's why we need you."

"Why's he in Paris anyway? What's there for him to do? I mean, what's he up to?"

Elton glanced nervously down at the folder, "We don't know." The silent man at Alex's side stirred briefly, nodding approvingly at the *we*. "We don't even know how he got there? Any ideas?"

"Don't look at me. Until a few weeks ago I didn't think he was going anywhere, I thought he was dead, remember?"

"Well, yes … I recall your telling me that. I hope you accept nobody at Torridon knew he was behind your … your …?"

"*Consigne?* Will that do? Or would you prefer *incarceration*?"

"A bit strong, but if you like. The fellow misled us. Unfortunate ..." Elton had a habit of talking himself into a dead end. He looked unhappily at the end of his pencil. "But you've got the wrong end of the stick. We don't want him back." He darted a glance at the other man, "Strictly speaking, he's nothing to do with Intelligence. It's true he worked for London Controlling Section, but that's long over."

"Sacked was he? Blotted his copy book? Or did somebody actually take the trouble to find out what he was up to all those days in the TPSU? Are you sure nobody's decided the reclusive Mr C is best out of the way altogether? One-way trips have been arranged before. I speak from experience."

"Look Alex, we appreciate you don't like him - no, don't say anything - and I can appreciate your reasons. But don't you think you might be getting things out of proportion? Let's leave it that I'm tasked to find out what Cabot's up to in Paris. That's my *consigne*, if you like." The tiny superior smile at his little joke was imprudent, "And all things considered, you seem to be best placed to find him." He risked a tiny theatrical intake of breath before tossing Alex the bait. "Besides, it's your chance to turn the tables on him. You realise that?"

"How's that?"

"What we thought was … well … it was your Mr Cabot ordered that *sine contactu* regarding that woman. Are you still looking for her? He must know where she is. Here's your chance to find out."

Alex stared venomously back at him, fuming. "Her name's Perry."

Elton had already relaxed, hanging onto his smile, knowing the game was won. He opened the slim folder in front of him.

"Now … liaison. I know it's clumsy, but we're stuck with intermediaries. No need to look like that, this lot are alright. Paris is full of amateurs now."

"I'll take your word for it. All the same, why not forget the spy games. He won't be all that difficult to find if I have the right authority. I can't see we have to involve the frogs at all."

"Can't be done, Alex. They say they want to look at you first. Resistance in Paris has been a bit passive up to now, open city and all that, but not for much longer. It's changing. You could find yourself in a shooting war."

The man at Alex's side had stifled a snigger at *passive*. He squirmed restlessly in his chair. The trap sprung, he had lost interest. Plainly, he wanted to go home.

"So I'm expected to wander round Paris in broad daylight, trading passwords with someone you hope isn't an amateur. You did look at my file, didn't you, Maurice? I've already been captured in France. Open city or not, when I last checked, Paris was under occupation. How long do you think I'm going to last?"

The silence was painful, all of them simultaneously conscious of faint sounds from the street outside.

A day. Perhaps two. Not longer.

"There's milice informers everywhere, Alex." Elton was getting his second wind, relishing this role as commissioner of operations. "That's why the French insist on seeing you. Slip up over that and we'll be walking you into a trap."

Something in Alex's face made Elton look away, leaving his words hanging in the quiet room. He stared defiantly at a picture on the other wall, one hand nervily playing with his bundle of papers. Alex felt suddenly light-headed, conscious of entering a kind of *folie à deux*.

"Walk me into a trap. Perish the thought."

"We're relying on the Yanks to get you into Paris." Elton's expression was uncertain. "There's a briefing for you about that this afternoon." He found another page in the bundle of papers, running his finger along a line. "You're to make contact in a place called Ranelagh Gardens. A chap by the name of Jules." He released an awkward bark of a laugh, "*Ranelagh Gardens*. Let's hope they don't mean the ones in Chelsea! You can look it up in the Map Room. It's in the sixteenth arrondissement."

"I don't need to look it up. I know where it is."

"Of course you do, I was forgetting. You know Paris, don't you? Right."

He leaned forward, passing Alex a sheet of paper. "The gen's all there. Baker Street sorted it out. You trade names as a pass phrase with the bloke in the Gardens. He's to give you the address of the circuit. You'll have to see what leads they have on Cabot. The problem is nobody knows what he looks like. Last we heard he was too close for comfort to the Vichy lot. Shouldn't be too hard to find." Remembering something, he waved at the paper. "Oh, yes, your safe house address. It's in there. If things go awry."

"What is there to go awry?"

"Nothing, nothing at all - just the usual fallback."

Alex stared blankly at the bit of paper.

The man at his side was already making for the door.

Thirty-Five

It was just past seven when he reached the Place Saint-Michel. When he was a boy, *L'Auberge de la Place* had commanded one side of the square, looking across to the fountain and beyond to the narrow twists of the rue Saint André des Arts. Close enough for what he needed, but not suicidally close.

Years ago Alex would weave his way between noisy tables right here, warm summer evenings reeking of aniseed and perfume, women leaning out to ruffle his hair as he hurried past, tugging at him to see the books he was carrying. An awestruck schoolboy late from class, hurrying to his Aunt Madeleine's.

Elton had been right about one thing: Paris had changed. *L'Auberge de la Place* had disappeared, war shrivelling it to nothing. Even the name had gone, leaving *Le Coq d'Or* scrawled in white paint across a single shabby glass door. Inside, lines of polished brass pumps on the long mahogany bar were all that remained of the old *Auberge.*

Albeit summer, the place was cold, everywhere the inescapable smell of bad drains. A reedy wireless bleated high up from over the door, a woman singing. Alex laid a coin on the bar, waiting for the stubby glass of red wine to appear alongside. The tables were empty:

you stood to drink at this time of night, scurrying home to listen to the news.

It was a quarter to eight.

Through a side window he watched an old man cleaning out a handcart on the corner of the rue Saint André des Arts, half climbing onto the boards, flicking bits of cabbage stalk down into the gutter. Two men in a shop doorway watched indulgently from the other side of the street, trading jokes, reluctantly breaking apart now and then as people pushed by.

A boy running down the narrow street found his feet skidding on fresh green leaves. He grabbed the handle of the cart, swaying to steady himself. Suddenly alert, one of the men stepped out onto the pavement, brusquely hauling the boy up, pushing him on his way.

The barman filled Alex's empty glass, exchanging the coin for a pile of copper, nodding as Alex left it lying there.

He carried the drink to a table by the door, opening an abandoned copy of *Soir*, letting street sounds orchestrate his glances outside.

A girl in a short white coat came out of the *Pharmacie* on the corner, gesticulating to someone inside until an illuminated sign went out. The old man began pushing his empty cart up the street, slowly disappearing from view. The wireless over the door fell silent.

It was eight o'clock.

A double whistle sounded from somewhere far away, barely audible. The kind used to control traffic, when there was traffic to control. Another - much closer. Close enough to bring the barman from behind his counter, pulling the street door open, stepping out onto the pavement, still polishing a glass with a white cloth.

Alex lowered the newspaper. The two men in the doorway had disappeared. Then he saw them. Further up the street, side by side among the cabbage stalks, pistols drawn. Frightened women with prams hurried past, trying not to look.

The barman came back inside, pushing his glass hard against an upturned bottle of Pastis behind the bar. He topped it up from the water jug, glancing across to Alex.

"Fucking milice."

Alex folded the paper back to the race results.

A little crowd had gathered outside, moodily silent, splitting into two as a car, one door hanging open, backed the wrong way down the rue Saint André des Arts. A gendarme jumped out, hanging on while the car slewed across the pavement, skidding to a halt. He walked to join the two men. They stood in line abreast, drowning in a stream of bicycles and perambulators.

The vegetable cart inched its way back, looking for somewhere flat to park, the old man kneeling to slip a wedge under the wheels. Failing to haul himself up, he gave in, sitting where he was, letting the crowd pick its way over his splayed legs.

A slight anonymous figure followed the stragglers down into the square, sauntering slowly, smoking a cigarette. The same shabby pinstripe suit, although he had abandoned the wire-frame spectacles. Seeing the three men he walked slowly across to shake hands. All four stood silently gazing up the street. As they climbed back into the car they were sharing a joke.

It was getting on for nine when Alex left the *Coq*, walking over two silent bridges into the embracing twilight on the other side of the river. He had watched the car disappear into the maze of streets beyond the square. It would have been tempting to follow, but he was in no mood for temptation. Soon enough – perhaps already - someone in London would know that Captain Vere had refused the bait.

A few men had drifted into the bar after the raid, nervously eyeing each other, drinking in silence. Alex sat on, nursing the glass of wine, remembering Inverness. Remembering Elton. Remembering Justine. Wondering what came next. As betrayals went, the affair had seemed dangerously inconsequential. Perhaps the man in the park guessed the cautious Captain Vere would have found it all too obvious.

In which case, why?

Elton's orders had been to make for the safe house. One thing was certain: wherever else he went tonight, it would not be within a mile of that place. In truth, he had settled that hours ago, even before he reached the Place Saint-Michel. For Alex, there was only one safe place in Paris. And that was somewhere neither Elton nor Cabot knew even existed.

At the top of the rue du Temple, three men were closing up a battered removal van, gas bottles strapped to its roof. Alex crossed to the other pavement, not risking his accent on a pointless greeting. They seemed in no mood for bonhomie in any case, sullenly waiting until he reached the corner before banging the van doors closed. He heard them drive away.

It was quieter here, a few passers-by hurrying to beat the nine o'clock curfew. Late evening sun coloured the upper stories of the buildings pink. Alex glanced back down the gloom of the empty street. It seemed unlikely he was followed, but he was in no mood for risks either. He slipped quietly into the stone portico of some municipal office, pressing into the shade, his back hard against the door. Ten minutes by his watch: an agony of time. No following footsteps. Nothing but grey tenements quietly dissolving into the gathering dark.

Aunt Madeleine's gallery was in the *Marais*, the old Jewish quarter. A double frontage next to a place that mended clocks in the rue Gravilliers. Every Wednesday, because school ended early and Aunt Madeleine was busy, he would go to the gallery for lunch. How long had he done that? Hard to remember: it seemed forever. All he could recall was a burly man in a leather apron, always carrying something. He tried to remember his name, but it wouldn't come. But his wife was called Sophie. A tall excitable woman who watched him eat, endlessly chattering - she would remember him, he was sure of it.

At the corner it seemed he had mistaken the way. The rue Gravilliers was always crowded. The shops were supposed to close, although somehow they never did. Even at night the place was crammed. A war would hardly change all that. He remembered squeezing past crowds to reach the gallery door, remembered walking home head-down past the first of the street girls, scared to see they were little older than himself. Sometimes they would stand in threes and fours, calling out as he scuttled past.

There was no one calling now. Apart from roaming cats, the whole of the narrow cobbled street was silent and deserted.

Aunt Madeleine's gallery had been boarded up, rough planks brutally nailed into the ornate carving. The huge double doors at the side were locked, a notice pinned to the little inset door: *Sealed on the Orders of The Prefecture of Paris*, the date impossible to decipher. An odd arrangement of steel wire was stapled to the frame, running round the metal catch, ending in a lead seal. Someone had cut the wire. The little door stood pushed in. Alex peered inside, a rotten smell of piss and abandonment blowing past him. A single gas lamp under a tin shade threw sickly yellow light onto rows of post boxes stuffed with neglected newspapers, limp with damp.

The Concierge's lean-to cell was deserted, a single broken chair lying on its side inside. A square of card had been pinned to the bottom pane of the window. He could read it from where he stood.

Gone away.

It took half an hour to reach Aunt Madeleine's apartment on the Faubourg Saint Honoré, walking faster than he should, barely controlling an obscure rising panic. He had been prepared for Sophie offering him that blank look that declared ancient acquaintance too dangerous to acknowledge, but hardly prepared for the gallery simply disappearing, wiped out, along with the rest of the street. Paris had changed, true enough.

He threaded an anxious way through streets he had forgotten he knew. Although well past nine, the restaurants were still crowded. Caught up in the crowd spilling out from a cinema, he found himself walking alongside a solitary German soldier. Almost too young to be in uniform, the man was limping heavily, leaning on a stick. He stopped to let people push past him, stepping down into the road, ceding them their pavement. As Alex squeezed past, their eyes briefly met: two men exchanging frightened glances, hurrying by.

The apartment on the second floor had acquired a freshly painted door. He stood erect in front of the glass bead of a spy hole, stoically composing his face against the possibility that she had long since moved, was dead even.

The door opened almost too soon to his knock, an elegant woman in a cloche hat holding it against the chain, peering through the crack, her face the sketch of someone he once had known. In his school days Aunt Madeleine had been unimaginably old. This elegant woman seemed barely his senior. She released the chain, pulling the door back, standing a long minute on the threshold surveying him.

"Aunt Madeleine," awkwardly extending his hand, "it's Alex ... d'you ...?"

She surged forward, filling the marble hallway with a cloud of perfume. "Heavens above! Yes, Alexandre. It is, isn't it? God in heaven!"

There was an odd pre-war flavour to her English, the accent slightly stilted. She sounded a little like his mother. She went on tapping her breast in surprise. "You're here alone? Yes, yes, of course you're alone. Why would you not be?" She frowned at a tiny watch on her wrist, pursing her lips in an exaggerated look of despair. "And I was on my way out. I'm late ... I'm always late. But come in ... come in."

He let her pull him by one hand into the lighted hallway, leaving the door behind them open. Little had changed. Persian carpets dotted an expanse of ancient parquet; the same two gilt-framed mirrors silently faced each other across the hall. A Chinese bowl of freesias on the little rosewood table spilled a cold scent into the air.

There were pictures everywhere, the walls crammed with canvasses. He was a schoolboy again, late for supper, satchel laced at his back, staring wide-eyed at more painted flesh than his thoughts could contain. Splayed legs, sprawling thighs like butcher's meat, terrifying pendulous breasts, nipples jutting red: everything too close, inexpressibly strange, the only common theme a kind of sophisticated menace.

She stood close to the mirror adjusting her lipstick, eyeing his reflection in the glass, one hand flailing behind for her handbag. As he rescued it for her, she turned and drew him close, exchanging kisses, left and right, laughing as he reared back to avoid the inevitable third.

She was digging fruitlessly into her bag. "Damn. I've left my case somewhere. Can you give me a cigarette? I assume you come armed with American cigarettes? It's alright, I know better than to ask questions."

Alex lit a cigarette for her, watching as she drew on it, her eyes widening. She exhaled a thin mist of smoke. "Terrible to say, but I needed that. My word, you choose your time. You are a dreadful shock, my dear boy. A good shock. When was it last? Before this damned war, that's certain. Now you make me think it really is ending. You're not the first, you know." She pressed her fingers to her lips like a child regretting a secret betrayed, "There, I'm saying too much. But you will know all that. Paris is waking up."

She waved a gloved hand to the glazed door opening onto the salon.

"You know where to go. I will be an hour, no more. You can bear that? I have a rendezvous … impossible to rearrange. My telephone has ceased to function again. It is always in that state now. *Paris*. Have you eaten? Are you a modern man - can you make an omelette? There are eggs in the kitchen. You can take two. You can find your room? Nothing has changed. I still think of the bedroom upstairs as little Alexandre's."

She was already past the doorway, calling over her shoulder, "I will take the stairs - the lift is too slow. I've a new girl. She'll be back very late – no one seems to care about the curfew any more. I don't trust these girls – heaven only knows who she'll be writing to when she finds there's a man here."

Her voice echoed up the marble staircase.

"Make yourself at home. There's drinks, just look. And eat something, you look starved."

A distant door below clicked onto silence.

There was a whisky decanter on the side table in the salon. Alex poured himself a drink. Beyond the window, Paris without its traffic exhaled an eerie silence. Madeleine gone, everywhere seemed unnaturally quiet. He drew the curtains back and stepped onto the little balcony, the scent of lime trees rising out of the warm dark to greet him. In the street below leisurely footsteps shuffled past, couples arm in arm, their voices no more than a murmur.

For the first time in many weeks he felt safe.

A tiny metal table was still set with breakfast things, presumably waiting on the maid Madeleine could not quite trust. He slumped into the chair, pushing a coffee cup aside, staring sightlessly over the grey clutter of leaded rooftops to the distant horizon, the Paris skyline etched black against the last bloody streaks of sunset.

A familiar obsessive incantation welled into his consciousness: thoughts of Justine. Even now, she could be watching this same darkening sky, perhaps not so many yards from here. She was here in Paris, he was certain of it. Calculations that had consumed him since Dundee wormed back into his mind. Five months pregnant in May: that must be so. Her baby would be an October child. Perhaps there was consolation in that: October was Alex's month.

A sudden cessation of the street sounds below brought him to his feet, staring dumbly into the silence, the memory of Major Gliess a pain even now he dared not acknowledge.

He turned to look into the lighted room, his back against the balcony rail. Nothing had changed. Furnished long before another war, the present war had left its shabby charm untouched. How many times had schoolboy Alex stood awestruck in the quiet intimacy of that elegant room, Aunt Madeleine's greeting unfailingly the same? Today, her greeting at the door had effortlessly erased the intervening years. It was as if he had never been away, as if she had been expecting him.

Already a pulse was jerking painfully in his neck, a sudden tension gripping his heart. There was no doubt about it: she had been expecting him.

Thirty-Six

For the second time that day he stood frozen, battling a rising surge of panic. He had been right: it had all seemed too obvious. Thinking to escape two traps, he had blithely hurried himself into the only one that mattered.

He had given lectures at Torridon on response to extreme stress, on the tendency to find sinister purpose in the inconsequential. One afternoon, on a whim, playing the good psychologist, he had given it an ironic name: *Agent's Paranoia.* Always good for a ripple of polite laughter.

Rotating his head to free the knot of pain in his neck, he forced his breathing into a textbook pattern, counting aloud on the exhale, trying to clear his mind, conscious only of danger, imminent and deadly, hearing his own voice floating thin and pointless onto the warm Paris air.

He stepped back into the salon, at once feeling naked in the light of the room, snatching the curtains closed at his back.

She had been expecting him.

If that were true, he was lost. So much for psychology: it was his turn to realise lectures rarely counted for much. How little anyone truly knew of paranoia. He had read the books: it was impossible for the subject to determine the truth of his own state. He had read the books: he never imagined the subject would be himself.

The paranoid imagine they are spied on.

What use telling that to a spy whose whole life is lived with spies?

The paranoid believe they are plotted against.

What use knowing that when your whole life has been lived in a hall of mirrors, bluff and counter-bluff endlessly reflecting themselves?

The paranoid falsely believe they are sincerely loved.

What use talking of erotomania to someone lost to love? To someone wagering his life in the search for the only woman he would ever love? For a woman who was certainly dead?

He walked out into the hall, his footsteps unnaturally loud on the polished parquet. The rucksack lay on the floor where Aunt Madeleine had tossed it under a chair, her careless gesture now dreadfully imbued with some other purpose. Kneeling down, he fumbled at the straps, frantically plunging his hand inside, feeling for the touch of the metal cold against his hand. Thank God: still there. He pulled the Model B out, turning it in his hand, seeing it for what it was, slowly unwinding the suppressor. Surely too late to fret about noise? It was a reassurance, all the same, this pistol. What was it she had said? *Armed with American cigarettes.* Perhaps she believed he had dared not risk a pistol, walking the streets.

He slumped down, legs outstretched, his back against the wall, feeling sweat rise hot along the line of his spine, trying to take stock, waiting for an odd light-headedness to pass, his mind invaded by a kind of sick hopelessness. The light above his head was too bright, the hall too exposed. Everywhere was too exposed. That business in the rue Saint André des Arts must have unsettled him more than he realised. That, and the endless wait in the *Coq d'Or.*

The day's pointless betrayals had had Cabot's fingerprints on them – he was sure of it. But surely Cabot could not have known an inconspicuous schoolboy decades ago had a habit of visiting his aunt after school? No one could possibly have known Alex would end up here.

A slight draught across the hall came cool on his face flushed suddenly with relief. He found himself smiling into space like an idiot, grateful Aunt Madeleine was late, that she had not come back to find some madman waving a pistol at her.

She could not possibly have been expecting him. Obviously, he had been wrong, fallen victim to some curious kind of recursive paranoia. He was letting Cabot loom too large, letting him infect his thoughts. No one could have predicted his coming here, least of all John Cabot. He had only made the decision himself an hour ago. To predict that would take somebody who knew him better than he knew himself.

It was only as he hauled himself up into a chair, the pistol still in his hand, that the true nature of his gullibility struck, turning his stomach. He had forgotten that bulging file with its pink sticker. Captain Alex Vere's whole life was in that file. You had only to trawl through it to see what might lead him here. *In extremis*, where else would he come? The address in the Faubourg Saint Honoré must be there. Buried, but certainly there. You would find it if you were persistent. And John Cabot was nothing if not persistent.

The more he thought on it, the more cunning this final betrayal seemed. Aunt Madeleine need know nothing of it. All that was called for were calculated steps to bring him here, and those had been effortlessly achieved. She need only return with whoever they chose. A car and two or three men, that was all it would take, and his charming reliable aunt would have innocently delivered him hog-tied to his death. Nothing theatrical, nothing elaborate. This elegant apartment would make for a quiet arrest and it was safe to assume the gullible victim would wait. After all, he had been complicit from the start. She might even apologise as they led him away.

He barely had the strength to stand. Hunger, stress, fatigue, fear - all of them – had sapped what spirit was left. Glistening beads of sweat made the smooth metal of the pistol wet. He had never known his hands to sweat like this. It seemed he was terribly unwell, too far gone to plan. He looked down at the weapon lying in his lap, vacantly registering that the safety flip was down. *You die for mistakes like that.* In some distant Torridon life he had been fond of that pompous phrase. How they must have tired of hearing it. He watched a disinterested finger resting on the catch, already knowing he would never fire the thing. Whatever had corrupted her was not worth her life; it was barely worth his own. Anyway, only a madman would try to shoot his way out of a second-floor flat. He would be arrested here. He would sit and wait. When it came to it, his only regret was that Justine would never know.

Aunt Madeleine was late. Steadying himself against the wall, he tried to focus on the face of his watch, the image of the glass rippling in time with waves of gagging nausea, everything oddly blurred. An hour, she had said, and it was long past that. She was very late. No, *they* were late. It was just a matter of how many. And something else she had said, her telephone didn't work. It came to him uncalled, another childish Torridon rule: *always check.*

He walked unsteadily down the narrow corridor to the study, surprised to remember the way. She had left the light on. It was hard to imagine she spent much time in this forlorn little room smelling faintly of furniture polish. Files were piled neatly on a desk facing the window, the telephone alongside, perched on a little stand. He heard the dialling tone even as he lifted the receiver from its cradle.

Her diary lay flung open, a huge affair in green morocco, a silver pencil lodged in the crease. He switched on the desk light, flipping the pages apart. Aunt Madeleine was not unoccupied. Every hour, it seemed, was filled with names, times, telephone numbers. Nothing in particular against today. No scrawl of *Alex*. Nothing either that might be a plausible code. But then, she hardly need remind herself.

There was a stack of thin manila folders on the desk. He picked one up, labelled *Bassano* in Madeleine's handwriting. Inside, nothing but typed pages, cataloguing paintings, columns listing title, size, medium, date, painter; annotations were inked in the margins here and there in the same irregular scrawl. The folders underneath were bulkier, one labelled *Lévitan*, the other *Austerlitz*, twenty or thirty typed pages in each, in the same style: title, size, medium, date, painter. But for the names, it seemed no more than an inventory of stock.

But for the names.

He found himself wildly scanning the room, searching for something that would do, *anything* that would do, a sudden scald of bile burning his throat. He was too late. He kneeled over the wicker basket, yellow vomit pooling over crumpled paper, liquid leaking round his knees. Everywhere, the stink of sour red wine.

The door along the hall was not locked. Years ago, visits to the little gallery had been a rare concession. He remembered a vast unfurnished room, bare white walls showing two or three canvasses, rarely more, sometimes only one. As he pushed at the door a flat fug of stale air greeted him, the windows shuttered and closed. The switch at the door threw stark yellow light onto heavy gilt frames jostling for space, a confused jumble rising to the ceiling.

White luggage labels dangled down, completed in the same impatient scrawl: Degas, Dufy, Sisley, Manet, Pissarro, van Gogh, Monet, Rouart. They were not displayed so much as hoarded there, the indiscriminate collection of some obsessive madman, wealthy beyond imagination.

The door swung back, revealing other paintings hidden behind. A brutal display of afterthoughts hung with no other thought but suspension, their faces to the wall. Stark bare canvasses on wooden stretchers, luggage labels dangling down, names swinging as the door clicked shut: Braque, Severini, Miro, Picasso, Chagall.

A painting was propped on a wooden easel in the centre of the gallery, covered with a dust sheet. Pulling at it, Alex found himself uncomfortably close to a little girl. Or, rather, a miniature adult framed in gold, its profiled figure too old for its years. A blue ribbon perched awkwardly in her hair, the ends falling away like the forked tail of some exotic fish. Her hands were placidly clasped in her lap, sophisticated eyes fixing something beyond the frame, seeing more than they ought. A metal plate let into the frame was engraved with the single word, *Bassano.*

Alex found the signature at last, lost in a mass of green vegetation high on the right, the letters not completely straight: *r e n o i r.* There was no label.

"*Here you are, then.* I was looking for you everywhere. What do you think? You think it's a copy?"

Madeleine was looking at him, her hair a little awry, standing at the open door, fighting to catch her breath. She pulled the coat from her shoulders, letting it fall onto a chair, startled eyes fixing the pistol in his hand.

"Alexandre, why are you in here? What's the matter?"

He gestured her to move from the door, straining to see beyond into the empty hall. She seemed to have come alone. Whoever had brought her must be waiting in the street below.

She dropped into a chair, nervously watching him walk to the door, her expression impossible to read.

"You look ill, my dear. Have you eaten? Can you put that gun away, it frightens me. God, Alexandre, where are you going? Come back. You can't walk the streets at this time of night. Not in that state. Don't you realise if you're found with a gun ...?"

He turned, searching for her eyes, her face oddly blurred. "Do you know why I came here?"

She frowned, slowly shaking her head. "Well, no, not really. I expected you would say. There have been many mysterious visitors lately ... we call them *visitors* ... you are not the first."

"Just listen to me, for God's sake. I came because I thought I'd be safe. Can you possibly know what it feels like to find somebody you trust ... to find somebody you trusted ... sells you out. And for what? No, I've a better question. *Why*?"

"*Sell you*? What on earth are you talking about? If you came here to shoot me, for heaven's sake get on with it. Do you think I care? Please put your ridiculous gun down."

"How many are there down there waiting? At least tell me that. It would cost you nothing."

"Ah, you mean there are people looking for you. I knew it would be something like that. No, no, I am careful. You are quite safe. Nobody was there when I came back. I am late. I waited for Stephanie outside the cinema until they switched the street lights off. The stupid girl shouldn't be out at this time of night, she'll get herself arrested. I was going to walk back with her. She wasn't there ... some man I suppose. Do sit down, Alexandre. You look really dreadful. I think you are ill. I'll go back down again and see, if that's what you want."

"You seriously think I'd let you do that? I'm not mad."

"Actually I think you are. At the moment … a little mad. Go down and look for yourself if you like."

She sat impassively, waiting for him to move, one hand plucking at her glove. "Do stop being like this, Alexandre. It begins to frighten me. Here, I've thought of something. You can see the street from the balcony in the salon."

She sprang up, standing alongside him, pulling at him, her arms round a dead weight. "Here we go, there's good boy. We'll both go and look."

At the touch of her hand he sank down to his knees, pressing the floor to steady himself, the room suddenly darker, closing in. It seemed there was little more to see than a patch of wood at the foot of the easel. His hands sank into the spongy mass of the parquet, watching his pistol slide away, skidding over the floor. The foot of the easel rose up to meet him, his forehead dissolving into it. Somewhere at the far edge of consciousness he remembered the yawning silence that precedes catastrophe, something huge embracing him. A momentary awareness of the surprising weight of glass. Shards of inflexible pain. Terrible pain. Then nothing. Nothing at all.

Thirty-Seven

The rattle of wooden curtain hoops filled the room with bright sunlight, a tiny breeze scented with lime carrying the murmur of street sounds into the room. A huge chamber pot, decorated with green and yellow dandelions, loomed over him, perched on top of the wooden *chevet* at his bedside.

Madeleine twisted the handle towards him.

"We thought you might need it in the night. More effective than a wicker basket. How do you feel this morning? You slept a long time."

Alex pushed himself up in the bed, wincing as the pillow snagged his neck, staring round, "How did I get in here?"

"Well, that was quite difficult. You have Stephanie to thank. She is stronger than I thought. You can also thank her for the bandage. It hurts?"

"No. Well, yes … it doesn't matter. Stephanie? I remember you coming back alone ..." Sunlight across the bed hurt his eyes, confused fragments of yesterday clamouring for attention. He knew where he was, there was that much to be thankful for, but how he got here remained uncertain. " … In the gallery. Is that right? I think I must have fainted. I remember I'd been thinking about Doctor Clérambault. Odd to remember that."

"Actually, you seemed to be thinking about a gun. Have you

forgotten?" She went to the window, fiddling with the cord of the blinds, her back to him. "This doctor with the complicated name. Someone in Paris? I've never heard of him."

"No, nothing like that. He was a psychiatrist, somebody I'd read about. I was a student of psychology before the war. Perhaps you knew?"

"No. Why would I know that? I can't believe you came to Paris to see this doctor."

"No, no, he's long dead. Committed suicide, in fact. He wrote a lot about manias."

She frowned, a tiny crease of skin between dark eyes, "So you decided to bring your *manias* here?" As she turned round he saw his pistol dangling awkwardly from her finger. "And does your dead doctor explain this?"

"Christ! Be careful! Let me see that thing."

"I think not. When I returned home it was pointing at me." She laid it carefully on the table in front of the window, "There is really no call to explain, Alexandre. At least not everything. I know why you are here. At least, I can guess. You are not my first, you know. I told you, Paris is filled with visitors now." Her look stripped him of years. She was Aunt Madeleine again, climbing the stairs to his little upstairs bedroom, standing at his bedside while he drank his special morning chocolate.

"The pistol … be careful."

"Stephanie made it safe. I could have done it myself, but it was entertaining to watch her. I was surprised she knew such a thing. I suppose it's the company she keeps. Well, you are here. Am I to know why?" She waited, raised eyebrows framing the question.

"Why I'm here? I was almost arrested yesterday. They had set a trap for me. Then it seemed coming here was part of another trap. I was not thinking very well. I convinced myself you were somehow part of the mess."

"*Me*? What is an *almost arrest*? And what has it to do with me?"

"I'm sorry, it has nothing to do with you. I just found myself betrayed one time too many. The life I lead can easily make you a little mad. You begin to see duplicity everywhere, nowhere solid to stand, nobody to trust. It's easy to say be rational, but betrayal has strange effects. You have to experience it to know."

"So you think I've not experienced it?" Her voice was suddenly hard. "You can't know much about Paris. Paris is nothing but betrayal. I will say I am sorry for you, if that's what you want. Now are you going to say why you are really here? No more nonsense about doctors. Or is it a secret? Usually it's a secret."

"No, not a secret. I was sent to contact someone. A man. Now I start to doubt he's here. Perhaps he's not involved at all. I realise now how much somebody wants me out of the way, both of us out of the way ..."

She came and sat on the little chair at his bedside as he stumbled into silence, waiting until their eyes met.

"Both of you? You mean this man? Or is there more to say? You forget, I know you. I remember when little Alexandre looked like that. Perhaps this man was not the only reason."

"Yes, there's another reason. A woman. Someone I worked with a long time ago. I was looking for a woman."

"*Was*? You mean you have found her?"

"Oh, no: the reverse. After yesterday I realise she was just the bait to get me here. I always thought it might be that. She's probably not even in Paris. That's why I woke up thinking about that dead doctor, as you call him. He wrote about people who waste their whole life looking for somebody. Searching for someone you can't find is a kind of madness."

"Yes, you looked a little mad. But this woman, did she have a name? That can't be a secret."

"Her name is Justine. Justine Perry."

"I like the name. French?"

"She spent most of her life in France." Something in Madeleine's face drew the words from him: "And something else ... there's a child. She has a child."

"Ah, Alexandre, this is a very French story. And this is your child? A little boy? Somehow I think of a little boy."

Seeing the pity in her eyes, Alex was suddenly consumed by a kind of weary resentment.

She reached out, patting his arm like a patient nurse, managing a brittle little smile, "Yes, you're right. Perhaps not now. I'll go and make us some coffee. Stephanie brought you some very early, but she left you to sleep. I will fetch your clothes. She did what she could with them. There was blood."

"I forgot. I should have told you. Last night, before you got back. I was in your office."

She stood up, making for the door, laughing, "Oh, we discovered that! But why were you in there?"

"The telephone, you said it wasn't working."

"Did I? It works now I think." She whirled round, her eyes wide with alarm, "God, you didn't use it? Oh, no! What is it you've brought down on me? You really are mad!"

"Of course I didn't use it. I'm not that mad."

"Aren't you? Have you forgotten what you said when I got back last night?"

"I'm not sure. Did I say I thought somebody was using you as bait for a trap? It's not as strange as it sounds, that's how these people work. They used Justine to lure me to Paris."

"*Lure you*? That sounds very dramatic."

"If you like. War is dramatic. When I realised they could work out I might come here, it's easy to believe you might be involved."

"Involved to do what? Anybody would guess you would come here. Where else would you come running? You were always a very transparent boy, Alexandre." She came back to the little chair, pulling it closer to the bed, the hospital visitor wondering how best to put something. "Let me tell you about the meeting I went to last night. I think it might concern you …"

"So there really was a meeting?"

She pursed her lips, suddenly impatient. "Are you always so suspicious? Why would I bother to lie about that? People of the *Quartier*. We talk about the future, about whether we have one. It's all we can do to stay sane. You have no idea, Paris is like a madhouse at the moment. Last night they were talking about a young woman who used to live not far from here. It seems she was a sort of spy. She worked for a German called Brunner. I know this Brunner. Slightly. A repulsive man, obsessed with what he calls the Jewish problem.

A couple of thugs picked this woman up yesterday afternoon. Our thugs, that is, not theirs. They made her tell them things. I don't want to talk about that, it's shameful enough having to think about it. In the end she told them about an English agent the milice were going to arrest. Now I think perhaps she was talking about you. Do you call yourself an agent? It sounds preposterous. She said she knew where this person was to be arrested."

"Where did she say?"

"The rue Saint André des Arts. I forget the number. Do you know that street? Near the Odéon. Not a very nice area."

"Oh, yes, I know it. Did she say when?"

"She thought it must have already happened. I don't think she knew much about it."

"Where is she now, this woman? Can I see her? Where are they keeping her? Do you think you could arrange for me to talk to her?"

"Where is she now? In the Seine, I imagine. They shot her." She shook her head, "No, I should stop being such a coward. The truth is, *we* shot her. We all agreed to it." She summoned up a weary smile, staring down into her lap, tugging pointlessly at the fabric of her skirt. "I don't know where they did it. That's what the New France has brought us to. We shoot French girls. Apparently she was quite brave when it came to it." When she looked up, her eyes were full of tears. "God, Alexandre, you know we can't keep prisoners. She knew that. It's a matter of surviving."

"But you *have* survived. The Americans will be in here in a week or two."

"And what then? You think our German friends will simply go home? Everybody is talking of an uprising, an armed insurrection." She glanced at the pistol on the table, "I suppose I am in a position to contribute a little now."

"The Americans won't march into that. Not street fighting. They've never wanted to come to Paris. Why should they? There's a garrison but Paris is mostly for old soldiers and wounded kids. All the Americans want is an orderly German retreat. They'll let them get out."

"How long have you been in Paris, Alexandre?" Not waiting for a reply, there was a strange ironic expression on her face, almost taunting him. "You seem very confident about your Americans. Did you cross a bridge coming here? You must have …"

"It was getting dark."

"Not too dark to see the explosives. They are intended to be seen. At The Hotel de Ville as well … all the monuments ... explosives everywhere." She crushed her cigarette into the ash tray. "And the galleries, of course. All of them. You forget what I do for a living."

"No, I don't forget. You sell pictures." Now he had reached the point, he was lost for what to say – only that her apartment was filled with imperishable masterpieces strung up on sagging cords like so many bits of junk. "You must know I saw those folders. It's stolen stuff, isn't it? Lists of looted stuff. And it's here. Are you surprised I was sick?"

She looked away, sudden patches of red appearing on her cheeks, her voice cutting through him. "No, you were not sick because of folders. You are being absurd. You were sick because you were ill, or frightened ... or deceiving yourself."

"Those names? Bassano, Lévitan … I forget the other."

"The other is Austerlitz. They mean nothing to you?" She was staring at him. "Frankly, that's hard to believe, but no, I see you don't."

"It's the paintings that need an explanation, not the names."

She stood up, smoothing her skirt. Making for the door, she suddenly changed her mind, holding on to the door handle, glaring back at him.

"So you want to know about pictures?" There was a kind of dismissive scorn in her voice. She was very angry. "Second tier stuff, in the main. Mostly from private collections, if you must know. You are quick to pose your questions. You think you can come here quizzing me? I'm not answerable to you. And since we come to it, you have not asked about the Renoir. Perhaps you remember?"

"The painting that fell on me?"

"You put your head through the glass. It's perhaps lucky for you that I dislike that painting. Life's not like that, he should have known better."

"*Second tier stuff*, I suppose?"

She flinched at the sneer in his voice, standing silent, her face set.

Alex pushed himself up in the bed, "I walked through the Marais last night. Whole streets deserted, houses emptied out, ravaged. You surely know somebody must own these paintings, even if they were abandoned."

"*Abandoned*?"

She shook her head, filling the silence with an exasperated sigh. "So you really are a child, Alexandre. Listen to me. I'll explain something for you. Although God knows why I should. Perhaps for the satisfaction of hearing what you have to say when I finish. You know nothing at all. Perhaps you are to be forgiven for that, but you'd better listen. Too many people hide behind ignorance."

She came to stand over him, restlessly wringing her hands, her pale face immobile. There was a horrible kind of suppressed tension about her. He might not have been there; she seemed to be explaining something to herself.

"When German troops arrived in Paris - I'm talking about the armistice - it seemed like a gift from God. We were not going to be caught up in another war. You can't believe the relief. Alright, we were to be saddled with the old fool Petain, but why not? There were worse options. And he had purchased us a sort of life. The war was lost, anyway." Her laugh was little more than a sharp intake of breath. Give the English a kicking while we're at it, that's what we thought. A kicking for being *têtu,* you know, wooden-headed."

She held on to a strange grave smile, no longer completely hostile, drawing him in. "And that's how it was at first. The Germans wanted the old Paris, the one in the books. They wanted their sex French, if you like. We began inventing a past for them to live in. We joined them there. Not such a bad thing."

"Apart from the Jews, the round-ups, the arrests. Apart from the slaughter camps. You're forgetting all that."

"You are running ahead. I'll come there, don't worry. And it will surprise you. One day a German officer came to the gallery. Only one leg. All dressed up for the visit, rather charming, you'd think he'd come courting. I was there that day. Do you know what he'd brought? A Fragonard. He'd got it under his arm, wrapped up in brown paper. A landscape. An early thing, really lovely. He wondered whether it was worth anything. What could I say? I told him he was unlikely to meet anybody with enough money to buy it from him. But that was just the start. Soldiers started turning up more or less every day with things, asking for valuations, always valuations. It's embarrassing having to explain the facts of life to your new masters ..."

"Facts of life?"

"If somebody arrives with a painting and no provenance, what's the first question you must ask?"

Alex hesitated. "I suppose you ask how they came by it."

"Exact. But since I could not ask that question, the best I could say was that things are often copied. And that is true, I can speak with authority on the subject, it is my profession. Take that Renoir you damaged. It was stolen from the family who actually commissioned it. It's a copy."

"Thank God for that."

"I mean a copy made by Renoir. He was always copying his own work. When the owner was arrested the painting was confiscated. Is *confiscated* a better word than stolen?"

"Arrested by the Germans, you mean?"

"I think so. But we soon learned to do our own arresting."

"The paintings are the spoils of war. Is that what you're saying? And that makes it legitimate?"

"Makes what legitimate? We are not at war, Alexandre. How can there be spoils when there is no war? I know for you English war is about battles, but Paris is not London, Warsaw – places like that. War has passed us by. How do you think that miracle came about?"

Alex looked down, embarrassed.

"You have nothing to say? That Renoir? The one you butted. You saw the little plaque on it?"

"Yes. The word, *Bassano*."

"And you really don't know what that means?" She was staring intently at him, watching his face, finally turning away to light a cigarette, pulling hard on it, muttering, "He knows nothing at all. It's hopeless."

"I'm not sure what I'm supposed to know. You mean the rue de Bassano? I know that's not far from here."

"Not far at all. The painting that came into contact with your head came from a house on the corner of the rue Georges Bizet. A fabulous place. A kind of palace. At the end of the last century the family commissioned Renoir to paint all three of their little girls. One of them was arrested not long ago. She was an old woman, of course."

"What on earth for?"

"Alright, not arrested. *Interned*, if the word consoles you."

"You mean because she's Jewish?"

"Jewish, yes. Although in her case, perhaps not sufficiently French would be better. When I was told they'd taken her away, I remember thinking, being painted by Renoir would protect her, give her some kind of immunity. Like being touched by God."

"She'll be released soon enough. I don't think the Americans will wear arbitrary arrest."

Alex became conscious of the expression fixing him, a sort of exasperated reproach.

"You think that, do you? I'm afraid release doesn't come into it. I know where they took her, you see. Too late for release, Americans or not. Well … release … it's a word you hear."

She pushed the chair at his bedside closer, perching herself half on it, the gesture a kind of conciliation. "You don't know what I'm talking about, do you? No point being angry with you. I'm sorry ... sorry for you." She turned aside, trying to catch her breath, suddenly short of air. "We're lost, Alexandre, don't you see? All of us. Living one sort of lie or another. And you talk about *release* …"

"But your paintings - I still don't understand …"

"They're not *my* paintings, for God's sake! Do you think I want to have anything to do with the damned things?" Her voice was choking, "Do you really think that?" She pulled a tiny handkerchief from her sleeve, pressing it against her mouth, finally pulling it away, her eyes blazing. "They bring them here, twenty or thirty pictures at a time … more sometimes. Forgeries, most of them. Nearly all of them. That's what I have to decide. I have no choice. A man comes every two weeks. A German, but not a soldier, he knows too much about art. He brings new paintings and takes the others away. These last few weeks he's started bringing work from banned artists. They are too easily copied, most of them … it's impossible now. If I am wrong, I will be relieved of the task. Do you understand what that means?"

Seeing the tears on her cheeks, Alex could think of nothing to say. He shook his head.

"I will be arrested. There are camps. I'll be sent to one of them." For a moment he thought she had finished. He watched her making for the door, mumbling to herself, "What's the point? He knows nothing."

"But I do know ..." willing her to turn round, "everyone knows. The death camps, hellish places in Poland, dozens of them. Of course I know. But …"

She turned at last, standing in the doorway, "As you say, death camps. But no, not Poland. We have our own. That's what you don't know. We have our own. Right here in Paris."

She had gone, quietly closing the door before he had time to reply.

Thirty-Eight

There was no one in the kitchen when he went looking for coffee. The pot on the stove was still warm. He poured himself a cup and walked with it into the salon. The long doors onto the balcony were wide open, Madeleine sitting in her chair, her head lolled uncomfortably against the metal rail. She started awake as he stepped out, fearful eyes opening full on his own, recognition arriving slowly.

"Ah, so it's you, Alexandre. The bath. Did you find the towels? I was asleep. I often sleep out here. Paris is agreeably quiet these days. Can you give me a cigarette? Your neck … you cut your neck."

He opened his case, holding it out to her. "The neck's alright, nothing serious. I've come to apologise. To say sorry."

"You know, when you were a child you were always saying sorry. It's an English habit. Irritating. I was overwrought, that's all, perhaps we both were. It's in the air at the moment, I'm used to it."

"But I mean it … I want to explain."

"Oh, of course you mean it, that's what is irritating. Explain about what? Your doctor what's-his-name? Or your woman? Come and tell me about her. Sit here."

"They come to the same thing. I think about Justine all the time. I'd like to tell you about …"

"No, I've changed my mind. We'll talk about her over dinner. I like talking about love when I'm eating. Stephanie made us something. Not much, I must say, but I'll find something good to drink. It's curious, I don't recall you having a girl when you were at school. Were you old enough for all that tiresome stuff? You were always here, but you never talked about a girl."

"No girl. I used to adore from a distance, that's as far as I got." He lit her cigarette, barely seeing her, his head filled with thoughts of Justine. "I remember how this place smelled. It's still the same, it smells of pictures. You know that smell, a bit like fresh putty? It used to scare me. It was not properly *domestic* somehow. It came back to me when you left me here last night. Standing in the hall … it was as if somehow I was a boy again."

"Is this part of your apology? The scent of paint?"

"You're laughing at me. No, but I remember the pictures. They were all so raw, you know, they looked barely finished."

"In those days some of them weren't finished, so you're correct." She was laughing, leaning her head back, squinting at him through half closed eyes, "Times change, you know."

"I suppose I thought proper pictures should be behind glass."

"Ah, I thought that was where you were going. You're leading me back to Renoir. I must say you are quite adept, Alexandre. Must we go through all that again? I am rather tired."

"I'm sorry, I suppose I was trying to be clever. It's what I do, if you want to know. My job, if you can call it a job. Teaching tricks like that. Interrogation tricks. And no, I'm not adept at all. I'm sorry." She shook her head at the word, crushing her cigarette into the saucer of her cup.

Alex leaned across the table, trying to catch her eyes. "What did you mean when you said there were camps? Camps in Paris?"

"Fetch me a drink, would you. Dubonnet. Put some gin in it if there's any there."

As he mixed the drink, she called through to him. "Pour something for yourself. That's not a man's drink."

When he came back onto the balcony she was sitting upright, her arms folded.

"That cushion. Behind my back. Now sit there while I think." She sat, fingers drumming the table, looking past him across the rooftops.

"I have to think where to start. Claude Pasquier, my framer? Why not there? You remember him? Or perhaps you don't?"

"In the gallery. I'd forgotten his name. An old chap with a leather apron. That one?"

"He wasn't so old, Alexendre. Not that much older than you. He started with me as an apprentice. You remember the shop in the Marais? Next to the clock-menders. If you could see that street now ..."

"The rue Gravilliers? But I have seen it - I was there yesterday. I'd better not say what took me there. The place is deserted. As if some kind of plague has hit it. And weird notices everywhere ... stuck on the doors."

"All that started over a year ago." She hesitated, eyeing her cigarette, frowning at a lipstick stain, an odd cautious expression on her face. "I ask myself, am I wasting my breath? How much does little Alexandre really know? I thought *agents* were informed. I would not like it if you were pretending to know less than you do."

"I know about the Jewish Laws. It's common knowledge. And the roundups, of course. But I'd not imagined what I saw in the rue Gravilliers."

"I can't remember when exactly they took Claude away. Time stops in a war, did you know that? It must be months ago. He's Jewish, of course. They took both of them on that account. You remember Sophie?" She was searching his face, waiting for him to acknowledge something, "Sophie, his wife?"

"*They* took them? You mean the Germans?"

"It was not always Germans. I think you know the man who took Claude. He was only a boy then, of course. You used to play with him. Veronique's son, I forget his name. A fat little boy, you remember?"

"Vaguely. He was called Camille. We used to rag him about his name, say he was really a girl, that sort of thing. Boys are cruel little devils. I went to the swimming baths with him once or twice. He was too fat. What about him?"

She reached down for her bag, placing it on the table, rummaging inside, pulling out his pistol. As he reached to take it from her she let it slip back inside. "He fancies himself with one of these now. And you're right, he is cruel. He has joined the milice. He was one of the group that arrested Claude. Him and a couple of thugs. He came visiting here the day afterwards."

"You mean to this apartment?"

"On his own. A private visit. Banging on the door like a maniac. Shouldering his way past me as if he owned the place, asking for my papers."

"You mean your *Carte*? What business is it of his?"

"He made it his business, and no, I don't mean my *Carte*. And why are you suddenly being so polite? You're thinking, *Why didn't she help Claude? Why did she let them take him away?* They are good questions. Why did I let a grubby gang of thugs do what they liked with my old friends?"

"I have no right to ask that question."

"God, you English. And you wonder why people hate you. Don't you realise how superior that sounds? You're so damned certain about everything. Well, I'll answer you anyway. I looked the other way. Do you think I'm proud of it? I knew what would happen to Claude and Sophie, and I looked the other way. The strange thing is, when those Jewish Laws came in, nobody thought much about it. You don't really believe things like that. Not even the church … well, they went on a bit about compulsory divorce, but even that seemed a bit rarefied. The truth is we didn't believe any of it. Not much of a defence, is it? We sold our souls for a chance of survival. I'm not sure *survival* means much if you're dead already."

"But we have it in England, it's the same everywhere. When war comes you're bound to ask about allegiances. Italians, Germans even. What do you do with them? Internment seems like rough justice, but when you're at war ... in any case, they weren't all French. Some are bound to be interned, deported even …"

"Is that what you think? Where do you deport people to in the middle of someone else's war? Let me finish about Sophie. In the first place, she's no more Jewish than I am. In fact, I'm more Jewish. My fool of a grandfather used to boast he was half Jewish, we were always telling him to shut up about it. No, Sophie comes from Perpignan. She has what they call a Catalan nose."

She stood up, leaning over the rail to watch a rare car creep down the street, trailing a cloud of black smoke. She did not turn round. Her voice was lost in the air. He could barely hear her. "The milice. These fat schoolboys with guns. They go by how you look now. You are arrested for looking Jewish."

She turned aside, her profile stark against the egg-shell blue of the sky, one hand poised over the rail, not quite touching it, the pose an exaggerated caricature of some painting he failed to recognise. "Do I look Jewish, would you say? What do you think of my nose, Alexandre? Should I die for my nose?"

"Aunt Madeleine, please. I'm sorry … no, I shouldn't say that. You don't have to tell me this. Nobody owes these butchers guilt. Monsters like that always claim others are responsible. God knows, I've met enough of them."

She leaned back, drawing on her cigarette, her expression closed in on itself, impossible to decipher. "I remember they let her telephone here," her voice flat, dissembling calm - she had told this story before.

"Of course they let her use the telephone. It was a way of getting my address, adding me to one of their damnable lists. That's how little Camille knew where to come. Sophie kept shouting down the telephone, *tell them I'm not, Madame. Speak to them. Tell them I'm not.* Over and over again. It broke my heart. I could hear them banging about in the apartment. You could hear china breaking on the floor, glass as well - it's dreadful to hear things like that. But nobody came to the telephone. And she's not Jewish, that's for sure. She'd even got one of those ridiculous certificates saying she wasn't, poor woman."

Seeing the question in Alex's eyes, she hesitated, wondering how best to put something, "Living in the Jewish Quarter like that, she thought it was best. But those certificates are a hopeless charade. The first thing they ask is why you think you need one. Then they tell you it's a forgery. And the truth is most of them are. Sophie left the receiver on the table. I could hear everything. You never imagine things could come to this, do you? Not in Paris. She was crying as they dragged her away. Not shouting, just crying. Like a little girl calling for her mother. I don't think I'll ever forget that."

"Where did they take her?"

She frowed at him, "Drancy, of course. Where else?"

"The housing estate?"

"Nobody would want to be housed there now. It's a kind of holding centre, a transit camp. You know what *transit* means? They picked up all their neighbours the same day, most of that bottom end of the street. Sophie should have known the risk, living there. The watchmaker next door, he was as Jewish as they come. That was when they started rounding people up by the bus load. It was a kind of obsession. The milice would arrest you then seal your house up, until they came back for the furniture."

"What do you mean, *furniture?* What about the furniture?"

"Yes, I can see you're new to Paris. It is another of the things we have learned not to see. Removal vans everywhere: hundreds of them. And we never see them."

"I saw one. On the way here. The rue du Temple, I think. I thought somebody was moving house."

"Paris is full of Germans, there are Americans at the gates, the English are dropping their damned bombs everywhere. And you think people choose such a time to move house?"

"I didn't think ..."

"Two days after they arrested Claude and Sophie, they came back to the gallery and made an inventory. They must have got the keys off Sophie, she always locked up. I was there that day. It was a removal company. Just two men and the municipal police. It's all legal. I suppose you can say legal. They had a paper from the Prefecture. They cleared the shop out, packed everything up. Much of what they took was mine, but when I asked, they told me to take it up with the Prefecture. They wanted me out of the way. I imagine they helped themselves to a few things. Hard not to, I suppose. That's how you end up with a Fragonard under your arm."

"But you can't just turn up and steal things ..."

"Can't you, Alexandre? And who is going to stop you? Think about it. If all these Jews are to vanish, it's only right their things should vanish with them. Food, for example. Best eaten up, wouldn't you say? Before it goes off ..." Alex went to take her hand, willing the anger from her. She pulled away. "They cleared the shop out. Took all the stuff Claude was framing for me."

"But took it where? There are hundreds of houses in the rue Gravilliers. All this stuff?"

"Yes, it's the right question. The answer will surprise you. When they'd cleared the gallery they went up to the apartment upstairs. Their little flat. I went and looked. Everything had gone. Sophie's clothes … all her little things ... even her underwear. The lino off the boards. Looking round I realised why. You know how places look when they are stripped like that? Sad little vacant spaces. Hardly worth the effort to have made a life there. They become nothing places. Easy to believe nobody was ever there."

"You were going to say about the furniture."

"You mean what happens to it? It goes to Germany. It's packed and sent to Germany as a kind of insane recompense. It gets sent to the bombed cities. Hamburg, Munich, places like that. To replace what was lost in the raids. Not just furniture - clothing, toys, books, everything. When it started it was on the wireless. They said it was only fair … a just reckoning."

"Except it's stolen, all of it."

"There are laws about that now. If you don't have the right to own something, it can't be stolen, can it? That's how they think about it. It's an enormous undertaking. Dozens of trainloads a week, mostly from the station at Austerlitz."

"Surely there are protests, resistance? It's not too hard to disrupt operations like that. I used to plan …"

"*Disrupt*? Oh, no, I thought you understood. There's something far more effective than disruption. We don't notice. Like the removal vans - we see them all the time, but we don't notice. It's difficult at first, almost impossible, but you soon get into the way of it. It's such a small price to pay, you see. That's how they were able to set the camps up. *Concentration camps*. Slave labour to pack the goods. They send people from Drancy to do it, some of the ones that are not to be shipped off straight away. So you see, the camps are not in far-off Poland, they're right here, in Paris."

"*Concentration camps*? But that's impossible … what I mean is … how long …?"

"Oh, a long time. And it's perfectly possible. You see, if you look the other way, you soon believe there is nothing to see." She reached across, patting his hand as if he were about to deny something, "There must be hundreds of people working in those places. God knows where they sleep. Or where they eat. Or what they eat, for that matter. They must be fed somehow. Or perhaps not. There you are - it's best not to ask."

"So you have all these people in prisons …"

"You can't pack furniture in a prison. No, you've seen where they are. Those labels you were so interested in."

"Bassano?"

"They send the best stuff there. Fine antiques, the best of the paintings, things that need specialists to repair. Specialist prisoners, that is. I think there's a special place they send pianos. You can't imagine how many pianos are being transported every day around Paris while your war is going on. And linen – bales and bales of linen – I believe they pack linen at the Lévitan store. Not that anyone knows it's going on, of course."

"You mean the Lévitan furniture shop? I remember that place. Cheap stuff. It was a sort of Woolworths."

"If you could shop there, you'd find it had gone up in the world." Seeing Alex's bewildered face her smile was ironic. "It's closed, of course, but not so cheap now ... not at all."

Thirty-Nine

They sat late into the night in a tiny island of candlelight on the balcony, drinking Chambolle-Musigny, picking at the salad Stephanie had set out for them, the city beyond a vast mosaic of flickering yellow pinpricks. Warm air rising from the quiet street filled Alex with an almost unbearable nostalgia, the scent of an unrecoverable time before the blight of war.

"This woman you say you were looking for." She leaned forward, resting on one elbow, waiting for him to light her cigarette. "She is English, after all? Does she have a family?"

"Her mother died when she was very young. She's half French, I think. Brought up by nuns. Somewhere in the South West."

"Nuns. My God! Poor soul!"

"Oh, I don't know. She said she was happy enough. She kept her faith, anyway ..."

"And ended up a spy. No, Alexandre, don't look at me like that. You can keep your faith out of revenge. There are nuns and nuns, believe me. What made you so sure she was in Paris?"

"They told her I had been posted here. Probably said I was in danger. That would be enough for her to try and follow me. It was all lies, of course."

"Now you're being mysterious. You make her sound very naïve, to come running after you. Why should she do that?"

"I don't know. Don't you understand? I don't know. In my job when things seem obvious, you get suspicious. All I know is Justine killed a German officer in France. They don't forget things like that."

"And this *they* you continually mention?" The sardonic look over the rim of her glass said she did not expect a reply. Her cigarette flared a tiny red dot between her fingers as she stood up, pushing the chair back. The lights of a solitary car below threw long shadows across the front of the buildings opposite.

"I see you're not going to explain. I remember you in this mulish mood." She glanced at her watch, "That girl is late again. It's getting damp. Shall we go in?"

Alex did not move, looking down at the tiled floor, mumbling. "He would have been born in October. I always think of him as *he*. I have dreams about him, you know."

"Does that sort of talk comfort you?" Standing behind him, she rested one hand briefly on his shoulder. "I understand more than you think. Your Justine cannot be here in Paris, that much is obvious. Not with a child – it's impossible. A romantic fiction. Who would send a pregnant woman ...?"

"Who's talking about *send*? Perhaps she had no choice."

"Shall we go inside? There is coffee."

Alex craned round, looking over his shoulder. "*Girl with Straw Hat*. You know a painting with that title?"

"Recent? You mean the Bradley painting? Of course I know it, I actually saw it last year. At the Palais des Beaux-Arts. I'd never seen it before. I was surprised he showed it there, mixed up with a dreadful lot of heroic nonsense."

"No, not that. There's a painting of Justine with that title, by an artist called Lucile Beyrou."

Madeleine frowned, shaking her head, "Beyrou? No, the name means nothing. Should it? Is she French?"

"No, she's English, but you won't know her by that name. She had to adopt that name."

"And the title? She put it in English like Bradley?"

"No, the title's in French, *Fille au Chapeau de Paille.*"

"Not particularly good French, I must say." She stepped inside the salon, calling back to him, her voice suddenly impatient, "There must be thousands of such paintings, Alexandre. French girls in straw hats. Renoir did his fair share. He was always painting them - regrettable things, but certainly full of hats. Why are you asking this?"

Alex followed her inside, standing awkwardly, waiting until she flopped onto the sofa, waving him into a seat opposite. "Beyrou - I'd better call her that - worked for years with Bradley in France. Ended up almost as famous as him. It got to be too dangerous living there. She was exfiltrated, *rescued*, if you like. They set her up in a place in Scotland. Dundee."

"Ah, you mean that English girl ... It's alright, I forget her name. There was an exhibition just before the war. Yes, her work was excellent. I was told she had been magically spirited away. So that was where you *exfiltrated* her to? The word is new to me. Why do you tell me this?"

"Because Justine was one of the agents who did the spiriting away. She actually lived with Beyrou in Dundee for a few weeks. I think that was how she was tracked down."

"And this so-called Beyrou painted her? From what I know of her work I can't see her painting portraits. Are you sure?"

"She said she did it as a kind of a consolation."

"Ah, I see. But you say your Justine is – how do you put it? - a secret agent, a spy?"

"She was an agent."

"But a portrait? Would that not be incredibly unwise? For the artist as well."

"Perhaps. But it was something private, between them. Then by some hellish mischance it ended up on display. Someone bought it."

"So …? You are being mysterious again."

"I told you I came to Paris to look for a man. In the world in which I work I count him as dangerous. He was the one who bought the painting, he would have recognised Justine."

"And wanted to avoid others doing the same, or find some way of exposing her. Is that what you're saying?"

"Either – but that's not the point. If he's in Paris looking for her it means she msut be here. At least, she's alive - that's the rock I am clinging to."

"And your child?" Her eyes were suddenly searching, "If it is your child? Is that your concern? Is it? This word, *consolation*. You say she is in need of consolation." Seeing the hurt in his face, she slowly shook her head. "It's hard to believe in this rock of yours. But listen, there is a man coming here tomorrow to collect paintings. He deals with the collection at the Bassano house, he is very knowledgeable. It's a tangled story, but I will see what I can prise out of him."

"Someone coming here?"

"In the morning. Yes, you're right, you cannot be here. He tends to wander about. Go and look at Paris for a few hours. Sit in a café somewhere. It is safe enough. Or go for a walk. Not too far. You may see some bread."

"But it's rationed. They'll ask for a card."

"Ah, but the strangest people sell bread. You imagine Paris can manage without bread? You have money I assume? Ask in a café ... if it looks safe."

"Is it safe to look at this Bassano prison? It can't be far to walk. There are people in London who would like to know about what's going on there. Is it safe?"

"No, it's not far. But there is nothing to see at Bassano. And it's not a prison. All you will see is a huge town house. God knows how many are locked inside, but you will see nobody. And no, it is certainly not safe, the street is too quiet. The furniture deliveries are mostly at the Lévitan Store. You might see something there but it's much too far to walk. Near the Gare du Nord."

"I don't mind walking. A railway station gives a good reason to be there. But if I'm stopped ... I don't trust my papers."

"Oh, you won't be stopped. Not any longer. We used to be harassed all the time - police, gendarmes, even German soldiers if they liked the look of you. Then a few months ago all that nonsense petered out. It's as if they've lost interest. More likely, they think it's no longer wise to take sides. Of course, you'll have the milice to worry about, but it's Jews they're after. Just try not to look like a Jew, my dear." She choked back a laugh, her face defiantly pink. “No, I agree. A joke in bad taste. Your disapproval is noted.”

“What right have I to disapprove? I’ve not lived through all this. I can’t imagine ...”

“Can’t imagine what keeps us amused in this madhouse? Is that what you mean? You’d be surprised. Sometimes it’s best to laugh.”

She stood up, pulling him to stand in front of her, placing two hands on his shoulders, straightening him as if he were setting out for school.

“You’ll pass. You look too respectable to arrest. Just one thing - you need a respectable hat to go out in. I will find one for you tomorrow. I have quite a collection of abandoned hats. And something for your neck, the neck spoils the impression.” She handed him a tiny visiting card. “Give them this address if you are very unlucky.”

She was already at the door. “Your gun will remain here. That way you can’t shoot anybody. Now I think I’ll go to bed.”

One side of the Faubourg Saint-Martin was filled with the early morning crowd streaming down from the Gare du Nord, past the stone facade of the Lévitan Store. Dusty plate glass windows streaked with bird droppings gave the place an unkempt air, somewhere that had known better days. Plainly, it had been closed for months.

Two soldiers stood between fake marble pillars, their backs against the locked doors, watching the crowd. Shabby uniforms, khaki and green, flashes of red high on the sleeve. It gave them a vaguely Russian air.

Alex fell in behind a press of women with prams, stopping as they stopped, turning side-on to gawp through grimy windows. Crude makeshift screens a few feet high set off tiny display areas inside, each with its collection of sofas, chairs, tables, beds - sad little caricatures of pre-war domesticity. Decorative lamps on tall stands, their dusty shades no longer straight, were lined up along the back wall.

A woman in front of Alex jostled into him, jerking her pram back onto the pavement as a removal van, braking hard, buried itself too fast down the steep ramp between the two narrow arches. She bellowed curses into the dark of the cavernous space.

The soldiers in the doorway came down the steps to look, nervously unhitching their rifles. They held their line as a stream of prams pushed towards them. Alex wandered a few yards down the vacant ramp. In the half light at the bottom, men were already swinging open the back doors of the van. It was stuffed with furniture wrapped in grey blankets, spindly kitchen chairs roped together, leaning out. A silent line of anonymous figures dressed in long striped aprons had already begun to unload, pulling out tea chests and cardboard boxes, mechanically passing them along to disappear through a doorway at the side. The driver stood aimlessly leaning against the side of the van. He flicked a cigarette into the yard, gesturing to Alex to move away.

At the top of the ramp the squabble had ended. The woman with the pram was walking slowly up the road towards the station. The guards had retreated to the huge glass doors. Uncertain for a second which way to go, Alex stepped out of the darkness onto the pavement, flinching back as something dark angled through his vision, momentarily blotting out the sun. A massive swish of air scythed past his face, some gigantic bird swooping on him, talons extended like thin gyrating legs. A sack of something soft thumped onto the pavement, a single sickening bounce bursting bits of coloured cloth out into the gutter.

It was over before he had time to move, before he had time to see. A mound of rags lay pressed against the pavement, red and black, pierced here and there with tiny beads. As he watched, a single naked arm flopped out, white flesh spattered to the wrist with blood.

The soldiers were already barging him aside, reaching down to the body, crumpled uniforms caked in grime, muttering in a language he had never heard before, their yellow complexion more Mongolian than German. One of them pulled aside a piece of the cloth, bending down to look. Part of an innocent pretty face was watching them from under a halo of light brown hair. She could not have been more than twenty, little more than a girl. And frail. You would have thought too frail to fall so fast.

A crowd had formed behind, hemming him in. Someone called, *Cover the poor soul up*. A man at Alex's side muttered, *I saw the whole thing. She jumped I tell you. Is it a woman?*

Blood had begun to seep from the bundle, a magenta stain spreading out from the woman's head. One of the soldiers grabbed Alex's arm, to steady himself, scraping at a fold in her dress with his foot to cover her face. He would not look down. A German officer appeared at the top of the ramp, pushing his way through the crowd. Alex freed himself, drifting to the edge of the pavement, hemmed in, forced to stand and watch.

The officer muttered something that sent the guards scuttling back to their post by the door. He lit a cigarette, standing over the body, head tipped back, staring at the row of tiny windows on the fourth level where the leaded surface of a flat roof reached out to a stretch of decorative tiles. He stood blowing smoke into the air, waiting.

An improvised stretcher appeared with two bearers, pistols tucked into their belts. They stood next to the mound of cloth, nervously looking across to the sullen crowd on the other side of the street. Perhaps the officer said something – it was impossible to hear. Someone called, *fucking milice. Leave the poor soul alone.*

A man at Alex's side ducked down, picking a stone out of the gutter. A wave of silence swept over the crowd, a gigantic intake of breath. He threw it hard at one of the plate glass windows high on the second floor. In the frozen moment they heard the sharp clink as it bounced down to the pavement. The officer kicked it away, grimacing as his shoes scraped the pavement.

As if the rattle against the unbroken glass had been some unspoken command, Alex found himself staring at a sudden line of faces at the window. Unnaturally white, like painted puppet heads, they hovered an instant then vanished, as if snatched away by hidden strings.

It could not have been more than a second, but Alex felt his world dissolve. Rooted where he stood, his head cocked absurdly back, he stared at the blank of the glass. The heads had long since gone. Perhaps a dozen, women all of them, faces white against the darkness of the space inside, all but one with scarfs covering their hair. Pressed in a milling crush of angry people he found he could not move, desperately clinging to the tiny fraction of time in which his eyes had locked with hers: time shared, certainty for ever sure. He stumbled forward as someone tried to drag him away, an odd surging sensation in his chest catching his breath. Standing his ground, it seemed he dare not move. Moving would shake the image away. Dark eyes, their expression fleeting desperation.

The men reluctantly loaded the stretcher, staggering back towards the ramp. The officer walked to the edge of the pavement calling to the crowd to disperse. Someone shouted, *Move off yourself. We live here*. He unbuttoned the holster at his hip, flicking the leather flap open and closed, facing them down. Conscious that it was in some obscure way a betrayal, Alex turned with the crowd, letting himself be swept back to the junction of the Faubourg Saint-Martin.

Forty

When he got back, Madeleine was sitting on the balcony drinking coffee. She seemed preoccupied, barely listening as he blurted out the story in an incoherent rush of words.

She looked up, as if seeing him for the first time, blinking.

"Wait. You say you were outside the Lévitan shop? We were a little drunk last night. I hardly believed you were serious. I thought you were going to a café. You realise that shop is a secret place? Guarded. There's nothing to see from the outside. It's just an empty shop, I was there last year to collect a picture. At least, you would think it was empty."

"You mean you've been inside? I didn't know that."

"Why should you know?" She snapped at him, sudden patches of red on her cheeks, "All I remember was the smell. An overpowering smell of unclean humanity. I suppose all prisons are like that, except this place seemed deserted. I was left to wait in a big hall. They called it the lobby, divided up into little private spaces. I suppose where they met customers, when there were customers to meet. My God, you took a risk going all that way. A risk for both of us. There's nothing out of the ordinary there, apart from the disagreeable smell."

"You don't think suicide out of the ordinary?"

"No ..." She paused as if the question demanded reflection. "Not particularly. Suicide is not unusual in Paris. You could say it's an occupational hazard for some."

"Soldiers on guard duty for an empty shop - not unusual either? They were certainly not French, not German either. I think the uniform was Russian."

"Ah, our famous Uzbeks. I'm not sure what country that is. Perhaps you know? They were deserters from the Russian front. Changed sides. It shows you are new to Paris, Alexandre. You meet them everywhere. Professional thugs the new masters use for dirty jobs they won't do themselves." She looked at him, shaking her head, the expression something he remembered from years ago – grudging disbelief barely disguising a faint approving smile for some act of infantile bravado.

"So little Alexandre walked on his own all that way? I begin to feel responsible for you. Perhaps you really are mad."

"What was I supposed to do? Alright, perhaps I drank a little too much last night, but you realise you were talking about concentration camps in the centre of Paris? It may be real to you, but it was always going to seem unreal to me, until I saw for myself. And thank God I did. If I hadn't …"

"So you went to see, and it is still unreal. You see phantoms. This nonsense about faces at a window."

"I saw her, I tell you. Justine is in that place. For God's sake, why don't you accept what I say?"

"Leave God out of it, Alexandre. You saw a face, just a woman's face. For a few seconds. You say you spend your life hoping to see this woman. You told me yourself it has made you a little mad, do you remember?"

"Not so mad that I imagine things."

"Mad enough to think you should wave pistols at me. What did you really see? A face. Tell the truth, how many times have you taken some complete stranger for your missing woman?"

"Her name is Justine. Dozens of times, I suppose. But …"

"There you are. Perhaps we can finish with this nonsense. The truth is, you *wanted* to see her."

"I don't understand. It's as if you want me to be wrong. As if you wish it. Why won't you believe me? *Why*? I understand these things, it is my profession. If I'd made a mistake, by now I would be doubting myself, starting to feel stupid. But I don't. Not in the slightest. We were looking straight into each other's eyes. It was Justine."

"Then God help her, the poor soul!" The ferocity in her voice struck him like a blow. He stood nervously looking down at her, aware only of the quiet flap of the table-cloth in the breeze. It was a long time before she spoke. "I'm sorry, my dear, I didn't mean to shout. It's been a difficult day. Come and sit down, I need to talk to you. About my morning."

"Of course. I forgot. The man who came for the pictures."

"Two men this time - the usual man and someone else. I have to tell you about him. He was not in uniform, but I know him. It was Herr Brunner himself. He's in charge of the Jewish clearances in the city. I met him once in the Lévitan store. I don't think he remembered me. I can't be sure. He is truly terrifying. Eyes everywhere."

"Too many questions?"

"Only one question, but it was enough. He asked whether he could admire the view from my balcony. How could I refuse?"

She waved despairingly at the table, her hands extended. "Two coffee cups. He saw them." She reached out resting one hand on his arm. "He said they won't be bringing pictures here any more. Some other arrangement is to be made. Then I had to listen to the two of them arguing." She seemed unable to go on, looking down at her lap, idly picking at a thread on her dress, mumbling to herself. "If I had known you were going to that place I would have paid more attention to what they were saying." She fumbled for a handkerchief, tears sliding softly down her cheeks. "There's no call to look at me like that. We all cry now. There is a lot to cry about. Listen. They were discussing the Lévitan Store. Apparently deliveries of food have stopped. Something about a strike. You understand me? There has been no food in that place for days. Brunner was ranting that he had no interest in bringing pictures here when there were prisoners to think about. His prisoners were more important."

"What d'you mean? You mean feeding them?"

"You think he cares about food?" Her voice cut through him. "What sort of a man do you think this Brunner is? God almighty, do you think I wanted to listen to this hideous German going on about his starving Jews? About *his* starving Jews, that's how he put it. It made me sick. He doesn't care whether they ever eat again. All he sees is the chance to ship one more consignment of the poor devils to their death. You know under French law the prisoners in the Lévitan can't be deported?"

"I know nothing about it. You mean because they're not Jews?"

"Not altogether. There are rules. Rules of definition. I'm ashamed to talk about it. We spend our lives now debating who's a proper Jew, who's half a Jew, a quarter Jew, and so on and so on. Even wife of Jew, as if it was something you could catch like the 'flu. You can die now for some scrap of paper your mother put away in a drawer."

She had talked herself into silence, staring blankly into space, breathing hard. She seemed unaware he was still there.

Alex sat down opposite her, leaning across the little table. "*The prisoners.* You were talking about the prisoners in the Lévitan store."

"Ah, yes ... you are thinking of your Justine?" Her tight little smile somehow set his heart thumping. "You think you really did see her? I'm afraid Herr Brunner has decided to tear up the rules that put her there. All the rules. I heard him say it right here. He was shouting at this other man, saying that calling people non-deportable was just a French trick. *Stringing things out*, that's how he put it. His French is very good. The orders have already been given. Half the prisoners are to be taken to Austerlitz tonight. All the young men. There is no appeal. No one to appeal to."

"To the rail station?"

"They will be loaded tonight for Poland. Convoy number 77. He kept saying that number. He was proud of it. I don't know why."

"And the others? The women?"

"He has told the women and old men they are to be released later today. It's a trick - he just wants them out of the way while they handle the men. They're to be given a *Quittance* and told to fend for themselves for food. They can find food from relatives, friends, anybody. Or a church soup kitchen. It's all a lie, of course, they will be rounded up tomorrow. Added to the convoy."

"But you said *released*. Once they're free ..."

"*Free*. Do you know what you're saying? Wandering about with just a meaningless bit of paper. You realise you can be arrested if you have no papers, Jewish or not? It happens a lot at the train station. They take them to the goods yard. It's best to pretend you don't hear the shots. Brunner's trick means he can arrest whoever helps as well. Whole families, men, women, children. No concessions for children, they take less space, you see. Trains loaded with children leave Paris all the time. So who's going to risk their life to help a starving Jew? Would you?" She looked up at him, her eyes dead. "I let them take Sophie away."

"But released later today? You said that?" He stood up, looking round, lost to a sense of weary desperation, searching for something in Madeleine's face that was not there. "You said later today? You did say that? So there's still time. I must go back ... find some way to keep watch ... somehow."

Hearing the panic in his voice she carefully eased herself out of her chair. As she made for salon she gave him a tiny patient smile, tugging at his sleeve, "Wait here a moment, I have to look for something. I will not be long." The click of her feet faded as she hurried across the hall and along the corridor. He heard the study door close.

"I have a friend with a shop near the Faubourg Saint-Denis. Not far from the Lévitan store." She had come back into the salon carrying a flat parcel tied with string. "Her name is Beatrice Verne - that's Verne like the writer. She sells art materials. If you're stopped, you're taking this to her gallery. It's an old print for framing. The address is on the parcel. It's not much of a place … on the corner, if I remember right."

"*Passage du Desir*." He looked up from the address on the parcel.

She gave an odd ironic snort of a laugh, "Not what you think. And no place for loitering. It has a reputation. Street girls use it. If the shop is closed …" she shrugged, "another roll of the dice. Tell Beatrice there is a letter from me inside the parcel. It asks her to frame the print and says Alexandre is delivering it. I used to talk about you, she might remember. Ask her if you can watch the Lévitan store from her upstairs window. You may see something, I suppose miracles happen.

At least you won't be outside inviting someone to arrest you. It's the best I can do. I am not rolling the dice."

The shop on the corner of the *Passage* smelled of turpentine and Madame Verne's incessant cigars. The place was cramped, just room to stand wedged against a long mahogany counter. The old woman took the packet from him, listening to his stammered request in unyielding silence, her back to the door, holding Madeleine's letter in two trembling hands. She led him painfully up three arthritic flights of stairs to a storeroom, standing in the doorway as he dragged a table to the window. He clambered onto it pressing his forehead against the dusty glass. She watched him for a while in silence, a puzzled expression on her face, until a bell tinkled at the shop door below. She stumped down the wooden stairs, leaving him alone.

Madeleine had been right – it was a good view. Beyond the corner of the street a sign: *AUX CLASSES LABORIEUSES* was picked out in glossy rain-washed tiles on the façade of the store. Far below, a soundless succession of removal vans, tiny as toys, laboured up and down the ramps. The morning guards still leaned against the double doors watching the vans drop out of sight. An endless stream of people from the station hurried past. No one seemed interested in deliveries to a shop that had been closed for years.

Pressed against his windowpane, Alex let himself fall into a kind of sleepy catatonia, the pain in his knees retreating to little more than a tolerable obscure ache. The endless afternoon wore on, the bell in the shop below his only connection with reality. No one left the Lévitan store.

D'you want to know how wars are won, Captain Vere? High explosive - the rest's just decoration. The words entered his consciousness from nowhere, jolting him back from a waking dream. That interview in Whitehall, it seemed years ago, the day Justine left; the day he lost her. Strange he should remember that military mandarin now. And hard not to smile recalling how he had used his tiny office, absurdly cramped, as warrant for effortless authority - you had to be English to carry that trick off. What would he make of Alex Vere now, keeping watch over a furniture shop in the back streets of forgotten Paris? Alex Vere fighting – and certainly losing – a wholly private war?

But he would have liked to explain, nonetheless. Every bridge was mined, every building of consequence wrapped in TNT, yet the war Paris had chosen to fight – his war - barely concerned itself with high explosive, had nothing to do with battlefields. It would be won or lost over the small mysteries occupying the heads of millions of quite ordinary people. A battle of the spirit with no certain outcome, to be fought out, even now, behind a grubby façade in the street below.

The patch of sky over the shop to the north slowly darkened to a deeper blue, Paris falling into twilight. It was already too late. Minutes had passed since a brief square of yellow light high on the fourth floor of the store had been snuffed out, someone tugging at a blackout curtain. A church clock somewhere close struck eight. He had kept watch the whole of the afternoon: no one had left the store.

The guards suddenly stepped forward, standing to attention as a polished Mercedes staff car slid silently to a halt. A German officer in dress uniform jumped down, pausing a moment on the pavement, arching his back, peering up to the roof. The driver scuttled round to open the rear doors, two women clambering out, sweeping up the steps, laughing at a cascade of ritual salutes from the guards. They disappeared inside through the double doors.

The officer seemed to call something to the guards, turning away to light a cigarette. He stood looking down at a dark patch where the pavement had been washed.

Two delivery vans had come and gone before the women returned, setting boxes and cartons down for the driver to pack, squealing in mock protest as a package was manhandled, tugging it from him, cradling it into the car in their arms.

It was getting dark, shadows falling over the silent store.

The officer watched the car drive off, pacing the pavement, pausing to check his watch. Not long ago crowds of people had been pushing past. They had gone now. With the chime of the clock an odd deserted air had settled on the street. A car drew up opposite, three men jumping out to join the waiting officer. They stood leaning against the car, looking across the street to the shop. Far below, Alex heard Madame

Verne pulling the shutters closed. She slammed the shop door shut, the bell jangling hysterically.

He jumped down from the table as she reached the landing outside his tiny room, wheezing heavily. She pushed past him, making for the window, peering into the street, calling over her shoulder, "There was an accident this morning. They are looking for witnesses. They will be coming here. Hurry, while they make their minds up. When you go out turn left."

"*Left?* I didn't come that way."

"They will block the Faubourg. Go down the *Passage*."

"But go where? Where does it go to?"

"Hurry Monsieur. Don't wait for me. You will arrive on the rue Lafayette. Can you find your way from there?"

"Yes, I think so."

"Just go straight down the *Passage*, that will bring you to the church. But hurry."

"*Church*? What church?"

"That's where they go looking for their food. The people from the store. The Lévitan. No, don't you go saying anything, you're looking for somebody, aren't you? You would have been better doing your looking at the church. I could have told you, but you said the front of the shop. They never come out that way."

The whistle sounded as he reached the first bend in the narrow alleyway. A single long blast, reminding him of the raid on the rue Saint André des Arts. Hearing the sound, a man coming towards him turned abruptly, walking away fast. They arrived together at the junction of three streets, the man glancing at Alex before scuttling down an alley to the left, his echoing footsteps cut off as he reached the turn. Alex looked back. The length of the *Passage* as far as the first bend was still empty. The whistle had stopped. Ahead, at the far end, traffic on the rue Lafayette ran left and right.

He was on a triangular patch of land in front of a church. A plaque declaring *Eglise Saint Laurent* was fixed to an iron gate closed with a rusty chain. Dead leaves and old newspapers had piled up under a mossy stone bench in an elaborate carved entrance. Weeds sprouted between the flagstones. No one had passed that way for months. The place had long since been abandoned.

Further down the *Passage* a restless little queue of people had formed outside a door, the murmur of soft voices reaching where he stood. They fell silent as a man with a wicker basket walked along the line handing out what looked like bits of paper. As Alex reached them the sociable murmur of talk fell quiet, letting him shuffle by. Seen from the junction his first wild thoughts had been of prisoners in search of food, but these were no cowed convicts. They were mostly women, dressed as if for some event. As he walked past, one, taller than the rest, turned towards him, a sudden glimpse of dark hair setting a frantic lurch in his chest. A hard-faced woman in her summer best despatched the thought with a brief anaemic smile.

Remembering Madeleine's final words, Alex found himself absurdly scanning one mild disinterested face after another, the rising sense of anti-climax almost comic. He pushed past, thinking only that the dice had been rolled and he had lost. Whatever these well-dressed people were waiting for, it was not food. Whoever they were, Justine was not among them. As he walked on, the memory of the faces at the window seemed to alter, taking on the quality of some dream he would never quite recall.

He glanced back hearing the slow shuffle of footsteps. They had disappeared, the swell of voices fading as a heavy door grated over stone. He was completely alone. For the first time since he had arrived in Paris Alex knew in his heart that Justine was irredeemably lost.

Forty-One

At the point where the *Passage* joined the rue Lafayette the street lights flared to life in a hiss of gas, the contrast plunging the deserted alleyway behind him into darkness. Two gendarmes were standing on the corner, silhouetted against the stream of traffic, blocking the way for those fleeing the raid on the Faubourg Saint-Denis. They turned into the *Passage*, walking side by side, black against the light, batons swinging in amiable synchrony, talking quietly together, close enough for him to hear. Alex had nowhere to go.

Walk not run. He turned and hurried back the way he had come, keeping close to the wall. As he passed a closed door, a faint line of yellow light sparked underneath it in a burst of muffled music. Heavily carved, the door was black with years of varnish, its pointless central knob polished bright. There was no keyhole – if it was locked, it must be from inside.

There was a slight bend in the *Passage* at his back. Once past that, the two gendarmes must surely see him. The steady beat of footsteps seemed very close. He pushed at the door, feeling it yield, slipping past the open crack into a cushion of warm air.

He was inside a tiny porch, bare stone walls stained green with damp, everywhere the overpowering smell of warm church mould. Facing him, a line of light leaked through a division in felt-lined double doors. Beyond, a voice intoned Latin into echoing space. A framed portrait of the ancient Marechal hung on a nail next to Christ, both a little awry. The outer door swung to, its catch resting against an iron lock. He pressed against the wall, straining to listen, the beat of his heart comingled with the placid voices of the gendarmes as they walked in step. They did not pause. Alex looked at his watch. He would give them two minutes, enough to know if they were coming back – then make a run for the rue Lafayette. He leaned against the door, breathing hard, to find it pushed in against him, throwing him off balance. An old woman stumbled inside, clutching his arm to steady herself. They stood swaying together for a second before she pulled away, still holding his arm, precipitating them both through the padded doors into a fug of candle heat and dim light.

They were inside a vast cathedral space, the tiny congregation barely visible, huddled into two scant rows near the door. Startled heads craned round as the woman clattered into a pew, pushing Alex hard against a pillar, hemming him at her side.

Penned in with no escape, Alex remembered little of the service apart from the sermon, a barely veiled call to arms, the priest reminding the tiny congregation how Cyril of Jerusalem had sold church plate to feed starving prisoners. It was received in silence. Alex scanned his ancient parishioners' startled backs. They seemed unlikely revolutionaries. It was hard to believe they knew many prisoners, starving or otherwise. They had probably occupied their Sunday pews for half a century.

As the Latin recommenced Alex thought of Archer's commemoration service, remembering *not impossible*, remembering a pile of opened letters, remembering feverish days of anticipation. Justine had not been there: she was not here either. He heard the service out in an agony of impatience, stumbling through a half-remembered final hymn. Hopes ebbed as the stained glass windows over the altar grew black. It was too late. Nobody had left the store after the two women had driven away. It would be madness to go back there now. Alex knelt as the woman at his side creaked down, the priest rattling through a benediction.

As the congregation filed out, a man leaned over to exchange a greeting with the woman, including Alex with a perfunctory nod. They lingered for endless seconds, finally easing out into the vacant aisle. She took the man's arm as the pair joined the straggling queue at the door.

Now he was free to escape, awareness of the futility of his search swept over him in a seductive wave of weariness. It was at least as sensible to sit on here, lost in the drowsy scent of incense, as to pointlessly wander the streets. He leaned back against the wooden rail of the pew, listening to the hundred tiny echoing sounds of an empty church. At the end of the aisle, the priest began to snuff the candles, spirals of smoke curling up into the still air. Reaching some secret switch behind a pillar, an echoing click returning the chancel steps to darkness. He shuffled on, extinguishing candles as he came.

That was when Alex saw her. Silhouetted against a yellow pattern of votive lights, pausing to adjust the scarf at her throat. She began to walk, feet soft on the patterned tiles. He waited immobile in his station, lost to the throb of his heart. She had reached him now, dark eyes lost in some hellish misery of their own. Eyes he had searched a million times fixed ahead on nothing at all. It seemed she might have walked on, compressed into herself, barely present, Alex willing her to turn, willing her to find him there, barely daring to break some hideous spell.

"Justine."

She turned to the whispered word, startled eyes wide alight.

A tiny escritoire served Madeleine for a dressing table. Ancient veneered wood polished to the colour of honey, the flap left pulled down to accommodate a jumble of little boxes and perfume flasks. A porcelain ring-stand, empty, kept a stack of opened letters at bay.

Far into the night Alex kept vigil at Justine's side, comforted by restless movements borne to his chair pressed hard against her bed. Settling her to sleep they had found a piece of paper crumpled tight in her right hand. A kind of crude *Quittance*, the names filled in on a dotted line, thanking Madame Isobel Fortieu, spouse of Corporal Thierry Fortieu, for service to the Republic, releasing her *Sine Die* from further service in the Lévitan store. An illegible signature appeared over yesterday's date.

She had pulled the sheets high against her chin, fists clenched against the cloth, tiny spasms of distress battling sleep. A bruise on one cheek had spread towards her ear like a smudge of purple paint. A tic at the edge of her mouth endlessly wrinkled her eyes with pain.

Hours earlier, Madeleine had brought him soup, bending over the bed, calmly examining the sleeping form.

"She will not wake tonight." She straightened up easing the stiffness from her back. "You too. You should sleep. I'll hear her if she wakes up."

Alex shook his head, the first true smile for many days. "When she wakes she won't know where she is. I'm better here."

Madeleine continued looking down at the bed, the expression on her face something he had never seen before. "So this is your Justine. She looks very young. Like a child. She is very thin. Strange to see little Alexandre's woman. I confess I never quite believed in her. All the same …" her smile was frank, "I ask myself whether this madman with a pistol deserves his sleeping princess. She looks, how shall I say it? Wholesome. Perhaps that's not the right word."

"Yes, it's the right word. And no, I don't deserve her. I never can."

She walked to the window, checking the curtains, the faint sound, *tch, tch*, his disapproving aunt of years ago. "No, Alexandre, you can't say that. She owes you her life. You must let her thank you for that. You are not heroic enough to be so modest. Now, I am going to find somewhere to sleep. It will be morning soon. Don't forget to eat your soup. The bread was fresh. Can you believe it? Impossible to find fresh bread in Paris."

She left the door ajar, an angled finger of yellow light reaching out to touch the edge of the sheet.

The sound of a rifle shot jolted him awake. A single shot so painfully close he thought at first it had been in the room. Hauled out of muddled sleep, finding nothing familiar, he was conscious only of the violent echo in his head. He fumbled at something slipping from his lap. He had been walking the empty corridors of Torridon in a dream of confused twilight, sporadic gunfire echoing from the snowbound hills. Checking room after empty room, searching for students, fretting he had forgotten what he must tell them. He woke with the guilty thought it was better they should never know.

Justine was sitting up in bed, smiling into his eyes.

"I'm afraid I ate your soup. My need was greater." She raised one hand to cover the bruise on her cheek, her expression almost embarrassed, oddly vulnerable. "God Alex, don't look so hard, you'll burn me." She stretched out a hand to him. "Good morning, Guffin … damnation, I knew saying that would set me off again. I've been sitting here weeping. It was lovely."

"How long have you been awake? I'm sorry, I was so sure I would never fall asleep. God, Madeleine? Have you …?"

"Been and gone long ago. Kissed me, said good morning, said she's your aunt, then said she was off in search of a ration of bread. If she's your aunt, Alex, that's good enough for me. I never knew you had an aunt. I must say she smells delicious. Apparently I'm in her bed."

She wriggled down until only her head was visible.

"I've been looking at my Alex. I think you were dreaming. Not about me, I hope. You seemed in a state. That blanket you pushed off was Madeleine's idea. She said you looked cold. Now, I'm tired of talking. I want to go back to sleep. Just for a while, my love. You can leave me … I feel perfectly safe. There's so much to tell you. But sleep first. I'm dreadfully tired."

Alex got up, awkwardly freeing the stiffness from his body. "I'm not far away. I'll hear you if you call."

As he reached the door she called to him, her remembered voice bringing tears to his eyes. "I did see you, you know. When was it? At the window. It's been a kind of miracle, hasn't it?"

Caught in the doorway, looking back, he found he could not reply. She was already asleep, a gaunt face white against the cover. She seemed calmer, her mouth settled into something like a smile.

Madeleine was in the kitchen making coffee in a saucepan. She put a finger to her lips, pushing the door closed behind him, whispering, "Stephanie takes Monday off. She has this diabolical thing she calls her Moka pot. I won't touch it. A saucepan will do for us. There were eggs at the bakers if you want to risk them. I can make an omelette." She glanced at the door, "Still asleep I suppose? Last night was like something from an opera. She seemed barely alive."

"Walking all that way, it nearly put paid to her. She's dreadfully weak. I thought I would have to carry her, but she held on, thank God. She kept saying the metro was too much of a risk. And she was right, there was a little band of thugs with pistols checking papers outside the Miromesnil metro when we reached it. Your milice chaps, I think. I saw them eying Justine but we walked past arm in arm. They were almost as nervous as us. They're not getting things their own way so much, people were arguing, telling them to stop pestering. They didn't stop us. It was single men they were looking for I suppose. We passed for a couple."

"But you *are* a couple, my dear. I've seen that for myself. And don't ever call those milice bastards mine. Did you hear the shot this morning? I was coming back with the bread. One of them was trying to get his motorcycle going. Somebody took a shot at him from an upstairs window. He took off like a frightened girl, pushing the thing along the road. Not too dignified. People in the bakers were saying the Americans will be here in a day or two. You must have seen the posters all over the place. *Victory is Near.* All of a sudden we're fighting a war. Victory – I ask you? You can't help thinking it's a bit late to be brave. God knows what's to become of us. Nothing's changed, the place is still full of Germans."

She came closer, suddenly serious, whispering. "You realise she is in dreadful danger? She has no papers. Nothing. I was thinking how we get her away. You as well, if you are to be a couple. That will be harder. How much does she know?"

"I don't know. She thinks she's safe here."

"And she is, for now. But I can't help wondering when Herr Brunner will remember that second coffee cup."

Forty-Two

He spent the rest of that day sitting alone on the little balcony, looking out across a patchwork of leaded rooftops wavering in the rising heat, the distant horizon curving slightly under an unflinching brazen sky. He was possessed by a sense of waiting for something undefined, perhaps something he had forgotten, filled with a restless vague anxiety. The street below seemed complicit: holding its breath, silent but for occasional furtive footsteps.

Justine came to the doorway behind him as the mantle clock in the salon chimed five. Barefoot, her hair still wet from the bath, she wore a patterned robe, a little too short. She stood poised on the threshold, breathing in the air.

Easing himself out of the chair Alex found himself closer than he expected, turning aside, embarrassed.

She took both his hands in hers. "Yes, I know. Odd isn't it? It's like we've just met. I feel new-born somehow. Very queer. As if I didn't know my dear old Guffin. Stay there, let me look at you. And it's the truth, you do look a bit different. Me as well. Of course I do, I see it in your face. Best not to look, not just yet. Come inside and sit with a friendly ghost."

Lost for where to start, he looked beyond her into the salon.

"Madeleine?"

"She said she had to go out. That's twice. I think she's being discreet. Very French. She's going to cook us something when she gets back. She says she barely remembers how, so we shall have to suffer. Her daily woman has stopped. Stopped being daily, that is. Run away to join the circus out there, I imagine. You can't blame her. I do like your aunt, Alex, she came and talked to me in the bath. Aren't mothers supposed to do that? I never had one, I know now what I missed."

It seemed she was speaking to fill the space between them, pouring words out to keep something at bay, anxious eyes darting across his face. She pulled him onto the sofa, jumping up to take another chair, sitting a little apart, hands gently crossed in her lap, an ironic echo of the SOE interrogation pose. As she straightened gaunt shoulders she saw the glint in Alex's eyes and looked away. "It'll pass, love. Not enough to eat. I ought to feel ravenous, but I don't." She grinned, a skeleton face wrenching his heart, "I know what, I shall let Captain Vere debrief me. Be warned, it's not a very flattering tale."

"You don't have to tell me anything. I can't even promise to listen, I just want to look. I'm happy enough just to sit here. Too happy, in fact."

"Oh, but there's things I have to explain. Things I owe you to say." She shook away his protest, leaning towards him, resting her hand on his, leaving it there. "The look a little less intense, Captain, please. It unnerves. That day in London. I thought of you coming home and me not there." She seemed suddenly lost, staring at her feet, struggling for words. "I'm a coward - that's what it comes to. No, don't interrupt ... I was going to tell you something that morning ... quite made up my mind to it. Then you were called to that damned meeting and I knew they'd send you away. You'd be posted away, God knows where. Suddenly, everything seemed ... what's the word? *Inopportune*. I couldn't ... anyway, I didn't."

She stood up, pulling the robe tight at her waist, looking down at him, her expression a kind of reluctant pity. "So there you are. I ran away. I can't forgive myself for it. Only don't look so hurt, Alex, it doubles the wrong." She managed a bright little smile, turning to walk away. "Confession over. Now I must go and find some clothes, this robe is a scandal."

He called to her as she reached the door. "You mean the child don't you? That's what you were going to tell me."

She whirled round, holding on to the doorknob, swinging slightly to and fro, fearful dark eyes painfully searching for his. "Yes …" She let the silence hang between them, a brittle tentative smile flickering round her lips. "Yes. That is what I meant. So you knew? Or guessed?"

Alex was about to speak when she cut across him. "It was those damned tulips - my Baker Street trophy flowers. And then when you said something about *eternal love* – that was what did it. I couldn't bear you saying that. I knew what you would think, the two of us pretending, like both knowing you had a secret mistress. Something like that …" She was weeping, tears running down to the crease of her mouth. She let them lie, staring him out, the tiny act of defiance defeating him.

"No, no, you're wrong. I guessed nothing at all. I'm not given to guessing. I suppose that's why I ended up with my job. Guessing discouraged: all that *trust no one* stuff, remember?"

She looked at him, slowly nodding her head, "Then how …?"

"Lucile Beyrou told me."

"*Lucy*? How on earth? When did you ever meet Lucy? But she promised …"

"Don't blame her. I went to Dundee to see her. I let her think I knew more than I did. It's an interrogation trick. I'm not very proud of my job."

She came across to the sofa, stumbling slightly, flopping down at his side. "If I don't sit somewhere, I'll fall over. Hold me, will you?" She buried her face into his chest, her voice muffled. "He's a lovely boy, Alex. Really lovely. Our boy." She pulled away, her face very close, her eyes fixing his. "Shall I say it again? Our boy. You'll see …"

"You mean he's here? But …"

"Not here, of course not. But I've got him safe alright."

She let him hold her close, two hands cupping his face, smiling into his eyes. "All those months in that dreadful place. Believing I would tell you this has kept me alive. Even when I knew I'd never see you again, I would keep myself sane imagining telling you about little Pascal"

"I knew you'd choose that name. I mean, if it was a boy …"

"Oh, of course a boy. So it was Lucy Beyrou? I don't mind. You can kiss me now. If you like. It seems opportune."

"That's why you left that ring behind, wasn't it? Lucile explained, but I'd already guessed. There - I do guess sometimes."

"She was a real soulmate in Dundee. The two of us comforting each other. I was sure I was going to stay there. Then those men turned up with the story about you in Paris. I suppose she told you?"

"Yes. But you knew I had never operated in Paris."

"Yes. Obviously it was a set-up. In fact, they barely tried to hide it. All the same I made the hell of a mistake. I tried to work out *why.* Why would anybody want to set me up? I forgot *why* is always the wrong question to ask. Trying to be too clever. God knows, I paid for asking it."

"It's only the wrong question because the victim never has any way of knowing. Tell me about these men. I can't help thinking John Cabot was involved. It was him shuffled me off to Scotland. I was well out of the way by then. But *Paris*?"

"Neither of them looked like him – not from the way you described him. No tubby Oxford chap with heavy glasses. They weren't the usual Baker Street issue either. One was RAF. At least, the uniform ..." She squeezed his arm before he could speak, "Yes, I know, I know - uniforms are cheap. To tell the truth he was rather fetching with his little French accent. You'd say a lady's man, except that sounds cheap. Actually he was very kind … attentive and kind."

"I used to give lectures about that in Torridon. Kindness can be a drug, a way of getting your brain to deny somebody is lying, even when it's obvious."

"They could see I was worked up because of you. That's what they kept playing on. You know - bringing news about Captain Vere, alive and kicking in Paris. Not that they were very specific."

"I was in Scotland."

"I was so relieved you were alive, even when I barely believed a word they said. That was what was so clever, they could see I knew they were lying and they didn't care. They knew I was desperate to believe them.

"It's classic Cabot stuff."

"They knew the hell of a lot about our operations in the South West, me being captured, pretty well everything. Went on about how impressed they were. They knew a lot of detail. Too much, now I think about it. Once or twice, I thought they might be fishing about that man Gliess, but you really couldn't say they were pumping me. Thinking back, I realise they were quite subtle, you know, slipping flattering things into the conversation, why hadn't I been decorated? Stupid stuff like that."

"This man Cabot is dangerous. He was involved, I'll stake anything on it. Schemes like that were his speciality: long range killing."

"But it wasn't a scheme, Alex, it really wasn't. And why would he go to the trouble of snaring me? Why would he do that?"

"You're asking *why* again. But I can tell you - Cabot thought I'd told you something deadly secret. Or rather that I could have told you. It comes to the same thing in his book. All those undelivered letter, remember? They thought you knew too much. You didn't, of course, but that doesn't matter. That's why it's pointless to ask why."

"They said they'd lost contact, casually slipped in the fact they'd lost contact with your Paris cell. They didn't seem too concerned. That was just before they left. I didn't imagine they'd come back."

"And you spent the following days getting more and more agitated, worrying about my mysterious cell being out of contact. I'm right, aren't I?"

"I suppose so. But they seemed so clueless, Alex, as if they didn't care all that much. It's hard to credit all that was a lie."

"No point of lying if you're no good at it."

"But you were right. They did come back a few days later. And by then I was so worried they could have persuaded me to anything. All I got were frustrating hints that you were still out of contact. One of them said the problem was none of the Paris circuits knew Captain Vere by sight."

"God, where have I seen that one before? Agents lost in the fog of war."

"I heard them say it would be risky to send a courier who didn't know you. It was obvious they were going to abandon you."

"So Justine Perry, resigned or not, volunteered. You're right, it was clever, even by Cabot's standards. They had you either way. After all, you'd operated in the occupied zone. You knew Paris. You knew me."

"Looked at their way, they were right, I was the ideal person for the job."

"Ideal, except for the minor matter that I wasn't in Paris. Let me guess the rest. Along comes this extraordinarily coincidental chance to get you in."

Justine nodded, a tiny rueful smile. "Don't sound so superior, Alex. I'm ashamed, but only because of how gullible they thought I was. It was humiliating."

"I know that feeling. I've known it all my life."

"They got me across on a fishing boat into Brittany two nights later. I was passed from one safe house to the next. I suppose they thought the pass-the-parcel business would blind me to what I was walking into."

"Which was?"

"I realised I'd somehow been kidnapped. Perhaps that's not the right word. But I'd ended up back in France, the last place on God's earth I should have been. Velvet handcuffs, if you like. I remember I was fiddling with a WT set one night. This French chap – they were all French – started barking at me to leave it alone. That was the moment I realised I was pretty well a prisoner."

"Where was this? Close to Paris?"

"I can tell you exactly. They said it was the final leg. Outside Drieu. Everybody was jumpy that night because the escort was so late. Then this awful shifty woman arrived. Kept going on about when was she going to be paid. That night I caught her going through my kit. She said she was looking for money and backed off, but I knew I was pretty well trapped."

"And once you were arrested, you would disappear in a cloud of glory doing a job you'd volunteered for. Volunteered, way beyond any call of duty. And everything you ever knew would go with you. Nobody would be responsible. That's how he works."

"You mean this Cabot chap? But I wasn't arrested. At least, not then. I slipped away while the escort was out scouting for breakfast, walked to the railway station and bought a ticket for Nantes."

"*Nantes*?" Alex was smiling. "You mean a switch?"

"I counted on them panicking, thinking I'd do something reckless. Once I'd bought the ticket I walked back into the village and caught the bus to Caumont. I shouldn't have got away with it, but I did. You have to be unlucky to have your papers checked on a bus. In fact a man helped me on board. Remember, I had a card to play."

He found himself blushing.

"Being pregnant is a passport in France, Alex, you should know that. A suitcase would have been even better, but I had my little shopping basket. The driver took my sous, kept everybody waiting until I was settled."

"*Caumont*. I've never heard of the place. What's there?"

"A school. Well, actually it's a convent, but it's a school as well. It was my old school. It wasn't far to walk."

"You mean they took you in, just like that? They'd take that risk?"

"I wish I could say all for the sake of my blue eyes. But it was money, of course. Before the war the Convent used to accept paying visitors, people looking for a retreat. All that had stopped and they were short of funds. One thing you can say about SOE, they don't stint on cash."

"If it was French money we probably printed it."

"They took it all the same, and kept quiet. That's where little Pascal was born. She pressed Alex's hand against her cheek. "Don't look so solemn, Guffin. You can do worse than be born in a convent. It was all perfectly satisfactory. One of the Sisters was a midwife. We managed. The nuns were kind and I had our little boy. Apart from wondering where you were, things could have been worse."

"And that's where he is now? This convent?"

"Pascal? Say his name, Alex. No, he's not there. It didn't take long for the rumours to start. Babies are hard to ignore in a convent. One day the Mother Superior told us she'd been denounced. Two letters apparently. The usual stuff - the convent was a sink of depravity, the Archbishop was coupling with the nuns, half the nuns were pregnant, and so forth. Not very inventive, but the poor woman couldn't let it pass. She offered to hide Pascal if I took myself off."

For a moment he thought she had stopped. She sat looking round the room as if searching for something. "Perhaps I'd have made a different decision, if they had given me more time." Something desperate in her voice made him look away. "I haven't seen him since that morning."

"But he's safe?"

There were lines on her face he had never seen before. Faint pencil marks of strain, tightening as she turned to him. "I believe so. Please don't ask me, please not. I don't dare say. Forgive me, my love. If they take me, I will die easily rather than say. I can't ask that of you. Yes, they say he is perfectly safe." She remembered something, suddenly smiling. "There's a little garden. I like to think of him in a garden."

Alex went to the window, stepping out onto the balcony. The sun had almost gone, the air suddenly damp. He called through to her:

"Everywhere is very quiet. It's like the whole place is waiting for something. Not a soul anywhere. Just a car the other side of the street. Nobody inside. It looks abandoned. I suppose you were picked up at the railway station? You must have known you didn't stand a chance."

She waited until he came back inside, settling himself close to her on the sofa. "It was a bus station actually. I'd walked to the village and was standing waiting in the little shelter at the *arrêt*. It's always the little things isn't it, Guffin? I didn't know Thursday was Market Day. They shift the bus stop somewhere else. It was a dreadful mistake. Nobody said anything, of course. I was too well dressed for one thing. Just kept looking at me standing there with my little case as if I was mad. In the end, a local police chap came up and asked was I going to stand there all day because the bus didn't come until half past seven. Not much of a policeman, the kind they sent to collect money from the stall-holders. It's always the little things, isn't it? He asked for my papers. Asked why I'd come shopping when my card was six months out of date. Had I been living in a cave? He had that stupid determined look, like a dog with a bone. I knew it was all up."

Forty-Three

"They took me to the Drancy transit camp. In a bus – quite civilised as arrests go."

She lay stretched out on the sofa, clutching the glass of water he had forced into her hands, staring into it now and then, as if surprised to find it there. "It's like a madhouse in there. You get called up one by one. In front of trestle tables - a bit like standing at the Post Office. They had my papers spread out. I thought they'd spotted something about the forgery, but it wasn't that at all. These two women were squabbling about what they called my *situation*, the queue behind getting longer and longer. Then they asked a man to arbitrate on the Nuremberg Laws, well, the French ones. I might have been a sick dog on its last trip to the vet. It's an insane version of The Last Judgement. In my case, God was a harassed little French chap with very bad breath."

"You mean the Jewish Laws?"

"He was perfectly polite about it. It was as if he didn't really believe what he was doing. I was supposed not to care whether they put me down or not. I'll always remember how polite everybody was, thumbing through your papers, thinking what best to do with you." She suddenly pulled away from him. "Do you really want to hear this, Alex? I haven't thought about it for ages. There's been so much since. Bringing it all back makes me tired. I'll end up weeping."

"You don't have to explain anything. Not to me. All I care about is you're here. Why don't you get some rest? We have to talk to Madeleine when she gets back, it's dangerous you staying here, you do realise that?"

"It doesn't feel dangerous. I trust your aunt. No, I'll sleep later. I owe it to all those poor devils who got sent away. Talking about it just made me lose heart somehow. All this sleep has made me weak. The truth is, after I was arrested I barely believed what was happening. There I was in an ugly housing estate in Paris, people discussing whether I deserved to stay alive. What they do seems so ordinary, you see. They hand you a little slip of coloured paper and tell you to take it to another table.

She was struggling for words, biting her finger like a child finding itself caught with a secret. "The Jews always got a purple slip."

"I don't understand … a purple slip?"

"A little purple slip of paper. Nothing else. Hundreds of people arriving every day at Drancy. You'd imagine people would ask why the place is never full - they never do. There, I've lost my thread."

"A purple paper …"

"Yes. You get one of those and wait your turn for the train to Pitchipoi. No Pitchipoi for me, I always got another chance to live. Every time. It was always a red slip for me, never purple."

"*Pitchipoi*?"

"It's what the Jewish children call the place the trains go to. You hear mothers talking about it to their kids. Trying to calm them down, you know, giving them a future to look forward to." Something was breaking in her voice, her eyes tormented, staring at him as if she barely knew him. "I'm not sure I can talk about this any more. It's disgusting. For heaven's sake, Alex, you know what I'm talking about. The camps. The Polish camps. Slaughter houses. Children clutching their little purple slips for the slaughter house. And do you know why I wasn't purple, Alex? Can you guess why? It's almost funny."

Alex shook his head, reaching out for her hands, "But you're not Jewish …"

"Of course I was Jewish."

"You mean your papers? But that would have been insane. London would never make that mistake."

"No, not Baker Street. But I wouldn't say the same for that French lot in Duke Street. They made the papers that woman at Drieu switched on me. If you think about it, that was all she needed to do. I was certain to be deported. God, why am I using that word? *Killed*, that's the word. One Jew the less, except …" She stared him down, a defiant flush on her face, "Except for my state. Whoever faked those papers thought it would be better for me to be married. I can just see some spotty clerk thinking that one up. Circumstantial colour, that's always the problem, isn't it? I remember you saying how Intelligence people always over-egg things. Can't resist being clever, I suppose. She'd dumped a whole wallet of papers on me: husband, marriage certificate, family photographs, the lot."

"You forget I was one of those spotty clerks. That's what I did in the TPSU with Cabot. We spent months inventing German officers."

"That's why I don't think it was Baker Street. Whoever did it, didn't check properly. Short of time, I suppose. The dead husband they saddled me with wasn't so dead after all. His name was on the list of captured combatants in the Russian campaign. He was logged as a POW. Decorated, what's more. That's the joke. They had managed to marry me to a decorated serving soldier ..."

"I can't see what difference …"

"To a decorated Ayrian serving soldier. I told you, they're terrified of breaking these Jewish Laws. I suppose it saves your sanity if you can pretend it's all about the law. And the law says you can't deport wives of POWs even if they're Jewish. So I ended up with a red slip every time. That's how I came to be in the Lévitan store. They couldn't gas me, but there was no reason why they shouldn't work me to death."

Pulling her close he became conscious of bones, aware of the terrible fragility of her body. He took her head into his hands, tentatively tracing the outline of the bruise on her cheek with his finger. "It's alright, I know."

She pushing him away, shaking her head, "No, Alex, you don't know. Things are not always the way you imagine them."

"Bruises like this don't just appear."

"Nobody hit me, if that's what you think. It wasn't like that. I got this bruise lifting a crate. That's what we do most of the time, shift crates about. Something fell on top of me - a piano stool I think – and half knocked me out. I was told off, because I held things up, but that's all. The guards won't come anywhere near us. They're a funny lot. Mongolian, I think. Very superstitious. You catch them eying us as if we were sacred somehow, the way people look at dying patients in hospital. Not so far off the truth when you think about it."

She lifted her face up to his, the kiss no more than a touch of dry lips against his face. "There, that's for a start. Now I don't want to talk about me any more. Can't we talk about you? Or not talk at all. I can just be here. We don't even need to speak. I was thinking in the bath there's only so much relief a body can take. Too much, and you start to feel queer. I do feel a bit queer. Can't I just be quiet and look at you? I'm tired of questions."

"Just one question. I don't understand how you ended up in that church."

"Madeleine said she'd explained. About that priest."

"She said people sometimes got food from the church. Nothing else."

"So the question is why *you* ended up there."

"It was a woman in an art shop. Madeleine's friend. She knew about the church handing out food. She told me to go there. I had spent most of the day watching the front of the shop. Until it seemed hopeless."

"Two weeks ago they stopped the daily food delivery to the store. There were days when nothing arrived at all. There's a sort of camp committee and we proposed they let us out overnight, at least, those that could get food. Brunner refused at first then changed his mind. He started sorting us into groups. The women and old men got this paper to take to the Prefecture tomorrow."

"Madeleine says it's so that Herr Brunner can fill one last Paris convoy. The men will have already been deported."

"You got these *Quittance* forms if you had family who would feed you or if you were registered at one of the church soup kitchens. I wasn't registered, but I turned up and told the priest I'd been working in the Lévitan store. I must have looked so dreadful he took pity on me. So I got some bread and honey. His own honey, he keeps bees. He's an odd sort of priest."

"I heard his sermon. He went on as if it was 1848 all over again, only this time it would be different. The usual stuff about the end of the ruling class and so forth. It was dreadfully careless talk, he was taking the hell of a risk."

"Not as much as you think. He used to visit the store to hand out tracts. He's quite a big fish in the Communist Party but the Vichy people think he's just a barmy old crank and leave him alone. He told me he knew about the plan to empty the Lévitan store and Brunner rounding up all the forced labour, Jewish or not, for one last insane convoy. He keeps a cache of small arms in the church for the *Front National*. For when the time comes and the uprising starts - not long now, that's what he said."

"Small arms against half a dozen German brigades. He must be mad."

It was evening before Madeleine returned, dumping her empty basket on the hall floor, standing looking at them, blinking herself into a show of recognition.

As Alex took her coat she brushed him away, sinking into a chair, sitting immobile, staring vacantly, her face like chalk. "You remember the night you arrived Alexandre? I told you about that informer they shot. I knew there'd be hell to pay. They're so naïve. Boys, that's all they are. They don't believe anybody would betray them. They've been listening to that fool de Gaulle going on about *mobilising a fighting force*. As if there was even a war to fight. It's completely mad. Fighting with what, I ask you? All we have is a few hand guns. There's a young chap called Marc. I suppose you'd call him the leader, not that they believe in leaders. He said he was organising the first patrol. In the Bois de Boulogne."

Justine fetched her a glass of brandy. Madeleine looked at it in her hand, forgetting to drink.

"I warned them you can't trust anybody in Paris. Shooting that woman was a dreadful mistake. They went off like schoolboys on a trip to the Bois. Twenty or more. Of course, the Gestapo were waiting. We've a new Governor. Only been here a few weeks. Called von Choltitz. He's responsible for all the explosives everywhere. He doesn't believe in prisoners. The first thing he did was ship off all the resistance in prison to a place called Dachau. It's sure they'll all be killed when they get there. Like my boys … Marc was the only one who got away. I talked to him when he got back. He said they'd made a run for it but they were between two machine guns. I think most of them are dead." She stood up, handing the glass back to Justine, walking wearily into the salon. She slumped into a chair, closing her eyes. She looked old.

"Are you there Alexandre? Come here. There's something I need to tell you. I have a dreadful headache. I must rest my eyes."

Justine kneeled down by her chair, one arm round her shoulders.

"You should lie down. Go and rest, I'll make us something to eat."

"Alexandre, can you hear? I was hoping to ask Marc about somewhere safe for the two of you. Impossible. I saw him when he got back. God help him."

"You mean the chap who got away?"

"They always see there's someone who gets away. It breaks morale. If you get away you must have been an informer. I refuse to believe Marc betrayed them, but who am I to say that? When I told him it was best to lie low he was so angry. Said I was accusing him." She shook her head, looking from Alex to Justine, "I suppose I was. Anyway, asking him for help is not a risk we can take now. We have to get you away and Marc was my best hope, my only hope." She glanced across to the open window, the sky jet-black outside. "Perhaps one more night. It seems quiet enough. If they raid the building, at least we'll hear them coming."

Alex looked at Justine. Neither spoke.

Forty-Four

They were sitting in the kitchen when they heard the sound at the door. Not even a knock, more a soft scraping double tap. Alex reached out, his hand on top of Justine's, pressing it to the table.

Madeleine stiffened, her head cocked, waiting. At the second scratch at the door she relaxed. "It's alright, I know who it is." She was whispering. "We use a sort of code in the building, just in case. It's the woman from the floor below. Asking about bread, I dare say. I can't help her much." She looked at Justine, her voice suddenly urgent.

"Go and sit in the salon. Not a sound. If she wants to come in, I always bring her in here. Alex, come with me, the sight of a man will keep her quiet for weeks."

Alex watched as Madeleine peered through the little spy-hole. Her shoulders relaxed.

"Yes, it's her." He heard the relief in her voice. "She's a dreadful gossip, don't say more than you have to." She slipped the chain and pulled the door open.

The woman was already scuttling away, a heavy black skirt trailing down the marble stairs. Two men pressed against the wall on either side filled the doorframe, closing ranks, pushing inside past Madeleine. Standard milice uniform: tight black jersey, brown leather bandolier, heavy, iron-clad boots.

"You have a worker from the Lévitan here."

A tiny wiry man, wrinkled simian face the colour of walnuts. He seemed too old for this work, resting his rifle on the parquet as if the weight were too much. He flapped an outstretched hand to the boy at his side, gangly, awkward, warily eyeing Madeleine, he could not have been more than sixteen. He hurriedly pulled a crumpled bit of yellow paper from his pocket, pushing it into the old man's hand. He passed it to Madeleine, snatching it back as she shook her head.

"Suit yourself. It's a warrant. Hurry up - we don't have all night. Where is she?"

Madeleine ignored him, stretching a hand out to the youth, letting it drop as he flinched away. "It's Thierry isn't it? How's your mother getting on? It's been a long time. Are you still living …"

"I don't know her." A strained hysterical squeak, eyes darting to the older man. "I've not seen her before, honest. You back off, old woman. What d'you know about my mother?"

Alex walked towards the old man opening his cigarette case, holding it out. "It looks like you've come to the wrong place. You're welcome to look round." He managed a laugh, "Mind you, does it look like we have escaped prisoners?

The man ignored the cigarettes, following Alex's eyes out into the stairwell, kicking the door closed behind him. He waited for the echo to die in the space outside. "And who might you be? As if we didn't know. You got papers?"

"I'll fetch them."

"No you won't. You'll stay where you are, and don't think I won't use this." He turned again to Madeleine, tiny eyes suddenly savage.

"Are you going to fetch her or do we start looking?"

Alex lit a cigarette, walking past him towards the door, "This is stupid. You've obviously come to the wrong place."

"Have we then? Next time you go to church, remember to put some money in the box. People notice things like that. D'you imagine we're all stupid? You were followed all the way to your little nest."

"She's not here I tell you, there's nobody here. Just us. You're making …"

The blow to his shin was executed so casually that for a moment

Alex was uncertain how the pain arose. He staggered against the side table, watching impotently as the vase tottered over the edge. Freesias scattered across the floor as it smashed. Madeleine stooped down to collect them, abandoning the effort as the man prodded her shoulder with the butt of his rifle.

"Leave it. We're in a hurry. Fetch the woman. Fetch her, or it'll be more than a china pot."

"*Who is it, Madeleine*?"

They had not heard Justine come in. She stood in the salon doorway holding out a sheet of paper.

"I heard you asking. Is this what you want? It's my *Quittance* from the Lévetan store. It's all perfectly in order."

The old man crumpled it into his pocket. "I don't know anything about that. You're to come with us. You'll need your coat for the star."

"They gave me a red slip."

He waved the warrant in her face, smoothing it out, squinting down at the few lines of print. "Listen, Madame Fortieu, you can sing your song when we get there. You're wasting our time. It says here they want you back." He whirled round, confronting Alex. "You. Papers. I asked for your papers."

"And I said I'll get them."

"Stay where you are." He brandished the warrant at Madeleine, forcing it too close to her face. "It says you live on your own, if you'd bothered to read it. *Sole Occupant*. Know what that means? Who's he?"

"My nephew. Just staying the night."

"I've never seen him before." The boy's stage whisper was for Madeleine's benefit. "He's not from round here. We should take her as well. She's a liar."

"Oh yes, why not take the lot of them?" The old man was laughing at him, "I'll tell you why not, son. There's not enough room in the bloody car."

He slung the rifle over his shoulder, throwing the warrant down onto the table, shrugging at Madeleine. "You - report to the Prefecture tomorrow. Take that with you. Him - he comes with us. Thierry, go with him, get his papers."

It took a long time to get the engine started, filling the inside of the tiny car with smoke, the smell reminding Alex of Inverness. He was squeezed in hard against Justine, the schoolboy leering nervously at them over the back of his seat, fumbling left-handed with the catch of a pistol, pushing it up and down, the thing absurdly large in his hand.

Approaching the junction, the car stopped. The old man got out, bending back inside for his rifle. "Keep an eye on them. I'm going to see."

"See what?" Kneeling on his seat, the boy craned round peering through the windscreen. One of the platanes at the crossroads was sprawled on its side across the road, dusty leaves rearing into the night air. "What's going on?"

"See for yourself. Road's blocked. The bastards have started cutting the trees down." The old man got back in, poking his rifle into the well between the two seats. "We'll have to go round. It's alright, I know the way."

"It says you can't go down here. There's a sign."

"Who's to stop us, then?"

The road widened out between cliffs of grey stone apartments. A fairground smell of hot food blew briefly through the open windows.

Justine leaned against Alex, her lips to his ear, "I know where we are. I know where he's taking us."

Alex pressed his cheek against hers, feeling it wet.

"What's that they're talking, Boris?" The boy sounded scared, kneeling up, leaning over the back of his seat, fat beads of sweat glistening on his face. "That's English. They're talking English."

The old man darted a glance behind, catching Justine's eye.

She stared back, shouting in German: "Take a good look imbecile."

He prodded the youth at his side, grinning, "Get down from there, she bites. And stop waving that bloody thing about. They can talk what they like. We're here now. Straighten up. Have you got the paper?"

They had turned sharply left down a steep ramp, pulling up behind a removal van parked for the night. A huge fire blazed at one end of a paved courtyard, green flames licking round bits of broken furniture.

Showers of sparks leapt into the night sky as a man tossed a child's high chair onto the fire, painted roses melting as it burned.

Two soldiers in uniform came out of a tunnel of darkness beyond the fire, walking slowly towards them. A German officer waiting at a side door reached to switch on a single electric lamp under a metal shade set in the wall. The three men gathered round the car peering into the back seat.

The officer glanced at the driver's warrant, passing a wad of banknotes through the open window, waiting impatiently while the old man counted them.

One of the soldiers opened the back doors filling the car with the scent of woodsmoke. Nobody spoke.

Justine's hand grazed his own as Alex let the solders shepherd them down a long sloping corridor to an open door at the far end. A hub-hub of agitated voices dipped momentarily as they came in. Forty or more people were crammed into a tiny anteroom. Unlikely prisoners, the men were mostly in dinner jackets, the women in evening dress. An improbable pall of cigar smoke hung over the hot little room.

A tall woman carrying a fur wrap broke away from a group, fighting her way through the crush. "Oh, Justine, my dear girl, you as well. I knew they'd never let us go. I knew it. But not so soon. You see how things are. I was walking through the Luxembourg this afternoon. Dead. All the shops closed. Even the cafés – shutters up everywhere. No police, just soldiers everywhere. I've never seen so many. And the metro. I walked down the steps just to look. Platforms packed with angry Germans. They looked as if they'd been there for hours, you could hardly see for smoke. The Luxembourg is always full of police, nice boys, gossiping. Somebody said they've been disarmed, so they're on strike. Can the police do that? Mark my words, that's what brought the Germans on the streets."

She pressed the back of one hand to her cheek, a curious theatrical gesture, widening her eyes. "I knew that madman would never let us go, but this … He's mad."

Justine stepped back, as if the woman's hysteria were somehow infectious. "Who's mad? I don't know anything. I've been asleep for a day or more. All I know is a couple of milice came to the apartment. They just ignored my *Quittance*." She turned to Alex, managing a thin little smile, "Alex, this is a fellow Lévitan inmate. Madame … Oh, no. Can I?"

"What? My name?" The woman laughed. "Of course you can tell him. I'm Cecile Arbout." She stared into Alex's face, finally swivelling a crooked smile back to Justine. "It's no use, my dear, he's never heard of me." She rested a plump hand on Alex's arm, briefly leaving it there. "You're forgiven. A long time ago I was in films. You're too young." The sudden bark of a laugh - too loud - brought faces turning to look. "God in heaven … everybody's too young to remember that." She pressed her hand against his shoulder, her face close enough for him to smell her perfume, something hot and flowery. "Our German friends don't know. Between you and me, Germans and actresses don't mix. Strange expectations, as we used to say. You think I'm going to risk that at my age?" She stepped back, making an odd little curtsey, grabbing him to steady herself. "I'm a seamstress now, believe it or not."

Something in her voice made him look away.

She turned to Justine, her eyes wild. "I think I've offended him. Here, young man, let the seamstress tell you all about our dress-making department. We have a really wonderful tailor." She was gabbling - a rush of hysterical words beating into his ear. "Jewish, of course. Germans don't believe in tailors unless they are Jewish."

Justine reached out, taking her hand, squeezing it, "It's alright, Cecile, it's alright."

"Bespoke suiting for the men ... did I say that? *Haute couture* for the women, of course. Even Madame von Behr … can you imagine that? Really wonderful stuff. And all completely free … completely free …isn't that a miracle?"

She had pulled Alex round, her face close to his. For a moment she looked insane. Seeing something in his eyes, she turned aside, drawing hard on a long-extinguished cigarette.

"This damned thing's dead." Her voice was suddenly calmer. "Do you have a cigarette, young man? I'm sorry. Did you think I was mad? It was the disappointment, you see. They rounded up my celebration party. Celebrating my release, can you believe? My theatre crowd."

"But rounded up for what?" It was all he could think of saying. He saw the panic in her face as people turned to his voice.

"Not so loud." Justine was whispering. "For God's sake don't attract attention. Sometimes there's a plant to listen in."

She pulled again at Cecile's hand. "You were going to explain about Brunner. What's this about Brunner?"

"You missed him. Our leader said he wants to check all our papers again. He actually deigned to walk among us. This was before you arrived. Stood on one of the ladders to give a little speech. We're to go back to Drancy to have it done."

Alex felt the heat of her breath again in his ear. "I'm not Jewish you know. We all say this, but it's true. I've always been a non-deportable, lovely expression, isn't it?" She had fallen silent, eyebrows raised, inspecting him, the expression too knowing to be comfortable. For a moment he thought she was waiting for him to say something but she simply stood, idly rubbing one hand against the other, apparently finding the action reassuring.

"You know the little theatre on the rue Saint Germain?" It seemed to Alex she was seeing him for the first time, a smile suddenly embracing him. "It's my husband's. They took him away ... all this was a long time ago. Two gendarmes came for him. Very smart. I remember it was a Saturday, perhaps they didn't care about that. I recall they saluted him – it seemed ridiculous. I haven't heard from him since. You know, when it started, Henri would read things out of the newspaper. *Not in Paris*, he'd say. I can hear him saying it now."

She freed herself from Justine's hand. "Herr Brunner, you wanted to know. A woman over there heard they started loading this afternoon. All the young men in the store. They were taken in a bus to the marshalling yard at the *Gare Austerlitz*. Do you think it's true? That damned maniac and his convoys."

"But the Americans ..." Realising she was not listening, Alex tried again, raising his voice, "The Americans ... I mean ..."

"*Americans*?" She looked puzzled. "What about Americans? You think Americans are interested in his convoys? Are you so sure? I think they will say *if that's what you French want, what business is it of ours*? Why should they stop it?" Sweat was running in lines down to the corners of her mouth completing the disintegration of her make-up. As she walked away he heard her mutter to Justine, *your young man seems very naïve.*

A guard pushed into the sweating crowd, making space, dumping piles of old clothes on the floor. Alex watched as people dipped down, looking for things, snatching particular bits from the pile. Women deep in conversation barely paused, slipping coarse striped aprons over their heads.

Cecile stood catching her breath before straightening a crude sacking tabard round her shoulders. A garish yellow star was inexpertly sewed to the breast.

A group of old men began plucking grubby overalls from a pile, awkwardly helping each other to pull them on.

Alex felt Justine's cheek brush his own, her whisper urgent. "It looks like they're going to make us work. Pray God it won't be all night. You'll need something to wear. Just take what's left. Look natural."

He dawdled to the back of the line, pulling something like a child's smock from the bottom of the pile and struggling into it. He followed the others and began sorting through numbered armbands strewn across a trestle table. As he picked one it was snatched from his hand.

"Mine, I think." The man at his side fished down into the pile, a chocolate theatre voice rumbling in Alex's ear, the accent impeccable.

"How about this? Poor chap won't miss it now."

An odd expectant silence had fallen on the room. Without any specific command they formed lines like obedient children, standing two by two as double doors at the far end of the room were flung back.

It seemed he had walked into a nightmare. The limitless space of a cavernous hall. Line upon line of feeble electric lamps dangling over a kind of madman's jumble sale. An exhibition consumed by its own excess: rows of tables set out with ghostly piles of starched linen: sheets, table-cloths, napkins, pillow-cases, towels, curtains, eiderdowns, bed-spreads. Everywhere the overpowering smell of damp cloth.

Wooden crates stood waiting between the tables.

"This was my room." Justine seemed not to realise she was already lifting towels from the pile, practised hands folding them flat. "Watch what I do. It's more organised than it looks. Only towels in this crate. They check."

She looked up, tears filling the dark eyes that met his own, lost to some familiar misery. "God forgive me, Alex. I've dragged you into hell."

Forty-Five

The chime of something like a school bell from the room above brought an end to work, a sudden surge of chatter breaking hours of silence. Linen lay abandoned where it fell, people slumping exhausted to the floor.

Alex perched awkwardly on the edge of a crate, breathing the fresh scent of cigarettes. An old man re-lit the stump of a cigar. From somewhere behind a tower of wicker baskets someone was banging a door, shouting *let me in. I need a bucket.*

Alex followed Justine across to a space on the floor where the windows had been boarded up. He sank down alongside her, his back against the wall. She seemed already asleep, the familiar tremor flickering across her face. She opened her eyes as he touched her hair, a tiny smile turning his heart over. "Hello Guffin. No, not asleep, just warding off misery."

"Cecile. The actress. You heard what she said?"

Something in his face made her look away, confused, feeling for his hand, pulling it to her body, holding it tight.

"Shall I tell you something. Guffin? There used to be children in the Lévitan store, you wouldn't know that ... no, of course, you wouldn't. Nobody will ever know about them. You heard them running about. They used to play on the floor upstairs, where they fix the clocks. One day Herr Brunner announced it wasn't a safe place for children. I suppose it was his idea of a joke. Let them all go to Pitchipoi. So that's what it came to. Can you think God made men like that? Can you?"

There was something dangerous in her voice. Alex pressed her hand, stroking it, willing her away from some desperate edge. She freed herself, sitting quiet, her head slumped down on her chest.

"The day they took the children away I thought a lot about Pascal. Normally I ration that, you understand, but I couldn't that day. I couldn't stop thinking of them locked in the waggons at Austerlitz. It was the only time I cried. I was ashamed. But you weep for children, don't you? What else? We watched them lined up in the yard. They were so small." She shuddered, leaning against him, shaking her head. "And I've brought you to this. I wish to God you hadn't found me."

He pressed her hand to his lips, tears starting to his eyes, "Quiet my love, don't say any more. I want to sit and think for a bit. I'll have to do it for both of us."

"*Think?* You mean about getting out? That's all we did in the early days. You think, this is Paris - how hard can it be to walk out of a shop? You think, that's the rue Saint-Denis just outside. Sometimes when it's quiet you can hear the trains in the station. But it's a waste of time, Alex. Nobody has ever got out. Well, apart from Sylvie. The guards are locked in with us. If we get to them, we all die."

She had fallen silent, her eyes closed. Alex tugged at her hand.

"Don't sleep yet ... we have to talk."

"Not talk about escape, my love. I've already had all that talk, months of it. It always comes down to the same thing – die now, or wait your turn."

There was a commotion as a door was opened on the other side of the room, a sudden crush of people milling to get out. Justine struggled to stand, falling against him with an exasperated sigh.

"Hell, I'm so weak. They've opened the back stairs up to crockery and silverware. There might be something to eat." She tottered back, steadying herself against the wall. "It's no good. I'll stay here. You go. There are a few camp beds up there."

"You think I'd leave you? Remember getting to Saint Aunix? I'll carry you again if I have to. Come on, lean on me."

She let him pull her upright, leaning unsteadily against him, her breath coming hard.

"You're a noble soul, Guffin. What did I ever do to deserve you? I was just feeling sorry for myself. You're right, we should get out of the stink. People have started using the buckets. It's the bastards' way of keeping you down - nothing like squatting over a bucket to humiliate you."

The floor above exchanged linen for mantle clocks, crockery, and glassware. China ornaments jostled together on avenues of trestle tables. Vases and pottery had been laid out on wider tables with tottering piles of photograph frames stacked face down. Towers of metal cooking pans leaned out from half-filled crates. A stained blue carpet in one corner was spread with cutlery, knives and spoons crudely tied together with bits of string.

Unsure where to go, Alex found himself stumbling against a wicker laundry basket stuffed with crockery, the plates on top alive with the glistening amber shells of feasting cockroaches.

Justine pulled him back. "It's where you put the things that still have food on them. It's not been emptied for days. I remember the first time I found food. I was rummaging in my crate, pulling things out, and there was somebody's breakfast still set out on its plate. It used to break my heart thinking that's when everything ended for somebody. They wouldn't have thought their life would end up here with us picking over it."

She held up one of a pair of silver candlesticks. "Pretty. You have to put anything that looks like silver to one side. It goes to be polished up for the display room downstairs, the lobby they call it. All the good stuff goes there. It's set out like in a regular shop, even cash registers, not that they work. Von Behr's wife shops there. *Shops*, that's how she puts it. As if she thinks it's less like theft done that way, less like armed robbery. Can you understand people like that? Greedy little children playing shops. I worked down in the lobby for a week, boxing things up for an officer's wife. They were furnishing their apartment. It was supposed to be a privilege. I was sent back up here to pack linen, for looking insolent."

An upright piano, thick in dust, had been pushed against the wall, next to stacks of frying pans, a single sheet of music entangled in its broken fretwork stand. Alex pulled it away. A child's study by Czerny, the fingering picked out in pencil. Somebody had written, *Try to get more legato in the left hand Patrice*, across the top with the date of the next lesson. June the ninth. Two years ago.

Justine took his hand, standing next to him, answering his thoughts.

"It's not that people didn't care. It took me a long time to realise that. Paris can't afford to care. The people made that choice years ago. In Paris it's always us or them."

"Which are we?"

She leaned across to read the label pasted on the lid of the piano. "This was a mistake. Pianos shouldn't come to Lévitan. They're supposed to go to the Palais de Tokyo. Don't look at me like that, Alex. How can I answer you? What would you do? Would you have the courage to make the right choice? Life always seems very precious."

Alex waved his arm into the dusty air. "Here's what happens when you look the other way. This is how it always ends."

"And the people made to do this hideous job? Hundreds and hundreds of us. You work until one morning you can't get up. Nothing dramatic. They take you to the hospital. Good word, *hospital.* It sounds restful. Soon there won't be enough of us left. Nobody will remember what happened because there will be nobody to do the remembering. Paris decided it would be convenient not to know. A city with a hole in its memory."

Alex realised he was still holding the scrap of music. Trying to perch it back onto the music stand it slipped down. He watched impotently as it fluttered off like a paper aeroplane, coming to rest under a chest of drawers. He left it where it lay.

"Is there water somewhere? I'm very thirsty."

"A tap by the buckets." She found a place on the floor, sliding down, her back against the wall. "But it's usually turned off. Water is their favourite punishment … that and night work. We've been lucky - that bell means they're not going to make us sort all night. Come and sit with me, Guffin. When they turn the lights off, it's pitch black. I don't want to lose you. We're quiet enough here. There's nothing to do but wait."

"Wait for what?"

The lights had been cut an hour ago, the click of some master switch reminding Alex of the church in the *Passage*. He stared into the darkness, trying to orient himself, imagining the narrow winding lane beyond the walls of the store. It could not be so very far, that church - only a few yards as the crow flies. The priest would have gone home by now.

Voices echoed up the stairwell, men calling to each other, no more than an amiable exchange of banter. The rattle of an opening door brought the smell of fresh tobacco, bright torchlight projecting shadows from towers of candlesticks, heavy boots clumping between the crates. They were counting bodies.

As the door banged shut, one of the men called out in a language Alex did not recognise, bringing an echoing reply from somewhere far away. The two men were laughing together in the corridor outside, moving slowly away.

Alex lay alongside Justine, gently pulling her close, listening to the tiny sounds of huddled humanity around him, knowing sleep would never come.

In the dead of the night Cecile's voice querulously cut someone short, a theatrical whisper echoing in the darkness. *No you old fool, you're not coming back. We're for the pit.*

Justine stirred, reaching out to him enclosing him, her voice in his ear part of the velvet dark. "Alex, love, I've been dreaming about that ring. I feel guilty there wasn't a proper goodbye. You knew, didn't you? About the ring? Why I left it?"

"That there was only us. Just us. Nobody else. That's nothing to be guilty about."

"It's just that I'd never loved anyone. Doesn't that sound shocking? Nothing ever like that for me until I met my Guffin. Took me by surprise." He felt her stir, her lips seeking his. "I mean a happy surprise. That and our little Pascal. Two of you in one go."

"You should have told me all the same."

“Is that a reproach?” He heard the smile in her voice. “No, my love, that’s the one thing I’m sure of. I wasn’t going to have you fret your days away thinking what if it’s not mine. Best think nothing at all than think all that sordid stuff.”

Holding her tight against him he could think of no reply, bright images of a little boy flooding his mind. Watching a tiny figure, head bowed, earnestly consumed by the intensity of play. Him standing somewhere he had yet to know. A garden perhaps.

Her breath against his cheek came easily now. “You still haven’t asked, Alex. Not right out. When I knew about Pascal. You remember the Russell Hotel? The night we lay in bed and watched that raid? I could have eaten you that night, quite gobbled you up. Did you not know? It was then. The next morning. Long before that monster Gliess. I would have never believed women knew such things.”

“Pascal? I was just thinking about him. Imagining him playing.” Hearing the name on his lips, he felt her move against him. “You say he’s safe. No, I’m not asking where. Just when …”

“Don’t say *when*, Alex. Not like that. We’ll spoil things if we start lying to each other. We both know what we’re in for. I just can’t forgive myself dragging you to this hell-hole. I’ll die with that regret.”

“You didn’t drag me anywhere. I found you. Do you realise that poor woman had to fall for me to find you …?”

“Sylvie? You shouldn’t think like that. You know she didn’t fall. You’ll understand if I tell you about it. We’d been sent to unpack clocks and toys that day. Sometimes the vans brought too many crates for the men. I remember Sylvie was on a table at the other end of the room. Brunner himself turned up that morning. They’d got us kitted out in clean aprons for the visitation but Sylvie missed out somehow. She was wearing this odd sort of gypsy skirt, red and black, very pretty. She’s not much more than a girl.”

She reached out, fumbling in his pocket for his cigarette case. Alex pulled it out, lighting a cigarette for her, her face flaring yellow in the flame. He waited, watching the glowing tip pulse red.

“Herr Brunner came sauntering over to my table. Stood there eyeing me up and down like a prize cow. He was all got up in his shiny uniform, smirking. You’re supposed to stand to attention for an inspection, turning your head so you're always looking at whoever. So he was tormenting us, striding up and down, flipping at a pile of pillow cases with his little cane. Suddenly there was this dreadful scream from the other end of the room. It was Sylvie. I remember thinking, why's he not looking? This expression on his face, as if he suddenly couldn't wait to get out."

"There were guards there? There must have been."

"Oh, yes, they were there. They were watching Sylvie. She walked into the middle of the room with this toy train in her hand. A big clumsy wooden thing. Home made."

"Oh, Christ, no …"

"She was shouting, *my God, my God, it's Paul's, it's little Paul's.* I'll die remembering that voice. Cracked, like it wouldn't work properly, like she'd never get it to work again. Then she sat down on the floor shoving the train back and forth in the rubbish, moaning to herself. Brunner was still there. We were all looking at him. That's what we had to do. He started shouting for the foreman, whacking at the piles of linen telling us to stop staring at him. But I couldn't. I just went on and on looking. It was like my eyes seemed to burn something on his face. Just for a second, before he walked away, there was this look ..."

"I know. I saw it somewhere this afternoon. I've seen it ever since I got here. Frightened. That's what you're going to say, isn't it?"

"After he'd gone, they brought the morning break forward on account of Sylvie. To calm us down, I suppose. There's a big flat roof up there. If it's not raining they let you walk about for a bit of fresh air. Sylvie came up with us. Nobody wanted to go near her, not even the guards. The poor woman walked up and down clutching her train, looking as if she was dead already. There were just the two guards that day, those strange yellow blokes that can hardly speak French. Sylvie went over to one of them and gave him the train. Then she straightened her skirt, gave an odd little smile and walked away. You wouldn't have wanted to stop her, Alex."

Forty-Six

Alex could only guess how long she had been asleep, her head pressed hard against his shoulder, one hand enclosing his in some desperate gesture of possession. She woke, drawing him closer as he fumbled in his pocket for cigarettes, wearily staring into the darkness, conscious of sleeping bodies around them.

"Alex, what's the matter, love? You should sleep."

"Listen."

She seemed to sense the tension in his voice, hauling herself up. "It's nothing. Just night noises in the building. It's always like this."

"No, hear what I have to say. About tomorrow, we have to plan while we can. Tell me what happens. As much detail as you can."

He felt the sag of her body as she pulled away. "All that's a fantasy, Alex. Don't even think about it. If we start anything, they'll shoot all of us. I know this place."

"Those two ancient Russians? I doubt they can do much shooting."

"There are German soldiers downstairs. They'll be in charge of transport to Drancy. Soldiers everywhere. A few enjoy themselves mauling the women onto the bus but the others always stay well back. Spaced along the back wall in the yard. They all have MP40s. There's a Bren gun in the yard. They're willing to take their own men down, if that's what's in your mind. A young chap made a run for it a few months ago and some poor corporal got in the way. We were worked nearly to death for that."

"No, not the loading – inside the bus, that will be the weak point. Think …"

"I've only been on the bus twice. There were armed guards. Two, I think. They stand on the conductor's platform at the back. Can you imagine a submachine gun in a bus?"

"When we get to Drancy?"

"If that's where they're taking us. Every time I've been, the bus didn't stop until it was inside the gates. The place is crawling with the Gendarmerie …"

"What d'you mean: *if that's where they're taking us*?"

"You heard what Cecile said. If they wanted to check our papers, why aren't they pestering us? You can see for yourself, nobody seems interested. She's right, Brunner has us lined up for his damned convoy. Rest on me a bit, Alex. Try to sleep. I want to sit quiet for a while."

He slept eventually, slumped against her body, conscious of the swell of her breast. A shallow restless sleep filled with a lucid dream. He was a boy again, consumed with familiar fear, his face pressed to the cold glass of his bedroom windowpane. Looking down on the angled stones of the Lévitan store. Light so bright it burnt his eyes, Mother prodding him to say the doctor had come to cure his thirst. Clinging to sleep among a clank of buckets, Mother pulling him back into the consoling dark, relentlessly prodding him, Doctor Clérambault's thick catarrhal cough strangely synchronised with her hand. He woke to a fierce thirst, a dreadful bitter taste in his mouth, his tongue shrivelled. A blaze of light cut lines through the thick blue haze of smoke. Everywhere, a vague disordered whisper: the sound of fear. Everywhere, the smell of raw shit.

Cecile was standing over him wriggling her shoe insistently into his back. "Hell, you sleep like the dead. Here, I've found us something to drink."

She pressed a tin into his hand, the label bright yellow, two children beaming between slanted English words: *Pineapple Chunks*. "Go on, have as much as you like, I have another. They were in one of the crates. Some poor soul must have been hoarding them."

"Justine?" He kneeled up, aware of a sudden pain in his side, staring in panic round the room. "Justine?"

"Over at the buckets. Best not to ask. Here, drink some. It's too sweet, but better than nothing. Don't look so tragic, the poor woman won't be long. God, this place stinks. Here's the other can." She held out a long bolster-case, weighed down with the tin. "You'll have to help me with it. I'll have to hide it or they'll accuse me of theft. You soon learn they have a sense of humour, our German friends. I'm going to hide it under my dress somehow. I'm fat enough. And yes I have something to open it with. Can you help?"

"I've a belt, we might do something with that, I'm not sure. I'm sorry, I'm barely awake."

"I can't take your belt. See whether you can find something over there. A piece of cord, that would do."

But Justine was already pushing him aside. "Cord? I know where there's some … let me."

Alex looked at Cecile. "Won't there be something to drink when we get there? At Drancy?"

She stood knotting the pillowcase round her waist, her expression bleak. "*Drancy*? That what you think? I've been wondering why that maniac Brunner isn't interested in our papers any more."

She rose up on tiptoes, starting to count heads, abandoning the effort, exasperated. "How many are we? Forty? Fifty? That's a bus load. Enough to fill his last damned convoy. No, we're to be number seventy-seven, alright. Sounds lucky, doesn't it? We're for the station at Austerlitz, you see. That's why they didn't bother with water. Why should they? We're dead already. For God's sake, do I have to write it all down?" He could smell the acid pineapple on her breath, something dead in her eyes. "All I know is they won't be loading me."

She took a few steps, an awkward stumbling walk, swinging her weighted skirt. "Don't worry. I bequeath you my tin. You can have it when the time comes. I'm going to run for it when they try to get us on the bus. There's always a muddle then. What? You think I'm a bit old for running? A bit fat?"

“No … no, it’s not that.” Alex was embarrassed, flailing, “But that’s precisely when it’s impossible. We know about these things. Just accept we both know. If there’s a chance, we’ll help you take it, but you can’t take chances with armed soldiers.” Seeing her start to shake her head, he pressed on, “You won’t get more than a yard. They’ll shoot you.”

Cecile hitched the load up round her waist, facing him, her mouth set. “Don’t take me for a fool, young man. I realise that perfectly well. I’ve realised it ever since they brought us back. One way or another, I’m afraid Herr Brunner’s convoy will be leaving without me.”

A door at the far end of the room rattled open. Not the door they had come in by, this was some kind of fire escape. A wave of warm musty air flooded into the room. Two men in uniform stood in the doorway, looking in.

“Careful.” Cecile was whispering in his ear. ”*Kreiskommandanturen* – that’s what they call themselves. Our resident German chums. The blond one is a sadistic devil.”

He had walked into the room, prodding reluctant knots of people into a straggling line with the butt of a submachine gun. He seemed harassed, sweat standing in beads on his forehead, endlessly pushing his cap back, sweeping locks of straw-coloured hair out of his eyes.

He stopped next to the buckets, retching violently, clearing his throat, spitting. The man in the doorway called him back, shaking the bolt of a rifle over a woman sitting on the floor.

A quiet voice, surprisingly gentle, counted them out as they filed past the guards onto a steep flight of concrete steps lit by a single electric bulb.

Alex supported Cecile, his back scraping the wall in a cramped space barely wide enough for two, people behind bearing down. At the final half turn they could go no further, a solid wedge of bodies unbearably compressed against double doors closed with a metal bar. A woman somewhere far above lost her footing, a wave of sweating flesh rippling down.

Cecile began to swear, a steady stream of obscenities, her face purple, fighting for air.

The woman higher up the stairs was calling now, adding to the bedlam, shouting she could not breathe. Over and over again, an hysterical sing-song repetition, conjuring herself into madness.

The guard shouted for her to shut up, unexpected French silencing her for a moment, only for her wails to resume in another key.

Stop it or I'll stop you. The other guard stopped laughing, bellowing over their heads. *It'll be worse on the train. Die Tür! We can't stay here all day.*"

Barely able to move, Alex wriggled his hand out pressing the iron rail, feeling solid wood resist. It swung free, grating across a concrete apron outside.

They were staring into the soft pink air of a Paris dawn.

A flood of people poured past, carrying him through the narrow door into a walled courtyard. As the guard closed the door, an old man hung on, scrambling back inside. The guard leaned over, swinging the butt of his rifle with one hand. No more than a nonchalant tap, the gesture something to check an errant child, barely worth the effort. The blow caught the old man on the back of his neck pitching him face down on the ground. A woman at his side bent to lift him a little, abandoning the effort as the guard prodded her to join the others. They stood in a mutinous circle round the door, muttering as the crumpled tortoise body shuffled itself backwards to lie unattended on the concrete.

Alex looked up to a patch of watery blue sky trying to get his bearings. They were at the foot of one of the ramps running down to the back of the shop, a massive circle of ribbed metal for turning the lorries filling most of a tiny courtyard.

Cecile walked across to the line of men standing against the far wall, reaching out, pressing her open hand against a bayonet, taunting the grinning soldiers manning the Bren gun.

Justine pulled her back. "Not here. Wait."

She tried to pull away, the whisper venomous, "I've told you. When the bus comes ... you'll see."

Alex stood alongside, taking her arm, pressing her tight between them. "You'll get a bayonet in your back. Now's not the time. You saw what they did to that poor devil."

He felt her shoulders fall, realising the truth of the matter. She had no intention of running. None of them had. When it came to it, courage was not enough. The night had taken something away from all of them. Fantasies of escape were all they had left. Imperceptibly, they had taken on their new identity, standing patiently in the pale sunlight like cattle, dimly conscious of their fate, vaguely restless.

Cecile faced him down, re-living some long forgotten piece of theatre, eyebrows framing a question he knew he could not answer. She sighed heavily, "Perhaps you're right. Wait for better times."

"Here's the bus!"

Painted in shabby green, there was something affecting about this relic of another age warily negotiating the steep slope. Someone had wound the windows down for the summer weather. It stopped at the foot of the ramp, bringing the bitter smell of half-burnt oil into the courtyard. The driver climbed down, walking towards the guards.

"Where did that thing come from?" They were managing in a sort of French, "A museum?"

"There's a strike on." The driver seemed offended. "You're lucky they let me come. It's no picnic backing this thing down there."

He pulled a sheaf of papers from his pocket. "I'm to give you this. It's the bill. How many to take?"

"Forty-one. They said forty, but we're one over. She'll manage the extra will she? Not too heavy?"

The driver looked nervously at the Bren gun. "You're not bringing that thing on?" He flinched as one of the soldiers pivoted the barrel, noisily cocking the bolt, calling out, *Boom!*

"Not that thing on my bus. There's no room."

"No grandpa, just me on your bus." He poked the barrel of his MP40 into the driver's face, "And my friend here." He shouted across to the soldiers slouching against the wall. "You lot going to stand there all morning? Get these bastards loaded." He swivelled round on his heel, facing the crowd, "Move, you lot."

Men stepped aside in a pantomime of absurd courtesies, letting the women stumble forward first, holding on to each other, unsuitable shoes slipping on the ribbed surface of the metal circle. They clambered onto their bus, neatly one by one, scuttling forward to settle on seats, as if compliance, even now, might ward off something worse.

Forty-Seven

Alex was the last to board, standing alongside while Justine pulled Cecile onto a seat, leaning across her, penning her between them.

The guard swung onto the platform as the bus moved off, yanking at the bell cord to mocking cheers from the soldiers in the yard. He gestured Alex to the empty seat across the aisle from Cecile, their eyes locking in a fleeting exchange. Alex stayed where he was, hanging onto the chrome rail next to where Cecile sat. The guard looked away, conscious he had conceded something, bracing himself, legs apart, the MP40 cradled loose across his arms.

They were running fast down to the river, morning sun giving the empty streets a pastoral air, softening the stonework. A couple arguing on the corner stopped to watch their progress - elderly tourists staring mutely back.

Alex bent over Cecile's head stooping to see through the window. They were in the old Jewish quarter, rattling past the deserted cobbles of the rue Gravilliers. He had stood in that street, when was it? It seemed a lifetime ago.

"He's turning down to the river." Cecile pulled at Alex's jacket, looking up at him, her voice drowning in a ripple of panic spreading down the bus. “This is the Boulevard de Magenta. It’s the wrong way. Now d’you believe me?”

She grabbed hold of his shoulder, pulling herself up, standing next to him, her breath warm against his ear. “This is the way to Austerlitz. That’s where they’re taking us. To the *Gare*.”

She freed the heavy pillowcase from under her skirt, pressing the twisted linen into his hand. “Here’s the tin. I’ll leave it for you two. Something to drink. They’ll not get me in one of those trains.” She tried to push him aside, “Now, for God’s sake, let me past.”

Seeing her move, the guard rose awkwardly on tiptoes, straining to see.

“Let me go!“ Her voice too loud, hoarse with the effort, “I have to get off.”

Justine pulled her back, Cecile feebly resisting, wrapping both arms round Alex’s waist, her face smeared with tears.

“Tell her to leave me be. Christ in heaven, what have I done to come to this? Let me out.”

At the bus stop on the corner a woman stepped into the road, signalling. The driver hesitated, veering over, the guard bellowing down the bus: *Drive on you bloody fool. We’re not taking passengers!*

Cecile stood up, swaying in the aisle, reaching up to the leather pull cord above her head. Hearing the bell strike as she pulled it, she pulled again and again in a demonic frenzy, the noise drowning the guard’s voice: *Drive on man, God damn you, drive on!*

The guard left the platform, shoving past Alex, swaying to keep his balance, transferring the gun to his left hand, standing hard against Cecile, the barrel pressed into her breast.

“I ask once. Sit down, old woman.” His broken French was menacingly calm, “Leave that alone.”

Cecile let go of the pull cord, seizing the barrel of his gun with both hands, pulling him close, almost an embrace, both staggering back as the bus careered into the kerb, braking hard.

The guard reached out, grabbing her hair to keep his balance, yanking it hard. For a moment as he fell back onto a seat a puzzled expression crossed his face, his hand coming away filled with the soft mass of Cecile's curls. She cried out, the sound like some tiny injured bird, covering her ears, the dome of her bare scalp rising between her hands, a few straggled tufts of dark hair across her head glistening with sweat.

The bus had stopped, bouncing slightly with the pant of the engine.

The guard laid the MP40 on the seat, sweeping the pile of hair to the floor, slowly unbuttoning the holster at his side. He drew the pistol out, turning it slowly in his hand as if trying to recall some detail of its operation.

Justine began sliding across her seat, reaching down to the slatted wooden floor to rescue the wig.

The guard kicked it away, motioning for her to stand next to Cecile.

"Go then." He leaned forward, his face set, waving his gun towards the conductor's platform. "Go."

Cecile walked slowly past him, pausing to push Justine back into her seat.

"No. Both of you. Go."

He turned slightly in his seat watching them pass, pulling the slide of the pistol back, cocking it. He stayed sitting where he was, the pose almost nonchalant, as if the task barely merited the effort to stand.

Justine reached the platform, her arm round Cecile's shoulder. As she leaned slightly forward, the gun barrel dipped, echoing her movement, waiting for her to rise.

Alex swung the weighted pillowcase round. Heavier than he expected, the weight almost defeating him, coming in from the side, landing low. A merciless blow, the edge of the tin took the startled guard full in the face. His mouth opened, silently expelling air. Like some unimaginable conjuring trick, a cavity appeared in his cheek, an atrocious concave wound, spouting blood. The gun exploded in his hand a single bullet striking the roof.

The second blow splayed the soldier's cap across his skull, felling him like a poleaxed beast. Blind with rage, Alex tugged to strike again, the tin caught stubbornly in the polished metal of the cap badge, a patch of blood, too much blood, spreading through the fabric of the pillowcase.

Behind Alex, a tall theatrical figure had eased himself tentatively out of his seat. An old man, making the best of his rumpled state, bow-tie not quite straight. He made his quiet way to the conductor's platform almost apologetically, turning to look back down the bus, eyebrows raised, waiting. An exodus had begun: passengers hurrying silently past the sleeping body, jumping down into the morning air.

Cecile walked back, rescuing the wig from the floor, standing for a second alongside Justine, squeezing her arm. They watched her waddle uncertainly into a disturbed ants' nest of aimless forms drifting round the stranded bus, slowly dispersing into the maze of side streets.

Alex panicked. "Justine, the driver. Stop him!"

"No driver." Her voice was calm against the silence in the bus. "He's gone. Made a run for it. Cecile as well. We'll not see her again. They've all gone."

Justine walked down the bus to see to the injured guard, stooping to prop him against the rail behind his seat, forcing his arms to support his body like some monstrous puppet. His mouth hung open, a thin clear liquid dribbling into it from one nostril. A mass of purple tissue spreading from the smashed cheek had sealed his right eye. As she let it go, his head banged hard against the rail.

"He's barely breathing. I think he's dying."

"He was going to shoot. I watched him cock the damned thing." Alex realised his hands were trembling. "What else could I do?"

"Nothing, nothing at all ... you saved my life."

She picked the submachine gun up, prising the pistol from the soldier's hand, handing them both to Alex. "We'll risk taking these with us. Let's hope we don't need them. I'm not sure where we are. Not that far from the river, I think. It will be the hell of a walk. But it's still early ... Alex, are you listening? You look terrible."

"He was scared, Justine. I saw it in his eyes when we first got on. I think he realised as soon as the bus started. There were too many of us for safety. He was frightened."

"What are you saying? You can't kill a frightened man? It was him or me. Perhaps there are honourable soldiers, I suppose there must be, but this man wasn't." She stood, pulling Alex up with her, leaning very close, her eyes hot with pain. "If you think we were the lucky ones, the ones who got away, don't forget those who didn't get away. I won't forget. Killed for their name on a bit of paper. Killed for existing. None of it has anything to do with war, none of it at all. Do you understand?" She turned away from him, "Come on, we'd better get out of this."

As she made for the platform at the back of the bus, Alex called to her. He was standing next to the driver's battered leather seat, his expression something almost a smile.

"It can't be harder than a jeep. If I can see how you get the thing started."

They abandoned the bus on the Faubourg Saint Honoré where another platane lay across the road, the air filled with the scent of newly sawn wood. A makeshift barricade of paving stones had been piled behind the tree. Strips of asphalt lay about like immense rolls of black carpet.

A single rifle shot from an upstairs window echoed into the silence, answered by the stuttering chatter of an automatic weapon somewhere to their right, filling the street with the stretched metallic whine of ricocheting bullets.

Fifty yards beyond the barricade, two German soldiers were crouched inside the pockmarked portico of an apartment block. One of them raised a hand to Alex, almost a greeting, ostentatiously sending his carbine clattering into the gutter. Perhaps he called out, they were too far away to be sure. He wriggled on his stomach out of the tiny stone cage, his arms outstretched in an absurd gesture of surrender. He looked like a drowning child. He rolled back, screaming, as a single shot turned one extended hand to a sudden splash of red. The men lay curled together against the stone steps like two children.

The firing stopped, an uncanny silence falling over the street. Not so far away, there was the sound of running feet, men's voices shouting, the smash of broken glass.

On the top floor of the apartment opposite somebody was furiously cranking a gramophone, pushing the mahogany box out onto a window-sill. The faint rickety sound of the *Marseillaise* floated into the street. It seemed somehow unused to the open air.

It took an hour to find a way to Madeleine's apartment. All that was left of the elegant glass doors to the street was a mosaic of splintered glass and wrought iron spread over the pavement. They picked their way through debris, broken glass grinding underfoot.

The metal lattice of the lift cage had been wrenched away, the tiny cabin inside draped with a frayed trade union banner, its circular medallion the hammer and sickle. A trail of cigarette-ends led to the turn of the stairs on the second floor. A discarded army boot, thick with fresh blood, lay at the head of the marble stairs.

Madeleine's door was open wide, a haze of brownish smoke drifting out, the sweet acetone smell of gunfire. Alex looked inside. In unshuttered sunlight the paintings in the empty hallway seemed oddly unfamiliar. Broken pieces of the Chinese vase lay scattered among fallen faded flowers. He bent down, lifting a piece of hollow pottery, puzzled it should have lain unattended for so long. It seemed months ago.

Down the corridor an excited chatter of men's voices suddenly stopped, the tiny frisson of silence broken by a single rifle shot, the sound too large for the space.

The salon door burst open. Madeleine stood frozen, staring at them, one hand clutching her breast.

"Dear Jesus - you here! I knew I'd never see you again. Either of you."

She started towards them, suddenly halting, looking beyond them into the hall, her eyes wild with sudden panic. "You're alone? God, yes … of course … on your own … it's a miracle." She wrapped her arms round Justine, looking into her face, smudging tears away. "We were talking about you this morning, well, dawn it must have been." She waved vaguely down the corridor. "My new tenants. Temporary, I hope. Talking about rescue. Nonsense, of course, that Drancy place is a fortress. They were just trying to keep my spirits up."

She reared her head back, catching Justine off guard, shrewd eyes suddenly too inquisitive. "And Drancy? They let you go? Has the fighting started there as well? Is that why? It started here this morning in the street. Men running everywhere. The police as well, they joined in. I heard a gang break in downstairs, rushing up the stairs, banging on the door like savages. I thought they would kill me for sure. But it was just a bunch of students. Communists. You have to be young to say that. They wanted my balcony to shoot from. Then we decided the studio window was better. They've been in there ever since. The mess is incredible. One rifle between the lot of us … to save Paris! I've told them it's a start, God will manage the end."

She released Justine, instantly changing her mind, spreading her arms round the two of them, pulling them close, tears running down her face, managing a choking sort of laugh. "They've started treating me like their mother. It was a mistake making them food, they've been here ever since. I came to get them something to drink. Come with me, I want to keep you where I can see you. I still can't believe you're here."

In the kitchen, the window looked across a narrow lane to the backs of another apartment block. The noise was louder, an incessant chatter of automatic weapons rattling the china on the dresser. There seemed to be no target, the tiny alleyway was deserted.

Madeleine uncorked a bottle of wine, rushing out, leaving them eyeing each other like unexpected visitors, neither daring to speak.

In the alley below, a lorry was inching towards a barricade, low gears screaming. Soldiers in the open back peered like penned cattle over an improvised palisade of slatted wood. One steadied his rifle on the cab, aiming high, tottering back as the lorry began to turn, clumsily shunting between the narrow pavements.

Alex flinched as something dark cartwheeled past the window. A bottle burst on the road, spraying liquid under the lorry. A second bottle landed inside the wooden pen, spinning round, unbroken. The soldiers kicked it away crouching to avoid a hail of bottles. There were bottles everywhere now, too many to count, the lorry standing on a carpet of green glass.

The soldiers in their wooden pen knew long before the smell reached the kitchen. Heaving themselves in panic over the sides, clambering into the mess of shattered glass, ineffectual arms covering their heads, grey shapes scuttling from one impossible shelter to the next. The kitchen reeked of the stuff now - petrol everywhere, fresh and raw on the air.

The bottles stopped. For a frozen second nothing moved, the men staring blindly round, dizzy in the heady scent. Something small, feather-white, floated down, twisting innocently to the ground, the street blooming into a mass of yellow flame.

Pygmy forms, alight like torches, filled the street, fleeing one another, each a screaming vortex of flame, collapsing into writhing mounds of smouldering cloth.

Alex felt his gorge rise. "God almighty. That smell …"

Justine stared blindly into the smoke, finally taking his hand, pulling him away. She was trembling. "I didn't realise. Paris has been a pretence, hasn't it, Alex? All that kept me alive was thinking I'd see Pascal again. But we won't, will we? Not now the war has arrived. We're not going to get away, are we? We're still trapped."

It was a long time before Madeleine came back. She had a young man with her, his face flushed with the excitement of unaccustomed power. He held out a hand to Alex then seeing it was black with oil pulled back, offering the sleeve of his overall, a peasant gesture, oddly touching.

"He wants me to go and talk to someone – I have to go out."

Hearing Madeleine speaking English, the boy glanced at Alex, unaccountably embarrassed.

"It seems they've taken a prisoner. Apparently not a soldier, but throwing his weight about in three languages. I think they want somebody to adjudicate. The man had my name and this address, and that's a mystery." She turned to Alex. "Will you come with me? I have no idea what it's about."

"Out in the street? They took our papers."

"Then best you stay here. He can't eat me, whoever he is."

The boy became impatient, addressing Alex in French. "Our prisoner is asking to see the Colonel."

Alex watched Madeleine's expression change, hardening. "What's he talking about? *Colonel*? Are there troops here?"

She pulled him to one side, throwing a smile at the boy, whispering. "He understands more English than you think. It's no use asking that question. They've organised themselves like the military, ranks, titles, and so forth. They all have arm bands. I suppose there has to be a hierarchy. You find it all juvenile?"

"No. I find it impressive, but you can't fight a war with armbands. Do they know what's in store when the garrison turns out?"

Another shot exploded at the end of the corridor, the first in minutes. Startled, Madeleine took the boy's arm, giving Alex a brief shrug. "You won't stop them now. You saw that business with the lorry? It's too late to stop. Too late. Now … where are you taking me young man? Not far, I hope."

"You know the bar. The *Leopard*. We have to go out the back way."

They watched them through the kitchen window, arm in arm, stepping gingerly through scattered broken glass. The street was ominously silent, the burnt-out lorry now part of the barricade. A plume of oily black smoke drifted languidly from one smouldering tyre. In the street beyond, tricolour flags sprouted impudently from the higher windows. At the corner, Madeleine paused for a second, turning to look back, steadying herself on the boy's arm. They walked out of sight.

Looking down, a nun with a tiny makeshift flag tied to a walking stick shuffled out from a doorway, the huge wings of her headpiece flapping white. Two men with a stretcher scuttled in her wake, bodies bent double against imaginary gunfire. They stood next to the soldier in the middle of the road. He had curled up like a sleeping child, unbearably still.

Forty-Eight

A Matisse hung on the wall opposite the empty fireplace in Madeleine's salon. Perhaps not a masterpiece, but her proudest possession. Alex could not remember a time when the reclining woman in red pyjamas had not been hanging in this room. She lay against a sombre pattern of red and blue, her face no more than a few bleak dabs of black, one arm raised to touch her forehead as if warding something off.

For reasons they dared not acknowledge they had left the door to the apartment open to the vague menace beyond the hallway outside, sitting together silent on the large sofa waiting for Madeleine to return, letting darkness consume the painted odalisque.

Outside, the revolution – if that was what it was - had contracted to no more than unfamiliar footsteps on the stairs, voices calling in the dark, now and then the sound of shattering glass.

It was late when Madeleine returned, hurrying feet across the tiled hallway taking them by surprise. A man's voice, echoed faintly from the floor below, *No, this is far enough. Goodnight, Madame.* Madeleine called back, conceding something. She hesitated for a moment at the door, perhaps puzzled that it was still open.

She was still smiling when she found them in the salon, dropping her coat onto a chair. "Sitting in the dark. I used to do that. But they say the blackout is ending. They say that. Shall we see? Go on, Alexandre, switch them all on." She let him take her arm, steadying herself against him, her breath warm on his cheek. "There, I can see you now. I'm afraid I'm a little drunk. They opened champagne to celebrate something. Being alive, I assume. They insisted I drink with them. After all, it was not their champagne."

She flopped onto the sofa, looking up at Alex. "Well, it seems it has begun. A very Parisian war, with breaks for refreshment. And don't the soldiers come young! Here, sit by me, I feel a little light-headed – expansive you might say. I have a story to tell, Alex. Bring a chair, sit close where I can hear you. Then we will eat - how I miss my Stephanie."

Justine sat next to her on the sofa. "Your mysterious man in need of adjudication – you saw him?"

Madeleine leaned back, one hand pressed to her eyes, against the electric light. She seemed to have aged since she went away: tiny spots of feverish red on her cheeks, a kind of slackening of the skin around her mouth. She sighed, as if speech would, after all, be too great an effort.

"*See him*? Yes, of course I saw him." She looked at Alex, searching his face, waiting for him to return her gaze. "But I heard him long before I saw him. Bellowing like a madman. Can people with squeaky voices bellow? The boys in the bar said he'd become tiresome, shouting like a bad-tempered schoolmaster. So they locked him in a storeroom upstairs. They asked me to stop him making such a noise."

She looked down at her hands, stretching them out in her lap, frowning slightly as if something about them was displeasing. "That was where I found him. A plump little fellow, full of hurt dignity, sitting among the empty beer bottles. I must say, after today it was hard listening to hurt dignity, even in good French. And yes, I admit his French was good."

She seemed to be waiting for Alex to acknowledge something, something unfathomable in her expression, a kind of provoking smile.

"At least, good for an Englishman."

Alex stared back at her, aware of slight movement about his heart, his pulse rising. "English? But he must have known you to send for you."

"I'd never seen him before in my life. But I guessed who he was even before they unlocked the door." The smile was still there. "He introduced himself, but shall I describe him? I said *plump*. Too kind really. *Fat* would be better. Quite short. Peering at me through his little spectacles. Ugly thick glass. Shiny face, *like a baby's bottom* as they used to say, his cheeks puffed out like an angry toad. When he saw they'd sent a woman visiting, he looked me up and down. I even got an insolent little bow, passing the inspection. I could have slapped his face."

Alex stood up, feeling a momentary dizziness, his heart oddly unloosed in his chest. He walked to the balcony doors, twitching the curtain aside, holding on.

She leaned back, calling to him, almost a provocation. "Where are you going, Alexandre? What do you think he said, this little English *bonhommne*? I wish I could imitate, it was really splendid. *I've so much wanted to meet you*. Oxford English, don't you say? I thought he was going to kiss my hand."

"What the devil are you trying to say? It was John Cabot, is that what you're saying? My God, that man's not a joke. But he doesn't know you. I can't believe it's him."

"I'm afraid you will have to believe it." She seemed irritated, half-turning in her chair, "And I can't see you if you stand there sulking. As for knowing me, apparently you are responsible for that. He explained that my address appears in your file. Do you really have a *file*?"

Alex came slowly back to his chair, slumping down, nodding wearily.

"*A file*? Yes … yes … of course. I knew that was possible. That someone could go looking. I'm sorry to wish him on you."

"Perhaps you may not be so sorry after all. He has proved useful. You know, he was not at all what I expected, this evil Moriarty of yours. To be in the presence of the devil incarnate and what do I find? A pompous little man locked up in a storeroom. I'm afraid he saw the disappointment in my face. Well, there you are, I could never hide my thoughts. You can't mend a thing like that. So we got off to a bad start."

Justine took her hand, glancing across at Alex. "You don't know about him. He deceived Alex. Badly. I think that was why he was looking for him."

Alex was blinking at his watch, as if he barely believed it, rounding on Madeleine, suddenly remembering something. "That young chap who came back with you? We heard him. Can I get to him? Can he take me? It's not that late."

"My escort? He was excusing himself. Not a very military excuse. He said he was late for his supper and his mother would be worried. You see, even communists have mothers." She pushed herself up, wincing slightly, pressing her head into the cushion. "I have a headache. No, you are too late. Your Mr Cabot left long before I did. A long time ago … a lot of champagne ago. Two men arrived in a car to collect him. Waving papers signed by General Gerow at us, as if we cared. They said they had to drive him back to Montlhéry tonight. I'm not sure where that is. Apparently there's been fighting there, that was why they were late."

"*Gerow* - but he's American …"

"American, yes. I assume that is how they managed to come. Apparently it is not impossible to come and go … a matter of payment. Mr Cabot works for them. No uniform, of course, but certainly American. You know the kind? A little too big for the room, very clean, smelling of chewing gum. You can imagine the excitement in the bar. Our first Americans. Even without the helmets."

"*Works for them*? He said that? How can he be working for them?"

Madeleine impatiently tapped the side of the sofa, interrupting him,

"There, I knew I'd forget. He asked particularly to be remembered to you. He said he was sure Captain Vere would recall. He had warm memories of a time you worked together. Is that right? You worked together?"

"Is this a joke? For heaven's sake, the man had me locked up."

"He said he arranged for you to be posted to Scotland. Is that locked up?"

Justine made room as Madeleine stretched out, closing her eyes, as if from some secret pain, her pose a curious echo of the Matisse on the wall behind. "He told me what you did in France. A little of what you did. What both of you must have done. I didn't know, I am ashamed. You are braver souls than me." She opened her eyes, looking down at Justine's hand, patting it, as if confirming some shared secret.

"Alexandre, my dear boy, Mr Cabot is envious of you, did you not know that? Or perhaps *jealous* is better. English is so difficult." She managed a watery smile. "I would kiss you for it, but I am a little tired."

She pulled Justine closer, her voice low, "I knew your *Alex* when he was just a child. He was always a modest little boy. You can kiss him in my place. Look at him now, staring at me in that disagreeable way. Alexandre, your Cabot man bears you no ill will, I know that."

"I'm sorry, you can't possibly know that. He had me locked away. How much ill will is that?"

"For your own safety, he said. Too much would be lost if you were captured. Surely you know war cuts corners? If you had lived here these past few years …" She shrugged, "War doesn't care about people, people just get in the way. Dear God, who am I to be explaining? Mr Cabot gave me a message for you. I am to tell you that his war has been at least as trying as yours. Life is too short to bear grudges, Alexandre. Don't you want to hear my news?"

"I don't care what he did to me. All that's over. It's what he did to Justine that I can't forgive."

Justine came to him, kneeling alongside his chair, her back to Madeleine, whispering, "Alex, my love, please don't. You mustn't jump to conclusions ... not about me." She turned to Madeleine, trying for a bright voice. "Yes, your news. He promises he'll be quiet. But you look awfully tired ... perhaps tomorrow …?"

"No, it's too important for that. Mr Cabot had arrived with orders for our arrondissement. The boys told him no one believed in those things any more ... orders, I mean. They wouldn't even let him read them out. And you can understand, because when he read them to me it was completely preposterous. Poor Mr Cabot, like a character in one of those sentimental American films that Stephanie adores. Americans believe such odd things about the French. I think it's because we don't speak English, it's seen as a kind of mental handicap."

She tried to straighten up, abandoning the effort, falling back onto the cushion. "Now, if you both promise not to interrupt me, I will tell you what Mr Cabot was doing while Alexandre was in Scotland. *Locked up* as you say. He was in the United States of America. Not locked up, I imagine."

Alex frowned at her, shaking his head, "No, no, no, that doesn't make sense. I'm sorry, I'm not interrupting you. It's just plain wrong. He was lying to you. You don't know him, he is a professional liar. It was Cabot who tricked Justine into coming to Paris. He is responsible for all of it. It was his trademark trick. He couldn't have done that if he was in the States. It would have been impossible."

Madeleine pressed on, barely listening, her voice hoarse with the effort. "At a training school in Virginia. He has been there until he arrived in Normandy a few weeks ago. Why should he lie to *me* about such a thing? It has nothing to do with me. But surely you can check if it matters that much. He said a place called Charlottesville. Do you know where that is?"

Alex sat mutely looking down at the patterned wood at his feet, a kind of defeat closing him in, contradictory truths leaving him slightly sick. "Charlottesville. Yes, there's an Officer Academy there. And yes, it's in Virginia." He summoned up one last desperate effort, his voice insistent, "But just because Cabot knows about the place doesn't prove he was there. There would be nothing sensible for him to do. His speciality is disinformation. That's a skill you can't export. The Americans have their own tricks."

"His work had nothing to do with disinformation." Her sudden feeble laugh took them both by surprise, forcing a faint uncomprehending smile to Justine's lips. "Although, *misinformation* might describe it well enough. He was training civilians to govern us. To govern France. The Civil Authority, that's what he called it. Do you believe me now? It would be a curious thing to lie about. In fact, I know he is not lying. We have known about this nonsense for weeks."

"When you say *we*?"

"Well …" She seemed to find the question embarrassing. "I thought I told you. People of the *Quartier.* We heard about this insane plan shortly after the invasion – after the *landings* as you call it. Americans going from town to town, claiming them in the name of Uncle Sam. Mr Cabot's pupils, one assumes. They have even printed us new money. French dollars, you could say."

"You mean dealing with the Vichy lot? Surely …"

"I mean no such thing. Why should they care about that? I mean settling who shall govern France. The Americans have decided – after all, it is their victory. And the answer is *not France*. Mr Cabot came bearing the names of people in the arrondissement selected to govern us." Seeing Alex shaking his head, she turned to look at the Matisse, her voice rising, "You surely see it's absurd … impossible? Thanking God to be rid of Germans, finding you are to exchange them for Americans. I imagine American curfews are much the same as German curfews, you still can't go anywhere. And he really imagined that, in Paris. I can tell you, people would rather die."

"People are dying already."

"I know that, Alexandre, you have no call to remind me. But this Cabot man. You say he is clever. I say he can't bear the thought that his mission has become a farce. People are laughing at him. He surely never imagined he would end up locked away with the empty bottles. I suppose that's why he poured his soul out to me. At least, he saved a little face. But, my God, he was so solemn, it was hard not to laugh. He kept saying, *you realise, Paris is doomed?*"

"But the man's got eyes …" Absurdly, Alex found himself defending Cabot. "He can see for himself what's going on. Do you really think a few angry students can end this? You think it's going to end well? How can it?"

"You mean my young men? Infant communists Mr Cabot called them. It's odd, he says he doesn't believe in them. Not particularly rational for a clever man. He says the whole situation is unreal. That was his word – *unreal*."

"He means how insanely unequal it is, that's what makes it unreal. Take this uprising, how many are involved? A thousand? Two thousand? Most of them unarmed. The German garrison is twenty times that. Armed soldiers with tanks. There must be fifty tanks or more in the city. There are scores of half-tracks, mobile artillery, the lot. How are a few ancient rifles supposed to liberate Paris?"

"Mr Cabot said he found the word *liberate* unfortunate. He is careful with words, your colleague. I must say, it was difficult to warm to him. Superior without anything particular to be superior about. Lecturing me about how France will be governed. I told him, we have had one military government and that was enough for a lifetime, we are not looking for another. He's a fool."

"He's one of the brightest people I've known."

"Then you have led a very cloistered life, Alexandre. I told him to go and ask those students the Germans were shelling this afternoon if they want some American who barely speaks French as their new Mayor. Ask the students near the Sorbonne if they want to take their city back, or live under some absurd *Pax Americana*? If it wasn't for the fact he could help me, I would have walked away."

"What help? Why should Cabot help anybody?"

"Ah, as to *why* I can only guess. He mentioned that painting you talked about. He seemed to think I understood. I told him we have to get you out of Paris. He had papers that allow passage at the Porte d'Italie. It cost him nothing to give me them. He was not at all unwilling. They are there in my coat." Trying to sit up, she fell back against the cushions. "If you would pass ..." Her eyes had closed.

Justine reached out, resting a hand on her knee. "I think she's fainted. She's not well. She's dreadfully pale."

"It's hot in here. I'll get some water."

"No it's not the heat. Look." Something in Justine's voice arrested him. "There's blood all over the cushion. God, we've been sitting here all this time and she's hurt. Her shoulder, I think. I'll see if I can lie her down. See what you can find in the bathroom. Hurry."

Forty-Nine

Alex carried Madeleine to her bedroom. She seemed unconscious, her eyes only flickering open as he laid her on the bed. Bending over her, he found mild blue eyes close to his own, a faint ironic smile wrinkling her face. "Hell, when did I last look up at a man like this?" She tried to lift herself, falling back, cursing. "I must have passed out. And where's this you've brought me?"

Justine began unbuttoning her dress, gently pulling it away at the shoulder. Madeleine pushed her off. "I can manage, let me. I remember now, I was feeling dizzy. I can't manage this button. Too feeble."

Justine leaned over to inspect the wound. "It's very raw. It looks like a bullet, but …"

"Don't go hunting for bullets, you'll find nothing. The boys already looked. A graze, they said. Quite deep, but just a graze. I remember the damned thing felt like a knife. Why the long face, Alexandre? There are some dressings in the bathroom. Go and see what you can find. It's not the end of the world. They said it was nothing."

"What would they know?" Justine sounded angry. "Kids playing soldiers. It's been bleeding quite badly."

"There was a crowd outside in the road. Drunk, I think. Somebody shot through the door of the bar. Hit the wall. This thing was a ricochet. Unlucky." The smile for Alex turned to a grimace, her teeth bared in pain. "You may fetch the dressings then you may go away. I'm not an exhibition. Justine will deal with me. Go to bed, you look very tired. Don't use all the hot water. I made your room ready this morning, a little act of supplication. We will talk about it in the morning. I intend to be still alive."

She rolled painfully onto her side as he left the room, reaching a hand out to Justine, her face drawn. "We'd better see what's to be done. A nuisance."

It was late when Alex finally climbed the narrow staircase to the floor above. He heard Justine laugh as he passed Madeleine's room, the two women talking over each other.

The scent of cedar wood on the staircase peeled away the years. How many times had he slept in the room at the end of this passageway? It must have been hundreds. His own little room, for surely no one else had ever slept there.

It had not changed: his homework desk still tucked between the two windows, the same tiny chairs parked on either side. Frail things, too delicate for sitting, upholstered in grey *toile de jouy*. Even the chamber pot beneath the bed. The picture was still there, filling most of the only free wall. Hard to imagine it anywhere else: a clumsy painting of water lilies, the signature, *Claude Monet, 1919*, optimistic. He had asked her once why she bothered with such a bad copy, remembering only now that she had never replied.

The bed was freshly made, sheets turned back, a double lace-edged bolster plumped and waiting. There was a pack of Sobranie Russian cigarettes on the little *chevet*. She had done all this today. Even the carafe of water with its scrap of beaded linen to keep the dust away. Futile rituals warding off the certainty she would never see him again, never see either of them ever again.

He woke to the sound of someone tapping at the door, starting bolt upright, flailing to find the electric cord, staring wildly at a figure silhouetted in the open doorway, barely knowing where he was.

"Oh, you're asleep. I startled you. Madeleine followed me to my bath. She wanted to talk."

"Madeleine, yes ... I'm sorry ... I'm still half asleep. Is all well?"

"The wound is nothing much. She's very professional about such things. There's things you don't know about your aunt, Alex."

"I know she's involved in some sort of Home Guard effort. Perhaps it's become more than that now. Those bandages in the bathroom were French Army issue. Surgical dressings. Not for when you cut your finger."

Justine walked to the window, looking down into the road, her voice muffled against the dark of the windowpane. She seemed strangely defenceless. "I left your aunt in her own bed." She turned to face him, her expression defiant, "She said I am to impose on you. She thinks she's being kind. And don't look like that, it's not fair. It's a ridiculous thing to say, but I feel shy. Turn the light off, I'll manage perfectly well in the dark."

He felt the movement of the bed as she settled alongside him, immobile on her back, bringing with her the fresh perfume of Madeleine's soap.

"Can we talk a little, Guffin? I'm dreadfully tired, but it will make me feel less odd. About Cecile and that hideous man Brunner. Do you think she could have got away?"

Alex reached out finding her hand. "Yes, I'm sure of it. You're asking about us, aren't you?"

"I suppose I am. It's all this madness starting. I realise I think about him all the time. Perhaps I'll go mad."

"About Pascal?" He felt her move at the name, turning towards him. "If what you're asking is should we trust Cabot and his papers, how can I answer? I've spent so long mistrusting that man. I seem to have lost my bearings."

"The Porte d'Italie. Is that far from here, do you know?"

"Not very. You could walk in an hour or two. Or one of those dog-cart things, if they're not on strike. But we can't walk through a war. This business will start again tomorrow, probably worse. Then what? How long before the German garrison is on the streets?"

"Madeleine is sure the Germans have no intention of holding Paris. No, Alex, that's what she says. Give me your other hand. If you'd only heard her. She is convinced she's right."

"But all she hears is hysterical rumour. The city must be full of it. Cabot is right about that much – it's all unreal."

"She said the Germans in Paris have lost heart. Perhaps she knows. She lives here. She told me about these two soldiers penned up in a house on the rue du Jura. This was yesterday. There was a crowd outside, fifty or more, baying for their blood. They shot themselves. Can you believe that? Shot themselves, rather than come out with their hands up."

"Two soldiers against a mob ... yes, but ..."

"It's more than that, Madeleine says it's like that everywhere. That's what Cabot didn't understand. It's not just a few thousand students, it's pretty well everybody now. Paris has fallen into a sort of madness. Nothing is going to stop it. If the Garrison starts a fight they will be torn to pieces whatever the cost, and they know it. It doesn't matter that nobody's armed. People are mad with rage."

Feeling him about to speak, she pulled him very close. "You do know I'm right about this, my love ... think … this morning on that bus … with Cecile. You remember?"

She turned over, curling her back against his side. "It's lovely having you here. I've been out of the way of being held. Hold me, Guffin, would you? We should sleep. I'll be here for you when you wake."

The air raid came before dawn, Alex swimming up into a blind confusion of sound, the drum of heavy engines, unbearably close. He sat up, searching for the window, a patch of lighter dark against the night. Two planes. Or three in close formation. It was hard to tell. Directly overhead now, engines whining in descent, the noise immense, unspeakably close. Justine woke beside him, gripping his arm, flashes of yellow filling the room with obscure shadows, the sky above the city outside vaguely luminous. Explosions rippled towards them like the slow tearing of wood, flexing the window glass.

It was finished before they had had time to move, engines straining in a steep climb. Towers of smoke reached up into a bloom of soft pink, low clouds shimmering alive.

"Is it over?" She was trembling, her voice unsteady, "They were ours, weren't they? I keep thinking how strange to be killed by our own bombs. Can you make out where they've gone? It seemed to be east. Perhaps they're not just bombing Paris. It did seem east, didn't it?"

"No, not ours. Not American either. The engines weren't big enough. Heinkels, I think. That would explain no ack-ack. I think they were bombing the Marais. I'm not sure about east, they were climbing away … probably just the one sortie. You're thinking of him, aren't you? Pascal. They'll have shelters, surely …"

Justine got out of bed, standing at the window, her voice flat. "I suppose so. You can only see sky from here, Alex. Everywhere seems on fire. You wouldn't think a few bombs could do that. The whole sky alight ..."

"It's their way of leaving little behind. Barely a trace, you'd say, not a rack. I start to think Madeleine's right. The Germans have decided to leave. Come back to bed, Justine."

"I won't be able to sleep. I'm not tired any more. What time is it?"

"I don't know. Very early."

He lit two cigarettes. They lay side by side watching the sky fade to the grey-pink of a Paris dawn. Somewhere in the street below a single blackbird began its morning song.

"It will be the same for the store, won't it?" She had been silent for so long her voice startled him. "I mean for the Lévitan and the other places? It will be exactly the same."

"The same how?"

"Erased. Forgotten. Not burned, just forgotten. Last night Madeleine said it would be like throwing letters in the fire. Things you don't want to read. An amnesic conspiracy she called it. The slave labour, the death camps, the endless misery, poor little Sylvie. All of them. It will all have gone."

"What do you think yesterday was about? If Paris survives …"

"Oh, Paris will survive. Paris decided to look the other way a long time ago, that's what Madeleine says. Decided to find something else to do. I don't blame them … misery piled on misery ... you reach a point when it's too much. Once you decide to forget something like that dreadful store, it can't be that hard, not if you never quite believed in the first place. You have to have been there, inside the horror, day after day, to understand."

"If it wasn't for John Cabot, you wouldn't have had to live through it. I'll never forgive Cabot for that."

"You don't have to forgive him, Alex. I don't believe he had anything to do with those men who came to Dundee. The mistake was mine. The mistake was visiting Lucile Beyrou."

"*Mistake*? Why was that a mistake? And if it wasn't Cabot, then who? The whole scheme has his fingerprints all over it."

"As for his fingerprints, yes you're right about that. It must have been planned that way. Mr Cabot can't be short of enemies. Perhaps they thought it convenient for him to get the blame. Revenge, if you like, but it wasn't him, I'm sure it wasn't."

"Then who?"

"I don't know. D'you think I haven't worried myself sick as to who? They must have worked out that Gliess story. Perhaps they got it out of Renault. They don't forget things like that."

"The Abwehr?"

"I think so. Or the Vichy lot. Apart from one of those first men in Dundee, everybody I met was French? Don't you find that odd?"

"But how could it ever work? You'd resigned. You couldn't be sent on missions, fake or not - it doesn't make sense. I'm not likely to forget that day you came back from Baker Street? The day you resigned your commission."

"But that wasn't true, my love, that wasn't true either. I saw you thought it, I saw you so much wanted to believe it, I hadn't the heart to explain, I just let you go on believing a lie. It's right, what they say about the Service - it's a sort of marriage. You're theirs for life. I'm not the first to find that you can't walk away. "

"But why shouldn't you see this artist? Why's it a mistake? I saw her myself. She knows nothing at all. To tell the truth, I've never understood all the fuss about her. All that effort just to exfiltrate an obscure artist nobody's heard of."

"Remember where she spent most of her life – the Gers safe house. But she's not obscure, my love, not at all. In fact she's horribly famous, you just don't know her name. Madeleine knew her work. Sometimes when I think she actually painted my portrait ..." She hesitated, "Alex, you're going to say I'm being mysterious. But I'm not. It's just hard for me to explain. About Lucy's picture of me."

"You mean the one Cabot stole? What's there to explain?"

"He didn't steal it, he bought it, and thank God he did. You knew the gallery had put it on show? Can't you see the consequence?"

"What? Because it has the same title as some painting by Bradley? Who on earth would make that connection? Justine, what's this all about? Why can't I know? Why the hell is everything always a secret? It's the story of my life."

She sat up, reaching across him to switch on the light, her face wet with tears. "But you can know, Alex, of course you can know. I hate hearing you say things like that."

She gave him a little broken smile, searching for a handkerchief.

"It's not really my secret either, it's something Lucy told me. All those years she spent years working with Bradley. One day, he told her about the woman in that painting of his, the famous one, the one in the straw hat. She was my mother. That's all. That's my secret – nothing so very important. My mother died bringing me into the world. Spanish 'flu. It sent him mad. Lucy said he was literally insane for a while. For years all he did was paint my mother. Dozens and dozens of paintings. He would finish them and burn them in the garden. Nobody had heard of him in those days. France was in ruins after the war. He was destitute, in and out of hospital. Perhaps he could have done something about me, but the truth is he didn't. I ended up handed over to nuns, just one more war baby. He never knew what became of me. I don't know, perhaps he never knew I existed."

"But if she was your mother …"

She smiled at him, shaking the hair out of her eyes, "Albert Bradley was my father. There you are, not so much of a secret, but secret enough. I think I was Lucy's only portrait."

"Yes, she told me?"

"It was a kindness reaching out to me, picking that title. *Fille au Chapeau de Paille*. Of course the word is *daughter,* not *girl*. But that's what made it so dangerous."

She lay silent for a long time. "That's what brought those men sniffing round her studio in Dundee, whoever they were. It wouldn't have been so hard to put two and two together. Mr Cabot had nothing to do with it. In fact, you could say he did what he could to mend it. He was too late, of course. By the time he bought it, I'd been propped up in a London gallery window for weeks. Lucy had even signed the thing with the name we gave her. She might as well have titled it *Portrait of an Agent* and included a map to the safe house."

Fifty

The sound of rain against the open window woke Alex to a fresh damp scent blowing past fluttering curtains. Justine's side of the bed was empty, her bedclothes thrown back. He stretched out one arm, paddling the cool sheets where she had lain, aware of an inexplicable feeling of contentment.

Madeleine was standing at his bedside.

"I've been watching you. You sleep like a little boy. Here, I've brought you your chocolate. A small cup, I'm afraid. All I've been permitted to carry. I've one good hand at least."

"Yes, your shoulder. I remember." He struggled to sit up. "You look better, quite cheerful, in fact. Have you seen Justine?"

She placed the tiny cup and saucer on the *chevet* at his bedside.

"Justine? Up and about long ago." She looked wistfully at his little homework desk. "I remember you sitting there. Would you believe I was weeping in here not so long ago? I'd found some cigarettes for you. Cigarettes you would never smoke. There I was, weeping for your lost princess. I was sure I'd never see either of you again. When she came down this morning she started weeping herself. No, Alexandre, calm yourself, tears of quite another kind."

"I've overslept. What time is it? Where is she?"

"Making the Colonel his breakfast. Stephanie was helping, so I ran away. I can't bear too many people in a kitchen."

"*Colonel*? You mean he's actually here? Is this about the air raid last night? I thought I heard shooting earlier, but a long way away."

"He came with my friend from the *Leopard*. Your Mr Cabot. The Americans had sent him back."

"Cabot here? And this Colonel, what's he want?" He scrabbled for the kitbag lying on the floor next to the bed, "If it's papers … is that?"

"Heavens, no! Not papers. Leave them where they are. He showed no interest at all in papers." She smiled benevolently down. "I'd say he was more interested in the three women in the kitchen. That's at least two too many. I'll let you get dressed. Now drink up before the day runs away: your grandmother used to say that. I'm going in search of milk and bread. I will try the *Leopard*, you never know."

As she reached the bedroom door she seemed suddenly to remember something, turning to face him. "I forgot. Stephanie said she was taking your German guns. The things you brought with you. You are famous, by the way, both of you. People make pilgrimages to your abandoned bus. It's become a sort of shrine."

"There was a German soldier … we had to leave him behind. Do you know …?"

"Your chocolate is getting cold. I remember you used to call it *cocoa* when you were a little boy." She came back to collect the cup, hovering over him, reluctant to leave. "Strange to be visiting little Alexandre's room. I could never bring myself to change the furniture. Another shrine, I suppose." She nodded to the vast canvas on the wall. "Even that Monet. Tucked away up here. Nobody ever sees the thing." She was unconsciously twisting the cup in her hand, lost for how to broach something, nerving herself to it. "It was always compromised, you know, the pleasure I took in having you here. Always a little compromised."

"I wouldn't worry, kids imagine they're important, the centre of the world. Demanding little devils. I don't think I've changed all that much, to tell you the truth. I suppose I was always getting under your feet. Funny though, I always thought of myself as an obedient little chap."

"*Obedient*? Yes, I believe so. I am explaining badly. What I mean is I envied my sister her little boy. Jealousy, that was the compromise. Playing at mothers is a very seductive game, a sort of drug. And now you're going to say, *Why not one of your own? Why not a little boy of your own?*" She shrugged, trying to smile, "Perhaps the day will come I tell Justine that story. I like talking to your princess." She posed herself on the edge of the bed, resting one hand lightly on his arm, her face taut with an odd intense expression. "The truth is I dislike responsibility. I prefer borrowing to owning. Perhaps you find that shameful?"

Alex stretched out for his cigarette case, smiling to himself as she avoided his eyes. "If I didn't know better, I would say my beloved aunt is being *adept*. Heaven knows where you learned that trick. There's really no call to steer me, you know. I'm only too willing to talk about him. About another little boy, that is. It's just that I daren't. Not yet. Justine says thinking about him is too much like tempting fate. She says he's safe, that's all I know. That's her particular rock to cling to. I realised last night, perhaps he was closer than I'd imagined. That raid upset her dreadfully. She asked me where the bombers were going next."

"Being responsible for someone like that … it's unbearable. That's the difference between owning and borrowing. You really don't know where he is? And now I feel guilty. Justine told me yesterday. She told me everything."

"I'm the one person she won't tell. I realise she wants us to find him together. I think I understand."

Madeleine squeezed his arm, easing herself up, gathering the cup again. She had pulled a handkerchief from her sleeve, bunching it tight into her other hand waving vaguely to the window. "There, the rain has stopped. Do you think that means our little war will start again? Come down when you're ready. Breakfast is in the kitchen. You will find your Mr Cabot there."

He looked up, puzzled by the tremor in her voice. There were tears in her eyes.

The hall downstairs showed no trace of yesterday. The parquet had been polished. Yellow roses, glinting with new raindrops, drooped from the rim of another Chinese bowl, filling the space with a gentle cloudy perfume. The same two mirrors examined each other, keeping silent watch. There were voices beyond the salon door, Madeleine explaining something in slow careful French.

Hearing the click of cutlery, Alex pushed at the door to the kitchen, peering inside.

John Cabot was facing him across the table, a starched linen napkin tucked neatly into his collar. He was eating an omelette with a tiny fork, pausing now and then to dab the plate with a piece of bread in his other hand. He scraped his chair back, half rising, nervously pushing the hair from his eyes.

He seemed greatly changed from those distant TPSU days. A veil of weariness had spun itself like a grey web over the familiar puffy face. Remembering the MO at Archer's ceremony, Alex wondered whether he also found his consolation in whisky.

"Alex. So here you are. I've been sitting here composing my opening sortie. Tricky thing, that …" Running out of words, he stared uncomfortably down at his omelette.

Alex looked on, obscurely aware he had secured some kind of advantage. Somewhere in another room there was the faint sound of Justine's voice. Watching Cabot frame silent words on his lips, carefully testing them out, he was filled with an overwhelming need to be somewhere else, anywhere but here, away from this sad, desiccated man.

Cabot lurched suddenly into speech. "Do say something, old boy, I start to feel lonely. Would you like some coffee? It's still hot. There should be a book about awkward encounters, don't you think? That translation of Apollonius Rhodius, you remember how it went? *Ill nature parted the conflicted foes*, something like that. Are we really foes, Alex? Were we? It's a hard word. I confess I *am* a little ill-natured, but you always knew that. It's an Oxford affliction. You're not still harbouring Scottish resentments, are you? Did you never think about it from my point of view? All those months we worked together, every single operation I was tasked to perform flagged me as deniable. If you're ordered to betray your friends, how d'you think *deniable* translates? I'll tell you. *Friendless.*" He pushed his plate a little away, fragments of egg left lying there, a tiny conciliatory gesture.

"Excellent omelette. Yours is keeping warm over there. She's gone, by the way, your aunt's cook. Off to do battle. Armed to the teeth. An MP40, if I'm not mistaken. That's a dreadful thing for a girl to be toting. I hope she comes to no harm. She seemed dangerously enthusiastic."

He tried one final time, his expression a kind of sad entreaty.

"You're looking frightfully well, old chap. Better than me. The flush of success? Your mission complete … that it?

"*Mission*? Which mission would that be, then?" Alex watched Cabot absorb his words, tuning himself to the forgotten voice, frowning slightly with the effort.

"No need to be so brusque. Winners are meant to be magnanimous – isn't that the rule? Although yes, perhaps I should have said *Major Elton's* mission. He wanted you to find me. You have found me. What next?" He grinned - the same puckish expression of years ago. It was difficult not to smile back. "I have news of your Major, by the by. He's been moved. We found him a billet where he can do a bit less damage. He did you a fair bit, I hear. What else? You'll be satisfied to hear Major Elton's forays into amateur espionage are over. Nipped in the bud. Hats off to you for surviving his efforts. More than most would have managed. But there you are, I'm afraid his passing means you now have nobody to report to."

"I can't say I care." Drawn in by the expression on Cabot's face, Alex found himself replying almost against his will. "Don't run away with the idea I was taken in by that man. The mission was misconceived from the start. I had my own reasons for going along with it."

"Your aunt started to tell me that story, but we were interrupted. I had to explain my return, my coming back to those oppressive children in the café. The Americans have blocked the Porte d'Italie. No passage for the likes of me, at any rate. By the way, did she explain I have a passenger? We seek refuge."

"If you think I came to Paris looking for you, you're wrong."

"No, I don't think that, Alex, I know you better than that. You wanted to find Mrs Perry, of course you did. And you did find her.

All the same, I should tell you about Elton's mission. Do you know what he thought he was doing?"

"Wasn't that obvious? He was interested in you."

"Right, as ever. Can you believe it? He thought if he could only discover what I was up to, his masters would heap favours on him. Maybe promote him. I think he had a medal in mind. The snag was his masters knew perfectly well what I was up to, it was their idea, after all. But I do blame you, Alex for all that. Just a little. You gave the little chap my name, I fault you for that. It set the poor fool thinking. Army Majors shouldn't think, it's a step too far for most of them. He was so proud of his scheme. Actually shared it with that Free French enterprise in Duke Street. Blissfully unaware that lot has been riddled with Vichy thugs since the word go. He actually invited one to your interview."

He looked up, catching Alex unawares, "But you knew all that, didn't you? How could you not?" He waited for Alex's reluctant nod, his gaze steady. "Strange, isn't it? Wars lost because some fool wants to inhabit a bigger office. God preserve us. Just to be straight, Alex. Don't blame me for any of that. I was far away."

"Virginia, Madeleine says. Is that part of your being straight? Should I believe her?"

"Oh, yes. It's true enough. Remarkable woman, your aunt, Alex. It must run in the family. I wish I had an aunt like that. An entourage of excitable young men waving guns about. She seems to have ended up as their unofficial commandant. Mind you, what isn't unofficial these days?"

"Should I believe you? Should I believe anything you say?"

"Please yourself, old man. Believe what you will. I was in Charlottesville for more than a year. There's your breakfast in the oven, and this coffee's getting cold. What's up? Don't tell me you're superstitious about breaking bread."

Alex rescued a plate from the stove, pouring himself some coffee.

Cabot sat watching him eat, leaning back, arms behind his head, suddenly confident, a comfortable expression on his face. "Have I put an end to all your dark imaginings, old man? I had nothing to do with the faithful Mrs P - apart from redeeming her portrait. And you can imagine the flap when we got wind of that. A novel form of homicide if you think about it, putting our enemy's targets on public display. Particularly that one. I was too late, of course. I'm sorry, Alex. That's the truth. I'm really very sorry. I did what I could."

"And that would be?"

"Well those two French heavies that chased her to Dundee won't be troubling anyone much, that was a start. Detained at the King's pleasure. No don't ask where. I gather they were hauled off a train at Crewe. Of course, our Duke Street friends kicked up the hell of a fuss, kept going on about dignity, but there you are. How are we ever going to manage without emergency powers? It fell to me to tell them it was *deemed expedient*. I'd always wanted to say that."

Someone had opened the salon door, Madeleine standing in the hall asking for something, her voice too soft to make out, a darker, voice surging out, *Would you? That's kind*, the words cut off as the door clicked to.

Alex got up, walking to the door. "Perhaps we can talk later. I rather think I'm wanted. That was Justine."

"Don't go, Alex. Please don't. You'll regret it. You're not wanted there. Honestly, I know you're not. It's just woman talk. I want to tell you something. We were talking this morning, Mrs Perry and I. About Paris. About what's to become of Paris. Don't you want to know what brought me here?"

"Something to do with the Civil Administration, wasn't it? That's what Madeleine said. She painted you as a true believer, but since the scheme is collapsing in ruins even as we talk I assume you were posted to the States to infiltrate it. To kill it off from within. That sounds more your line."

"She took so much pleasure in my gullibility, it would have been heartless to disabuse her. But in truth we didn't need to do all that much. I think it was Mr Churchill who pointed out what a wonderful weapon we had in *misplaced enthusiasm* ... it needs English hands, of course. I offered lectures on European history. Rather a lot of them. All impromptu, I may say. You could see interest waning."

"The Americans will hardly thank you for that. Aren't they supposed to be our allies?"

"They really are endearingly naïve." It was the old Cabot again, eager face thrusting forward, eyes bright with the chase. "They can't seem to make up their mind whether they've liberated France or conquered it. Either way, they're hell bent on pulling the strings. And they don't care a damn which puppet they hang on the other end. Come on, Alex, we can't have that. For God's sake, let the frogs sort their country out. They'll bugger it up, of course, but it's theirs to bugger. Anyway - American soldiers against French politicians. I'd have said that looks like *No Contest*. It didn't need much help to come unstuck."

"It worked in Italy."

"The Allied Military Government, you mean? *AMGOT*, as the Yankees put it. Americans are remarkably wedded to ugly acronyms. But no, I don't think it has worked. They always forget the OT at the end. *Occupied Territories*, old boy. Who's supposed to do the occupying in France? No, it was worth every bean we spent to kill that off. British perfidy at its finest … when will people finally wake up to the fact we're good at it?"

"Aren't you running a bit ahead of yourself? A little matter of the German Garrison."

Cabot shook his head, "You were up very late, Alex. You missed the show. We stood on your little balcony, all of us, watching the cars go by. One was tempted to wave. Mercedes nose to tail. Think of all those poor bloody corporals up all night polishing. Generals in the back, dressed to the nines. A sort of gypsy caravan, bits of furniture sticking out of the boot. It says a lot, that last infantile bit of theft. Floozies at their side, of course. Admirable word, that. Your aunt used it. I gather you must be blond to qualify."

He reached out, sharing the last of the coffee pot between the two cups. "No, I never thought it possible, but your aunt will get her city back. The conquerors are off without a squeak. Top Brass first – it could start a trend."

"The place is still mined … all the bridges … on the Governor's orders."

Cabot looked at his watch. "In a little over an hour your new Governor is to declare a ceasefire. I heard the news last night while squabbling at the Porte d'Italie. He's negotiated safe passage through the Swedish Consul. *Safe passage*. Prettier than *surrender*, don't you think? Von Choltitz has been busy about his reputation for days. Giving little parties, boasting that the man who flattened Sevastopol could do the same for Paris but has decided not to. He calculates he'll be forgiven. At least, forgotten. Paris is good at forgetting. He may write a book about it."

"*Negotiating*? Who with?"

"Doesn't the victor get to do that?"

"You mean the Americans?"

"Do I?"

He got up, rummaging in a coat thrown over a chair, finding a crumpled packet of cigarettes, shaking one out for Alex. "Here, try this bit of circumstantial evidence. They're called Chesterfields. Give me a packet of Players any time."

"And this Colonel you brought back with you?"

"Our little Colonel? With your women, I think. Probably craving male company by now."

In the salon, the door to the balcony had been flung back. Puffy clouds blew across a watery sky, pale yellow sunlight slanting now and then across the breakfast table.

Madeleine was asleep, breathing damp Paris air, head lolled against the metal rail of her chair.

Justine was kneeling on the floor, one arm supporting a little boy. He had long outgrown a curious sleeveless coat fashioned from some rustic fabric. It gave him an odd clerical air. He sat on a patterned carpet, tiny legs outstretched, his head solemnly bowed over a pile of cowrie shells, slowly pushing them into piles, consumed by the intensity of play.

Hearing the salon door open, Justine looked up, her eyes alight, pressing her fingers to her lips.

www.ingramcontent.com/pod-product-compliance
Lightning Source LLC
Chambersburg PA
CBHW070757030726
47504CB00003B/588
9781999694111